ASSASSIN'S REIGN

Also by Michael Arnold

Traitor's Blood
Devil's Charge
Hunter's Rage

ASSASSIN'S REIGN

MICHAEL ARNOLD

JOHN MURRAY

First published in Great Britain in 2013 by John Murray (Publishers)
An Hachette UK Company

1

© Michael Arnold 2013

The right of Michael Arnold to be identified as the Author of the Work has been
asserted by him in accordance with the Copyright, Designs and Patents Act 1988.

Maps drawn by Rosie Collins

A CIP catalogue record for this title is available from the British Library

Hardback ISBN 978-1-84854-756-8
Ebook ISBN 978-1-84854-758-2

Typeset in Bembo by Hewer Text UK Ltd, Edinburgh

Printed and bound by Clays Ltd, St Ives plc

John Murray policy is to use papers that are natural, renewable and recyclable products
and made from wood grown in sustainable forests. The logging and manufacturing processes
are expected to conform to the environmental regulations of the country of origin.

John Murray (Publishers)
338 Euston Road
London NW1 3BH

www.johnmurray.co.uk

For my niece, Bethany Gunn

Summer 1643

Royalist territory

Parliamentarian
territory

Inverness

Aberdeen•

Perth•

Edinburgh

Newcastle

Carlisle•

Bridlington

York•

Lincoln

Newark•

Chester•

Nottingham

Lichfield•

Worcester•

Colchester•

Pembroke•

Gloucester•✠

Oxford•

Cirencester•

London•

Bristol•

Taunton•

Portsmouth•

Launceston•

Plymouth•

✠ Gloucester was a Parliamentary garrison
in the middle of Royalist territory

N
W   E
S

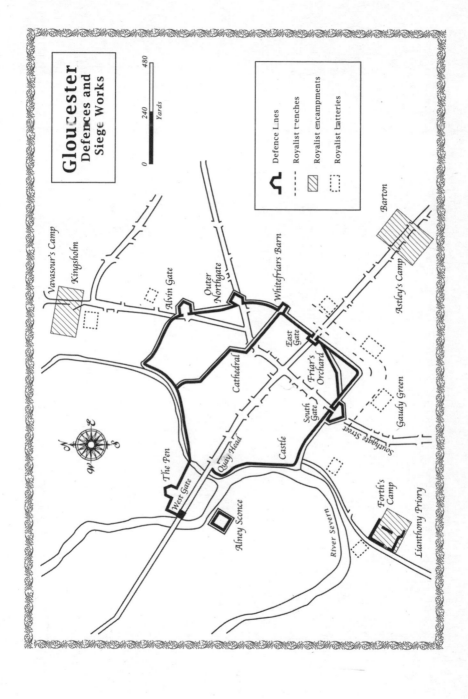

Gloucester
Defences and Siege Works

0 240 480
Yards

Defence Lines
Royalist trenches
Royalist encampments
Royalist batteries

N
W E
S

Vavasour's Camp
Kingsholm
Alvin Gate
Outer Northgate
Whitefriars Barn
East Gate
Friar's Orchard
Cathedral
South Gate
Castle
Quay Head
The Pen
West Gate
Alney Sconce
River Severn
Gaudy Green
Southgate Street
Astley's Camp
Barton
Forth's Camp
Llanthony Priory

PROLOGUE

The Bath road, east of Bristol, 26 July 1643

Jonas Crick cursed softly as his shoe snagged on a raised root.
He glanced down instinctively, and then he glanced back
along the road. It was empty, save for the phalanxes of trees
standing on either side of the thoroughfare, and the darkness
was so impenetrable, it was fit only for thieves.

Crick allowed himself a small smirk. 'Lost you, you fat old
bastard.'

And then a crack, like a muffled pistol. No: a snap. A branch
under foot.

Crick's pulse quickened. He swallowed back a jet of throat-
singeing bile, and shrank into the darkest part of the road's edge.
He opened his eyes wider to draw in any chink of light that
might be had, feeling the sting of the cool air. But nothing
emerged from the gloom. No winged demon or fanged ghoul.
No creeping enemy with sharpened blade and blackened heart.
Only stillness. Enveloping, suffocating stillness. He glanced up
through the heavy canopy above, catching the movement of
clouds as they scudded in vast, charcoal smears across the night
sky. There seemed to be no moon at all.

Another sound sent manic prickles racing across Crick's
skin. He tensed, willing himself to become one of the trees,
until with a rush of relief he realized that it was just the hoot
of an owl. He let out a huge breath as he stepped back out
on to the road and swore harshly, thumping a thigh with his
balled fist.

The blow when it came was not heavy, but sharp, precise. Even as the pain settled between his shoulder blades, he could sense the power leaching from his limbs. He lurched forward wordlessly, a dull ache spreading through his body as the sound of drums began to thrum in his skull. Staggering sideways suddenly, he managed to turn to face his assailant. What little breath he had caught in his throat.

'Hello, Jonas,' the man's voice said evenly. 'Or should I say Judas?'

'We have failed,' Crick managed to murmur, the words sounding eerily distant to his own ears. 'Bristol has fallen. It is over.'

The big man grunted his amusement. 'No, Jonas. The plan has not failed. It is merely altered. We shall await his next move.' The dark shape of his shoulders bunched as he shrugged. 'Perhaps Gloucester? Or even London? An opportunity will present itself, be sure of that.' He chuckled deeply, and the sound seemed to reverberate in the darkness. 'But you shall never know of it. A shame.'

Jonas Crick stared up at the large form looming like a cliff face before him. He made to respond, but his mouth simply flapped open and shut like a landed trout, no words reaching his lips. A dread cold trickled down his spine, spreading out like icy talons to coil about his arms and legs. His face was suddenly numb. And then he was falling.

CHAPTER 1

Lawford's Gate, Bristol, 27 July 1643

Dawn was only a few minutes old when the scarred and battered gates groaned open.

A single face peered out from behind the studded oaken barrier, like a mouse venturing from its hole, nose tilted up as if to sniff the sulphurous air, eyes wide and alert. It was the face of what had once been a young man, now turned black and haggard by a night spent in hell. A night illuminated by fire and the dragon-breath flashes of musketry and ordnance, its silence shattered by the screams of the wounded and the sobs of the dying.

Gradually, the head grew a neck, shoulders and torso. The buff-coated body – dressed in what had once been the finest quality – was as black as the face, caked in the grime of powder smoke and sweat. The man edged further out until his shabby form was free of the gate's protection.

And the noise began.

It started as a low thrum, like a distant thunderclap bounced among the dark Mendips that loomed to the south. But far from fading, this thunder grew, gathered power, hostility, until it shook the pockmarked walls and charred timbers of Bristol as though some gigantic beast had been sent by God Himself to devour the city.

The man at the gate winced and shrank back. His ears still rang as though crammed with chiming church bells, but now they were overwhelmed by the collective voices of his enemies.

3

They were the voices of demons, laughing, jeering, grotesque. Tones made hoarse by a night screaming their Cornish war cries into air clogged with black powder and roiling smoke. And now, as the streets still stank of rotten eggs and burning timber, those Cornishmen – finally victorious with the surrender of these last desperate rebels – craned from windows and doorways, spilled from the mouths of narrow alleys and lined the muddy streets, all determined to give the departing rebels the farewell they felt was so richly deserved.

The man whispered a short prayer, took a deep breath, straightened the dishevelled tawny scarf at his waist, and peered back over his shoulder. Beyond, within Bristol's beleaguered inner sanctum, massed ranks of pale, moon-eyed faces clustered together like a vast flock of sheep. He tried to meet as many of the frightened stares as he could, and injected his tone with a bravado he did not feel. 'Steady now. Do not let the dogs smell your fear.'

'Colonel Fiennes, sir.'

Fiennes looked to his left, where a hollow-cheeked junior officer clutched his horse's reins in a trembling fist. He took the leather straps and forced a smile. 'Thank you, Masterson.' He glanced back at the exhausted defenders. Soldiers and townsfolk together; not just men, but women and children too. His people. They had been finally overwhelmed, pushed back into this last enclave until there was nowhere left to make a stand. There had been no other choice in the end, and he thanked God for giving him the wisdom to spare their lives. It did not have to end in slaughter. This was not Germany. He swallowed hard, suddenly wondering if Westminster would see it that way.

And then he gave a curt order for the gate to be thrust wide, a final gaping breach the Royalists had failed to make themselves, and the defenders surged forth, abandoning the town they had held at such a high cost.

Colonel Nathaniel Fiennes, Parliamentarian governor of England's second largest city, clambered up on to his creaking saddle, and urged his whickering mount into the muddy street, hot tears pricking his eyes.

The lieutenant weaved along the street for twenty jelly-kneed paces, shouldering his way through the baying mob, cannoning from surly musketeer to glowering pikeman like a saker ball fired down a narrow alley, until he spied a sturdy-looking water trough. He staggered to it quickly, studying his feet to keep from tripping, slumped against the cold stone, and vomited. For a moment the nearest soldiers, dressed in an array of coat colours that reflected the eclectic nature of the king's army, turned harsh glares towards him, ready to damn his eyes – or worse – as the acidic stench singed their nostrils, but quickly turned away as they recognized him as an officer. The lieutenant did not care, for sweet relief had come with the violent evacuation of his stomach.

'Praise God and Jesus and everyone else,' he hissed through sore throat and gasped breaths. 'Praise God indeed.' He wiped a dangling tendril of mucus from the end of his long nose and straightened tentatively, still propped by an elbow against the trough, and peered between the shoulders and heads of the crowd. The throng was convulsing now, lurching forward as if with one mind as the defeated Roundheads marched sullenly past. A hail of insults, threats, spittle, stones and mud greeted them, a final gauntlet for the trudging enemy to run. Penance for their collective treason.

Gulping down another jet of bile, the lieutenant managed to straighten, determined to witness the end of Parliamentarian resistance in this grand old city. The head of the column was made up of officers, all mounted and straight-spined, though each with an expression as black as Bristol's walls. The lieutenant had never seen any of these men in the flesh, but he knew their names right enough. It would be Colonel Fiennes at the very front, with his brother, John at his side. Popham would be there too, flanked by the brightest lights of the bloodied garrison. Brave souls all, followed by the exhausted ranks of fighting men, and many women too, sooty faces flashing between the clamouring bodies of the lieutenant's own army. Despite himself, the lieutenant felt a pang of respect for these crestfallen people. They had been beaten, it was true, but the cost to the king's army had been huge. Even now, a day following the truce, the dead of both sides were still being retrieved from streets and houses.

'Get back eastways, and keep yer arses away!' a hulking musketeer three or four paces from the lieutenant bellowed suddenly, shying a clump of dried mud at the column.

'Tell yer Parly-mant!' another bawled, waving his musket aloft like a club. 'Keep its fackin' nose out, less'n it wants it chopped off!'

'Run away, boys! The king's lads'll give ye another batterin'!'

Men pushed through the crowd then, brandishing their scarred tucks to clear a path through the heaving mob. The lieutenant's natural empathy for the departing rebels made him wince at this, for he knew what was to come. The Royalist soldiers wanted recompense for their troubles. Regimental pay was an undependable thing at the best of times, and it was generally accepted that a victorious army would take as much reward in plunder as through legitimate means. These forbidding warriors were part of the army's Cornish contingent, judging by their accents, and the lieutenant knew that they more than anyone else would want to extract a high price for their pains. He had witnessed their assault at first hand, had been there in that charnel house of an alley known as the Christmas Steps, when the snarling men of Kernow had launched themselves at the desperate defenders. Through the self-induced – and never more welcome – wine haze, the lieutenant had ricocheted from one dying man to the next, screaming for his mother and weeping for himself, as whistling shot carved up the air all around. It had been a nightmare. A living nightmare.

The lieutenant looked on helplessly as the grim-faced Cornishmen waded directly into the Roundhead column, pushing and shoving the cowed rebels, snatching purses, rummaging in pockets, emptying snapsacks on to the road in the hope of finding something precious. Swords and daggers were taken, hats plucked clean off flinching heads, pipes, tobacco and coin spirited clean away.

'St-stop that!' the lieutenant bleated, though he could sense how feeble he must sound. The protest earned him not a single glance. The world suddenly spun. He vomited again.

'Get away!' a new voice echoed about the lieutenant's swirling skull, and he forced himself to look up. 'Get away, I say! Damn your skin and bones, I shall run each of you through myself!'

Abruptly, the lieutenant saw him: a huge man atop a huge horse, filthy from the grime of battle but nonetheless dressed in finery. He was narrow-faced, almond-eyed and long-nosed, with flowing coke-black hair that cascaded from beneath a wide, feathered hat in a veritable explosion of curls.

'Leave them unmolested!' Prince Rupert of the Rhine snarled again, laying about the nearest men with the flat of his long, glittering sword. Most of the looters scattered immediately, fearful of the young general and his near mythical reputation. The king's nephew was known to be brave, reckless and utterly ruthless.

'But m'lord!' one brazen plunderer wailed. He stood his ground before the prince's mount, clutching a snapsack close to his chest as though it were a newborn babe. 'These is ours by rights!'

Rupert swept his blade downwards in a flashing diagonal arc. The flat connected with the Cornishman's helmet, felling him like an elm in a gale. 'Anyone else?' the prince dared his surly troops. 'The terms are clear. They march away unmolested.' He stood in his stirrups, raising the sword with deliberate menace. 'Make me break my word, and I will stretch your necks!'

The lieutenant gave a wry smile as the looters evaporated as quickly as they had appeared. He coughed briefly, spat a gobbet of sour-tasting spittle into the trough, and turned away. 'Bloody animals.'

'Can you blame them? It was a bad fight.'

The lieutenant looked up in surprise. He was standing before the charred ruin of a house, around which were gathered dozens of infantrymen. They wore red coats, most faded to a pale pink, in the main. Some sucked on clay pipes, others chewed scraps of desiccated meat or inspected new wounds, while many sharpened tucks that had been battered and blunted in the assault. He felt his pulse quicken with a stab of apprehension. He had lived through the storming of Bristol, a hard, bloody, terrible fight, and yet – compared to these men – he knew that he was yet as green as April grass. These were veterans, men who had fought together through this summer of blood and survived. They had charged up that lonely hill at Stratton, and had stood shoulder-to-shoulder at Lansdown. Some might even have been on that vast killing ground beneath the ridge at Edgehill. Their faces were lined and weathered, their expressions implacable; they had the easy nonchalance only experience could give. And they were terrifying.

But in the midst of this pack of human wolves, sat on his haunches against the worm-eaten door frame, was the man who had spoken. He was the most fearsome man of all. It was all the lieutenant could do to keep from gasping, such was his shock at looking into that face. It was the narrow, hollow-cheeked face of one accustomed to hardship. A face that might have been handsome once, but which now carried the telltale lines and divots of a lifetime spent in battle. A face that lacked its left eye, that space – and most of the left side – now consumed by swirling, mottled scar tissue, as though the man had dipped his head directly into flame.

The lieutenant returned the scarred man's stare as he casually rose to his feet. 'But the terms . . . sir?' The lieutenant was uncertain as to what manner of man he addressed. The scarred man was tall, filthy and ragged. He had long hair the colour of raven feathers, tied at the nape of the neck, and a woollen coat of the same shade. His lean torso was protected by a sleeveless doublet of dark yellowish hide, split diagonally by the broad leather of a baldric. The lieutenant's father had warned him of men such as this. Land pirates, brigands turned soldiers, men without morals who sought only blood and plunder. This man fitted the mould perfectly, but for his boots and sword. The former were clearly expensive; supple leather, lovingly cut and stitched, then blackened and stiffened at the rigid tops to protect the thighs as though he were a cavalryman. His sword was more impressive still. A long, broad blade sat tight in its scabbard, swirling basket hilt blooming like a bouquet of silver flowers from the snug throat, a gleaming ruby-coloured garnet winking at its stout pommel. It was not the weapon of a common footpad.

The man lifted a hand to worry at the scabby edges of a recently healed wound that ran horizontally across his forehead in a livid pink line. He smiled kindly enough, though the older scarring mutilating his eye socket pulled taut, turning the expression ugly. 'They lost many friends, sir. Hundreds, by my reckoning. That's a deal of scores to settle, wouldn't you agree?'

'I suppose, sir,' the lieutenant muttered, deciding this frightening fellow had the bearing and speech of a man accustomed to command. He would err on the side of caution until he knew better.

'No matter,' the tall soldier said. 'Their fear for the prince outweighs their greed.'

The lieutenant nodded, felt his guts lurch again, and doubled over, coughing up a stream of bright bile that spattered his boots.

'Bumpsy bloody stripling.'

It was another man who had spoken, though the sound was more a deep croak than a human voice. The lieutenant forced himself to look up, ignoring the world as it swam before him. The new speaker, leaning against a blackened wall some three or four paces to the pirate's right, was not what he had expected at all. He had never laid eyes on such a – such a what? The lieutenant did not know how to describe him. He was dressed as a warrior, swathed in a suit of grey, with the hilt of a dirk protruding from the top of each of his long boots, and a sword hanging at his waist. But that sword was improbably short, deliberately cut away and reshaped for an owner who could have been no taller than four feet. The lieutenant's first impression was of a child. But then he saw the eyes, bright with wisdom, yellow like those of a cat. And he noticed that the skin of the imp's face was as creased as old bark and as tough as the baldric from which the toylike blade dangled.

'Sir?' the tiny fellow rasped again, the hint of challenge in his bright eyes.

The lieutenant realized he was staring, slack-jawed and wide-eyed. 'Beg pardon,' he muttered, blinking quickly to regain focus. He was immediately embarrassed to have apologized to an enlisted man, but something in the grating tone and twinkling menace of the gaze had extracted the words from him before he had time to think. The dwarf smirked, an expression of pure evil to the lieutenant's eyes, and he turned quickly to the man he had taken to be in command.

'Bumpsy, sir?' he said, recalling the original insult.

'Mister Barkworth implies the wine carried you through . . . Ensign?'

'Lieutenant, sir,' he corrected, forcing himself to straighten. 'Lieutenant Thomas Hood. Lately of Slanning's, but imminently—' He stopped short as a dozen invisible daggers jabbed at his guts, the wine twisting his innards to knots.

The tall man shot a sideways glance at the voice-throttled dwarf, producing a jagged-toothed smirk from the latter. 'You are, are you not, in your cups, Mister Hood?'

Hood felt his cheeks burn. 'Was, sir. No longer.'

The scarred face smiled its grimace again, his lone grey eye piercing the younger man like a lance through a hog. 'There's no shame in it, Tom. The taking of a city is a terrifying ordeal, and no mistake. And the officers lead the charge, yet they are no more shot-proof than the next man. None would blame you for drowning your fears before you faced the guns.'

Hood nodded. 'Kind in you to say, sir.'

'And a sympathetic commanding officer would doubtless pat your back and fill your cup before plunging into a breach.'

'I'd like to think so, sir.'

The tall soldier stooped, plucking a wide-brimmed hat from the ground and propping it on his head at a slight angle. When he looked at Hood again, the grey eye seemed to flash silver. 'Sadly for you, Mister Hood, I am not a sympathetic man.'

Lieutenant Thomas Hood felt his jaw loll. 'C-Captain Stryker . . . sir?'

The fearsome man in black stalked forward and offered his hand. 'Well met, sir.'

Hood took it and winced as his fingers were crushed. 'Sir.'

'Welcome to Stryker's Company of Foot, Mister Hood. Your new family. Fight well and we shall be friends.' He released Hood's hand, glowering in a manner the lieutenant's father would have branded demonic. 'Drink after battle in future. If I see you at the wine barrel before a fight again, I'll drown you in it myself.'

Bristol smouldered through the night. Buildings were smoking shells, the carcasses of homes and livelihoods. Ravens and kites circled endlessly, their beady eyes scouring the savaged land for the remnants of the fleshy feast upon which they had gorged in the hours following the slaughter.

Roads – strewn with the dead less than a day before – were still stained dark where blood had pooled in the ruts. It was summer, and the rain had been thin enough, but it had been constant, falling in diagonal blankets that filled the narrow streets and turned the ground to a morass. And those viscous thoroughfares, which yet bore the ragged gullies carved by thousands of scrabbling shoes, had also retained the flotsam of battle in a macabre parody of the Severn shoreline just a few miles to the west. Twisted spurs jutted from the mud, severed and abandoned beside broken dirks and buttons, buckles, scabbards and shot. Glinting litter to gladden any magpie and sadden any heart.

The city was quiet. The crows of the victors, matched in their volume by the melancholy wails of desperate citizens, had

waned like the watching moon. Soldiers – ebullient and vengeful in the hours after the truce – had felt the excitement of
assault drain away, replaced in equal measure by the stark reality
of a long butcher's bill and acute, throbbing exhaustion.

Captain Innocent Stryker stooped a touch to clear the lintel
of a tavern in Bristol's broken heart. He removed his hat and
stepped inside. The shutters at the windows had been blown or
smashed clean off during the assault, but still the gloom was
immediate, oppressive, and his single eye took several moments
to adjust. Gradually the light won out, aided by a couple of
stinking tallow candles at the taproom's far corners and the
chinks from some unseen light above, battling to leak between
the floorboards in thin beams.

The room was busy. Men clustered in groups to brag of the
fight, compare wounds, share in one another's relief and toast
fallen comrades, for they were the lucky ones. Near a cold
hearth at one end, half a dozen fellows in yellow and white coats
rolled dice and growled at the numbers, spitting oaths and slapping backs as fortunes spun with the carved bone cubes. A man
with a mangled nose perched on a low stool, fiddle nestled
against his bandaged chin as he played a lively reel. His mate,
a red-haired monstrosity with arms like culverins, danced an
ungainly jig, face ruddy and eyes glazed, ale slopping haphazardly from the pot in his big paw.

Stryker pushed his way to the counter, finding a spot that was
not soaked in beer to prop his elbow, and turned back to squint
into the room. The men largely ignored him, officer though he
was, but the few to catch his eye dipped their heads in acknowledgement. He did not care. This was where he wanted to be,
well away from the polite congratulations of fellow officers and
the snide machinations of the army elite. Even now, he suspected,
the gainsayers would be whispering. They would gather in the
corridors of power, both here and at Oxford, the king's new
capital, and recount the butcher's bill with macabre relish. Losses
had been heavy, and Prince Rupert's jealous rivals – of which
there were many – would be making merry with that fact.

'Cap'n Stryker, sir?'

Stryker had to twist his head to see the speaker, who had approached on his blind left side. 'Aye.'

'John Reece, sir,' the man said. He was a fresh-faced fellow, of lean frame and fair hair that crested his narrow head like a straw bird's nest. 'Musketeer in Trevanion's.' He clutched a wooden ale pot as though his life depended on it, raising it in ragged salute. 'And we were with you, sir. At the Steps.'

Stryker's mind darkened at the memory. What a fight it had been. Prince Rupert's ambitious assault had seemed doomed to fail. His huge army, spearheaded by experienced infantry brigades, had stormed Bristol on three sides, hammering and tearing at the defiant rebels on the walls. But those rebels, inferior in number, had been staunch and undaunted, and their courage proved as resolute as their aim. From the blazing walls a hail of shot had poured down, smiting hundreds of the king's best men, wounding and killing a sickening number of his most promising commanders and dissolving morale as though it were a pillar of salt in a flood. And yet somehow a determined squad had found a way over a thinly guarded section of wall, and their escalade, unlike the rest, had been completed unscathed. Stryker remembered the shouts of amazement as – stone by stone, timber by timber, barrel by barrel – the defences had crumbled, torn away by the unexpected storming party from within the city. The cry had gone up, excited, shrill, blood-freezing. A breach. A goddamned breach! And they had surged; swarmed forward into that small but crucial crack, forcing their triumphal way into the burning streets and spreading in all directions like a wave through a rock pool.

Stryker's company had been in the forefront, reaching a dark alley, treacherously steep and claustrophobically narrow, down which the defenders had scurried. He shuddered at the memory of plunging into those hellish depths on the heels of the enemy, bathed in flame and flayed by lead. The rebels had made their last stand in that bloody place, a place Stryker now knew to be called the Christmas Steps, and the passage had become a

13

moonlit charnel house. Eventually the human dam broke, the tide of vengeful king's men bursting through by sheer weight of numbers, and the city had fallen. But at such cost, by God.

It was all done with now, though. Bristol was in Royalist hands. Finally, painfully, the great port had capitulated. Like a bulbous black canker, poisonous and festering, it had perched between the king's heartlands of Wales and the south-west, a symbol of rebel defiance and a hub of their power. The canker had been cut away by Prince Rupert's knife, cauterized by the joined armies of Cornwall and Oxford. It was a great victory, Stryker knew. And yet he could not feel a victor's joy. He felt only a sense of despair. Of emptiness.

'So you were,' Stryker said eventually, pretending to remember the man and his courage. 'And how fares your colonel? Shot in the leg, was he not?'

Reece's face visibly drooped. 'Dead, Captain.'

Stryker swore softly. It was always a terrible blow to lose a competent officer, but the identity of this particular casualty made it doubly worse. Stryker had served with the Cornish forces in the weeks before its amalgamation with Hertford's Western Army, and he knew that the men from the deepest corner of England revered their commanders with a zeal that was unmatched.

The tapster slid a pewter cup towards Stryker, followed quickly by a blackjack of strong beer. He filled the cup and lifted it to his lips. 'Trevanion.'

Reece nodded and took a long swig of his own drink. 'An' Colonel Slanning's mortal wounded too, sir.'

Stryker shot the young musketeer a hard stare. 'You're certain?'

'Not dead yet, thank the good Lord, but we hear he's dire poorly.'

And that, thought Stryker, could spell the end of the grand Cornish army, as sure as any defeat on the field. 'I pray he survives.'

Reece took another deep draught. 'Was all so glorious after Stratton, sir. We marched up that bloody hill and drove those bastards off like they was an army of chil'en.' He offered a wan smile. 'But then so many fell at Lansdown, cut down and left to rot. Our beloved Sir Bevil among 'em. And good General Hopton blinded so cruelly.'

Stryker nodded bleakly. Sir Bevil Grenville had been one of the most charismatic men he had ever served with. His bravery and ambition at Stratton had been the driving force of that most unlikely of victories. A pole-axe had split his skull at Lansdown, while the Royalist general, Sir Ralph Hopton, had been caught in an explosion after the battle and was still laid low by his wounds.

Reece sighed. 'Fortune's turned against us, sir.' He glanced around the taproom. 'We can all sense it. Trevanion now gone, Slanning on his way.'

A hollow feeling formed deep in Stryker's guts, for he knew what the musketeer was intimating, even if it could never be uttered. The Cornish had had enough. Their triumphal march east had not been inspired by loyalty to the monarchy, but by devotion to their local leaders. And those men had been gradually whittled away. Morale would surely follow. He tilted back his head and drained the cup, letting the welcome taste of beer ease his troubled mind.

'The miserable,' a new voice cut across him, 'have no other medicine but only hope.'

Stryker turned. Reece had gone, melted back into the mass of bodies from whence he had come, to be replaced by a different visage altogether. This face was round and red-cheeked. It carried none of the telltale marks of campaign and disease that others bore, yet Stryker knew that its owner was no less a veteran than himself. He tried to smile, but failed. 'Shakespeare?'

Captain Lancelot Forrester's cherubic faced creased in a warm grin. 'Of course!' He moved to Stryker's side, removed his battered hat, and ruffled his thinning sandy hair with a chubby hand. 'Though dear William was wrong in this instance.' He caught the tapster's eye. 'Ale, sir, and make haste about it!' When cup and coin had been exchanged, Forrester took a swig, wiped his lips with a grimy sleeve, and belched. 'You are an elusive fellow, old man.'

Stryker frowned. 'Where I said.'

'You said the White Hart.'

'I said the Two Boars.'

Forrester shrugged, evidently deciding it was not worth an argument. 'Well, we're both here now, so we can commence the long overdue toast.' He drained his cup, peered into Stryker's blackjack, and waved at the tapster again.

The man sidled across to the two officers. 'Sirs?'

'More ale, my good man,' Forrester demanded. 'The most potent brew you have. A jug a piece, and no short measures!' Satisfied, he glanced at Stryker. 'Let us drink to him, for it has been a long time coming.'

'I'm in no mood for it, Forry,' Stryker said, immediately regretting the gruffness of his retort.

'And I'm in no mood for your woes, old man. Not today.'

Stryker looked up from his newly replenished blackjack, and, for a fraction of a heartbeat, felt as though he might launch himself at the man before him. He was in a mood blacker than Bristol's singed walls, made darker still by drink and grief, and no man spoke to him in such a way. But almost as quickly, a rush of remorse washed through his veins, shaming him utterly. Lancelot Forrester had fled his aristocratic upbringing as a young man, choosing the allure of a mercenary's life; one of whoring, drinking and fighting. Thus, his path had crossed with that of Stryker, and they had learned their trade in the Low Countries, fighting for the Protestant League against the combined forces of the Counter-Reformation. He had fought alongside Stryker all over Europe, witnessed the same horrors at Edgehill, and faced the same dangers in this new kind of war. There were not many men who might address Stryker thus, but Forrester was one of them.

Stryker offered a resigned nod. 'Very well.'

Forrester lifted his cup as he beamed. 'Then we'll drink to Lieutenant Andrew Burton of Sir Edmund Mowbray's

Regiment of Foot. A callow youth he enlisted, a true warrior he departed. May he rest in peace.'

'Aye,' Stryker echoed, drinking straight from his blackjack, entertaining the forlorn hope that the liquid would somehow assuage his guilt. It did not, and his mind whirled with the image of young Burton on that blood-soaked hill in north-east Cornwall, a glistening hole in his forehead where a pistol ball had entered. The lieutenant had been his protégé, his friend, and, though he had not fired that fateful shot, Stryker nevertheless felt culpable.

'And may his murderer rest in pieces!' Forrester added, indulging in a prolonged draught and belching again. He grinned wolfishly. 'Young Andrew would have been in the thick of it, eh? Wading through the blood and smoke with the rest of us.'

That was true, thought Stryker, and he let slip the ghost of a smile.

'By the by,' Forrester went on, 'the giant will be with us soon, I fear, so drink up before the thirsty bugger asks to share ours.'

'I told him to see to the men,' Stryker said.

'And it is done, by all accounts,' Forrester replied brightly. 'So Mister Skellen tells me, leastwise, though he probably lies. Still, my greatest hope is that he has discovered a cache of tobacco somewhere betwixt Devizes and here, and it will be about his person when next we meet.'

Stryker took another swig. 'They say the King comes to Bristol.'

'Joy of joys,' Forrester muttered. 'Here to awe the townsfolk with his regal majesty, no doubt. What will be his next move, d'you suppose?'

'Next move?'

'I'll stick a groat on the capital.' Forrester answered his own question before Stryker could think of a reply. 'A dash to London, and victory by Christ-tide.'

'Precisely what we were saying last year,' Stryker chided, 'was it not?'

Forrester blew out his ruddy cheeks. 'I suspect it was. God's nailed hands, but I hope I'm right this time. Do you know how long it's been since I donned the garb of Caesar?'

'I believe you're about to tell me, Forry,' Stryker replied resignedly, knowing full well that an attempt to avoid Forrester's tales of his days in the theatre was an utterly futile gesture.

'Near a full two years! Can you warrant such an outrage? Two years of slogging about the damnable countryside, when I was born to tread the boards. The Candlewick Troupe will have missed my skills tremendously.'

'The Candlewick Troupe will have been closed down like the rest.'

Forrester shook his head angrily. 'Bloody Puritans. It is worth winning this war, if only to oust them and their dour ways.'

'How fares your company?' Stryker asked, deftly steering the conversation in an alternative direction.

'They're well, Stryker.' Forrester shrugged. 'Well as can be expected after such tribulation. Lost a dozen on the Steps alone. You?'

'Fifteen.'

'Jesu! We'll have no men left if this keeps on. Rupert's tactics are successful, I grant you, but, zounds, they're damnably dear. And where do we find replacements? Seems every lad of fighting age is either enlisted, dead or turning Clubman.'

'Aye.' He had encountered the same obstacles. Recruiters worked feverishly in town and village, swelling the ranks of Cavalier and Roundhead alike with any man able to heft a pike. Bribes, promises and threats were all fair tools in the battle to keep an army from withering away. And now a third faction was growing with each passing month. The Clubmen – those who took up arms to protect their homes and livelihoods from marauding soldiery of any allegiance – were beginning to look like an army in their own right. He wondered how long it would be before their influence was truly felt.

'Though I hear you have one replacement,' Forrester remarked pointedly.

'Thomas Hood.'

'It's about time, eh? More than two months since—' he hesitated. 'I am sorry.'

Stryker waved him away. 'No matter. I needed a lieutenant.'

Forrester's round, blue eyes narrowed. 'But did he need you?'

Stryker looked up sharply. 'What have you heard?'

'That you frightened the very bones out of his body this morning.' He drank deeply, offering a wry smirk when his gaze returned to Stryker. 'And ain't spoken with the poor lad since. He may benefit from poor Burton's demise, but it was not of his doing.' He turned suddenly. 'Aha! Sergeant Skellen, well met indeed. Have you—?'

A gigantic man had stridden into the tavern. He was of lean, tough frame, like an ancient tree, with long, powerful arms and huge hands. His eyes were heavily hooded, sepulchral in their deep sockets, and his hair closely shaved, through which a myriad of tiny white scars could be seen, crisscrossing his scalp like the lines of an old map. He was a head taller than anyone else beneath the gnarled beams of the Two Boars, and he moved across the room with a languid, almost predatory confidence. Stooping briefly under the lintel before straightening with a nod in Forrester's direction, he held up a small, brown object between thumb and forefinger, proffering the captain a black-toothed grin. 'Took a while to find the good stuff, sir.'

Forrester clapped his chubby hands together. 'Then let us pack our pipes and drink the smoke, damn your sluggish ways!'

'Where is Barkworth?' Stryker asked as Sergeant William Skellen approached, handing Forrester the plug of sotweed.

Skellen shrugged. 'Got 'imself into a scrap with one o' the Cornish. Happy as a dog with three pizzles, sir.'

'And the men?'

'Settled, sir.'

'In their cups?'

'Well and truly, sir. Old Seek Wisdom's ranting at 'em with every swig.'

Stryker offered a rueful smile. Seek Wisdom and Fear the Lord Gardner had joined the company as preacher shortly after the Battle of Stratton two months earlier. He was eccentric – some said insane – but Stryker liked him. He often wondered if his haranguing of the men was more for his own amusement than to save their mortal souls. 'If he comes in here, you have my permission to shoot him.'

'Right you are, Captain,' Skellen said, his face serious. 'Beer here!'

'As for Hood,' Forrester said quietly, as Skellen dealt with the tapster, 'it will get better, Stryker. He comes well recommended, and will do well for you. I'm told he is competent.'

'That is not—'

'It will get better!' Forrester exclaimed suddenly, slapping Stryker between the shoulder blades. 'And we will continue our glorious ways!'

'Glorious?' Stryker echoed bleakly. 'How many died for this wretched place?'

'You know it needed to be done as well as I, Stryker,' Forrester said, wagging a reproachful finger. 'We have the West. *Finally*, we have it. Now we shall surge into Parliament heartland and make a road of rebel bodies for Charlie to stroll across. All the way to the capital. Come now, old friend. They cannot beat us! The Prince has them running like frightened kittens, and we have swept all before us since Stratton, have we not?'

Stryker was unconvinced. 'Aye, well, things change quickly in war, as well you know.'

'No no no. The king's name is a tower of strength, as the Bard would say! More victories await us, Stryker. The rebels scatter like mice, and we will catch them one at a time, if needs be. An army of tomcats!' He dropped his voice to a conspiratorial whisper. 'And then you will have your way.'

'Oh?'

'Come now, old man, I'm no fool. You are London-bound, for that is where your heart lies.'

Skellen peered down at his captain. 'She still there, sir?'

Stryker nodded. 'Aye, the last I heard.'

Forrester chuckled. 'Seething, I shouldn't wonder.'

Stryker did not doubt it. He had been assigned to aid her. Had planned to travel direct to London in the earliest weeks of the summer. But the campaign in the west had shifted, become more dangerous, more bitter, more bloody. Priorities had changed, though he knew Lisette would not understand. 'Her mission foundered when Hopton was wounded.'

'Perhaps now you'll be unleashed, eh?' Forrester suggested.

'Perhaps,' Stryker agreed, and hoped his friend was correct. For that was truly where he wanted to be. London.

CHAPTER 2

London, 1 August 1643

Lisette Gaillard peered out from the depths of her heavy hood as the wherry rocked. It was a wide, stable boat, but one of her fellow passengers – a fat, shiny-faced man in a scarlet robe – could not seem to sit still for more than a matter of seconds without feeling the need to shift his huge rump. Thus the vessel lurched like a warship in a storm, great waves of brown Thames water slopping over the bows to dampen shoes and spirits alike.

Lisette whispered a vicious oath beneath her breath, a silent hand snaking to the hilt of a dirk within the voluminous folds of the cloak, but she knew she could not challenge the plump fool. No one would recognize her here, of course, but London was still the capital of her enemies. Parliament's headquarters, its heartland. The vipers' nest. A knife-wielding Frenchwoman would not go unnoticed. She stifled a smile at the thought, nevertheless.

'Blackfriars!' the waterman called suddenly, lifting his oars from the river. He leant back to rest briefly while the vessel slid gently to its berth.

Lisette stared out across the water, scanning the shoreline for danger. There was none, and, as the wherry touched the submerged shore, she waited her turn while the rest of the passengers rose to alight. The fat man stood, a catastrophic motion that caused the boat to rock wildly, and she gripped the damp timbers to steady herself, but soon he was on the stairs, puffing and grunting his way up the slick wedges of cut stone. Lisette – last off – shuffled forwards. She lunged for a cold ring of iron that dangled from the dank staircase, letting it take her weight as she steadied herself, and twisted back to toss the waterman a coin. He nodded his thanks, wiped his long, glistening nose with a crusty sleeve, and pushed off towards Southwark. Lisette Gaillard watched him go, crossed herself beneath the concealing cloak, and scuttled quickly up Black-friars Stairs to street level.

She moved swiftly, keen to keep out of the prying gaze of surly apprentices or Parliamentarian troops. They roamed the streets in these dangerous days, eager to spy out men – and women – who might say or do something that marked them as Royalist. Lisette was not unduly worried, for her training made her hard to track and harder to fight, but this was the very epicentre of the rebellion. The place where the enemy was strongest and most numerous. Plenty of Londoners would harbour sympathies for the king, she did not doubt, but those voices had been hushed, at least for now.

Moving up to a large stone building that had once been part of the old Dominican friary, Lisette made for an alley on its far side. She plunged into the narrow thoroughfare, thankful for its protective gloom, and scuttled its muddy course, skirting a stick-toting child terrorizing a small dog, a couple of large women squabbling over some trivial matter, and the outstretched legs of a prostrate drunk. And then she was in full daylight again, bathed in late summer sun, and enveloped by London's chaos.

It was still early, yet already the city broiled with life. There were bustling shops and slant-walled homes, and squawking peddlers, barrow-boys, servants and well-to-do personages with their noses thrust up at the clouds. Piles of dung looked like small, steaming islands in the vast ocean that was the road, their stench stinging the eyes in the balmy heat. Above, and looming like God's own sentinel, was the grand edifice of St Paul's Cathedral, and Lisette made straight for it, glad that she might use the vast church to plot her course. She had been in this cursed place since June, but, preferring to spend much of her time amongst the less salubrious, and, by turns, less closely watched neighbourhoods on the Surrey side of the river, she still struggled to grasp the infuriatingly intricate web of London's streets and alleys. Best, she had decided, to keep the city's land-marks at the forefront of her mind. To travel directly south from Smithfield would take her to the safe house on Pie Corner, while aiming for the spires of the Tower would, regardless of the road she chose, ultimately lead to the little gilder's premises beside Custom House that was used to pass messages between the king's agents. St Paul's, though, was the greatest marker of all, and she knew that keeping the big, squared-off tower to her left would guide her on to Carter Lane, which was where the latest rendezvous would take place.

Lisette saw Christopher Quigg long before he noticed her approach, and the fact irked her immediately. She could accept that some of the king's agents had been thrust into this life with-out prior knowledge or training, but still their amateurish nature astonished her. Quigg was not the worst – not by a long stretch – but he remained an ill-judged conscript for the world of the spy. Nor, she reflected as Quigg loitered conspicuously beside a small pie-seller's stall, was he a good choice if his recruiter had been aiming for one who might blend in with the folk on London's busy streets. He was of average height and build, which, at least, was of benefit, but the rest of him left a great deal to be desired. His face had been ravaged by smallpox, the skin pitted so deeply it was as if an army of mice had feasted on his cheeks, chin and neck. His teeth were all but rotted away, leaving empty discoloured gums with which to chew, and his nose was severely canted to one side. But most startling of all were his eyes. They positively bulged. Great chestnut and white orbs, shot through with fine tentacles of livid scarlet, seemingly exploding from his pitted forehead as though there were simply no room in his skull.

Quigg finally spotted Lisette when she was half a dozen paces away, and hailed her heartily. She walked straight past, leaving the bulbous eyes to strain in her wake, wet lips flapping mutely. Eventually she ducked into an alley, turned, and doubled back, reaching the bewildered spy before he could speak. The knife she held beneath her sleeve was pressed firmly at Quigg's side.

'Hush your breath or you will feel it leak between your ribs.'

Quigg winced, blinked like a great toad and nodded. 'My apologies, mademoiselle,' he muttered hoarsely. 'It is all rather new to me, truth told.'

She removed the blade and cast him a withering gaze. 'Let us go somewhere more private to speak.'

Quigg nodded again, though she had already walked away.

They reconvened beside a cartload of purple plums. The heady smell – earthy but sweet – filled the space all around, lingering in the warm breezeless air and overcoming some of the Thames' stench of putrefaction.

Lisette Gaillard breathed deeply, letting the plums take her back to France. How strange it was that the place could invoke such longing. Normandy had been the scene of so much horror for her, such grief, that at one time she had vowed never to return. Yet here she was, revelling in memories conjured by overripe fruit.

'Mademoiselle?' Quigg asked tentatively.

Lisette waved him away. 'No matter. I have been here all summer with no success. I grow frustrated.' Stepping close to whisper, she leaned in, all the while raking her gaze along the road for signs of trouble. 'I did not wish to threaten you before, Monsieur Quigg. But, you understand, a Frenchwoman in London brings suspicion, for she may be *Papiste*.'

Quigg nodded. 'Understood.'

'A woman alone in London earns the suspicion of the Puritans, for they accuse her of harlotry.'

He nodded again.

'And a woman in a heavy cowl, bearing concealed weapons, earns the suspicion of the Roundheads, for she may be an enemy of their cursed Parliament.'

Quigg swallowed nervously, big eyes darting to the floor. 'I shall be more discreet in future.'

'*Bon*!' Lisette flashing her sweetest smile. 'If not, I will slice off your stones and toss them in the Thames.' She watched Quigg's face, gnarled as the apples in the cart, convulse briefly before continuing. 'Now, I understand she has been moved.'

'Just so,' Quigg chirped, clearly relieved to have the subject turn to business.

Lisette swore harshly. 'I have been gone three weeks. Three goddamned weeks, and they move her.'

'Beg pardon, madame, but might you have been meeting your friend?'

'Friend?'

'The one you said was coming. The captain. Strider, was it? Strifer?'

Lisette tensed at the name. She gritted her teeth. 'Stryker. No, he has not come.'

Quigg's insect eyes widened further. 'But I thought he was coming to help us. To rescue the girl.'

Lisette felt her cheeks flush, and hated herself for it. 'Well, he is not.'

Quigg looked at his boots again. 'A shame.'

'Indeed. Forget Stryker. I have.'

'Then why no contact? I thought you might be dead. Caught out by some enemy patrol.'

'An ague,' Lisette said simply, though in truth the sickness had laid her very low. There had been moments as she sweated on her palliasse in the Surrey safe house, digging desperate finger-nails into her griping guts, when she had expected to expire with her very next breath.

'You are recovered?' Quigg asked.

'*Oui*.' She grasped Quigg's sleeve suddenly. 'Where did they take the girl?'

'Some old monastic building up beyond Moor Fields.'

'Certain?'

Quigg nodded firmly. 'I watched 'em leave. Followed the lot of them up through Cripplegate with me own eyes.'

And what eyes, thought Lisette. 'The lot of them? How many?'

'The girl, obviously,' Quigg replied, gnawing the inside of his mouth as he spoke. 'That pasty-faced colonel . . .'

'He's a general,' Lisette corrected.

'And a score o' soldiers in black coats. Seems a lot of steel for one lass.'

Lisette ignored him. Quigg did not need to know the identity of the girl. 'But why? Why move her now?'

Quigg shrugged. 'Getting twitchy, I reckon.'

Lisette frowned at the unfamiliar word. '*Twitchy?*'

Quigg reached back into the cart, plucking a plum from the heap and sending others tumbling in a purple avalanche. He bit into it, wincing as the tart juices hit his tongue. Before taking a second bite, he looked down at Lisette. 'There's been a lot o' bad news for Parliament coming out of the West Country. Heavy defeats, 'specially at the hands of the Cornish, who they seem to fear beyond all logic. And William the Conqueror's army smashed over at Devizes. Now Bristol's fallen, by all accounts.'

'I heard as much,' Lisette said. She kept her expression blank, but her heart was racing. Bristol. That was where he had last been. She and Stryker had not spoken directly for weeks, but her contacts within the Royalist intelligence network provided reasonably accurate information as to his whereabouts whenever she made the request. He had been with Hopton's army in the west since April, chasing the rebels from Cornwall and Devon into Somerset, Wiltshire and beyond. The battles of Stratton, Lansdown and Roundway had, by all accounts, been bloody affairs, and she had thanked the Holy Mother for Stryker's continued survival. But Bristol was different. Rumours had reached the capital. Rumours that whispered of fire and carnage on a new scale. Even now, it was said, the tattered and humiliated Parliamentarian garrison were on their way back to London, hounded and mocked by the country folk along the way, losing men by the hour to the twin enemies of gangrene and camp fever. A sudden pang stabbed at her guts. Maybe Stryker had been one of those to fall in Bristol's narrow streets, stripped naked and stacked with the rest of the corpses to turn black in the summer sun. The image brought cold dread to her mind, and she shuddered involuntarily. She forced the feeling away. God damn Stryker. He had abandoned her, left her here to face this cursed city. He had broken his word.

She blew out her cheeks, clearing her thoughts. 'What are you saying, Quigg?'

'The people fear for their very lives, madame,' he replied in hushed tones, 'for they see the King's gaze turning back to London. The war is lost, they say. The rebellion will be smote once and for all, Parliament dissolved again, but this time for good. The people are terrified, and every day comes news of more lives lost. The women want their husbands and sons back. The merchants want peace in which to trade. They want an end to it.'

A sudden thought struck Lisette Gaillard. 'Pamphleteers.'

Quigg stared, eyes bulging. 'Mademoiselle?'

'Pamphleteers, Quigg,' she replied urgently, stepping closer. 'Printers. Do we have any in our pay?'

Quigg considered the question, spat the plum stone on to the muddy road, and nodded slowly. 'One or two I could name.'

'Do not name them, for God's sake,' Lisette hissed earnestly. 'Pick the best. Take me to him.' For the first time in months, she felt hope surge within her, for she had had an idea. An idea that would finally bring this miserable mission the success she so craved. She almost laughed aloud, because in the heart of this most rebellious city, she was going to start a rebellion of her own.

Hartcliffe, near Bristol, 1 August 1643

'Stryker's boys here!' bellowed the tubby man, red coat straining about his ample gut. He pointed at the nearest of a chain of ramshackle houses. 'On this row.'

'All of us, sir?' a musketeer asked incredulously, earning a venomous scowl for his trouble.

'*All*, you cheeky beggar!' Quartermaster Richard Kinshott snarled. He leaned back, craning his oak trunk of a neck to inspect the tumbledown homes. 'Reckon you'll get—' He was thoughtful for a moment, scratching the wiry tuft of russet hair that served as a beard in his near chinless face. 'Half a dozen in this'n.' He snatched a stump of chalk from behind a hairy ear and scratched six vertical lines on the door. He repeated the action with the next house, and the next, until a woman came bustling angrily from within one of his targets.

'Six?' She spat the word. 'Six soldiers in my home, sir?' The portly quartermaster ignored her, and she grasped at the tail of his coat, furious.

Kinshott rounded on her. 'Have a care, Goody, or you shall have a dozen 'neath your roof!'

The woman was mortified. 'You cannot—'

'Cannot?' Kinshott mocked, placing hands on broad hips. 'Well my apologies, your ladyship, but I can do as I damn well please. To your pots, for you have extra mouths to feed this eve.'

Anger turned to worry as the woman's weathered face seemed to age visibly. She fiddled nervously with her coif as her gaze drifted across the red-coated horde that had descended upon her village. 'But, sir—'

Kinshott cut her off with a raised palm, his watery, dark-green eyes drifting beyond her shoulder to settle on the open doorway of her home. 'Your boy's a strapping lad, ain't he?' He brandished a malicious grin as the silhouette of a young man slunk rearward into the gloom. 'How many years? Sixteen? Slot straight into a pike block, I'd wager.'

'Thirteen years only, sir,' the woman replied defiantly. She stepped back, positioning herself between the quartermaster and her home. 'A boy. Just a boy.' She forced a smile. 'I will make pottage, sir.'

Kinshott beamed again. 'That's the spirit. For good King Charles and his fighting lads!'

'Ho, Dick!'

The quartermaster spun on his heel. '*Sir*, to you, Stryker.'

Captain Innocent Stryker lifted his hat in deference. 'Quartermaster Kinshott, sir. Well met. Do you have me a choice billet?'

'I do, sir, I do,' Kinshott declared proudly. 'The finest I could find.'

A tall man came to stand at Stryker's flank. 'Couldn't swing a bleedin' dwarf in there.'

'Mind your tongue, Skellen, you gangling clodpate,' Kinshott bawled. 'The King arrives in Bristol, so the likes o' you must make way.'

'Aye, mind your tongue,' Stryker agreed.

Skellen cast a glance back over his shoulder, winking at the company's shortest man, Simeon Barkworth.

'Permission to see if we might swing a lanky sergeant in there, sir,' Barkworth croaked. He might have been tiny, but he was one of the best fighters under Stryker's command. Former bodyguard to the Earl of Chesterfield and member of the feared Scots Brigade before that, Barkworth had enlisted with Stryker's company after the Battle of Hopton Heath, and he had already shown himself to be an able man. But his fiery pride and powder-keg temper had proven a dangerous combination on many an occasion in recent months, and Sergeant Skellen took unholy relish in goading the little man.

'Denied. Enough of this.' Stryker looked back at the quartermaster. 'Thank you, Dick. It will serve nicely.'

Kinshott nodded and, with a final, mischievous smirk at the crestfallen woman, bustled away to secure more quarters for the men of Sir Edmund Mowbray's Regiment of Foot.

Stryker turned to the woman, who stepped back involuntarily under his Cyclops gaze. He was accustomed to the reaction. 'Goodwife, we thank you for your hospitality.' He offered a low bow. 'My men are rough-hewn, but they require only food and shelter. We carry no fever, and will pay you all respect. Upon my honour.'

She swallowed hard, peering up at Stryker. 'Honour, sir? Soldiers have no honour.' Her mouth hardened. 'They are a plague on us.'

'My word, madam.'

The hostile gaze left him and raked across the men who gathered along the road. 'And I suppose you'll tell me you keep no women of the . . . lewd sort?'

Stryker smiled as kindly as he could. 'No, Goodwife, I will not. We have many. But they are yet in Devon, with the tail of our baggage train. You have my word that your home and family will be safe.' He set his jaw, 'But we *shall* rest here, that is decided.'

The hue and cry went up almost as soon as Stryker had taken his seat. Even as the sweet relief of rest surged up and down his weary legs, he was compelled to rise again.

He had selected the defiant goodwife's home for his own quarters, letting her bustle around the small ground-level room as he and five of his most senior men unslung baldrics and bandoliers. Skellen was there, with his second sergeant, Moses Heel, and Simeon Barkworth. Ensign Chase, the company's standard bearer and most junior officer, had joined them, speaking in hushed tones with the newest recruit, Lieutenant Thomas Hood. Stryker was glad the pair were beginning to forge the beginnings of comradeship, for he had been remiss in his dealings with Hood since the young man joined them. He had needed a new second in command to replace Burton, and complained continuously to Colonel Mowbray upon the subject, but when one had been forthcoming, his reaction surprised even himself. It was as if Hood's appearance had triggered the grief Stryker had carried since Burton's death, and he found it barely tolerable to so much as meet Hood's eye, let alone fulfil the excitable officer's enquiries about Edgehill, Hopton Heath and Stratton.

Stryker had been staring at the large cauldron rocking gently above the soot-shrouded hearth when the door rattled, a heavy fist belting it from the roadside. It was a struggle to tear his gaze away from the dancing steam, but the beating became more insistent.

'What is it?' Stryker snapped, as Skellen moved swiftly to open the door.

On the road, shifting his weight from one foot to the next in agitation, was Harry Trowbridge, one of Stryker's best musketeers. 'Enemy, sir.'

'Where?'

'Out on the tree line to the east, sir.'

Stryker followed Trowbridge's outstretched arm, his lone eye settling quickly on the place, perhaps a hundred paces beyond the last of Hartcliffe's modest buildings, where a large group of his men were beginning to gather. The road through the village ran away to the east, and his men seemed to be peering into the cluttered foliage hugging its wooded northern verge. 'How many?'

'Hard to say, sir. Score?' He shrugged apologetically. 'They's in green.'

All at once the crackle of musketry reached Stryker's ears, and he pushed past the anxious redcoat and out to the road. He followed the sound, bounding along the cracked mud of the village's main thoroughfare, passing a couple of the regiment's wagons and several frightened-looking locals. Skellen and a dozen of his men were at his heels, all squinting to assess the burgeoning engagement, though they could discern little beyond the pall of smoke that thickened with every shot loosed. There was no breeze at all, and the gritty gouts from each weapon simply roiled around their masters like stinking haloes.

Eventually Stryker was able to make out a few of his redcoats around the periphery of the acrid cloud. Some stood, others knelt, but all were focussed on the opposite side of the road, where large trees provided cover for this unknown and unwelcome force. They were firing, reloading and firing again. All the while bright tongues of orange licked the air from amongst the trees, illuminating the enemy hiding places for the briefest of moments.

The first soldiers Stryker encountered were his pikemen. He had twenty-five of them in the company, nearly a quarter of the fighting force, but at this moment they were an irrelevance. The skirmish was chaotic in its rhythm, with men firing their weapons as and when the long-arms could be brought to bear, but still the lead flew with a consistency that made his pikemen sheer away like a flock of sheep in the face of a rabid dog. They were impotent in this scene, unable to reach an enemy obscured by trees, and unwilling to charge into the hail of bullets.

He turned, his gaze falling on Sergeant Heel. 'Get them formed up!'

Heel, the bullock-shouldered Devon man who had traded Bible and plough for sword and halberd, spun on his toes to engage the pikemen. 'Form up, you lazy bastards!'

The men began to shift, jockeying for position within four short lines, morion pots adjusted, tucks swept clear of shuffling legs. In seconds they had formed a small square, the block of man and spear that made them appear as a gigantic, malevolent hedgehog.

'But do not advance till you have my word, Moses,' Stryker added, as he plunged into the smoke. 'You hear me?'

'Right enough, sir,' Heel bellowed at his back.

Stryker had marched across countless battlefields, breathed deeply of the sulphurous air that such places produced, and stormed more burning, smoke-veiled towns than he cared remember, but, even after so many years, those evil humours of war still blistered his eye and throat. He screwed up his face, straining to make sense of the obscured fight amid the yellow-ish, roiling fog, until, as if dropped there from on high, Skellen appeared before him.

'Will, get them into some order.'

Skellen knuckled the upturned fringe of his Monmouth cap. 'Right, you tardy-gaited bravos!' he snarled, transformed by action into some demon in this unholy mist. 'On me, and make it lively!'

'Stand your ground!' Stryker bellowed, as his men began to step back from the more advanced positions on the road. He craned his neck left and right as Skellen continued to bellow orders, fretfully scanning the ground in the grim expectation of discovering red-coated bodies. To his relief, he saw none, but that would not remain the case if the situation went unaltered for much longer.

'All yours, sir!'

Stryker had to twist his entire head to see the speaker, as the voice had come from his blind left side, but saw that Skellen had arranged the musketeers into two broad ranks.

Stryker moved to the end of the line, wincing involuntarily as the air pulsed beside his face. Somewhere behind, he heard a thump as a musket-ball met a doorpost. 'First rank only!' he roared. 'First rank, I say!' He drew his broadsword, held it aloft so that all might see the ornate Toledo steel and know it was him, and swept it downwards in a scything arc. '*Fire!*'

The world seemed to crack in half. The noise was ear-shredding, reverberating about Stryker's chest like the beat of a thousand drums, and he had to take a step back to steady himself. But it had been exactly what was required. A single, thunderous volley at close range. All at once a gust of fresh air swept down from the village, funnelled first between houses and then between ancient trunks. It dispersed the powder smoke as though it had never been there. The view was abruptly, starkly clear. Green-coated bodies moved amongst the trees, sure enough, but Stryker could see that they were falling back in the face of an organized onslaught that had evidently been unexpected.

'Hold your fire!' he snarled at the remaining ranks. He turned to the waiting pike block. 'Sergeant Heel! Get them into those bloody trees!'

But even as he saw the great, tapering, razor-tipped shafts of ash fall to chest-height so that they might charge the green men beyond the roadside, Stryker knew that his pikes were not needed. The cacophonous volley, coupled with the terrifying image of the advancing pike block, had worked its magic. Less than a minute had passed since the muskets had rent the air, yet already there was no return fire from within the tangled branches. Indeed, the rebels showed only their backs.

*

34

The ambushers scattered like sparrows before a buzzard. Their dark green coats melded superbly with the lush summer woodland, but their movements could be seen well enough, as so many blurs against lichen, branch and trunk. Stryker watched as the enemy soldiers plunged deeper into the foliage, scrambling to save their skins like a herd of hunted deer, but he called for his own men to hold their position. It was tempting to race after the fleeing rebels, to put them to the sword as they had been put to flight, but he did not know what was beyond the wood. Perhaps these men were not a terrified and isolated unit, but the bait in a bold Roundhead trap. He doubted it, but that did not mean he was interested in finding out. Some of his men strode between the gnarled trunks, fanning out into the shadowy world to ensure there were no remaining threats within musket range of the road, and Stryker let them wander, but most he ordered to stay back.

'Where's Barkworth?' he asked of the nearest men. One pointed to his right, further along the line to the eastern extremity of the village. Sure enough, out on the far side of the musket line, he saw a diminutive figure dressed in grey, holding a short sword and spitting unintelligible oaths.

'Sir?' Barkworth rasped as he came running back towards his captain.

'You're the fleetest of foot, Simeon.'

Barkworth grinned, displaying a mouth full of mouldering, crooked teeth. 'I am, sir.'

'Get into that damned forest and see what they're about. Have they retreated far, or do they linger close?'

'I will, sir.' Barkworth's sharp yellow eyes narrowed as he scanned the deeper forest. He pointed with his sword. 'Might like to ask him a few questions while I'm gone, eh?'

The rebel had not fallen far from the road, and that was his undoing. A near miss from a Royalist musket-ball had caused him to lose concentration and his foot had snagged an exposed tree root. The fall, it seemed, had knocked the wind from him, and by the time he recovered his senses, Stryker's advance party had reached a point beyond his hiding place, cutting off his escape.

'Richard Port, sir,' the man, who looked to be in his early twenties, had replied to Stryker's first question. 'Musketeer, Purcell's Foot.'

Stryker glared down at the captive. He knew that the circle of redcoats hemming in the kneeling Parliamentarian must have been a formidable sight, and he set his jaw, hoping his glowering expression and glinting grey eye would cow the fellow as it had so many others. He placed a hand on the swirling metal of his sword-hilt, leaving it there as a reminder of violence held, for now, in check. 'Purpose here?'

'Luring us in, sir,' Lieutenant Thomas Hood had spoken at Stryker's right hand, and he shot his subordinate a hard glance.

'No, sir, not that!' Port cried suddenly. 'Never that!' He had been stripped of his weapons and held his good right hand up at Stryker in supplication. The wrist of the left had been damaged in the fall, and he let that lie across his lap. His cap was lopsided, his eyes round as newly cooled musket-balls and his skin slick with a cold sweat. 'An accident is all. No design, sir, 'pon my life.'

'What lies beyond these trees?' Stryker asked.

'Another road, sir,' Port bleated. 'Just a little track. We are a patrol out of Keynsham, sir. Stumbled into your force, and—'

'Thought to bloody our noses.'

Port offered an apologetic shrug. 'Aye, sir. But nothing more sinister. There is no more than two score in our whole unit!'

Stryker kicked him in the chest, flinging him on to his back, leaves billowing in all directions like fine ash before the breath of bellows. Port cried out, curled into a ball like a woodlouse, and began to rasp breathless prayers into the earth. But the Royalist captain was astride him in a heartbeat, kicking his injured left arm free and placing his boot heel directly on the wrist.

Port's scream was shrill and desperate.

Stryker eased his weight on to the boot, feeling the rebel's pinioned limb sink into the ground until the soil was compact enough to resist. The wrist began to audibly crack.

'Please!' Richard Port squealed like a piglet at Smithfield. 'Please, sir! I beg you!'

But Innocent Stryker could not relent. He knew he should, and yet it was as though his leg would not heed his conscience. In that moment he felt like a cooking pot left too long over a flame. All the darkness of recent weeks, the anger, the melancholy, the guilt and the abject, spiralling sense of loss bubbled to the surface in a great torrent. He had to hurt, as he had been hurt.

'Sir,' a man muttered at Stryker's back. It might have been Skellen, it might have been Heel. He did not care.

'Once more, damn your hide! What is your purpose here?'

'An ambush, sir!' Port wailed, eyes glistening. 'Nothing more! 'pon my son's life, nothing more!'

Son. The very mention of the word thrust a lid on the cauldron, a jug of water on the flames beneath. He met Port's wide gaze, lifted his boot, and stepped back. Christ, but what was he doing? He took a deep breath, shook his head, and addressed the captive again. 'Is there a larger body of men in this area, Musketeer?'

'No, sir,' Port murmured, lying on his side now, clutching his agonized wrist to his breast as he gasped like a drowning man. He forced himself to look up into Stryker's face, his breaths heavy, laboured. 'A chance raid. Ill-judged as it were, God forgive us.'

Stryker heard the approach of rapid footsteps and turned to see a newcomer reach the group. 'What say you, Simeon?'

Barkworth panted from the run and his constricted voice rasped like a whetstone on a new blade. He glanced with interest at Port, then looked back up at his commanding officer. 'There's a track beyond the trees, Cap'n.' He pointed to the north, where the forest was thickest. 'Half mile that way. Nothin' there now, so the buggers are long gone. No great army, though, sir.' He glanced again at Port. 'Just these sorry bloody greencoats.'

'Got more than they bargained for,' Lieutenant Hood put in.

Stryker ignored him, looking instead at Ensign Chase. The standard bearer had been quietly taking account of the aftermath of this most hectic skirmish. 'Bill?'

Chase had evidently left the company flag out on the road with the rest of the men, for he held a naked blade in one hand. With the other he scratched at his wiry brown beard. 'Just two, sir. Both theirs.'

Stryker nodded his thanks before scanning the assembled faces for his most senior non-commissioned men. 'See to the dead, Sergeant Heel. Skellen, truss this one up and bring him back to the road. We'll let Quartermaster Kinshott find a wagon.'

Richard Port peered up at his captors nervously. 'Sir?'

'You're for Bristol, fellow,' Stryker replied. 'You can beg the King for mercy.' He nodded at Skellen.

Skellen lent his ferocious halberd against a nearby elm and stooped to hook a gloved hand round Port's tensed arm. 'Up you get, son.'

The rest of the group began to pick their way back to the road. Stryker was forced to skirt a dense thicket of bracken, the route bringing him close to Thomas Hood, and he heard the younger man chortle at something Ensign Chase had said.

'Stand the men down, Lieutenant,' Stryker snapped, cutting short their shared jest, 'and be sharp about it!'

Hood swallowed hard, casting his eyes to the ground. 'Aye, sir.'

Stryker instantly regretted his tone. Indeed, he regretted the very words themselves. He raised a hand in his new subordinate's direction. 'Thomas, I—'

'Christ on His Cross!' The raging blasphemy echoed through the trees like a pistol shot. 'Come 'ere, you fucking little bastard!'

Stryker and the men at his flanks turned as one to gaze upon a scene engendering such surprise that they simply stood and stared. William Skellen was on his backside in the dirt and leaves, knees hauled up to his chin, huge hands cradling his right leg at a point midway up the thigh. Even from this distance, dark tendrils of blood could be seen oozing between his gloved fingers. He rocked back and forth like a bedlamite, hooded eyes fixed upon the trees to the north and cursing.

And already some way off, leaping bracken and weaving branches like a deer with a green hide, Musketeer Richard Port made good his escape.

CHAPTER 3

Bristol, 3 August 1643

Stryker leaned forward to pat the sleek neck of Vos, his sorrel-coloured stallion, as he and his eight companions trotted steadily through the Frome Gate and into the battered city. Vos whickered contentedly, his right ear twitching slightly in time with his master's hand, and Stryker muttered something soothing as they drew closer to the heavily armed guards milling malevolently beyond Bristol's walls. The place was clearly nervous, the sentries watchful and suspicious, and Stryker wondered if the king's arrival had set them on edge. An attack on Bristol now, however unlikely, was indeed something of which to be mindful. If the enemy could wrest back control of England's second city while the sovereign was inside, then that might end the war at a stroke. He was glad to be quartered out in the relative calm of the countryside.

The time had slipped by without incident since the skirmish on Hartcliffe's hitherto sleepy roadway. Stryker had taken pains to be pleasant to the folk of the village and had enjoyed his hostess's simple but comfortable home. Indeed, the delights of a home-cooked meal, rather than the charred remains they were normally given, was something to be savoured. Thus, when the summons had arrived, he had been most reluctant to leave the pleasant billet. Colonel Mowbray, however, had been clear that no dissent would be tolerated. Stryker had had Vos tacked and made ready for the ride.

'Still, old man,' Captain Lancelot Forrester chirped at

Stryker's right side, 'there are advantages to being back on the road.'

Startled, Stryker glanced across at his friend. 'You read minds, Forry?'

Forrester ran a gloved hand along the coke-black mane of Oberon, his big gelding. 'It is quite clear from your expression that you would rather not make this journey.'

Stryker raised his lone eyebrow enquiringly. 'For the sake of argument, what are these so-called advantages?'

'It does no good for a soldier to sit around on his arse for days on end.' Forrester craned his torso forward, saddle creaking in complaint, to peer across at the fellow riding on Stryker's left flank. 'Besides, we may thank the good Lord above that Sir Crannion, here, has been offered a task to which to set that maudlin mind.'

William Skellen chose to ignore the remark and instead kept his dark eyes fixed on a place in the middle distance. Forrester's point was well made. Skellen had bemoaned his injury almost constantly since the unseen blade had entered his flesh in Hartcliffe Forest. It occurred to Stryker that Richard Port evidently had more about him than the innocent terror he had seemed to exude. The concealed knife, a small thing but sharp as the finest poniard, had torn a neat little hole in Skellen's lower thigh. He had been lucky, for he had not sensed the fateful movement of Port's arm, nor made moves to avoid it, and the weapon might have been a great deal bigger, the blow more damaging. But that did not make the furious sergeant grateful.

'You're right, Forry,' Stryker said, loudly enough for Skellen to hear, 'the whining scold seems to have finally found his peace. I was beginning to wish the devious greencoat had run him through, for my ears hurt so.'

'Forgive me, Sergeant, but why are you here?'

Skellen, Stryker and Forrester turned as one to look upon one of their party who rode a handsome piebald beast some yards behind. It was Sergeant Major Cornelius Goodayle, and, though he made the remark in good humour, it was a

41

reasonable enough question. The group was made up of the regiment's eight company commanders, less Colonel Mowbray himself. Lieutenant Colonel Baxter led the way, followed by Goodayle and the half-dozen company captains. Skellen dipped his head in acknowledgement of the regiment's third most senior man, and answered with due deference. 'Protection, sir. We was attacked two days back. Ambushed. Roads ain't safe. My job, as I see it, sir, is to keep m' captain's skin intact. Sir.'

Goodayle smiled wryly. 'If Captain Stryker requires a bloody bodyguard, Sergeant, then I resign my commission, for the roads really are too hazardous.'

Snorts of laughter followed, and Stryker saw fit to defend his man. 'I gave him permission to come, sir. We languish in our billet, and Skellen is a man of action.'

'And,' Forrester added impishly, 'he was bound to be murdered by his own men, such is his bellyaching of late. Stryker protects Skellen in this, not the other way around.'

'It is Mowbray,' someone said with sharpness, and the chatter died away. Baxter tugged on his reins to slow the group, and, sure enough, from amongst Bristol's busy streets cantered a big bay horse upon which perched a small, well-dressed man with flowing russet hair and neatly kempt beard and moustache. Sir Edmund plucked the feathered hat from his head, waved it at his approaching officers, and absently glanced down to check that his royal-red scarf was neat and conspicuous about his gleaming breastplate.

'Fastidious as ever,' Forrester muttered quietly, though without a trace of malice. He was fond of the colonel, as were they all.

'Ho there!' Mowbray bellowed when he reached the group. 'The men?'

A chorus of positive, if impatient, murmurs answered the colonel's predictable enquiry, and he nodded happily. Stryker felt his own mouth begin to twitch in a private smile. Mowbray's staccato movements and clipped speech never failed to put him in mind of the sparrows that had danced about his window as a boy. He cleared his thoughts quickly as the man who had founded and funded the regiment leaned forward purposefully in his expensive saddle.

'I apologize for wrenching you all back to this poor city,' Mowbray began, voice high-pitched and nasal but clear as a bell. 'But I am come direct from Council.'

'What is to become of our grand alliance, sir?' one of the assembly asked in the accent of the Low Countries, and all eyes fell upon a pale-faced man of willowy frame and twisted, broken nose. Aad Kuyt, the regiment's first captain, was a toughened veteran of the wars in his homeland, a professional soldier and one of the best Stryker had served with.

'We came together as two armies,' Mowbray answered promptly, placing the hat back on to his head with a light tap of his fingertips, 'and we shall depart as two armies.'

Kuyt's pale brow rose, forehead rippling beneath his thick blond curls. 'We are to divide, sir?'

Mowbray nodded at the Dutchman. 'Aye. The Western Army marches south and west with Prince Maurice.'

Kuyt exchanged a wary glance with Sergeant Major Goodayle, and the latter spoke, his deep tones incredulous. 'They're allowing the Cornish to leave? We heard some units had already departed, but not the entire force.' Goodayle stretched his broad shoulders and rubbed a meaty hand across his chin. The stubble scraped loudly. 'My God, but they're our hardiest scrappers by far.'

Mowbray spread his palms. 'And they would rather scrap in their own towns than in some far-away place. Moreover, Trevanion is killed; Slanning grievous wounded.'

Lieutenant Colonel Baxter blew out his thinly bearded cheeks. 'That after Grenville fell at Lansdown.'

'They haven't the stomach for it any more,' Mowbray went on. 'His Majesty has two choices. He may let them march back through Devon, reasserting his dominance in that region, or he may force them to remain with the Oxford Army.'

'And have them desert in their droves every night,' Baxter agreed, removing his hat to expose thinning iron-grey hair and

43

fanning his face with the brim, 'till they've melted away to dregs.'

Stryker cleared his throat. 'What of the rest, then, sir?'

Mowbray fixed him with a steady stare. 'The Oxford Army – of which we are now a part – will march upon Gloucester.'

Stryker felt his heart pound harder against his ribs as he recalled Bristol's dark streets lit by hellish, tremulous flame. 'Another storming?'

'Perhaps, Captain. Though the losses here seem to have set many a mind against another such course.'

'A siege, then?' Stryker asked, realizing he had been holding his breath. He let the air ease out through his nostrils as his pulse began to calm.

'Starve the buggers out,' Forrester added with relish.

Mowbray offered his clipped shrug. 'It is not yet known. The Council was called to determine two things. Firstly, whether this grand alliance would part or march on to the next design.'

'And second?' Forrester prompted impatiently.

'What that design,' Stryker interjected, 'should be.'

Mowbray let his intelligent eyes drift to his second captain. 'You have it. The first decision was made with little fuss, as I have already recounted.'

'And the second was not such a smooth voyage.'

The colonel's pinched face cracked in a rueful smile. 'Well put, Mister Stryker. The King's chorus sings not in harmony but in grievous discord. One faction pushes for the subjugation of the Severn Valley, Gloucester being the final obstacle to that design.' He glanced about at the black-tinged walls and lead-pocked buildings. 'Rupert took this place in no time, and it is stout compared with Gloucester, by all accounts. I hear their garrison numbers no more than that of Cirencester, and we stormed that in half a day. But many others argue for a direct march upon London. They see Gloucester as a distraction.'

'I can see their point of view, Sir Edmund,' Goodayle boomed. 'Before the spring, the rebels held sway across most of the west. Devon, Somerset, Dorset, Wiltshire.' He counted each region on a thick finger. 'They garrisoned Bristol, and sent the Severn Valley's riches direct to Parliament's coffers in London. But now what do they have? Stratton took care of Lord Stamford's army, and Roundway destroyed Waller. The Roundheads are finished here.'

'He's right, sir,' Stryker agreed, casting his mind back to that bloody hill overlooking Devizes where Sir William Waller's forces had been utterly smashed by the famed Royalist cavalry. The last major Parliamentarian field army had been crushed without hope of recovery, placing the momentum firmly with the Cavaliers. 'Gloucester is no longer the northernmost tip of a vast rebel heartland. It is a lone island in a sea controlled by the King. Why waste our time in its taking?'

'Because with Gloucester we have control of the River Severn,' Mowbray replied, 'allowing us to supply Shrewsbury and Worcester from the port of Bristol. And because,' he added with a half-smile, 'it is populous and wealthy.'

Forrester snorted in amusement. 'Tax the buggers till coins pop out their backsides.'

Mowbray nodded. 'Precisely. So we must take the city, mop up the region, then look east.'

'To London,' Sergeant Major Goodayle growled.

London, 3 August 1643

'You have heard of the Peace Party?' Christopher Quigg asked as he and Lisette Gaillard strode northwards along Fish Street. They had rendezvoused on London Bridge, hoping the crossing, tightly packed as it was with homes and businesses, would be teeming with the comings and goings of the day. Sure enough, the bridge had provided ample cover for their clandestine meeting, and quickly they were on their way into the city.

'*Naturellement*,' Lisette replied, unable to prevent the derision that coloured her tone.

He frowned. 'You dislike a faction who would shift against the Parliament in their own town? I imagined you'd be their greatest advocate.'

Lisette looked up at Quigg. 'I dislike a faction who would sue for peace, in any form. The rebellion must be crushed, not negotiated with.' She saw the puzzlement in his expression. 'You think me a hard woman, yes? You do not know me, monsieur. You have not seen what I have seen.'

Quigg shrugged. 'And what have you seen?'

'*In*,' she rasped suddenly, hearing stentorian tones coming from beyond the street corner, some twenty paces up ahead. She snatched a handful of Quigg's doublet and dragged him through the nearest open doorway.

'What in God's name is that stink?' Quigg blurted angrily, unhappy at the manner with which the woman had manhandled him, and repelled by the vile air that greeted them.

Lisette touched a finger to her lips, indicating the roadway with a jerk of her chin. Immediately the voice she had heard rang out again, louder this time, and Quigg's bulging eyes widened with terror. Now the fool understood, she thought, for he could tell a sergeant's bellow as well as the next man.

The squad marched by. It was a small unit, perhaps a dozen men in the distinctive egg-yolk-coloured coats of the capital's Yellow Regiment. At their head was indeed a man who probably held a sergeant's rank, for his gloved hand gripped the shaft of a well-maintained halberd. Lisette held her breath, almost gagging from the stench that had pervaded her nose and throat. She peered back into the gloom of the building, realizing by the stink that they were in a tallow chandlery. At the rear of the workshop she could see the startled face of a man who had been hefting a stack of candles from one bench to another. He stared at them with a mixture of confusion and fear. She pushed the hem of her long cloak aside to expose the hilt of a dirk that protruded from her boot. The man sank back into the shadows.

She looked up to see Quigg's pocked cheeks rapidly flush. He was evidently struggling with the noxious smell too. But the patrol had no interest in the building or its occupants, and quickly their thudding progress fell to a whisper as they turned down a side alley and away. Lisette let the acrid air seep from her nostrils, releasing her white-knuckled grip on Quigg so that he might rush out into the open.

Lisette followed in his gasping wake, calling a word of thanks over her shoulder. She had no idea whether the chandler's disappearance was an act of mercy or fear, but the effect was the same, and she thanked the Holy Mother for his silence.

'Now?' she asked as she reached Quigg's side.

Quigg pointed to the street corner from whence the patrol had come. 'Turn right there, on to Little East Cheap. It is a short way after that.'

'Then let us make haste.'

'We were speaking of the Peace Party,' Quigg said as they rounded the corner. 'You may not like them, madame, but they are the key to this scheme of yours, mark me well.'

'They are up in arms?'

Quigg scratched at his crooked nose. 'Not yet. It is mostly the womenfolk, truth be told, but the resentment festers, nonetheless.' He brandished his empty gums in the semblance of a smile. 'The pot bubbles, so to speak. A touch more heat and we could have a proper uprising on our hands.' Without warning, he took Lisette's elbow, steering her down a narrow alley that seemed to taper with each step. At a point where it was nearly impossible for them both to walk along the passageway shoulder to shoulder, he abruptly stopped by a low, studded door. 'And here,' he said, rattling the stout timbers with a distinctive knock that she guessed was some kind of code, 'we shall meet the man who will bring our pot to the boil.'

The door groaned loudly as it swung inwards, and Quigg bent beneath the wizened lintel. Lisette followed more slowly. Inside, a pair of fat candles flickered in placings on the wall, but they did not offer a great deal of illumination. There was also a window, open to encourage some semblance of a breeze, but it was high and small, and the result was a stiflingly muggy interior.

Lisette loitered near the threshold as a woman closed the door at their backs, increasing the gloom all the more. But by now her eyes were becoming more accustomed to their new surroundings, and she studied the woman closely. She was about forty years old, with mousy hair swept away from her high forehead and carefully captured beneath a coif. That garment, like the long apron that covered the rest of her bony frame, was stained with smudges of black. The woman acknowledged Lisette with a nervous nod.

'This,' Quigg announced, 'is Goodwife Greetham.'

'God save you, Goody,' Lisette said.

'And I,' came a voice from deeper into the room, 'am Henry Greetham.'

Lisette and Quigg turned to see the speaker. He was tall; perhaps, she thought, similar in height to Stryker, but of a far leaner build. His face was cadaverously hollow, with cheeks like craters dug beneath deep-set eyes and jutting cheekbones. His jaw was heavy with stubble, darkening the skin around a narrow mouth.

A smiling Quigg approached him, making to grasp the man's hand, but Greetham shook his head with a wry smile, lifting palms vertical as though he pushed open an invisible door. They were black as jet, shimmering like the surface of a deep pool in the guttering light. 'A hazard of my trade, I am sorry to say.'

Quigg turned to Lisette, grinning toothlessly in triumph. 'Printer's ink.'

'I can see that,' Lisette replied testily, though Quigg's speed at arranging this meeting had been impressive.

They moved further into the room, and Lisette was instantly overwhelmed by the smell of the place. She caught her breath and waited a moment to steady herself.

Greetham seemed to read the discomfort on her face, for he grimaced. 'The paper and ink make for a most rich odour, do they not? But you are most welcome.' He beckoned to them, and they followed him into an antechamber at the rear of the dwelling, Mistress Greetham busily tidying the little house in their wake.

At the doorway to the rearmost room was a young lad of about ten. He, like his parents, had blackened fingernails and deeply stained clothes. He was red-haired, thickly freckled and as skinny as his father.

Greetham patted the boy's head, striding past him into the room. 'My son, David. He is my apprentice. One day my successor. It takes skill and diligence to work her, but he learns daily.'

Lisette frowned. 'Her?'

Greetham let them move into the antechamber, where the smell of ink was that much riper, and moved aside to provide a good view of the interior. '*Her*,' he said grandly, sweeping his arm back as though he were introducing a play at one of London's (albeit now defunct) theatres.

Lisette looked beyond Greetham. There it was, the reason she had made this journey.

'You wanted a printing press,' Quigg boasted, 'and I found you one.'

She ignored him, her attention instead focussed upon this thing that was so alien to her eyes. It was a machine. A vast skeleton of ink-stained wood and iron that squatted in the room's centre, ugly and dominating, a huge screw rising from its very core like the ominous dorsal fin of some biblical sea creature. That screw was suspended between two broad wooden pillars, rising vertically from their fixings in the floor and connected by leather straps to the ceiling.

'This here is my pride and my joy,' Henry Greetham declared, moving to place a hand upon one of the press's stout uprights. 'My pet. My baby.' He moved across to one of the stone walls and snatched a long apron from a hook. The garment might have been white once, Lisette supposed, but it was now as black as his stained paws. He deftly fastened it around his neck and waist, and returned to pat the machine fondly, as though it were a beloved dog.

'You are an experienced newsmonger, sir?' Lisette prompted.

'Learned the trade in Holland, mademoiselle.' He looked

lovingly upon the press once more. 'Brought her back to these shores piece by piece. Assembled her in this very room, for she would not have fit down our alley, let alone through the door.' He beamed. 'But she was worth it.' He clapped his hands together smartly, startling his guests. 'Is she not a thing of rare beauty?'

Lisette and Quigg exchanged mute glances, but already the newsmonger had darted across to stand beside the huge contraption's mechanical core. Slowly, almost tenderly, Greetham began to caress the vertical screw with his dark fingertips. 'See here; the spindle sits snug in this collar.'

The collar, as far as Lisette could ascertain, was a metal ring that covered the entire circumference of the screw, holding it in place. A long bar jutted from that collar, curved at the insertion point but straight after that, and she watched – more than a little discomforted – as Greetham let his hand snake up and down its length.

'The bar,' he said, 'may be pulled down to lower the spindle and, being raised, will lift it. When we pull her thus, she will exert a great force, but precise for all that.' He demonstrated briefly, easing the bar towards him so that the screw moved directly downwards into the very heart of the press. 'The consequence is neat, legible, lettering.' He grinned again. 'News-sheets, pamphlets, decrees. Anything a man, or *woman*, could wish for.'

Now that was what Lisette had wanted to hear. 'You will print what I ask?'

'God save the King,' Greetham intoned in a low voice.

'*Bon*,' Lisette said, her mind already wandering. She was standing beside a low table strewn haphazardly with sheets of paper, and something on those sheets had caught her eye. She noticed they had already been used, crammed from top to bottom with neat letters, all encircled by an elaborate floral border. She picked one up, scanning the printed pages with interest.

'Oh, madam,' Greetham stammered suddenly, unease inflecting his hitherto jaunty tone, 'do not mistake—'

'*Joyful news from Kent*,' Lisette read aloud, scanning the page for the next piece of pertinent information. '*Troops loyal to God and the Parliament suppress heinous uprising by Papist plotters.*' She dropped the pamphlet, casting Greetham an acid look. 'You shift for the Parliament, sir?'

'No no no,' Greetham protested, the words tumbling from his narrow mouth. 'I swear I do not. A more loyal man could not be found in this troubled city, I swear it.'

Lisette looked at Quigg. 'What manner of man have you enlisted, sir?'

Quigg's eyes darted down to search her hands, perhaps checking for the knife he knew she carried, but before he could respond, Henry Greetham had moved to the table, keeping his eyes on the Frenchwoman. He carefully gathered some more of the news-sheets, tapped them on the table gently to bring them into some kind of order, and handed them to Lisette. She leafed through them silently.

Greetham drew a lingering breath. 'My cover, madam. I am a printer. There are not many of us hereabouts, thus we are all known to the authorities. What would you have me do?'

Lisette looked up from the papers, each one printed with a new anti-Royalist report. 'Do not print this filth.'

Greetham's face creased plaintively. 'But I must print something, do you not see?' He glanced at the press. 'She cost me every groat I had. She is not something a man buys only to leave dormant. There would be more Westminster eyebrows raised were I to leave her silent. So I work her. And what does the Parliament require of me?' He reached out, tapping a long, stained finger on the news-sheets in Lisette's grip. 'This drivel.'

Lisette paused a moment, then made to speak, but the news-monger cut across her hesitation.

'But in amongst the chaff,' he went on, 'you may find the occasional sheaf of purest wheat.' He crouched suddenly. Lisette stepped backwards, reaching for her concealed weapon, but he was digging his long fingers into the crack between two large stones in the floor. He lifted one of the stones with a grunt, flipping it over. In the exposed hole was a small cloth sack. He snatched it up and handed it to her.

Lisette pulled the throat of the sack open, taking out more sheets of paper, all similarly inscribed with elaborate borders and stark, black lettering. She scanned the first, noting how the language carried the same triumphal tone as the rest. But the message itself could not have been more different: '*Joyful news from Cornwall*,' she muttered. '*Being the true copy of a letter sent from a captain in Sir Ralph Hopton's army to his wife in London, dated May 17th, 1643*.' She looked up. 'A report from Stratton Fight.'

Henry Greetham stared directly into Lisette's eyes. 'From the Royalist side.' He took the sheet from her and pushed it gently into the sack, then stooped to return it to its hiding place. 'Those,' he said, straightening, 'are my true works, madam. They are distributed throughout the land by the King's couriers. His agents, like yourself. If I am caught with them, my life would be forfeit. But I am a loyal servant of King Charles.'

Lisette looked from Greetham to his printing press and back again. She nodded. 'Then we have work to do.'

Near Bristol, 3 August, 1643

Sir Edmund Mowbray had further business in Bristol, and turned back into its winding streets as soon as his impromptu gathering had been dismissed. The rest of the men began to wend their way towards their billets at Hartcliffe, and soon the pack, hampered as they were by supply carts, returning refugees and troops of various denominations, found itself splintering. Goodayle and Baxter, the most senior men, set a brisk pace up ahead, with captains Kuyt, Taylor, Fullwood and Bottomley some distance behind, chatting happily and evidently enjoying the open country.

'I cannot believe,' the regiment's fourth captain, Lancelot Forrester, muttered in low tones, 'you had the audacity to join this party, Sergeant.'

The man trotting at his side on a lean-limbed bay mare sniffed the air as though he were a hound. 'Rain again soon, I reckons.'

Forrester rolled his eyes in exasperation. Stryker rode some twenty paces ahead, and he stared at his friend's back. 'It wasn't for protection, was it? Why you came, I mean.'

Skellen looked at him then. 'It was, sir. Though not in the way you think.' He joined the captain in watching Stryker. 'Out in the woods, when that bugger stabbed me . . .'

'Someone stabbed you, Sergeant?' Forrester exclaimed in mock horror. 'By the nail holes of Christ Himself, man, you should have told us!'

'Out in the woods,' Skellen went on as though Forrester had not spoken, 'the captain was—' He hesitated, watched all the while by Forrester's searching gaze. 'He was angry, sir.'

'He's always angry.'

Skellen nodded, though his face remained troubled, an expression Forrester had rarely seen. 'Always angry, sir. But not this. This was . . . vicious. The man who stabbed me, sir. Mister Stryker broke his wrist.'

'Quite right too, William. Decent sergeants are hard to come by.'

'Thank you, sir, but he did it before the bastard drew his dirk.' He shrugged. 'Was more than that. The hate. The cold fury in his face. He's not right.'

Forrester glanced from sergeant to captain and back again. 'You stay with him to protect others,' he said in sudden understanding. 'You're afraid he'll get into some scrape on account of that temper.'

Skellen nodded. 'He's not right.'

Forrester turned back to Stryker, who still forged ahead out of earshot. 'Cuts a lonely figure, does he not?'

'Wasn't his fault, sir.'

'It was that damnable greenback's, Sergeant, I agree.'

'Not the skirmish, sir,' Skellen said, instinctively touching a hand to the place on his right thigh where the steel had

53

punctured. 'The lieutenant. Witch-catcher pulled that trigger, and none else.'

Forrester let out a long, sad sigh, remembering Lieutenant Burton's murder on that dusk-shrouded hill. He could still see the blood spatter in all directions, could hear the thud as first the young man's knees and then his beaten torso collided with the ground. Those staring, lifeless eyes. 'That being so,' he replied quickly, 'Stryker nevertheless feels responsible for his men.'

'Lost a lot o' men over the years, sir.'

'Haven't we all,' said Forrester. 'But Burton was different, William, you know that. More like a brother – no, a son – than a subordinate. And they'd quarrelled of course.'

Skellen sucked at an unseen tooth, wincing slightly. 'Aye. Up on that bitch of a tor.' He looked across at Forrester. 'They'd resolved it, mind.'

Forrester sighed with a hint of impatience. 'But young Andrew's death was due to his recklessness. And that reckless-ness was nothing if not an attempt to regain some favour with the good Captain. Stryker knows that truth well enough, no matter what muttering platitudes we might offer to absolve him. He feels it as keenly as that wound in your leg.' He dipped his shoulders, fixed Skellen with a stern stare and let his voice drop to a hoarse whisper. 'If only you'd not quarrelled in the first place. That is what his mind whispers in the darkest hours.' He straightened again. 'And that quarrel, as you must know, was perhaps of Stryker's own making.'

The sergeant's dark eyes searched the horizon, a ghost of concern snaking across his features. 'Couldn't say, sir.'

Forrester studied the man, ordinarily so laconic and unflap-pable, and knew he was troubled. He wondered if the sergeant recalled the company's time on Gardner's Tor, hounded by a furious cavalryman and a vengeful witch-finder. They had rescued a young woman, quite by accident, and had taken her with them on to the tor. And there, so the rumour mongers said, she had come – irrevocably and, perhaps, fatally – between

54

Stryker and Burton. Skellen would never articulate the rumours, of course, but every man had heard them.

Forrester shook his head. 'Nor should you, Sergeant. Either way, that is how our friend sees it, so that is all that really matters.'

As if the very act would clear away the evil humours such a conversation had conjured, the pair kicked forward together, cantering to close the gap between themselves and Stryker. Almost immediately Forrester saw that they need not have bothered, for the lone officer had slowed to a virtual halt. He was looking across at a group of mounted men passing on the other side of the road, though they too were tugging on reins to hold their charges still.

Forrester looked from the group – numbering around twenty – to his friend, and realized Stryker's face, visible now that he had half-turned, was rigid and strained. He had removed his hat in an evident show of respect, but something about his expression did not seem right. And then Forrester's heart began to quicken, for he noticed that the coats worn by the troopers were dyed a rich yellow. He scanned the group, searching the faces for the one he feared was amongst them, until, with growing horror, he laid eyes upon a man he had prayed he would never again see. It was a countenance obscured by the three vertical metal bars of a gleaming cavalry helmet, but Forrester could nevertheless identify the white beard and thick, wet lips, and, as he and Skellen drew ever closer, hear that terribly familiar voice.

'Shite,' Sergeant Skellen intoned grimly.

Forrester swallowed hard. 'Artemas Crow.'

Captain Innocent Stryker had been thinking of Lisette Gaillard. Dreaming of her as the stones of the road passed beneath Vos's reddish bulk. They had not seen one another since early April when, after a night making love in the warmth of the Lion Tavern in Oxford, they had once again parted. Stryker had gone south and west with the army, sent to bolster Sir Ralph Hopton's campaign against the Devonshire Parliamentarians, and she had gone . . . where? She had not been willing to say, but some well-placed threats in the corridors of the king's new capital had given rise to rumours of Paris, or Rome or Madrid. But then she had returned, for he had been ordered to join her in London for the rescue mission on Cecily Cade, the girl with knowledge of great treasure. The girl who had been taken by the enemy from under Stryker's nose. The order, of course, was counter-manded almost immediately, as Waller's great rebel army had threatened Hopton's progress, and Stryker was denied the chance of seeing her again. Lisette Gaillard. He revelled in her image. Tried desperately to see her in his mind's eye. See the faint white scar on her chin, the blue eyes that seemed to look right through him. Christ, he missed her.

'By God!'

His dream instantly shattered. In a heartbeat those lovely images had disintegrated into a thousand shards, tumbling away like a great church window under an iconoclast's hammer. What replaced them was a reality as bleak as it was dangerous. And it came in the form of a man. A short, plump man with tiny blue eyes and a flat, bulbous nose.

'By God, I say,' the voice of Colonel Artemas Crow rang out again. That voice. That shrill, furious voice Stryker recalled with the most terrible clarity. It was as though it drilled a hole into his very skull. He felt instantly sick, even as Crow tugged the helmet from his head, tossing it to one of his stern-faced dragoons. 'If it ain't the Prince's little hero.'

Stryker simply stared, dumbstruck and frozen in his saddle, as Crow grinned his way down from atop his fine mount, grunt-ing as his tall boots hit the mud. He was just as Stryker remembered; short in stature, stocky as a mortar and angry as a hornet. His white beard positively glowed against the livid red of his fat nose, and his huge lips glistened in the afternoon sun.

'See how he conducts himself?' Crow sneered loudly so that his troopers could all hear. 'Sits when his betters stand. I'd expect nothing less. A rogue, this one. A rakish cur, good for murder and deserving of the gallows.'

'Was not Captain Fantom sent that way only recently, sir?' one of the dragoons replied.

Crow glanced back at him. 'Aye, Samuel, that he was.' He looked at Stryker. 'Did you ever meet Carlo Fantom, Captain?' When Stryker nodded mutely, the colonel went on. 'He was a superior cavalryman, none could deny it. A Croat, I believe. Veteran of the Low Countries, like yourself, and a notorious killer. Again, like yourself.'

'Sir, I—' Stryker began.

'But,' Crow cut him off sharply, 'he overreached himself, didn't he? A devil in a man's clothing. A beast who fed on slaughter and rape. His own army – *this* army, Stryker – had him dancing the noose-jig for his evil ways.'

Stryker shook his head defiantly. 'Fantom was a ravisher, sir.'

'And you are a murderer, sir,' Crow replied slowly.

Stryker's first instinct was to dive at the ruddy-cheeked colonel, beat him to a pulp with his fists alone. His mood of late had been volcanic, and he was inclined to let it erupt. But the exaggerated clearing of Forrester's throat somewhere at his back made him think twice, and he managed to rein in his temper. Reluctantly, he snatched off his hat and dismounted, fixing his gaze on an invisible point just beyond Crow's shoulder. 'I had hoped,' he stammered, his heart thumping each word up to his mouth.

Crow's blue eyes, small and malevolent, searched Stryker's face for what felt like an age. 'Hoped?' he echoed the word with a malicious grin, stepping closer so that Stryker could smell his acrid breath. 'Hoped, you say? And what had you hoped, Captain? That I had forgotten you? Forgotten your arrogance, your smug smirk? Forgiven you the casual murder of my sons?'

The mention of that fateful night in Cirencester brought whirling memories to the fore. A pair of yellow-coated brothers had died in a makeshift stable, one at the end of Stryker's sword, the other impaled on a pitchfork wielded by Sergeant Skellen. Stryker remembered their eyes, glinting with such malevolence. Like their father. 'Saul and Caleb Potts were—'

'Were mine!' Colonel Artemas Crow erupted in sudden, spittle-drenched rage. He took a pace forward, as though he would lash out. Instead, he levelled a quavering finger in Stryker's face. 'They were mine, you cur,' he hissed so that only Stryker might hear. 'Not my heirs, certainly, but my flesh. My blood. And you stole them from me.' He turned back, raising his voice. 'Here, my lads, is the murderer of poor Saul and Caleb! The killer of brave Major Edberg. Look upon him as you would Satan himself.'

'Colonel,' one of the dragoons, still mounted, kicked forward, drawing his carbine in the same movement. He said nothing more, but Stryker saw the look on his face, and unsheathed his sword.

Crow smirked as more of his men brought weapons to bear, urging their horses on until they formed a rough crescent around colonel and captain.

Stryker lifted his blade, letting the tip dance in the air in front of the animals' faces. He knew it was a feeble gesture, for the dragoons were seated high and hefting muskets and pistols, but he would be damned before showing his apprehension to Artemas Crow. 'One at a time,' he said, feeling reassurance in the arrival of Skellen and Forrester at his back, 'or must you hold hands?'

To his surprise, Crow began to laugh. It was a sound he had not heard before, and its screeching tones were even more penetrating than his speaking voice. 'Hold!' he ordered, raising an arm to curtail the ambition of his yellow-clad disciples. 'Not here, my lads. Not now.' Crow threw Stryker a derisive sneer. 'Put that little hanger away, Captain.'

Stryker hesitated at first, but the evident cessation in hostilities gave him pause for thought. To be seen holding a blade before a senior officer was not wise, and he gradually lowered the point to the throat of his waiting scabbard.

Colonel Crow spun abruptly on his heels and stalked back to his horse. 'No, sir,' he declared when he had clambered back into the saddle, 'I have neither forgotten nor forgiven, and your time will come. By God it will.' A thought seemed to come to him then, for his amphibious lips parted in a sudden grin. '*Captain* Stryker. The title is a disgrace. This courageous swash-and-buckler man, they say. How can he not be a major in our grand army, or higher still? *Pah*!' Crow rocked back as though his chest had been hit by a pistol ball. 'Well I know, Stryker. You are no gentleman. No leader of men. You are a peasant.' He jabbed the air with an accusatory finger. 'You are a common brawler. A *murderer*. The Prince cannot protect you forever.'

'I'll be waiting, sir,' Stryker said, instilling his tone with a confidence he did not feel.

Colonel Artemas Crow hawked up a sticky gobbet of phlegm and spat it on the road a few feet from Stryker. 'Of course you will,' he said simply, and pulled hard on his mount's reins.

CHAPTER 4

Hartcliffe, near Bristol, 4 August, 1643

The tip of the match-cord glowed bright orange in the murky dawn. It wavered at chest height like a flaming wasp, swaying left and right in small arcs, menacing in its promise of instant death.

The little man approached it steadily, pacing along the road with his arms held aloft in a show of supplication so that the man carrying the weapon would not shoot. The picket stepped forth, musket still levelled, his features resolving from behind the bright match, but the object of his suspicion merely swept back his hood and muttered a single word. 'Killigrew.'

The picket nodded, suddenly at ease. He closed the long-arm's pan cover and averted the menacing gaze of the muzzle. 'On your way, sir,' he said, lifting the musket a touch to blow on the match, careful to keep it ready should a shot be required.

Ezra Killigrew offered a nod of thanks as the match-tip raged fiercely, and replaced his hood, moving on into the village. He smiled to himself. He was not a large man. Indeed, his short stature and dumpy torso had been the object of ridicule as a child. He was no rake-hell or dashing *cavaliero* like his master. But he had power. Strangers did not know it, would never believe it, but Ezra knew it, felt it, wielded it. Those, like the picket, who knew his name, quaked in fear. And that was enough. As aide to a great man, he would arrange things, would speak to people at court, would whisper in the appropriate ears and hiss the necessary threats. He smiled again.

Killigrew skirted the row of tawdry, sagging buildings as quickly possible, keeping to the dark crevices of the new dawn. He might have been in the army, but he was no soldier. He hated the rank and file, old soaks intent only on brawling and rutting, men born for this life and who God had doubtless chosen to perish in battle or of the pestis. No, Ezra Killigrew was not one of them, and his goal in life was to have as little to do with the low-born sort as possible. On occasion, however, business forced him to brush up against society's underbelly. He gritted his teeth, pulled his cloak tighter and prayed none of the worst kind were yet out of their beds.

He had been told Hartcliffe was the place and, sure enough, the red ensigns of the regiment could be seen leaning up against the window panes of homes at regular intervals. The colonel's plain colour was not here, of course, for Sir Edmund and his company had remained in Bristol, but the rest were all present. The lieutenant colonel's standard, a copy of his colonel's with the added cross of St George in the corner beside the staff, was the first he identified, and he snaked past it quietly. The next was the sergeant major's flag, which carried the added device of a pile wavy, a tongue of white flame issuing forth from the St George canton. He knew he was getting close when he saw the colour of the regiment's sixth captain; half a dozen white diamonds filling the red field. He peered down the street, brown eyes straining in their puffy sockets, looking for the colour that carried just a pair of diamonds at its centre.

'There you are,' Killigrew whispered, spying the object of his search just a little way down the road. 'Now, Mister Stryker. I do hope you are not abed, for this day will prove a busy one.'

Malmesbury, Wiltshire, 4 August 1643

The building was a substantial affair of small red bricks. It was a storehouse, with large lower chambers crammed with hogshead casks and two airy rooms above. The upper windows were unglazed, split by vertical mullions of moulded brick, and the roof beams were black with soot, the telltale sign of life before the stout chimney had been added.

The large man stared up at the beams as he reclined in a high-backed chair that creaked at his every movement, his pudgy fingers laced across his vast belly in the manner of the iron rings fastened around the barrels in the chamber below. 'Fetch me some of that beer.'

At once, another man shifted. He pushed himself away from the mullion against which he had been leaning and went to a low table that held three battered blackjacks. He lifted the first, weighing it in his hand before selecting the second, which was evidently more full, and decanted some of the rusty liquid into a goblet of crumpled pewter. He moved slowly across the room, careful that his pronounced limp and crooked back would not cause him to spill the ale, and handed it to the fat man. 'Why here?'

The fat fellow leaned forward and yawned, scratching at his beard as he did so. It was a rich chestnut colour, matching the curls on his head, which were still thick, though they were beginning to abandon his forehead and temples. He jerked his head to the side, so that his oxlike neck cracked loudly, and took the cup. He sipped, closing his eyes contentedly. 'They say,' he replied when he had taken his fill, 'the malignants will march upon either Gloucester or London. From here we may react to whichever course they choose.'

The crookback winced, his right eye flickering uncontrol-lably. 'What if he don't go wiv 'em?'

'An acceptable risk, Nobbs,' the fat man said. He picked a small hair from the rim of the cup. 'What else would you have me do?'

Nobbs offered a slanted shrug. 'Buggered if I know, sir.'

'And that is why you do as I say.' The fat man set the goblet on the floor, careful that it balanced evenly on the worn timber slats. 'Of course, if you wish to question my authority, you may do so.'

Judging by the grimace, it hurt Nobbs to shake his head, but he did so anyway. 'No, sir. Not a bit of it.'

'Good. A shame Jonas did not share your wits.'

Nobbs swallowed hard. 'Sh–shame indeed, Mister Slager, sir. Stupid bastard, he was, sir. Brains of beef and the heart of a mouse.'

Slager simply grunted in reply. 'How about we take a look at the piece, eh?'

Nobbs scuttled in his crablike manner across the boards, stopping when he reached a stout hogshead beside the closed door. He had dragged it up from the storeroom upon their arrival, just one of threescore such barrels in the building's inner sanctum, but his master had been quite specific about which one it had to be. He glanced down at the small cross that was chalked on its side before taking the dirk from his waist and prizing open the already loosened lid. 'I thought—' he began, peering into the musty interior.

'You thought it was a musket?' Slager interrupted correctly, jerking wobbling chins towards the barrel.

Nobbs took the prompt, and dipped his hand into the hogshead. What he drew out was a metallic stock, etched with intricate swirls and images of prancing stags. It was small, not even the length of his forearm from elbow to wrist, and set into its far end were a pair of neat limbs of polished steel. Between them, crossing the stock horizontally, was a thick cord of twisted hemp.

Nobbs turned. 'A crossbow.'

'A balestrino. The assassin's bow. It is favoured in the Italian states. Guns are too risky for our needs.'

'Risky, sir? I heard some cur put a ball through Lord Brooke's eye from atop Lichfield Cathedral.'

'A lucky shot, Nobbs,' the big man said dismissively. 'He could not have repeated it had he tried a hundred times. And besides, a matchlock would be too awkward for our mission, not to mention too large.'

'Pistol, then?'

'Too unreliable. Even if we were to get close enough, it could well misfire, and our chance would be gone. This,' he said, gazing at the weapon still held in Nobbs' hands, 'gives us the best opportunity. Small enough to bring close to the target, but accurate enough to make the shot. And no flash in the pan.'

Footsteps sounded from the corner of the room behind Nobbs, and he turned sharply. Before him was a handsome but painfully thin man, with a mop of straw-coloured hair, shining brightly against his suit of all black, and a square chin so cleanly shaven that it looked as though no beard grew there at all.

'Christ, Robbens,' Nobbs hissed, 'must you lurk so? I almost shat m' britches!'

'She is a beauty,' the newcomer, Robbens, said in heavily accented English, as he moved closer. He lifted a hand to fiddle with the strands of silk that had been threaded through a piercing in his earlobe. The ear-string was his only flourish of colour in an otherwise sober ensemble, and he pulled the threads together, laying them in a bright bunch across his shoulder.

'That she is,' Slager, still leaning back in his chair as though it were a throne, agreed. 'Cost a pretty penny, I can tell you.'

'The Union were happy to fund,' Robbens replied, his ice-blue eyes never leaving the crossbow.

'They were indeed,' Slager said. 'They cannot have England sit any longer on the sidelines. Things are desperate.' He set his meaty jaw determinedly. 'This will change everything, so they say.'

Robbens dipped his head piously. 'I pray they are right.'

'Unless he misses,' Nobbs added nastily.

Robbens cast him a withering gaze. 'I never miss.'

'In your hands, or mine,' Slager said to Nobbs, 'the bow is dangerous enough. It is spanned using a screw built into the rear of the stock, so that a killing draw-weight can be achieved.'

'Small, though,' Nobbs said, his eye quivering again as he studied the steel weapon suspiciously. 'The bolts must be like needles. One o' those couldn't knock m' granny off a piss pot.'

Slager nodded. 'It would not penetrate armour, you're right, which is why it needs to be aimed by an expert if the throat or eyes are to be picked out. Fortunately, held by our Dutch friend here, it is unerringly deadly. It is the best balestrino bow money can buy. Robbens is the best shot money can buy.'

Nobbs sneered. 'He looks half starved. You sure about that?'

Robbens' eyes seemed to gleam, but he chose not to take the bait. 'I can wield the piece well enough, friend.'

Nobbs dropped the crossbow back into the barrel. 'Still need to get bloody close, though,' he replied belligerently, 'Don't care how much you tighten the screw, it can't fling anything too far. It just ain't big enough."

'I will get close,' Robbens said. 'If Mister Slager can arrange the opportunity, I will take it.'

'It will be arranged,' Slager said. 'Have no fear over that.'

'And they'll kill you,' Nobbs added, a little too happily. 'Soon as you loose the bolt, they'll cut you to scraps.'

Robbens closed his eyes. 'I have made my peace with God.'

Nobbs shook his head, nonplussed. 'Bloody antick.'

Robbens' eyelids snapped open, his thin face creasing in a smile devoid of warmth. 'With two bolts, Mister Nobbs, I wager I could pierce each of your stones. Would you like to take the bet?'

Slager leant forward for the first time. 'Enough, sir.' He looked at Nobbs. 'I hope you are not losing faith.'

'No, sir, 'course not,' Nobbs said quickly. 'Just that m' mammy always told of the old longbows.'

'That they had the greatest range, were the most accurate?' Slager asked. 'And where would we find a bowman of the calibre to shoot it? The draw–weight on a longbow is more than a normal man can bear. It takes a lifetime to wield one properly. But this,' he glanced at the cask. 'This can be brought to bear by any man. The only question is the man's aim. And I have brought Robbens all the way from the Continent because he never misses.'

Nobbs nodded reluctantly. 'What now, sir?'

Slager sat back. 'We wait for the Cavaliers to make their move, and follow them to whichever poor town is next to face their wickedness. We take Master Robbens with us, and he takes the new bow. Sooner or later the malignants will make a mistake, and he will be allowed close enough to the mark.'

'And then,' Robbens added quietly, 'I will put a bolt in the mark's Romish throat, and the war will be over.'

Slager threaded his hands behind his head, easing back into the chair, a smile of contentment spreading across his fleshy face. 'And another war can begin.'

Ashton Vale, near Bristol, 4 August 1643

Colonel Artemas Crow's throat itched. He imagined a doctor might tell him the humours of the inn, so pungent with sotweed and filthy bodies the previous night, had irritated his lungs, and that fresh air was the only remedy. But he knew better. His throat always itched, and his heart always pounded and his jaw and gums always ached from the grinding of rotten teeth. All because his mind had turned, as it so often did, to an infantry-man with long, rook-dark hair and one grey eye.

'Stryker,' he said aloud. He lifted the wooden cup, rim worn pale by a generation of use, and took a long drag of the small beer, hoping it would jolt him awake. He was seated at a table that had been pushed hard against one of the White Hart Inn's grimy walls. From there, he gazed over the vessel at his men, good troopers all, as they began to stir, groaning and yawning and stretching as sleep began to give ground to the new day. He did not approve of this kind of place. He despised the strong drink his men imbibed, detested the dice that had been thrown and the bawdy songs the merry dragoons had bellowed to the rafters. His small, battered Bible had felt suddenly heavy in one of his coat's breast pockets, as he had watched the serving-girls throw themselves at his lads, and he had prayed aloud as he had swived one of the fairer little punks himself. But what could he do? He had been billeted here, his men thrust into Satan's jaws, and there was little to be done but suffer it with humility.

Now, though, as the morning sun climbed up from the eastern hills, his cloudy mind was once again captive to that man who made the night's sufferings seem tawdry. 'Captain Stryker,' Crow said again, turning the words on his tongue as though they formed some wicked incantation. It disgusted him that such a man might hold a blade in the king's grand army. 'Let alone a fucking commission!'

'Colonel, sir?'

Crow glanced to his left. There, sat at the adjacent table, rubbing the dregs of sleep from his eyes with broad, calloused palms, was a black-haired man of muscular physique and square, heavily bearded face.

'My nemesis, Major Triggs.'

Triggs thought for a moment, rubbing the pale gully of a deep scar that bisected his right cheek from earlobe to nostril. 'The plodder we ran into yesterday, sir?'

'The very same. Captain Stryker is his name. A more wicked cur you will not encounter.'

It surprised Crow, this hatred. Sometimes he would catch himself brooding on the one-eyed infantryman, noticing the familiar itching in his windpipe, the whitened knuckles or grinding teeth, and he would have to physically shake his head to rid his mind of the demon. It was a burning resentment, a never-dying ember that would flare unexpectedly to scorch his mind and mood. Christ, but he hated Stryker.

Crow considered himself to be a reasonable fellow in the main. Quick-tempered, admittedly, and his late wife would often accuse him of ill-humoured irascibility, but times were difficult, and war had the power to bring tension to the most sanguine of bodies. He was a hard man, but a fair one, and that, Crow felt, was all that could be asked of him. But Stryker had come along, had strutted into his life in the smouldering ruin that was Cirencester, and murdered his two beloved illegitimate sons. His wife might have been pleased at the thought of Saul and Caleb finally being cut from their lives – and any pretension to inheritance – but Artemas Crow had loved them as his own.

Separated from him by society, he had used war to bring them closer, providing them with posts within his new regiment of dragoons. He had always enjoyed the fact that he had used conflict to unite his family, even as it tore so many others apart. Yet all that joy, all that possibility, had been stolen from him on a single night.

'The 2nd of February 1643,' he muttered.

The major scratched a knot of dried pottage from his whiskers. 'Sir?'

'The night Stryker made my life crumble to ruin. I have never forgotten that damnable warlock's face, or the wrongs he has done me. But then it was there, wasn't it?' He remembered the moment he had looked upon Stryker on the road outside Bristol. He had feared his heart might stop in that very instant. 'The 2nd of February 1643. That date will remain with me,' he tapped a finger against his temple, '*branded* up here, until the day I'm put in the ground. It is the day I will avenge.' A thought bloomed in his mind's eye, glittering and radiant, as the sun bloomed beyond the White Hart's dank walls. 'No, Samuel. It is the day *you* will avenge for me.'

Triggs nodded eagerly. 'Gladly, Colonel. Tell me where he is and I'll run the bastard clean through.'

Crow offered an appreciative smile, but shook his head all the same. 'He is protected by men you would not wish to cross.' The proud face of Prince Rupert replaced that of Stryker in his mind, and he shuddered. That Teutonic rake-hell was the murderer's patron, and not even Crow would dare make an enemy of him. 'Rupert and his brother, Prince Maurice, are two of the most dangerous men in the land. They would not be kind to a man who had hurt their little lap dog.' The king's strutting nephews were the worst kind of Cavaliers to Crow's mind. Brash swaggerers both, darlings of court and army. Unbeatable fighting popinjays. Men clamoured to be in their regiments, men's wives clamoured to be in their breeches. Artemas Crow was not about to move against their favourite soldier with such audacity.

'Besides,' he said, thinking back to the aftermath of Stryker's original crimes, 'I have followed that course already, and failed.'

'Major Edberg,' Triggs replied grimly.

Crow nodded. 'Your predecessor underestimated Stryker's lust for blood, and was himself murdered. Stryker is one of the Cavaliers who poison the King's cause as sure as Pym and his dogs cock their legs against it. Not of the same lofty breeding as the princes, and certainly,' he mused with a half-smile, 'a damned sight uglier than the sons of the Winter Queen. But he is a man of action, I am forced to concede. Touched by luck and blessed with Rupert's patronage, and that makes him extremely dangerous. The knife we wield must be subtle. Do you have a man, Triggs? A trusted fellow? One who might watch Stryker, get close to him, engaging only when the moment is right?'

Triggs breathed loudly through his nostrils and tilted his head back to look at the ceiling. Eventually he dropped his gaze again, meeting his commanding officer's small blue eyes with the merest hint of satisfaction. 'Aye, sir. I believe I do.'

Hartcliffe, near Bristol, 4 August 1643

Stryker did not much care for Ezra Killigrew. He thought the fellow a pompous, self-important prig who enjoyed wallowing in his master's power as a dog might roll in fox shit. But he knew it was unwise to ignore the summons and now, just an hour after sunrise, he found himself following Killigrew along a narrow track through the fields to the south of the village.

'How far?' he growled in irritation.

Killigrew did not look back. 'Not far, Captain, not far at all.'

'Christ, man, do you ever grow weary of your games?'

Killigrew gave a nasal chuckle, flattening down the slick black hair that was glued firmly to his pate by pungent lavender oil. 'Never, sir.'

'I am in no mood for this.'

Killigrew stopped and turned. 'When are you ever, Captain? His Highness says you have been tiresomely maudlin since Stratton.'

Stryker felt himself tense. 'Mind your tongue, Killigrew, or I'll—'

The pudgy shrew's face creased in an unpleasant smile, revealing crooked teeth and gums that were red-raw. 'You'll what, sir?'

It was a good question. What Stryker would like to do to Ezra Killigrew and what he had the courage to do were worlds apart. He breathed deep, feeling his heart quieten, and forced his fists to uncurl. 'How far?'

Killigrew winked a thick eyelid and pointed to a dense stand of trees at the far end of the field. 'Just beyond that copse.'

The rendezvous point was a grassy glade, accessed by three or four small tracks but invisible from the main road. A clandestine spot if ever there was one, Stryker mused, as he skirted the last of the trees in Killigrew's scuttling wake. Up ahead he could see a collection of horsemen milling at the glade's centre, all facing inwards, collective attention taken by something – or someone – within. There were a dozen of them, all dishevelled and mud-spattered from a hard ride, but, even at a distance, it was clear that these were no mere cavalrymen. The beasts they rode were well bred and heartily fed – big, sleek and muscular – while pommels gleamed like sceptres from ornate sword-hilts and cloaks flashed as gilded thread caught the light. Stryker felt his ruined eye socket tingle, the patchwork of mottled pits feeling constricted at the edges, contracting in time with his quickening pulse.

'He has his entourage, I see,' Stryker muttered.

'Not your favourite fedaries, Captain?' Killigrew answered dryly. 'There, at least, we find common ground. Still, the Prince will ever draw a following, be it a troop of strutting toadies in the field or a gaggle of breathless young maidens at court.'

'Damn the spavined villains!' the voice exploded like an incendiary shell at the epicentre of the glade. Stryker glanced at Killigrew. The supercilious aide proffered that irritating wink once more, stooped in a low, mocking bow, and moved quietly aside.

Stryker stepped forward, swallowing hard. The horsemen parted like the Red Sea as they made way for one of their party. Even atop his mount it was clear the man was tall. He had a slim frame, though broad at the shoulder like an acrobat, and a long face made predatory by a sharp nose and dark, intelligent eyes. His buff-coat was well worn, weathered and crusty, but it could not hide the fashionably laced suit of blue and yellow beneath, or the ostentatious scarf of bright red that was tied in an enormous knot at the small of the man's back. The upturned bucket-top boots were dirty but clearly of fine quality, and the red ribbon in his wide-brimmed hat was shot through with silver thread that seemed to shimmer against his long, tar-coloured hair.

Prince Rupert, Count Palatine of the Rhine, Duke of Bavaria, Knight of the Garter, General of all His Majesty's Forces of Horse and favourite nephew to King Charles, let his vast black stallion lope out to greet Stryker, who offered a low bow that the prince entirely ignored. 'Each one a veritable piss-a-breech, Captain, by my very honour!' Rupert snarled in the curiously accented voice that described his famously itinerant upbringing in the courts of Europe. He leant forward in his saddle, crossing his long arms to prop himself against the animal's muscular neck.

Stryker felt the scab at his forehead start to itch as his skin began oozing sweat. Rupert's mount was bigger than most, and the general was himself gigantic. His great shadow seemed to loom like some vast thunder cloud.

'The Council, Your Highness?' Stryker ventured.

Rupert peered down at Stryker as an eagle might eye a hare. Stryker was not a man to be easily intimidated, but this young soldier – only twenty-three years of age – was to be genuinely feared, and he quickly found himself staring at the prince's brightly spurred boots. 'Not His Majesty, Captain, but those who would pour craven words in his ears.' The prince sat upright

71

suddenly, plucking the glove from his right hand so that he might scratch at his lace collar. 'Do you know where next we march, Stryker?'

Stryker replied that Colonel Mowbray had told him of the ambition to take Gloucester.

'In which case, you will know that *gentler*,' Rupert hissed as though the word itself tasted of acid, 'means are to be employed upon the engagement of our next conquest.' The black stallion took a sudden step forward. Stryker flinched. Rupert glowered like some mythical beast, half man, half horse. 'I took Bristol in three days, Stryker. Gloucester is the lesser thorn of the two. It would be plucked from my uncle's flesh in a matter of hours if he would only leave me to my own devices.'

'And he will not, sir?'

Rupert fiddled with the silver lace that glittered at the fringes of his buff-coat. 'It is judged Bristol was too bloody an enterprise. Can you warrant such a thing?'

Stryker certainly could, for the storming of the port city had been costly indeed, if not in the quantity of men killed, then the quality. But he knew such an argument would be lost on the general. Prince Rupert had fought at some of the bloodiest engagements of the wars on the Continent in his efforts to wrest his father's Bohemian throne from the Holy Roman Emperor. Regimental commander at the age of fourteen, battle-hardened veteran before he could so much as shave, Rupert was not a man to waste time ruminating upon the butcher's bill.

'It is a travesty, sir,' Stryker muttered, engendering a chorus of sycophantic murmurs from the gathered horsemen.

'I am glad you see sense, Captain,' Rupert replied, his slight Germanic accent becoming less pronounced with the apparent cooling of his ire. He arched his back, stretched like a gigantic cat. 'There are those at court who would have us charge head-long at London.' His dark brow rose as he noticed Stryker's cheek twitch. 'On the contrary, Captain, I am not a member of that faction. Not yet, leastwise. We should take the capital, of course, but we must subjugate the Severn Valley in the first instance. It does not take great wit to understand.' He lurched forward suddenly, thumping his bare right fist into the gauntleted palm of his left. 'Secure the region, tax the hides off the rebellious locals, advance into the Associated Counties, castrate the strutting knaves who infest those parts – Cromwell and the like. And then crush London once and for all.'

'To secure the Severn Valley,' Stryker said, 'we must take Gloucester.'

Without warning, Rupert twisted his neck and shoulders to address the waiting horsemen. 'Leave us.'

There was a moment's hesitation, but the group let their mounts take them away along one of the waiting tracks. Only the prince, Stryker and Killigrew remained.

Rupert stared back down at Stryker. 'We must, as you say, take Gloucester. But I am not permitted to storm the contemptible place, thanks to my uncle's council of cowards. So which way must I turn?'

Stryker met the younger man's piercing gaze. 'Betrayal.'

The prince laughed, a rueful bark of a sound, at this. 'You are a clever man, sir.' He rubbed his proud chin with neatly manicured fingers. 'I must convince His Majesty to take Gloucester, Stryker, lest my enemies at court steer him on a different course. But I may not propose the strategy with which I am most at ease.' He shook his head mirthlessly, black curls quivering at his shoulders. 'It appears I must turn spymaster.' He paused to fish for something at the top of one of his boots, pulling a crumpled rag from beneath the leather. Lifting it to his face, he blew his nose noisily. 'What do you know of Edward Massie?' he asked eventually.

Stryker shrugged. 'New governor of Gloucester, sir. Appointed in Stamford's place. Young, but with experience in the Low Countries.'

'Like us, eh?'

'Sir,' Stryker acknowledged, though at thirty-two years, he hardly considered himself to be young.

'And it is rumoured,' Rupert added, 'a man with more than sympathy for our blessed sovereign's cause.'

Stryker considered the prince's words. 'He will surrender?'

Rupert took the glove from his lap and absently pulled the exquisite garment of kid hide back over his hand. 'We do not know for certain, but that is the hope. And that is where you might do us a great service.'

'Oh?' Stryker replied cautiously, feeling his blood begin to chill.

Rupert spread his palms wide. 'A request only, Stryker. I would not order you on such a task so soon after your heroics on the Christmas Steps. And besides, we are aware of your recent . . . loss. But,' he added quickly upon sensing Stryker's discomfort, 'we require further intelligence. A . . . *view*, if you will, on Massie.'

'Forgive me, sir, but it sounds like you have a view already.'

Rupert offered a wry smile. 'We have many views, and that is our problem. One man suspects the slippery knave will turn his coat, another is adamant he will not. The King does not know which voice to heed, and all the while time ebbs by. I would take Gloucester, Stryker, but it must be done quickly. Essex's army is to the east. They are laid low by some plague, unable to respond to our threat. But that will not last forever. So I would offer my uncle a new opinion, in the hope of expediency. An experienced opinion. An impartial one.'

'You would have me parley with Massie?' asked Stryker warily. 'But he will tell me whatever he feels I need to know, sir.'

'Not parley, Captain,' the prince said, twisting a fraction to gaze at the scores of smoke funnels that traced their way above the nearest trees, marking Bristol's distant hearths. 'That order has already been given, and will be carried out by a suitable ambassador in a day or two. I would not waste your talents on such an errand. No, sir, this calls for something less conspicuous.'

So, Stryker thought, he was to sneak in to the rebel stronghold. Not something to be taken lightly, but he had always preferred action to sitting around in fever-ravaged camps awaiting an army's next lumbering move. Especially as this particular army contained Artemas Crow.

He could not prevent an image of the colonel of dragoons resolving in his mind like some taunting demon. The snow-coloured hair, spike-like hackles, cheeks flushed crimson with that simmering rage, and eyes that seemed to blaze with raw, unquenchable hate. There was a debt of two sons lost in the ruins of Cirencester to be paid that could only be wiped clean by the demise of a tall infantry officer with one grey eye. Perhaps, he thought, it was right to take the opportunity to leave the army now. But he already had one mission on his mind. 'What of London?'

Prince Rupert of the Rhine had been gnawing at the inside of his mouth, but at the mention of the capital his face suddenly became a rigid mask. 'It is not high on the Council's agenda at this moment, Captain.'

'But Miss Cade—' Stryker blurted.

'Miss Cade?' Rupert replied sharply. 'Or Mademoiselle Gaillard? She is leading this task, is she not?'

Stryker shrugged in response. It was a shrewd thrust. The rescue of Cecily Cade had become something of a personal mission since it was from his company that she had been kidnapped. But he had to acknowledge that much of his guilt over remaining in the West Country was borne of the knowledge that Lisette was waiting for him in the capital.

'Miss Cade,' the General of Horse went on, his voice calm but stern, 'purported to know where her father's wealth was hidden, and we should very much like her to share that information. But she has not been liberated. The cursed rebels have her well veiled, and Mademoiselle Gaillard's attempts to track her down have come to nothing. Zounds, man, but we have not received so much as a whisper from her in near a month.'

Stryker gritted his teeth. He was tired of the argument. Lisette was the queen's most trusted operative, and she had been sent to discover Cecily Cade's whereabouts so the Royalists could send a rescue party. But that clandestine search had, by all accounts, proved fruitless, and Stryker had found himself helplessly teth-ered to Mowbray's regiment as the weeks trundled on. Things might have been different, he suspected, if the mission's chief architects – Sir Bevil Grenville and Sir Ralph Hopton – had thrived with the king's fortunes, and without their patronage the impetus had waned. Stryker inwardly wondered whether the remaining voices at King's Council even truly believed Sir Alfred Cade's treasure existed, but he resisted the temptation to say as much.

'Mowbray was right to keep you with the army,' Rupert was saying, 'for you are too important for us to lose. You will not be wasted chasing wild geese in London when you should be here making yourself useful.'

Stryker balled his hands into tight fists. 'Tiptoeing into Gloucester will be useful, General?'

Rupert's big horse lurched forwards again. 'Have a care, Captain Stryker,' the prince said levelly, though his taut tone put Stryker in mind of the treacherous currents he had encountered playing in the Solent as a child. Sheer ferocity concealed beneath a millpond surface. 'Have a care. You have served me many times, sir, and I am all too aware of your recent tribulations. For that I will ignore your tone on this occasion. But do not presume to speak above your station.'

Stryker dipped his head. 'Highness.'

'And who said anything about tiptoeing?'

The prince's sudden brightening threw Stryker off balance for a moment, and it took him several seconds to answer. 'With—with Bristol fallen,' he said carefully, 'the folk of Gloucester will be nervous. It will be difficult to break through their defences undetected.'

Rupert of the Rhine grinned broadly. He had a dazzling set of white teeth, and his ees sparkled with effortless confidence. 'And that, my dear Captain, is why you shall abscond.'

Stryker stared into the prince's brown eyes in surprise. 'Desert, sir?'

'*Ha!*' Rupert barked, clanging his gauntlet against the pommel of his ornate sword. 'Ingenious, is it not? Have the rebellious bastards welcome you to their bosom.' With that, he offered a sharp nod and tugged on the stallion's reins, compelling the animal to turn as though it were no more than a child's pony. He kicked it to a gentle canter, meaning to rejoin his now far-off entourage, but glanced briefly back over his shoulder. 'To discover if Massie will turn his coat, my dear captain, you must turn your own!'

CHAPTER 5

Gloucestershire, 5 August 1643

The sun cracked across the horizon as the three riders moved steadily eastwards. They did not speak a great deal, for they shared a creeping suspicion that this enterprise might well make an end of them. Men turned their coats often in this conflict where a true foe – or friend – was difficult to distil from the various competing interests that scrambled to fill the void left by a sovereign gone from London. But still the business of abandoning one cause to join another was fraught with risk, and not something to be taken lightly. For his part, Stryker's caution had been matched in equal measure by a sense of relief. He had considered, albeit fleetingly, a rejection of the mighty prince's decree. The waning interest in the mission to rescue Cecily Cade had been a bitter blow, and part of him had wanted to spit on Rupert's expensive boots and simply walk away, but such a reaction would have been tantamount to suicide. He had also had time to reflect, particularly upon the exchange with Artemas Crow and his baying dragoons. The yellow-coated colonel was a powerful man with impressive connections, his troopers well trained and dangerous, and the raging man's words still rang in Stryker's ears. Crow meant him harm, and, by turns, meant his company harm.

Consequently, the darkening hours after he had stridden from the glade had seen him busy with preparation. The genesis of the plan might have been Prince Rupert's, but the young general was not a man for detail, and it was Ezra Killigrew's quiet efficiency that marked the hastily made arrangements. He had been given leave to speak to Mowbray so that, should the mission end in failure, his reputation within the ranks would not be tarnished, but beyond that he was not to tell a soul, save the men who would share the short journey. Stryker, Killigrew had dryly observed, would not be the kind of man to desert alone, given the level of loyalty he seemed to inspire in others. The acerbic little aide had remarked that the captain's entire company would probably have followed him to the gates of hell, let alone the crumbling walls of Gloucester, if he asked it of them, but such a thing was obviously not desirable. Thus, it had been decided that Stryker would be accompanied by two confederates; one of his own choosing, and a second assigned by Killigrew.

'It is not that we lack trust, Captain,' Killigrew had explained once the horses had been tacked, 'but I have other tasks that must be carried out within the city. Messages to convey, and suchlike. My man will see to those, while you and your sergeant look to the mission at hand.' They were in a vast stone barn on the outskirts of Bristol, and he let his small eyes dart from Stryker to Skellen, who waited patiently close by on a bay mare. Killigrew's eyes narrowed as he examined the tall sergeant in the gloom. 'This is the man you chose?' he muttered dubiously.

Stryker had given a terse reply of confirmation, though he doubted the sergeant would have taken no for an answer, had he selected another for the task.

'Well I wish you all success,' Killigrew said as he released the bridle of Stryker's loaned gelding and stepped aside. 'You are comfortable with your mission?'

Stryker kicked a little harder than was necessary so that the huge chestnut beast lurched forward more quickly than Killigrew had anticipated. He tried not to smile as the aide struggled to keep his feet. 'I am. Turn my coat, enlist with the rebels and discover Massie's intentions.'

Killigrew had responded with a sharp nod. 'And if he means to surrender?'

'Come and tell you.'

The aide sighed heavily. 'If you cannot break out?'

'Make for the ancient wall to the east of the city. Wait for mid morning, and catch the sunlight upon a piece of glass.'

'How many times?'

'Thrice for surrender. A fourth and fifth if he is like to defend.'

Killigrew had set his jaw. 'I'll be watching.'

'See that you do.'

Thus, the trio of cloaked riders cantered out through the pale meadows to the east of Bristol and never looked back. Stryker wore his usual feathered hat, though the red ribbon he had fastened to it at Bristol had been replaced with one of plain black. Skellen and the third man, one James Buck, ordinarily wore Monmouth caps, but Stryker had convinced them to don hats with wide brims so that, come the bright morning, their venture into the rising sun would not prove too blinding.

Desertion, it transpired, was surprisingly easy. Stryker did not know what he had expected. Some stoic pickets, perhaps, challenging them in the darkness. Poised black gun muzzles thrust in their faces, metal locks gleaming in the moonlight like cut coal. But this army was too big to be contained by Bristol's smouldering walls – being a fighting force of near ten thousand men, all needing food and shelter – and it had spilled out across a huge swathe of the Severn Valley. The comings and goings of infantry squads or the thundering evolutions of mounted troopers were commonplace, the army's perimeter security necessarily fluid. Moreover, the king's grand horde did not suffer the same tribulations that had seen the Earl of Essex's rebel force thrust so low. They were a winning army, flush with confidence after Stratton, Lansdown, Roundway and Bristol, and – now that the restless Cornishmen had marched their cold feet back to the south-west – not many in their number were yearning to abscond. As the sun rose to illuminate the dawn, Stryker, Skellen and Buck forged east without hearing so much as a whisper of challenge.

James Buck, it transpired, was an intelligencer. An ardent Royalist, he had joined Ezra Killigrew's carefully constructed network of spies, enforcers, runners and code-breakers as a low-ranking informant, made useful by dint of his knowledge of Somerset and Gloucestershire.

'The terrain, sir,' he had said when pressed on the subject. 'Father was a drover. As a stripling, I'd follow as he drove herd or flock to market. One town this day, another tomorrow. Soon I knew every hillock, ford and shortcut for a hundred miles.'

Stryker could well imagine that such an intimate knowledge of the landscape had proven invaluable to Killigrew's covert machinations. 'In time,' he said, 'other, more complex tasks were entrusted to you.'

'Quite so, sir. And now here I am, serving the great Ezra Killigrew.'

Expendable pawn, Stryker thought. 'A deal of responsibility held by young shoulders,' he said pointedly.

'I have recently reached my nineteenth year, sir,' Buck replied with a half-smile.

Stryker looked across at him, assessing this new compatriot keenly. Buck seemed a plain sort, of sallow complexion, sad eyes and greasy hair that was the same colour as his mount's liver coat. He appeared a trifle moody, certainly for one whose career apparently excelled with the deepening of war. Not badly natured, as such, but somewhat aloof. Perhaps, Stryker wondered, he felt aggrieved to have been assigned a mission that would involve following orders given by a one-eyed, battle-worn soldier, rather than the smooth-tongued spymasters to which he was evidently accustomed. 'Did you see the escalade?'

'Bristol?' Buck asked. 'Aye, sir, I did. From the inside.'

'You were in the city?' Stryker replied, unable to hide his surprise.

'Mister Killigrew's business, sir, as ever. I went in to coordinate efforts with our people amongst the defenders.' He shrugged as though it no longer mattered. 'The Prince stormed the walls before I could work my way free.'

They reached a narrow stream, its clear water gurgling over grey pebbles, stretching ragged tentacles of green weed horizontally. One by one they led their tentative horses down the gentle slope to the grassy bank, paused as the beasts drank, and urged them across.

Stryker had been first to cross, and he halted in order to wait for his companions. His long hair had been tied tightly at the nape of the neck with a thin length of leather so that it fell between his shoulder blades like a tar-coloured tail, and he lifted a gloved hand to play at the fastening knot. 'How fares that leg, Will?'

Skellen was safely across by now, and he let his horse lumber up to whicker at Stryker's mount. Instinctively, he peered down at his damaged limb. 'Hurts like hell's flames, sir.'

'How did you come by the wound, Sergeant?' Buck asked when he had joined them.

'Stabbed by a crop-head.'

'I'd wager he didn't live long enough to wipe his blade, eh?' Buck said in a strained attempt to sound jovial. When Skellen failed to respond, he added, 'Rather you than me, Sergeant. I prefer my fights to be cloaked and shadowed.'

'Curious, then,' Stryker interjected, 'that your blade is so well used.'

Buck followed the captain's interested gaze to his sword-hilt. 'This thing?'

Stryker nodded. 'The grip is nicely worn, by way of a man's fingers.'

Buck's eyelid twitched for a moment. He blinked hard. 'Borrowed, sir. I am no swash-and-buckler man, I can assure you. Intelligencing is my life, and I would not change it.'

At midday, the party turned north. Killigrew had said that a military presence, from both sides, was heavy on the coastal road. Thus they had pressed a number of miles eastwards before joining the highway that would take them near Nailsworth and Stroud. It was a small detour, but one that was doubtless worthwhile, and now, finally, they were travelling in the right direction, for this rural conduit would lead directly to the rebel city.

They made good progress through forests and meadows fairly bustling with wildlife now that, and even the horses seemed to keep a high-kneed pace, as though the fresh air of this relative wilderness were a welcome antidote to the sulphurous miasma of Bristol. Civilization was scarce. They passed the odd hamlet, the comforting scent of wood smoke lacing the air, but didn't encounter a living soul. Stryker imagined parents ushering their offspring into their homes with fingers pressed tight to lips, urging silence lest the strangers were out in search of loot – or worse. Crossing the brow of a low hill, they looked down upon a farmstead that appeared utterly deserted. Its grounds were overgrown, the enclosures untended, and one of the outbuildings looked to have been ravaged by fire, judging by its blackened roof timbers. The three stared silently down at the scene as they rode by. Perhaps the owners had fallen victim to marauding soldiers not too dissimilar to themselves.

As they reached the rolling foothills of the Cotswolds, they noticed a small cavalry unit crossing the horizon. The troopers trotted along the crest of a far-away hill, their helmets like a string of tiny pearls against the blue sky. The three would-be turncoats dismounted, coaxed their horses to the edge of the road where they would be obscured by the low-lying branches of oak and ash, and scanned the distance for further danger. Nothing came, save for the cavalrymen, who seemed not to have spotted them and were instead content to continue their progress behind a little fluttering cornet.

'What shall we do if we are sighted?' Buck enquired when they were back on the road.

Stryker shrugged. 'There is no safe way to turn one's coat, Mister Buck.'

'I thank God,' Buck replied earnestly, looking Stryker up and down, 'you saw sense, and discarded your company coats.'

Stryker smiled briefly. 'When Sir Edmund raised his regiment,' he explained, 'his funds went towards the purchase of arms and armour rather than the pristine, matching garments you will see elsewhere in the army.' It had been one of the reasons why Stryker had been so comfortable in accepting his commission, for he reckoned the colonel was clearly a man of sound judgement, compared with many of the Whitehall cockerels who had courted him upon his return from Europe. 'We were quick to establish ourselves as a solid fighting force, reliable in both garrison and tertio. But the colonel always harboured the ambition to have his men march in one, uniform colour.' Indeed, thought Stryker, it was no secret that Mowbray had always felt the prickle of jealousy when his men were compared with the smart-coated ranks of the King's Lifeguard, Rupert's Bluecoats or the men enlisted with Earl Rivers. 'Upon Cirencester's fall, we captured divers stores of cloth. Enough for many units to replenish, replace and repair their kit. Since then, we have been in red, in the main.'

'In the main?'

'Utmost in Sir Edmund's mind is the comfort of his fighters. Those of us wishing to remain in our chosen clothes were given leave to do so.'

Skellen thumbed his own threadbare coat that had, if Stryker remembered rightly, started life the colour of seaweed, but which was now more a garment of brown, due to the many patches it had endured. 'This old thing's been with me right across the Low Countries. Killed a Bavarian dragooner for it.'

'Surprising a colonel would allow it,' Buck said.

'A good commander,' was all Stryker said, for it was all Buck needed to know. In reality, he reflected, it was the intervention of Prince Rupert that had secured Mowbray's reluctant acquiescence. Upon hearing of Sir Edmund's plan to purchase red cloth, the fearsome young General of Horse had insisted that a select few of his men remain in their neutral colours. Stryker had become a valued tool for the prince. His ban-dog, Forrester often wryly observed. A man to order upon certain tasks; those of a lethal kind that most other men would shirk. Stark red would not do for such operations.

'I am told you join us for your knowledge of the city, sir?' Stryker said, steering the conversation away from his own brand of intelligencing.

Buck nodded. 'Aye, sir, you're in the right of it. A Gloucester man, born and raised.'

'And now rallying to the defence of his home town,' added Stryker, 'even at the peril of his king.'

'Quite so. Once I am given my liberty, I can execute my duties for Mister Killigrew.' He seemed to sigh; a soft, wistful sound. 'It will be pleasant to see the old place again, though she is at low ebb.'

'Does any village or town thrive?' Stryker replied bluntly. 'I think not.'

Buck looked at Skellen suddenly, perhaps as uncomfortable with this subject as Stryker was with the last. 'You mentioned the Low Countries, Sergeant. So you are soldiers of fortune?'

'Aye,' Skellen answered with a glint in his eye. 'Mercenaries.'

The young man shot a cautious glance at Stryker. 'That is how—'

'How I came by this?' Stryker replied quickly, tapping his forefinger at the ravaged hole where his left eye had once been. 'Indeed. Black powder and lit match is not a poultice I would recommend for one's face. But that was long ago. We were called home by war.'

'And not stopped fighting since,' Skellen droned.

Buck stared at the desultory clouds. 'The logical choice for this mission, I suppose.' He flushed suddenly. 'Er, beg pardon, sir. I spoke out of turn.'

Stryker waved him away. 'No matter. You're right enough. What better than a local man and two soldiers of fortune? The King does not pay well enough, so we seek to offer our services to Massie. He did the same, I'm told. Preferred the royal cause but was not offered high enough rank, so he went over to the rebellion.'

Buck nodded. 'Hence, he can hardly condemn us for plotting the same course.'

'That is the idea, Mister Buck, certainly.'

*

It seemed as though dusk would never end, the high summer sun lingering above the Severn far to the west, but eventually the jagged shadows lengthened, softened, melded into one, and lay like a dark blanket over the rolling Cotswolds. Those hills were where Stryker led his companions, for they climbed towards Stroud, Gloucester looming like a storm cloud beyond, both beckoning and defying them. But first they needed rest, and the verdant slopes and valleys would offer the most protection during the impending night.

'I was thinking,' Skellen grumbled as they urged their mounts, three abreast, along a sunken track that seemed to plunge endlessly into one such valley, 'it'd be nice to have a sign.'

'A sign?' Stryker echoed incredulously above the trill of a thousand hidden grasshoppers. His horse's ear twitched and he reached out to stroke it. 'Gone religious on me, Will? I shall ask Seek Wisdom to minister to you.'

Skellen wrinkled his nose in disgust. 'Do that, and I really will turn my coat. I meant a field sign, sir.'

'But we don't know it, Sergeant, and a guess would be yet more hazardous. Wear a black feather in your hat, and they'll all be wearing white. Plump for a sprig of oak leaves, and it'll turn out to be beech, like as not.'

Skellen sniffed. 'Just a bit o' tawny rag, then.'

'We're deserters, Sergeant. Why would we have anything of that sort to hand?' he shook his head. 'We're safer with nothing, and we'll have to plead our case.'

'Well I hope you're right, sir,' the languorous sergeant muttered, his tone strangely absent. His steed had stopped her casual stride, her reins twisted taut about Skellen's knuckles. He was staring along the track, his hooded eyes transfixed. 'Cos I reckon we're about to do some o' that pleadin'.'

Stryker glanced across and followed Skellen's gaze.

The cry split the night like an axe through rotten timber. It was a human voice, the tone hard, urgent, lancing up from the place where the track vanished into night. All three men lurched forwards in their saddles, squinting hard at the inky depths.

Skellen's keen eyes had already seen something, and his face was rigid. 'Cavalry,' he said sharply. 'Dozen, maybe more.'

Stryker forced his eye to strain into the abyss, desperate to gauge the threat for himself. It was not often that he felt the lack of an eye, for his mind had adjusted to the disability in almost every way over the years, but at times like this, when failure to pierce the impenetrable darkness might result in death, brought reality starkly home.

And then, in one more aching heartbeat, he saw them too. Horsemen exploding from the low-lying darkness to the north. They were still a good way off – perhaps as much as half a mile – but even from this distance it was easy enough to catch the dull gleam of the russetted armour that encased their chests. These were fighting men, right enough. Well-equipped harquebusiers, doubtless brandishing pistols, blades and carbines.

'Trees, sir?' Buck asked, though the way he was already moving to the roadside made it clear that he expected only one answer.

Stryker shook his head. 'Wait.'

Buck's eyeballs looked as though they might pop from his skull. 'For protection, sir, surely?'

'If we run, they'll make assumptions we cannot afford. I'll not have them taking pot shots before they ask questions.'

'God 'elp us,' Skellen droned, for the riders were closing the ground between them with thunderous efficiency. They were competent horsemen, galloping hard, and already the whites of the animals' eyes could be seen like dancing sparks.

Stryker kicked ahead of his companions, thankful for his horse's calm courage, and positioned himself as conspicuously as he could in the centre of the road. He was careful not to appear threatening, leaving his sword in its scabbard and doffing his hat. But the riders did not slow their charge, and the foremost of them drew his long cavalry blade, held it stretched at arm's length as though it were a lance, and stood high in his stirrups.

'Jesu,' Stryker whispered. It was too late to run, and a fight would be bloody, rapid and futile.

The cavalrymen sped along the sunken road like floodwater through a drain, the iron shoes of their mounts rumbling despite the soft earth. More swords were drawn, and Stryker could see the faces of the riders now, taut and ferocious. Their eyes were narrowed to slits against the rushing air and their lips were drawn back to expose teeth gritted for battle.

'Oh God!' Buck wailed somewhere behind. 'We'll be slaughtered like piglets!'

'Captain?' Skellen said evenly enough, though Stryker could hear the anxiety in his tone.

'Hold,' he replied, not looking back. With one hand he patted the horse's neck. He let the other slip to the hilt of his sword.

They were just yards away. Stryker still gripped his sword, squeezing the shark-skin handle, but with his free hand he waved frantically, deciding to take a chance on the allegiance of the cavalrymen. 'Friends!' he bellowed. 'God and Parliament!'

'Parliament!' Buck and Skellen echoed somewhere behind.

One of the riders kicked ahead of the rest. Stryker noticed that he wielded a wicked-looking pole-axe rather than a sword, and he held it at his shoulder, poised to sweep it across in a short, murderous arc. Stryker drew his sword as a matter of instinct, levelling it in front to parry the blow, but even in that moment he knew that the axe-man's comrades would make a swift end of him nonetheless.

And then the rider was past him, the wind pulsing at his flank in the wake of the snorting destrier. Stryker twisted hard, watching the cavalryman rush beyond Buck and Skellen and wheel his mount round to face them. The rest of the harquebusiers followed suit, sliding swords back into scabbards in high-speed manoeuvres that were evidently meant to impress, and in moments they had encircled their quarry.

The man wielding the pole-axe, evidently the group's leader, let his heaving mount trot forwards. He glared down at Stryker, perhaps deciding whether to split his skull there and then. Through the vertical bars that obscured his face, Stryker could see that the man might have been around thirty, with a small, triangular beard and beautifully waxed moustache. The man nodded. 'Captain Robert Backhouse. Army of Parliament, Gloucester garrison.'

Stryker returned the gesture. 'Stryker. Hitherto army of King Charles.'

Backhouse's eyes narrowed. 'No longer?'

Stryker shook his head firmly, glancing at William Skellen and James Buck in turn. 'Nor these fellows.'

'Rank?'

'Captain, as was.'

Backhouse seemed dubious. He licked cracked lips slowly. 'You would join our cause, sir?'

'I would, sir,' Stryker said enthusiastically, sheathing his sword as he spoke. 'I am disillusioned with the King. There is talk of Popery in our ranks. The Queen brings more and more Romish gold and men to this land, and I will not be party to something that so offends our Lord.'

Backhouse gave an almost imperceptible nod. 'I am glad you see reason, sir.'

'Besides,' Stryker ventured with the hint of a conspiratorial smile, 'I have heard tell of great reward for men of ambition in Parliament's ranks.'

'That is often possible, Mister Stryker. We lack professional fighting men, and are keen to enlist them where we may.'

Stryker forced a grin. 'Then I'll fight for King Jesus and His brave men of Gloucester, Captain.'

Backhouse spurred forward suddenly, calling for his troop to follow with their three captives in tow. Stryker did not know whether to be relieved or terrified They were heading northwards. To Gloucester. To the enemy.

Captain Stryker had turned his coat. He was a Roundhead.

London, 6 August 1643

Lisette Gaillard held the fresh paper sheet up to the light that streamed relentlessly through the window. They were in Henry Greetham's house-cum-workshop off Little East Cheap, she and Christopher Quigg having made the hazardous journey from their safe house before dawn, and now, in the stifling little room, she was inspecting the newsmonger's handiwork. The characters were strong and stark, blocks of authoritative blackness against the pale paper, and she scanned each line with a growing sense of triumph.

'*Dread news from Bristol,*' Lisette read aloud.

The tall, cadaverous presence of Greetham loomed behind her, though she sensed by the constant shuffle of his feet that he was tentative. The hastily commissioned pamphlets had been produced during the night, the printer and his son churning out the various reports with remarkable speed, but clearly he was keen to attain her approval. 'You like that one? My wife's idea, truth be told.'

Lisette nodded. She placed the sheet on the table beneath the window, and picked up the rest of the thick stack. It was the only pile worth reading, Greetham had told her, for the rest of the table was full of the pro-Parliamentarian sheets he was obliged to print. She inspected the top leaf, again reading the largest print aloud: '*A true account of the destruction of Sir William Waller's army beneath Roundway Down.*' She cast her gaze down the rest of the report. It spoke of death and devastation on a grand scale, painting the Parliamentarian troops as craven rogues and incompetent buffoons. At the foot of the page, the newssheet made a strongly worded plea to the leaders of the rebellion, beseeching them to spare London from the coming tide of Royalist retribution. She noted that the plea made particular reference to a feared onslaught of men from the despised Welsh and Cornish regiments, and went on to hint at an imminent arrival of Catholic soldiers from Ireland.

She slid her thumb down the side of the ream so that the papers sprung forth like a fan. As they moved, she caught sight of new revelations. More easy victories for Prince Rupert and his demonic dog, Boye. A likely assault on the Thames Valley by the Marquis of Newcastle's northern Royalists. Tales of desertion and chaos amongst the Roundhead ranks. In short, the pamphlets and news-sheets were designed to strike terror into the hearts of Londoners. It was as though Greetham had distilled every nightmare and paranoia held by the capital's jittery populace and printed them all in this one, beautifully horrific stack of paper.

Lisette looked up from the sheets, staring into the anxious newsmonger's crater-like eyes. '*Parfait*, Monsieur.'

Henry Greetham swallowed hard, his skeletal head bobbing happily. 'All is well, then.' He looked back to one of the room's dingy corners, where his wife and son loitered, offering the ink-stained pair a warm smile.

'Now let us be away.'

It was Quigg who spoke, and Lisette turned to him. 'You have the names?'

The top half of Quigg's coarse face had been caught in the beam of light, and his huge eyes glistened. 'A score of contacts, aye. Ready to distribute our . . . *information* . . . at a moment's notice.' His amphibian gaze narrowed suddenly. 'We shall give the Peace Party something to shout about, eh?'

Gloucester, 6 August 1643

Stryker could see Gloucester's defences from two miles away. Even from this distance, it was clear that the city was a hive of activity, with a range of large-scale earthworks being thrown up across the whole of its north-eastern fringe.

'You see?' Captain Robert Backhouse, trotting out front, pointed at the tiny figures moving across a vast hill of soil that dominated the horizon. 'They raise walls from God's very earth.

Bastions too, so that our guns will wreak havoc upon your former allies.'

Backhouse had proven a pleasant enough captor. He had been suspicious of Stryker's claims of desertion, but Gloucester's cause was not one overwhelmed with competent soldiery, and he had evidently decided to give the three strangers the benefit of the doubt. As such, he had been happy to chat with the newcomers in the hours before dawn, explaining that the city's defences were partly made up of an ancient stone wall, but that the said wall only extended as far to the east as a place called Whitefriars Barn. From that place, where the wall thrust abruptly west towards Gloucester's epicentre leaving the northern half of the modern city unprotected, a new work of earth and ditch had been constructed. Commissioned by the city's common council and supported wholeheartedly by Massie, the military commander, it enclosed the entire northern part of Gloucester, snaking around the line of the River Twyver until it reached the natural protection of the mighty Severn to the west.

Captain Backhouse had chosen to approach the city from the north. The simpler route might have been to use the better-laid southern road, but Backhouse had stopped to speak to a local farmhand when they had come within five or so miles of Gloucester, and that man had warned him of a large body of horse and foot massing on Tredworth Field, an area of open ground immediately south of the city limits. Deciding upon a path of caution, Backhouse had chosen to give the southern road a wide berth, for it seemed likely that the unknown army were members of a Royalist advance party, and he had taken his men – and their three guests – across the hilly terrain to the north.

Now, as noon approached, that decision appeared vindicated, for the guards at the road's turnpike barrier were full of the news.

''Tis Gerard,' one of the sentries, a sergeant with cheeks blotched crimson from some disease, said as he doffed his montero in acknowledgement of Backhouse.

Backhouse squinted away to the south-west, evidently hoping to spy this force, but the sprawling mass of Gloucester's suburbs obscured his line of sight. 'An attack?'

The sergeant shook his head. 'No gunfire as yet, sir. Talk says they mean to trade captured nags.'

Stryker had reined in directly behind Backhouse so that he could hear the exchange. He followed the captain's gaze, staring at the patches of colour that were the wooden-framed dwellings of the city suburbs, which spread out beyond the old walls like the tentacles of a giant octopus. He could see the pale line of the wall itself rising above those homes and imagined the colours of Gerard's Northern Brigade hanging limp in the weak breeze in the fields beyond. Captured horses. It seemed an incongruous thing at so tense a moment, and he recalled Prince Rupert's mention of a clandestine parley with Governor Massie. Perhaps this was the excuse. He wondered if, even at this very moment, Massie was considering whether to hand the city to the king.

Backhouse took off his helmet, revealing a thatch of auburn hair that stopped abruptly in a thick wedge at his earlobes. He propped the helmet in between his thighs and ran a hand through his sweat-darkened fringe. 'Well, keep your wits about you. The enemy are never above treachery.'

'That I shall, sir,' the sergeant replied smartly, moving out of Backhouse's path and motioning with his halberd for the barriers to be removed from the road.

'We are a compact city,' Backhouse said to Stryker as they cleared the turnpike. Ahead was another smaller barricade, and then the imposing edifice of what the troopers identified as the Outer North Gate. It was not a gate in the traditional sense, for the ancient stone walls – designed to enclose a much smaller city – did not stretch this far north. Rather, this was a huge, gated, bastion of soil and wooden stakes that loomed malevolently over the road.

'You seem proud of that fact, sir,' Stryker replied, drawing up beside the cavalryman. He could see figures scurrying at the crest of the works like a frenzied colony of ants, digging, piling and preparing the slopes.

Backhouse's helmet was now back in place, and he looked across at Stryker through the protective bars. 'A small town is easier to defend than a big one, is it not? We are not as strong as Bristol outwardly, but we have a smaller area to defend.'

Stryker considered the assertion. 'Aye, that is one way of seeing things.'

'We have the Severn protecting us from a land assault to the west,' Backhouse went on brightly. 'And the River Twyver is no mean obstacle to the north, not to mention the marshland thereabouts.'

Stryker again turned to look over his left shoulder. 'Much building work has gone on in the land to the south, sir. I'd wager it is higher ground, and therefore a deal drier.'

Backhouse shrugged nonchalantly. 'But we have our walls, sir. You can see them clearly from here, such is their stature. Two storeys in some places. And six feet thick.'

Stryker wondered whether Backhouse knew that large siege cannon would puncture six feet of stone in no time, but he kept his peace. What struck him more, was the Roundhead's seemingly boundless confidence, which was not what he had expected.

'I had thought to join a retreating garrison, if I'm entirely honest,' he ventured.

Backhouse gave a deep snort of derision. 'No, sir. We shall fight!'

Skellen was riding close to the rear of the pair, and Stryker thought he heard the laconic sergeant mutter something about heads being full of bees, but fortunately his mount's well-timed whicker sufficiently obscured the words.

He thought a suitably vigorous reply was in order, and raised a fist. 'Praise God, sir! It gladdens my heart to hear of your courage, Captain. But,' he added cautiously, 'the King's forces are strong.'

Backhouse looked defiant. 'As are ours.'

'Come now, sir, I am no spy.'

The cavalryman seemed to think for a moment, sucking at his well-kempt whiskers, but evidently decided that he would not be revealing anything that Stryker was not about to see for himself. 'Our strength is less than we might have hoped, 'tis true.'

That was an almost laughable understatement, Stryker thought. Ezra Killigrew had told him that the garrison now numbered little more than fifteen hundred men, comprised of a hotchpotch of units with varying degrees of skill and experience. Some of Stamford's solid bluecoats were apparently behind the walls, and that, he accepted, posed a reasonable threat, but they were bolstered by a local regiment drawn primarily from the town's Puritan elite, very few of whom would ever have fired a shot in anger. Ranged alongside, Killigrew had heard, was a single company of trained band foot, augmented by around a hundred dragoons who had abandoned their base at Berkeley upon Bristol's capitulation. By contrast, Stryker reckoned, if King Charles came to Gloucester, he would have more than ten thousand men at his back.

'But we have foot,' Backhouse continued, failing to read the misgivings that Stryker assumed were branded across his face, 'and horse, powder and cannon. And, of course, the good men you see here.'

'You have served before?'

Backhouse shook his head. 'Alas, sir, but I am green in the ways of war, to my shame.'

That would explain his blind faith in walls erected before black powder had been invented, Stryker thought. 'You are a local man, then?'

'A lawyer by profession. Though I hope to blood my troop soon enough.'

Christ, Stryker thought, you'd better hope they are not tested against Rupert's cavalry, for the blood spilled will be their own. But he forced himself to nod happily. A man who understood the scantiness of Gloucester's chances would not have deserted his own army for a place in its feeble ranks.

*

They passed through the Outer North Gate without hindrance, though Stryker could feel the hard stares of the men up on the bastion. They were musketeers in the main, for pikemen had no use within a besieged town, and their weathered faces and faded blue coats told Stryker that they must have belonged to the Earl of Stamford's regiment, of which Edward Massie had recently taken command.

'They'll get 'emselves smashed in no time, sir,' William Skellen whispered at Stryker's side, as Backhouse spurred further forward to lead his troop home. 'With Bristol—'

'This is different,' Stryker said, risking a glance up at the men on the bastion. 'They'll have heard what happened to Bristol. Heard of the storming and the looting, like as not. If Backhouse is right, and they choose to resist, they'll fight like cornered badgers.'

Skellen grunted, evidently dismissing his superior's concern, but he instinctively dropped back as the troop forged on into the very core of the rebel stronghold. The road was lined with houses, some set on robust stone footings, their upper storeys projecting ostentatiously on jetties, but most were of the simple wooden kind, their antiquated timbers slanted and drooping. From windows and doors, faces emerged. Women and children, gaunt in the shadows, peered curiously at the newcomers like dark-eyed ghouls, each citizen seemingly assessing the riders for themselves.

'Wary lot, aren't they?' Skellen said quietly.

'Gerard's brigade is camped outside,' Stryker replied in the same hushed tone. 'Wouldn't you be?'

But it was not long before the more forthright among Gloucester's folk stepped out to go about the day's business. Some waved at familiar faces within Backhouse's proud group, greeting their men as though they were conquering heroes; others gave simple shouts beseeching God to protect their city and the far-away Parliament for which they might soon have to fight. It was a strange ambience, to Stryker's mind: nervousness for certain, but tempered by a vein of steel that made him uneasy.

Gloucester, as Backhouse had insisted, was ready and willing to defend itself.

Up ahead, the road was blocked by another barrier, but this one was built in real stone. Backhouse twisted to address his companion. 'Part of the original medieval defences, sir. See there? It joins the cathedral walls.'

Stryker followed Backhouse's outstretched finger. The wall, like those they had seen to the south of the city, climbed higher than most of the surrounding buildings. Behind it, the vast Gothic bulk of the grand cathedral sat in domination of the city, its tower soaring heavenward. Stryker gazed at it, wondering how long it would remain intact if the king's fire-workers were brought before the makeshift bastions. He remembered the roar of Sir John Gell's mortar at Lichfield, its incendiary shells punching through the cathedral's eaves with impunity. It made him shudder.

At the point where the wall blocked the road there was a stout gate, reinforced with iron and flanked by two musketeers in blue coats. Backhouse hailed them casually, spurred forward to speak with them for little more than a few seconds, and turned back to Stryker. 'This, as you have probably surmised, is the Inner North Gate. It takes us into the heart of our fair city. You will come with me, if you please, and I shall find you lodgings.' He shrugged apologetically. 'Under guard, you understand.'

'Of course, Captain,' Stryker nodded, hardly expecting to be afforded freedom to roam.

'The men,' Backhouse went on, indicating the blue-coated sentries, 'inform me he is indisposed today. His time is taken with the parley. But after you and your companions have rested the night, I may be able to arrange a meeting with him on the morrow.'

'A meeting, Captain?' Stryker replied cautiously. 'With whom?'

'Why, Colonel Massie, of course. Your new master.'

CHAPTER 6

Gloucester, 7 August 1643

The officer was slim and tall. He wore a simple suit of brown, clamped tight beneath a smartly polished breastplate, allowing only the flourish of a finely woven falling band collar. His features were delicate, his skin pale and his eyes large and dark. His hair, which was a shade lighter than his eyes, was straight and thick, but tousled from dirt and sweat; it reached all the way to his collarbone. This morning he wore a large hat with a simple ribbon tied at its crown, and he took it off as he walked, fanning his face with the wide felt. 'What say you, James?'

The man at the officer's side blew out his cheeks and followed his companion's gaze. 'Wouldn't like to storm it m'self, sir, that's for sure.' He offered a crooked smile. 'But you're the engineer, Governor, if you'll forgive me.'

They both stared up at the newly erected bastion that would, they hoped, protect the Alvin Gate, which was the main route into the city at the north-eastern corner. This part of the city had not been fortunate enough to fall within the protective embrace of the medieval walls, and the defenders had been compelled to construct fresh defences. Thus, a massive earthen rampart had been built following the course of the River Twyver, a steep glacis running down its outer face to make an assault by infantry extremely challenging. Even now, the officers looked on as Gloucester's volunteers – men and women desperate to protect their homes against the feared destruction that

98

would come close on the king's heels – struggled to place spiked storm poles along the rampart's crest and in the palisade below.

Lieutenant Colonel Edward Massie, Governor of Gloucester, chewed the inside of his mouth. He was indeed an engineer, having served with the Dutch on the Continent, and knew what he was about well enough. But Gloucester was his to protect. The people had placed their trust on his twenty-three-year-old shoulders, and suddenly he did not feel quite as confident in these new works as he had when the first soil had been broken.

'Well, James,' he said in his perpetually soft voice, 'they will have to do. The scouts bring news from Bristol. The enemy come hither, I suspect.' He turned suddenly, waving a white hand in the direction of a small, portly built fellow with thinning red hair and a permanent squint. 'Master Baldwin, if you please!'

The man who had been inspecting some of the storm poles waddled smartly over. 'Governor Massie, sir.' He bowed to Massie's companion in turn. 'Captain Lieutenant Harcus. I hear you intend to lead a sortie later today.'

Harcus grinned. 'Our brave bluecoats are restless, sir. We hear the malignants are near Wotton. I mean to find them and bloody their noses. A matter of morale.'

'God preserve you, sir,' Baldwin said dutifully, letting his eyes switch to the taller of the officers. 'You summoned me, sir?'

'You are our Surveyor of Defences.' Massie looked back up to the bastion. 'What say you? Will she hold?'

Baldwin rubbed thick fingers across his chin, the calloused skin sounding loud against his stubble. 'I am a mere stonemason, Governor Massie.' He paused, but Massie did not flinch. 'Aye, sir, she'll hold. Besides, the terrain to the north is too marshy for a landward attack. If the King comes, he'll look to the south, I'd wager.'

Edward Massie grunted, stole one last glance up at the bastion, raked his gaze southward along the line of the new rampart, and turned away. *Jesu*, he thought, but what a web he had woven for himself. He had joined the Parliamentarian faction because it had offered greater prospects of advancement to an ambitious man, and in short order he had found himself deputy governor of this rebellious city. Stamford had been defeated down at Stratton, events had moved on apace, and now, as if his own ambition was mocking him, he was the sole military leader of the grand old place. It would have been a dream position but for the succession of recent defeats that had left his modest garrison alone in a sea of enemies. By day he looked to the defences, refurbishing the ancient walls left over from long forgotten wars, erecting the new ramparts, positioning cannon for the expected tribulation and rallying the terrified citizenry with promises of stout and Godly defiance. At night he lay awake, listening for the distant sound of cannon fire, always expecting to see Prince Rupert and his Cavaliers on a flaming horizon. God, but he was a long way from his father's home in Cheshire.

His thoughts often drifted to darker realms: treachery and betrayal. The previous day's appearance by Gerard's Northern Brigade to the south of Gloucester had masked a more clandestine meeting. A personal plea from Colonel William Legge, an old comrade now fighting for the Royalists, had made it clear that the king fully expected him to do his sacred duty and surrender the city. Massie had refused, but the night had passed without a wink of sleep.

'Guv'nor, sir!' someone called down from the rampart. Massie looked up to see a skinny fellow in the clothes of a labourer. 'Comin' on nice, sir! We'll stop them Popish bastards, sir, in Jesu's name we shall!'

Massie blinked hard, forcing the gnawing doubts from his mind. Around him men, women and children, soldiers and civilians, scuttled this way and that, some carrying clods of turf to bolster the growing glacis, others hefting bushels or dragging the newly carved storm poles. The sight gave him heart like nothing else. He might not have been a zealot when it came to religion or politics, and part of him still hankered to join the sovereign and his all-conquering armies, but the people of Gloucester were worth fighting for. They had come out in their droves to plunge elbow deep in mud as the ditches were scoured from the earth, and they had not ceased in their eagerness to help make their city more defensible. The city corporation had been a thorn in his side, of course, questioning every penny that went towards tools, weapons or materials for a siege that was still just a possibility, but he could expect nothing less from such blinkered bureaucrats. They were the silver-haired, sober-faced aldermen that knew much about coin and nothing of war. But the common folk had been invaluable in their support, and he found himself wanting to lead them to victory, however unlikely that might be.

'God bless you, sir!' a woman shouted from one of the houses hugging the road beside the Alvin Gate. Massie gave his most confident smile, added a little bow that made the woman coo like a pigeon, and moved on, Harcus grinning broadly at his side.

They continued, intending to follow the line of the rampart down to the Outer North Gate. Massie looked at the younger man. 'They'll come for us soon enough.'

Harcus seemed to beam at the prospect. 'We'll send them packing, sir.'

Massie could not help but laugh. 'You're like an excitable puppy, James.'

'Thank you, sir.'

Times were perilous, Massie mused, but which path would truly reward the ambitious man? He could be a junior officer in the victorious Royalist army, safe but wing-clipped, or the unlikely champion of a seemingly doomed cause. He took a deep, steadying breath, and strode on. Perhaps he had taken leave of his senses. Or perhaps this city would be the making of him after all.

'Sir!' The man who had hailed was on horseback, and he rode towards them at a brisk canter from the direction of the cathedral.

Massie halted his progress and turned to lift a hand in greeting. 'Captain Backhouse,' he called as the rider drew close. 'Welcome home. How went your patrol?'

'Governor, sir,' Backhouse said breathlessly, swinging a leg across his saddle and slipping nimbly to earth. He moved quickly to where Massie was waiting, removing his helmet and offering a snappy bow. He was several years older than the colonel, but shorter by three or four inches, and had to crane his neck to look up at the city's military commander. 'A successful patrol indeed, sir. Returned last evening, and I shall take them out again imminently, with permission.'

'You have it,' Massie replied.

Harcus stepped forward, unable to control his enthusiasm. 'And you say the last was successful, sir. You saw action?'

Backhouse glanced at Harcus. 'We did not engage the enemy, alas, but we return with spoils nevertheless.'

Harcus seemed to shiver. 'Oh?'

Backhouse propped the newly polished helm beneath his armpit and turned his gaze back to Massie. 'Deserters, sir. Three of them, taken out to the east.'

'Ours or theirs?'

'Theirs.'

Massie was not surprised. Regiments leaked men like water from a cracked bucket. On garrison duty, marching with an army or quartered for winter, the common sort would always prefer the comforts of home than a rough regimental billet. Not to mention the risk of disease or battle that came with it. 'Will they turn their coats? I cannot afford to feed prisoners.'

'Oh yes, sir, that they will.' Backhouse could not help but brandish a smug smile. 'But these men are not just the usual rabble, Governor. Not a bit of it.'

Stryker sat before the cold hearth on the ground floor of a large, timber-framed house on a road Robert Backhouse had identified as Westgate Street. The lawyer-turned-harquebusier had told him the previous evening that the building – quite grand in this modest area – was owned by a Dutchman named Commeline, but Stryker had not seen the man or his family. There were, however, telltale signs of his occupation. He was, according to Backhouse, a wealthy apothecary, and the room in which Stryker, Skellen and Buck had been locked for the night was indeed replete with shelves that were themselves crammed full of strange-coloured jars and vials.

'Moses' stones!' Skellen hissed beside one of the shelves. He was clutching a large jar at arm's length, covering his nose with his free hand.

'I told you not to go poking around,' was Stryker's reply.

'You were right in that, sir,' Skellen muttered, hastily returning the jar to its perch and backing away as though the entire shelf had assumed a sinister air. 'Stank like Satan's pizzle!'

Stryker could not help but laugh, though it was a tired sound even to his own ears, and he leaned back in his creaking chair and dug a filthy palm into his eye. He wondered what Backhouse had told his superiors, and whether they would believe the story. They had not yet been shot or hanged, which, he supposed, was a good sign, but the night had been a sleepless one nonetheless. The lock had turned in the door as soon as Backhouse installed them in their temporary lodgings, and the shuffle of feet in the corridor beyond told them a pair of guards had been detailed to keep them inside.

'What now, sir, if you'll allow the question?'

Stryker blinked until his eye stopped stinging and turned his head towards the large window that faced the street. 'Wait, Mister Buck. Bide our time. Convince the authorities here that we are committed to the rebellion.'

James Buck had been peering forlornly out of the window since dawn, watching the comings and goings of Gloucester's people like a dog chained outside a butcher's shop, desperate to be on the opposite side of the glass. 'I had hoped they would not lock us up like common criminals.'

'Not like criminals,' Stryker replied, lacing his hands behind his head. 'Deserters. Which is what we are. They will not give us freedom to roam until they can give us their trust.'

'But I have—' Buck blurted, his sallow face creasing with consternation.

'You have Ezra Killigrew's muck to shovel, I know,' said Stryker, his voice dropping to a whisper. 'But you know this game, sir. You are an experienced player. It is never simple.'

Buck ran a pale hand through his oily hair and paced into the room, his own voice suddenly constricted. 'I do not like being unarmed.'

Stryker frowned. 'Nor do I, sir, I can assure you. But you cannot have expected anything less.'

Buck's slim jaw quivered as he gritted his teeth. 'No.' He shook his head. 'No, you are right, of course.'

'We must be patient, Mister Buck,' Stryker said calmly. In the corner of his eye he noticed Skellen leaning against the wall, arms folded, studying Buck with something akin to amusement. 'There is nothing else for it.'

'Patience.' Buck repeated the word, sighing heavily. 'And what will you do when we are free, sir?'

'Initially I had thought to speak to the other officers,' Stryker said, glancing at the door, voice still hushed. 'Gauge their feeling. Whether they have the stomach for a fight.'

Skellen moved in from the wall. 'No longer, sir?'

Stryker looked up at his sergeant. 'Now, it seems, I will meet Massie himself.' He shrugged. 'According to Captain Backhouse, leastwise.'

Skellen wrinkled his battered nose. 'The chief bastard himself. Doubt it. Backhouse is full o' piss an' wind if you ask—'

A sharp metallic crack of a turning lock cut the sergeant's words off in his throat. The three men turned to stare at the door. At its foot, where a chink of light streamed in above the threshold, they saw shadows dancing to the rhythm of shifting feet. Stryker stole a quick glance at his companions, noticing that, where Skellen's brow had lifted in intrigue, Buck's entire face had become rigid, like a corpse, and he had shied away to his old place at the far window.

The door swung inwards, screeching painfully on its hinges, light flooding in its wake, and a group of dark figures filed into the room. Stryker rose to his feet, waiting for his eye to adjust to the gushing brightness that so far obscured the newcomers.

'Mister Stryker,' a familiar voice came from the doorway.

Stryker squinted at the party that now numbered five. 'Captain Backhouse?'

'The very same,' Backhouse replied, moving further into the room so that he could be more easily identified. 'You are well rested, I trust?'

'We are, sir, thank you,' Stryker lied. His sight had regained its sharpness now, and he dipped his head to the other men, none of whom he recognized, though three were blue-coated musketeers that presumably served as an escort. 'Your servant, gentlemen.'

'Forgive me,' Backhouse said, suddenly sounding awkward. 'I must introduce you, sir, to the—'

'Worry not, Captain,' another man said. It was a young voice, but delivered with an unmistakable tone of authority. The speaker moved out from behind one of the grim-looking bluecoats, took off his dusty hat to reveal brown hair that framed a narrow, pallid face, and returned Stryker's short bow. 'You are Captain Stryker, sir? *The* Captain Stryker, formerly of Mowbray's Foot?'

The man was almost the same height as Stryker, who looked him directly in the eye, cocking his head to the side. 'You have me at a disadvantage, sir.'

The young gentleman's thin mouth twitched at the corners. 'Edward Massie, sir. Governor of Gloucester.'

Stryker stared at Massie for longer than he had intended, but he could not help but be taken aback. This was not what he had expected. The plain clothes, a complexion that would have better suited a light-deprived miner than a soldier, those big, sorrowful eyes and the sheer youthfulness of the man together served to give Massie the image of callow, world-green inexperience.

But what had Stryker been expecting? Some sword-toting knight, clad in medieval armour and twirling a mace like a twig?

Perhaps a rakish cavalier, all lace and colour and bravado, more akin to the king's Teutonic nephews than this soberly dressed young gentleman who looked as though he might be more at home behind a clerk's desk. He chided himself for the preconception, but the thought that Massie might be more suited to writing poetry than commanding a garrison continued to gnaw at him.

'Governor,' Stryker said, having to force the words into his mouth, 'it is good to finally meet you.' He glanced at Backhouse. 'The captain, here, has mentioned my service to you?'

'Not a bit of it, Stryker,' Massie replied. 'Your name is known to me. At least, your family name—'

Stryker shifted his feet uncomfortably. 'I prefer simply Stryker, sir.'

Massie gazed at him in mild bafflement, but shrugged nevertheless. 'A veteran of the European wars, like myself.' His large eyes, like gleaming brown coins, seemed to bore right through Stryker's head, as if scouring his very mind. 'I learned my trade with the Dutch.'

'As did I,' Stryker replied, wondering how many years such a young man might possibly have accumulated. 'The Swedes, too.'

'Just so,' Massie said, pressing the hat back atop his head. 'That is where you came by your—' he hesitated for a moment, '*injury*?'

Stryker felt the scar twitch slightly in the place where his left eye once sat, as it often did when unwanted attention was drawn to it. 'Sir.'

'And you mean to join our great cause?'

Stryker nodded. 'Aye, sir, I do.' He glanced over his shoulder at Skellen, who had been silent in the shadows. '*We* do. This man is my sergeant, William Skellen, and—'

'James Buck, sir,' Buck stepped forward so that his frame was suddenly black against the window light. 'Not a confederate of these fine men, insomuch as we ran into one another in the country outside of Bristol, but I am of the same mind. The King's cause is rotten, sir. Parliament's just. I would enlist with you forthwith.'

'Good, good,' Massie said, bobbing his head, though his face remained unreadable. 'And what service might you bring our God-fearing city, sir?'

'I was a mere clerk, Colonel. I am little use with powder or steel, but I had hoped you might find some employment for me.'

Massie pursed his lips briefly, tilting his head to the side. 'Your fingers are impressively clean, Mister Buck.'

Stryker saw that Buck's pale skin had suddenly taken on a strawberry hue. He half expected the young intelligencer to make a run for it there and then. 'Fastidious fellow,' he said, deciding to lend some assistance. 'Washed his hands and face in every brook and stream we crossed, isn't that right, Sergeant Skellen?'

'Had a jest or three about it, sir,' Skellen replied without hesitation.

'I . . . I do not like the ink stains, sir,' Buck offered weakly.

Massie smiled. 'Then perhaps clerking is not the vocation for you.' The smile faded as quickly as it had come. 'And what of our mutual enemy? What can we expect?'

'Sir?' Buck blurted uncertainly.

'You were a clerk, sir, so you would have seen papers. Messages passed between generals, ammunition orders, requisition orders for supplies. What is our misguided monarch planning, sir? Are we to face him? If so, when? Or does his gaze fall elsewhere now that Bristol has fallen?'

'I am a simple regimental clerk, sir. Slanning's, as was. The only orders I see are those for new tucks or extra musket-balls. Nothing more mighty than that, I assure you.'

'Slanning's . . .' Massie repeated the word slowly. 'A Cornish unit. But you are not Cornish, sir.'

'My father was, sir,' Buck replied. 'From Truro, but we moved to Somerset when I was a child. I thought I would make him proud if I enlisted with Sir Nicholas.'

'And?'

Stryker was impressed to see Buck's look of utter consternation. 'He died, sir. Heart gave out a week before Kineton Fight.'

'I am sorry for your loss, Mister Buck, of course,' Massie said, before turning to Stryker. 'And how was it? That is to say, how was Bristol?'

'A cauldron of horrors,' Stryker replied solemnly. He saw intelligence in Massie's eyes, and it made him uneasy. He wondered what thoughts whirled in the governor's mind, and whether the young colonel had truly swallowed Buck's story. 'Too many souls lost. And for what?'

Massie's face seemed to betray a ghost of amusement. 'For King Charles, sir, surely?'

Stryker felt his heart begin to gather pace. 'For a king corrupted by the poisoned words of his advisors. I would not enlist with a rebellion that seeks to depose a rightful sovereign. But, rather, one resolved to remove those who would lead him astray.'

Massie smiled warmly enough, though his eyes twinkled. 'Well said, sir.'

'God save me,' Stryker went on, 'but I fought at Bristol. Added to its misery. My scales, as it were, have since fallen away.'

Massie glanced over Stryker's shoulder. 'And Mister Skellen?'

Skellen did not flinch. 'I follow my captain, sir.'

'Just so,' Massie replied. He glanced from Skellen to Buck, letting his gaze linger there, before finally letting his attention settle upon Stryker. 'I shall not dissemble, Captain. I am short on manpower, on leaders, on men who can shoot a musket or wield a sword. Mister Buck, the City Corporation runs civilian life here, and they would, I feel certain, be delighted of any assistance you might give.'

'Of course, sir,' Buck said with a small bow.

'Do the three of you pledge to fight for God and for Parliament, against the forces of King Charles?' Massie asked grandly. He was rewarded with immediate murmurs of assent from Buck and Stryker.

'I miss m' halberd, sir,' Skellen droned.

Massie's wide eyes swivelled to peer up at him, the slight creases in his ghostly cheeks deepening as he smiled. 'I'm sure one can be located for you, Sergeant.'

'Grand, sir. I'm all yours, sir.'

Massie's smile widened. 'Then I welcome you to your home within our new walls. And may God preserve us.'

Stryker had half-expected to be ordered to the official garrison, where he would be given a rank and the blue coat of the Earl of Stamford's Regiment of Foot, and detailed to a specific role within the anxious city. Indeed, representatives of the Common Council, the body responsible for organizing the manning of the defences, had apparently been sniffing around since word of Stryker's arrival reached them, but Massie had expressed only disdain for their bureaucratic machinations.

'You will be given a degree of liberty, Captain,' he said, as the two men strolled south-eastwards along Westgate Street, Skellen limping awkwardly in their wake.

'Thank you, Governor,' Stryker replied, noting Massie's use of his old rank.

'I'll not consign an experienced man such as yourself to goddamned guard duty because some grey-bearded clerk says so. Not right, sir, not right at all.'

Stryker was pleased the governor felt that way, but inwardly wondered whether James Buck was as content with his lot. The young spy had been taken in a different direction as the group filed from the apothecary's rooms and into the morning light, led by Captain Backhouse and one of the musketeers to meet his new colleagues in Gloucester's small but, according to the governor, energetic administrative community. Stryker and Skellen had shared a stolen glance as he disappeared around the first corner, each wondering whether Buck would have the gumption to execute whatever tasks he had been assigned by Ezra Killigrew.

'I am grateful for your trust, sir,' Stryker said truthfully.

Massie looked at him, one corner of his mouth twitching in a sly expression. 'I have little choice, sir. I need every fighter I can muster, and if your reputation is only half true, then you will be worth ten men if the enemy comes. Besides,' he said, attention returning to the street, where men and women seemed to move from his path like the Red Sea before Moses, 'you will be closely watched, Captain. Any wrong move—'

'Understood, sir.'

The day was becoming stifling, and Stryker took off his cloak, slinging the battle-worn garment across his shoulder. For the first time since they had been accosted by Backhouse's patrol, he felt some semblance of calm about the affair, for they were being afforded a level of respect and freedom he had not foreseen. Moreover, Massie had ordered their weapons be returned immediately, and the pendulous weight of the sword at his waist was a comfort indeed.

A portly woman hefting a stout hogshead waddled past them, and Massie stepped aside to let her through. She garbled her thanks, sweat pouring from her brow to cascade in large rivulets across bright red cheeks. 'They all play their part, however simple it may be,' Massie said as he watched her drop the barrel into place beside a score of others. A party of men emerged from an alley between two houses. They were naked from the waist up, sinewy torsos gleaming in the heat, and acknowledged the young governor with waves and nods before each stooped to heave a hogshead on to his shoulder. Massie returned the greeting with a silent wave of his own, and pointed so that Stryker would notice the growing rampart that rose at the alley's far end.

'You believe the king's men will come, sir?' Stryker ventured.

Massie pursed his lips in a gesture that made it seem as though he weighed his next words carefully. 'A fellow came to me yesterday under a flag of truce.'

Stryker's pulse seemed to skip a beat. He focussed on the distant rampart that crawled with gangs of labourers, like maggots over a dead bird. Some carried shovels, others dragged sharpened stakes up to the crest, but most bore baskets of earth on their backs to pile on the outer face of the artificial glacis. 'From the King?'

'From his council, certainly.' Massie blew out his cheeks. 'Offered me generous terms to open our gates. I rebuffed the villain, naturally.'

'Then they will come.'

Massie nodded, his soft eyes suddenly brightening with diamond hardness. 'They will. And we will fight the scoundrels off until our last man – or woman – is dead. His Majesty will witness our resolve with his own eyes. I have made certain of it.'

'God save us,' Stryker said, wondering what that last comment had meant. He looked further along the road to where a pair of small children pushed a barrow-load of turfs between them. The vehicle lurched from side to side, and the boys yapped at one another angrily as they wrestled with their unwieldy bounty. 'Whole families work at the walls?'

Massie shrugged. 'The palisade must be constructed by hand. The ditch in front is more than ten paces wide, and if you were to stand at its base and I perched on your shoulders, I would not see above it. That takes more manpower than I have at my disposal as military leader, so the Council must engage the common folk, too.'

Stryker looked at the streets and houses around him. It was a strange scene, for, though the area was crowded, Gloucester's citizens were not employed on what he imagined to be their daily business. As he was beginning to understand, normal life seemed to have been suspended in the wake of the threat of an impending attack. Every man, woman and child was engaged in the defence of their property. In defence of their very lives.

Massie halted outside a top-heavy building that leaned to one side, its upper floors piled precariously on a wood-framed jetty that looked as though it could never bear such weight. 'This is where I must take my leave.'

Stryker stared up at the building. 'A tavern, sir?'

'Just so,' Massie said with a grin. 'The Crown Inn. Sadly, though, she is to be transformed from alehouse to command centre, much to the tapster's chagrin.' He gave one of the musketeers a flicker of a glance. 'Corporal Dodd will escort you from here. Now, if you'll excuse me, gentlemen.'

The bluecoat gave a silent nod, Massie offered his hand for Stryker to shake, touched a finger to his temple to acknowledge Skellen, and vanished within the tavern's gloomy interior.

'We're in,' Skellen muttered as soon as they were moving again. The bluecoat tailed them conspicuously, but mercifully out of earshot. 'Now what?'

They turned down a wide thoroughfare lined with shops, narrowly avoiding a group of shoeless urchins haring out from a side alley as though an invisible culverin pounded at their heels. They were laughing and shoving and prodding one another, very much like any gang of boys one might have seen in any of England's towns, but, as they shoaled instinctively to skirt the menacing pair of soldiers, Stryker noticed their bare feet were as mud-caked as their hands and forearms.

'Look at them,' he said to Skellen. 'They've been on the defences.'

'Cheeky beggars.'

'No, Will. *Working* on the defences. The whole city really is involved.' He picked at the scab on his forehead without thinking. 'We were told Massie may have a mind to surrender.'

'And?'

'And I think he did.' He paused, tilting back his head to meet Skellen's hooded eyes. 'Until yesterday, or during the night, or when he saw the sun rise this morning.'

'You don't think he will now?'

'No.' Stryker noticed the bluecoat had slowed his stride, but not halted, and was drawing too close for comfort. 'The parley with Gerard,' he said in a low voice as they resumed their progress, 'was a cover for the real message. The one designed to cow Massie into submission. But he seems to have hardened his resolve.'

'And the folk are right up for a brabble.'

'Aren't they just?' Stryker squinted along the length of the road, trying to see even one person not apparently busy with the industry of rebellion. He found none. Even those whose arms were not piled with material for the rampart seemed focussed and deliberate in the way they scuttled about Gloucester's warren-like core, and he supposed they would be conveying orders on behalf of the military leaders, or passing messages between the political elite. Every person had a role to play. And then there was the man at the top. 'Jesu, I look into his eyes and I see determination, not fear. I look at the common folk and they're digging the blasted ditch. Even the striplings are set to work. If the King comes before the walls expecting the city to capitulate, he'll get a nasty surprise.'

Skellen sniffed. 'What do we care, sir? If he comes, he'll come with plenty o' lads. They'll trample through these bloody ant-hills in no time.'

'If Rupert takes command, yes. But he feared His Majesty would not countenance another escalade after Bristol.'

'Make the signal, sir,' Skellen said, casting a quick glance back at the glum-faced musketeer and offering a friendly nod. 'Gloucester ain't likely to surrender, so Longshanks'll need to smash a hole in its pretty new walls.'

'Or,' Stryker replied, thinking back to his discussion with the prince, 'the King will avoid this place altogether and strike instead at London. I fear Rupert will not welcome our news.'

'Might as well tell him before they finish their defences,' Skellen said, 'in case he can convince his uncle to give him the reins.'

'Aye.' Stryker looked up at the sun, realizing the day had raced away while he had been exploring the city. 'Killigrew said mid-morning. He won't be watching for the signal now. We will have to do it on the morrow.'

Skellen's leathery faced cracked in a rotten-toothed grin. 'Just so, Captain. Just so.'

CHAPTER 7

Gloucester, 8 August 1643

By mid morning it was already sweltering, and the two men sweated profusely as they strode along the busy street. And busy it most certainly was, for news of the enemy had reached Gloucester and been retold by its most senior men, right down to the gossips and newsmongers, goodwives and children. The king's men were on their way, it was said, in tones ranging from high excitement to tremulous panic. The all-conquering Royalists were sweeping up the Severn Valley and would be at the city's walls in less than two days. And after all the talk, all the preparation, the fresh earthen ramparts, ditches and bastions, it was really happening. War was coming to Gloucester.

But ahead of that fearsome army would come its outriders. Its vanguard of cavalrymen and scouts, atop oat-fed destriers that could outrun any but the very best animals, and they would encircle the rebel stronghold, plumb its protective rivers, assess its strengths and weaknesses, prod its turnpikes, harry its pickets and plot its downfall. With those men would be the king's intelligencers, all hurriedly feeding information back to the oncoming army, taking notes, sketching maps. One man amongst them would be watching a stretch of the south-eastern wall where it loomed over a broad swathe of heathland known as Gaudy Green, and it was here that the two men now went to make contact.

'He'll be watching for us?' William Skellen said under his breath.

'Him,' Stryker replied equally as softly, all too aware that their watchful guard paced a short distance to the rear, 'or one of his people.'

'There,' Skellen pointed to the end of the street, where they could make out the pale grey of the wall marking the termination of alleyways that ran between blocks of houses. Above the man-made structure rose the distant hills, a patchwork of greens in the summer sun, though they were ominously empty of live-stock, the sheep and cattle having long since been driven down and into the city to bolster supplies. 'So how to shake that bugger off.'

Stryker glanced back at their blue-coated shadow. Corporal Dodd was a wiry, red-faced fellow, with a flaxen moustache and triangular beard that appeared almost white against his ruddy skin. He might have been anywhere between twenty-five and forty, Stryker reckoned, and his green eyes seemed to look in different directions, giving him a disconcerting stare that one could never quite return.

'This should do,' Stryker said when he had turned back, and he steered Skellen into a small crowd of people who were gathered about a team of bony looking oxen. There was a growing murmur of voices from within the group.

'*Oi!*' Corporal Dodd, face even more red, if that were possible, yelled at his charges' backs as they pushed through the bodies, making direct for the oxen. 'I can't see you, sir! Back 'ere, if you please!'

It did not please Stryker, so he forged on, careful not to look as though he were actively running from their guard, but briskly enough to put distance between them and Dodd. He and Skellen eased some shoulders aside, downright shoved others, until at last they reached the team of weary beasts, hides streaked with pale lines where rivulets of sweat had cut mock valleys down their dirty flanks.

The object round which the curious townsfolk had gathered was an artillery piece: a forbidding cylinder of black iron the length of two men lying top to tail and mounted on a wheeled chassis that was connected by a series of thick traces to the exhausted beasts. It was a demi-culverin, a formidable thing weighing three thousand pounds, and Stryker guessed it had been moved here from some other placement on the walls, explaining why the crowd had not seen something of this size before. Whatever the reason for the noisy curiosity, he was thankful for it, and pushed on through the chaotic mass, skirting a gang of children who were taking turns in providing piggy-backs for their friends to see over the taller adults. Eventually he made it to the far side of the furore, turning to see Skellen emerge at his heel, slightly stooped to make himself less conspic-uous. Further back, still at the centre of the crowd, Corporal Dodd jostled and cursed his way through, his musket bobbing high above the throng.

'On me,' Stryker said, more casually now as the noise of the crowd near drowned all other sounds. He twisted quickly away, checking all around for suspicious faces, and led Skellen from the cannon and its admirers. The pair plunged into one of the narrow alleys that ran, like rat holes, in between the multitude of timber dwellings, and strode quickly south and east, making for the old medieval walls that inevitably blocked the far end.

'If he sees which way we came?' asked Skellen, breathing fast.

Stryker nodded to a white-coifed woman who squatted in the threshold of her home preparing vegetables, the peelings collected by a small child, half naked in the heat, for some later meal. When they were well past, he spoke: 'We'll say we did not realize he had lost us. We have not fled from him, have we? We are simply strolling out to see the defences we will soon be manning.'

The wall had been impressive once, back when it enclosed Gloucester completely, a ring of stone blocks that were too thick to break by hand and too high to climb. But those walls had long since ceased to stretch beyond this single section of the modern city, and siege cannon would make short work of the most robust stone. With Massie's leadership, though, Stryker had seen how the citizens were volunteering in their droves to make the best of what they had, and here it was no different. The rest of the city perimeter had seen more frenzied work thus far, as the need to raise a rampart where there had been nothing was far greater than the desire to shore up the existing defences, but the governor's construction teams had nevertheless begun to pile heaps of soil at the foot of the stone face in order to give the wall extra strength in the event of a Royalist bombardment. Moreover, they had erected wooden scaffolding along the inside of the wall to provide a firing step and continuous vantage point, and it was here that Stryker headed.

With a furtive look back across his shoulder, he saw that the alleyway was empty, save the woman and child, and he made straight for an old groaning ladder that bowed disconcertingly under his weight. He paused to check that it would not break up beneath his boots, nodded to Skellen, who waited patiently for his turn, and scrambled up to the platform above. The tall sergeant joined him promptly enough, though the climb was not so easy with his wounded leg. At the top they paused to check the walkway.

There was just one other man close by, about twenty paces along the platform, and the roofs of the nearest houses obscured them from being viewed from ground level. They approached the lookout without delay. The hammering of their boots on the fresh timbers sounded unnaturally loud, and he must have heard their advance, but he did not bother to turn. Evidently not expecting an enemy at the rear, the man instead squinted into the sun-drenched horizon, intent on being the first to spot the bright banners of a Royalist force on the surrounding hills. He wore the clothes of a civilian but was armed with a standard tuck, the kind issued to infantry recruits, and a matchlock musket. The firearm looked to be of fine enough quality, but was old-fashioned in style, with a barrel that reached at least four feet in length, and would, Stryker guessed, require a rest on which to place it when firing. In short, he supposed the fellow was one of the city's volunteers rather than a member of the better-trained garrison men Massie had inherited from Lord Stamford's regiment, and that was a blessing indeed.

From the corner of his eye, Stryker saw Skellen's big hand move to his sword-hilt, and he shook his head rapidly, staying the sergeant's movement without a sound. Instead he indicated a piece of wood that nestled against the palisade a couple of feet from where Skellen stood. It was the length and girth of a man's forearm, and Skellen darted forward with impressive agility to snatch it up.

The lookout was still diligently studying the eastern terrain when Skellen thrust the makeshift club into his lower back, aiming for his fleshy side and the kidneys beneath. The impact sounded like wet meat slapping a butcher's block and the man doubled over, air gushing from him like giant bellows in a foundry. He tried to twist back to face his assailant, gasping for breath, face horribly contorted, but Stryker was there, knocking his high-crowned hat free and grasping a fistful of lank, sweaty hair. He hit the man once in the face, pulling the blow to protect his own fingers, but allowing enough force to knock the terrified guard senseless. In that instant he feared his victim would scream, but his lips, peeled back in shocked anguish to reveal long, yellow teeth, simply flapped mutely. He gave one final shudder and keeled forwards, his face colliding with the dusty timbers of the walkway.

Stryker looked around as Skellen tossed the club aside and dragged the inert body behind a row of soil-filled bushels. No one came running, no screams sounded from the packed lanes below them, and no boots thundered along the wall, yet his heart sounded like an ordnance volley inside his skull.

'Reckon he saw us?' Skellen asked.

Stryker shook his head. 'God-willing, he won't be found any time soon. And we'll be long gone before he wakes.' He breathed deeply, noting the sun was high and strong before them. 'Glass.'

Skellen fished in his snapsack. He had surreptitiously knocked one of the larger jars from the apothecary's crammed shelves soon after they had woken at dawn, making great play of his own dull-witted oafishness when the alarmed Corporal Dodd had burst through the door, musket in hand. Embarrassed laughter and profuse apologies followed, during which performance a wicked shard the size of the sergeant's palm had been secreted amongst the cold detritus of the hearth, to be collected once Dodd had taken his leave. It was this shard that Skellen now produced, gripping it carefully lest its keen edges nick a finger. He rubbed it against the hem of his buff-coat to clean away the smears of ash, and handed it to Stryker.

Stryker leaned against the cool stone, lifting the glass in front of his face and adjusting its angle until he was certain it caught the sun. When he was happy that the glint would be unmistakable, he tilted the shard gently, letting it reflect the bright light in the direction of the hills. Five signals, Killigrew had said; five flashes to let him know that Edward Massie intended to defend the city. After he had sent the message, he waited for perhaps thirty seconds, though it seemed like an age, exposed as they were on the platform, before repeating the sequence.

And then it was over; his mission was complete. A gush of relief poured through his veins, and he let out a long breath that he had not known he had been holding. 'Let us take our leave, eh?' he muttered, looking up at Skellen.

'Or praps not, sir,' the sergeant said, staring over his shoulder, his hooded eyes as wide as Stryker had ever seen them.

Stryker turned slowly, expecting to see a blustering Corporal Dodd, but instead he found himself looking into another face he knew. This one was that of a man in his twenties, dressed in a green coat, with dark eyes, clean chin and auburn hair below a green montero cap. The man grinned broadly, but it was an expression of predatory triumph rather than mirth.

'You,' was all Stryker could think to say.

'Stay your fucking flam, sir,' the greencoat growled. He was flanked by two others who wore the blue of Lord Stamford, and they snorted their delight at his insolence. The man ignored them, instead looking at Skellen. 'How's the leg, Sergeant?'

'Why, you goddamned—' Skellen began, stepping forward quickly, hand falling to his hilt, but one of the greencoat's companions instantly levelled his musket at the sergeant's chest, halting his advance. Skellen seethed, balling and unballing his fists manically. 'I should have killed you in the woods, you poxy little hector.'

'Peters, was it?' Stryker said suddenly. He thought back to the skirmish at Hartcliffe where they had driven a brazen group of greencoats into the forest after a sharp firefight. He remembered the lad clearly, the fear in his eyes as Stryker interrogated him. 'Musketeer Peters.'

'Port,' the man said, and now the grin was gone, replaced by a tight-mouthed expression of pure malice. 'Richard Port. And I remember you, sir. Oh, how could I forget your ugly fucking face.' He lifted an arm, and Stryker noticed that the wrist and hand were tightly bound with grimy bandages. 'Broke my fucking arm, *sir.*'

'We have turned our coats, Port,' Stryker said quickly, hoping to assuage the man's ire. 'We are up here—'

'I don't care a rat's privy member for what you're up to!' Port snarled. 'You could 'ave been made governor and I'd still expect my debt paid in full. Bones?'

One of the bluecoats, a burly, lantern-jawed man with no neck and fists like bear paws, stepped forward eagerly. 'Aye, Dicky?'

'Ding the culls.'

Bones nodded, reversed his musket so that he brandished it with the heavy wooden stock out in front. 'Right you are, Dicky.'

Off Bishopsgate Street, London, 8 August 1643

The building was silent, save for the tapping of heavy boots as the sentries paced the path that encircled the entire complex like a flagstone moat. Thirty yards to the south, in a stand of withered trees that cast shadows the shapes of elderly, stooped men, two pairs of eyes glinted from behind the low hanging canopy. They watched the musketeers as they marched in groups of three or four, gauged their pace and numbers, searched the soaring walls behind for weaknesses.

'This is it?' Lisette Gaillard asked, not turning to look at the man who crouched at her right shoulder. 'You are certain?'

'Of course,' Christopher Quigg muttered indignantly. He reached out to ease aside a branch that obstructed his view. 'The old hospital o' Saint Mary without Bishopsgate. Private buildings now, naturally. All sold up by King Henry.'

The wide thoroughfare of Bishopsgate Street Without cut through the land immediately to their left, and the ominous rumbling of a cart made them both flinch. They shrank back into the shadows, barely breathing until the creaking of the wheels had died away.

'You had better be right,' Lisette hissed testily, turning her attention back to the ancient monastic estate's formidable stone-work.

'You see the damned guards,' Quigg shot back. 'Do you believe they are here to take the air?'

Lisette grunted but offered no argument. Quigg, she knew, had tracked her quarry here himself. They might have been moved again, but the presence of the granite-faced sentries suggested otherwise. And these were no ordinary musketeers. The afternoon sun was high, and must have been baking their woollen-coated backs without mercy. Trained Bandsmen or raw recruits would have left their posts to search for shade. These men had not so much as flinched, despite the sweat she could see gleam at their cheeks. No, these were soldiers of a high calibre. The kind who might report to a man of power. And she knew just who that man would be.

She knew Major General Erasmus Collings to be a fragile little man with porcelain-delicate features and skin as white as chalk. He dressed in dandyish fashion, more like a courtly cock-erel than one of the chief architects of the rebellion, and, though Lisette had never met him, she had been told his voice was as soft as a child's. Not, then, a typical power broker in these ever more bloody days, especially for the Parliamentarians, who seemed to be increasingly in favour of forthright, muscular kinds of leaders such as Cromwell in the east and Fairfax to the north. Collings was different; special. The Royalist high command had dispatched Lisette on this mission with warnings of his infamy ringing in her ears. He was a spymaster, one of Parliament's best, and a man who neither forgot a slight, nor forgave one. A major general with as much influence as the Earl of Essex or Sir William Waller, but one whose power was wielded in secret. In short, Erasmus Collings was a dangerous enemy for whom politics and treachery were to be embraced, and it was he who commanded the guards here.

Lisette had been sent to rescue Cecily Cade from the rebels after she had been taken from Stryker's company in a Roundhead ambush just before the unlikely Royalist victory in a corner of north Cornwall she had never heard of. The girl was by all accounts the spoiled daughter of a Royalist sympathizer who happened to be filthy rich, but those riches made Miss Cade important to Lisette's superiors, and that in turn made her important to Lisette. The early days of the task had been relatively positive, for Lisette had been promised that Captain Stryker would be joining her to rescue the girl – quite rightly, to Lisette's mind, seeing as it was from under his not so watchful gaze that she had been kidnapped – and that thought had filled her with excitement. But he had not come, and from there on things seemed to worsen. Major General Erasmus Collings, it transpired, was Cecily Cade's gaoler here in London, and he was proving a difficult adversary. His personal squad of musketeers had been an ever-present barrier, preventing her from getting close to Cecily, and his penchant for moving the imprisoned girl ensured that Lisette spent a great deal of wasted time staring at empty buildings across the breadth of the city. The problems had been compounded by the sickness that kept Lisette in her bed for so long, which meant she lost all contact with her superiors back in Oxford. Indeed, at her lowest point she had truly wondered if this mission would prove to be the death of her. But, by the grace of God, she had gradually recovered, and made contact with Quigg, who, for all his faults, had managed to locate the prize again. And now, as she stared out from the copse to look at the stone-built compound, she offered a silent prayer of thanks to the Holy Mother. The game was not yet up.

Quigg was pointing to the small door positioned in the nearest wall. 'She is in there.'

'How can you know which building holds her?'

'I saw them enter through that very door. Why would they use the back entrance if it were not the quickest route to her cell?'

'Maybe he saw you following,' Lisette mused aloud.

'Impossible,' Quigg retorted hotly. 'There are little rooms beyond that entrance, my people tell me. That is where they will be keeping her.' He rubbed at his disease-pitted neck. 'To think, that grand place used to be home to all those lazy bloody monks.'

Lisette was inclined to stab her companion then and there for such a comment, but instead she chose to bite the inside of her mouth hard, the metallic tang of blood crawling across her tongue. The Protestants continued to crow about the decline of the monasteries, even though a century had passed since their fall. Establishments such as this once beautiful one had been plundered, dismantled and sold to the highest bidder, raped and robbed by Fat Henry and his vile lackeys, and the thought hurt her deeply. The suppression, she felt sure, had ruined Britain. Crushed its spirit, and left it akin to an open wound, festering and destined for a juddering, painful end. But Quigg was, after all, just another misguided Englishman, and she had grown accustomed to them, despite her antipathy. 'Bloody heretics,' she muttered.

'Heretics?'

Christopher Quigg's bulbous eyes had swivelled like a pair of spinning plums to search Lisette's face.

Lisette shook her head. 'Nothing.'

Quigg's eyeballs rolled back to the hospital buildings. 'Like a damned fortress with those guards always on the lookout.'

Lisette looked up at the pale facade. 'Even Magdeburg fell eventually.'

'Pray God your pamphlets prove a tad more expedient than the emperor's guns.' Quigg produced a handkerchief and mopped his temples. 'Magdeburg held out for six months.'

Lisette chose to ignore him. 'The Peace Party is emboldened, you said.'

Quigg nodded. 'Aye, that is what I hear. The lords Holland, Bedford and Clare sue for negotiation at Westminster, while their supporters are out in the streets. The voices of dissent grow with every passing hour. They want the war over, finished.'

'Then my pamphlets are working.'

'They are certainly doing us no harm. The common folk would have it ended by any means.'

Lisette looked at him. 'And you have every agent assigned?'

Quigg placed a pudgy hand across his heart. 'By my honour, madame, I have every available contact whispering doom for the rebellion, stirring trouble where they may.'

She returned her stare to the compound. Its pale stone walls and gargoyle-fringed roofs shone in the afternoon sun, making the old place appear as though it had a veneer of solid gold. She imagined the clergymen bustling along its corridors, in and out of elaborate cloisters and across green courtyards full of vegetables and beehives. A truly wondrous place, built amid worship and contemplation, designed to help the needy, back in a time when England knew its true place in the world. But for all its beauty, the hospital remained a formidable place. The walls were thick and the intricate carvings peered down from heights too lofty to scale. There were not many guards – Lisette had counted twenty in all – but there were only four or five visible entrances for them to protect, and each man appeared to be well armed and vigilant.

She needed a distraction, a disturbance big enough that the guards would be compelled to investigate. She doubted that anything, save an assault on the capital by the Oxford Army itself, would make them abandon their posts, but the Peace Party and their increasingly vocal supporters might, she had hoped, cause enough of a furore to draw the guards' collective attention elsewhere. And that was where Henry Greetham and his printing press had come in.

One of the guards, black-coated, with a white kerchief fastened around his hat and armed with a halberd that was propped against his shoulder, paced across the walkway in front of them. His face was almost entirely obscured by a thick beard the colour of fox fur, but Lisette could see the tiny pin-pricks of light dance across his eyes as he checked the area with a worrying level of care. He paused by the small door, almost as though he sensed the eyes watching it.

'Bastard whoreson,' she hissed bitterly, a sudden feeling of dread washing through her. 'It will never work. He does not give a damn for the protests.'

'Your major general?' asked Quigg. 'He will.'

Lisette breathed deeply, embarrassed at her show of concern. She found herself wishing it was Stryker at her side, and the thought made her angrier still. 'How can you be so sure?'

'The mood is darkening,' Quigg said confidently. 'I have told you our people are in the streets. They are in the taverns, in every tannery and wharf and shambles. They whisper what we tell them to whisper. They ensure the pamphlets are seen, passed around. The protests will only grow. Eventually the guards here will be unable to ignore them.'

Lisette rose from her crouching position, feeling the burning pain in her cramped knees, and backed away into the trees. 'I pray you are right, monsieur.' She sketched an invisible cross in front of her chest. 'I pray you are right.'

Alveston, Gloucestershire, 8 August 1643

Captain Lancelot Forrester watched the fire spit and hiss from the fat that pattered the lurid embers; it was like watching raindrops falling on leaves. He stared hard as the flesh around the blackened ribs curled back, those charred bones, like a row of tarred twigs, pushing out beyond the bronzed carcass of the sow. She, together with her squealing brood, had been taken by the regiment's foraging party to feed the swarm of men flooding north along the Severn Valley. They were officially commandeered in the name of the king, of course, but the few shillings that found their way into the farmer's bony palm had not served to mollify him one bit. Forrester guessed the poor man would be throwing in his meagre lot with the Clubmen before winter.

A man cleared his throat suddenly, and Forrester glanced up to see his colonel beyond the flames. Sir Edmund Mowbray was not in the habit of sharing victuals with his men, preferring to maintain the dignified distance required for command, but this evening was clearly different. Forrester wondered what news was about to be imparted.

One of the regiment's pikemen had been summoned to tend to the pork, and Mowbray shot the young, sallow-cheeked lad a quick nod to indicate that the flesh should be carved. 'Not the least pleasant way to end one's day,' the colonel said as he waited until a large wooden bowl had been filled with thin strips of the greasy meat. As soon as the food was offered to him, he dismissed the pikeman, ensuring that the soldier was well out of earshot before he spoke again. 'As you're no doubt aware, Aston and Gerard are already at Painswick, just six miles short of the city. For our part, we will be at Gloucester's south-west fringe in a day or two.'

The gathering was exclusively made up of Mowbray's most senior officers. Lieutenant Colonel Baxter sat at his colonel's right hand, with Goodayle, the gruff sergeant major, to his left. Across the sumptuously fragrant smoke squatted Kinshott the quartermaster, Humfrey Patience, the regiment's provost marshal, and his three highest-ranked captains, Aad Kuyt, Job Bottomley and, in Stryker's conspicuous absence, Forrester.

The latter received the bowl in turn, picked out the fattest strip he could find, and lifted it to hover before his lips. 'I hear Vavasour,' Forrester said, waving the meat as he spoke like a conductor before an orchestra, 'diverts horse and foot from his siege at Brampton Bryan.'

Mowbray nodded. 'And we have more reinforcements coming from Banbury, Worcester and Oxford.'

Forrester popped the food into his mouth, chewing as he spoke. 'A veritable horde, sir.'

'Aye,' Goodayle agreed, his deep tone rumbling through the grey dusk. 'And His Majesty rides across the Cotswolds.'

Forrester smirked. 'Didn't fancy slogging with us, then?'

Goodayle's eyelid twitched as though he fought to suppress his own amusement. 'He feels it important to rendezvous with the reinforcements from Oxford.'

'Or find a big house with a feather bed and a pretty view,' Forrester replied sourly, before immediately regretting the barb. He felt himself colouring as his colonel leaned forward purposefully.

'Have a care, Captain,' Mowbray warned.

Forrester finished the meat, though it felt as though he gulped down thorns. 'Sir.'

'The decision is made, then, sir?' Aad Kuyt said quickly, sensing his friend's embarrassment. 'We storm again?'

Mowbray screwed up his already shrewish face, lips disappearing behind his neat moustache. 'Not as such. It is still wagered the governor, one Massie, will surrender the town with little ceremony.'

Kuyt scratched his crooked nose thoughtfully. '*Still* wagered, sir? Something has changed?'

'As you know, Colonel Legge's message was officially rebuffed,' Mowbray confirmed, 'but not privately.'

'It is the talk of the camp, sir,' Kuyt said. 'There was a second message. A secret reply from Massie that hinted at his willingness to surrender.'

'If the King himself appears before the walls,' Goodayle rumbled.

Mowbray nodded. 'That is so. But—' He stared up at the darkening sky. 'Matters have been complicated this day.' The colonel pulled at his moustache for a moment as he chose his words. 'Massie is suspected of double dealing, of saying one thing and whispering another. The mixed messages received by Legge have only served to confuse. For that reason, another man was sent into the city to see for himself. Get a feel for the preparations, and the morale of the place.'

'And we have received word from him?' Forrester asked.

'We have,' Mowbray said with a grimace. 'He advises Massie will not surrender.'

It was Forrester's turn to stare at the sky as he attempted to unravel the absurdity of the situation. 'So we have his official response to Legge, stating that he will not surrender, followed by a secret message suggesting the opposite, and yet another contradicting that.'

Mowbray offered a pained smile. 'I fear you are correct, Captain.'

'Meaning?'

'Meaning the King is unsure as to how we must proceed. We will nevertheless appear in strength, His Majesty himself at our head, and allow Massie to throw open his gates.'

Kuyt offered a rueful laugh. 'And that is our plan?' he said, not bothering to conceal his disbelief. 'His Majesty will stride up to the walls and call upon Gloucester to surrender, all the while knowing our agent has given information to the contrary?'

Mowbray's little head flinched in a nod. 'Aye.'

Kuyt shook his head. 'So we will not attack, but nor will we leave them be?'

'The losses at Bristol,' Mowbray answered the Dutchman tentatively, 'were adjudged too great to risk again while there is a chance of a peaceful resolution. But the King would neverthe-less capture the city before he considers a move upon London.'

'Jesu,' Kuyt muttered incredulously.

Beside Mowbray, his second in command, Francis Baxter, let out a heavy sigh. 'Politicking is a curious thing, is it not?' The lieutenant colonel had a thick head of gunmetal-grey hair from beneath which a pair of abnormally large ears jutted. His eyes were bright blue, but the lines at their corners betrayed his world-weariness. 'We have Rupert's faction advising the King to take Gloucester, the Queen's toadies arguing for an assault on London, and in the end, he chooses to satisfy neither party.' He offered a tired smile, arching his back to crack broad shoulders. 'I wonder who was architect for this middle way. I would not wish to be in his boots.'

'Sir John Colepeper,' Colonel Mowbray replied. 'And yes, he seems to have earned the enmity of almost everyone at Council.'

Baxter smiled. 'In an effort not to offend, the King offends all.' He glanced around the circle of officers. 'So we must hope this Massie fellow proves our agent wrong, and will indeed sympathize with our esteemed cause.'

Mowbray lifted a hand to stroke his compact beard, his face pensive. 'We must pray that is the case, aye.'

Baxter cast a wry glance at his colonel. 'You believe the agent is correct, sir?'

Mowbray paused, seemed to consider his response carefully, but eventually spoke in a low voice, 'This Massie has already shown himself to be a duplicitous rogue. The man in Gloucester is not.'

Lancelot Forrester had been eyeing the bowl that was rapidly becoming depleted of pork, but he jerked his head up at the comment, staring hard at his commander. 'It's Stryker, isn't it, sir?'

'Captain?'

'The agent in Gloucester, sir,' Forrester persisted. 'With the utmost respect, Colonel, I do not believe for a single moment that he has deserted.' It had been a difficult few days. His friend had gone one morning, simply vanished along with Sergeant Skellen. At first he had suspected foul play, a quiet murder by Crow's dragoons in the middle of the night, but somehow he found that unlikely, given the fact that the pair had not, he was told, strayed from their company for so much as a minute. And then it had emerged that their belongings and weapons had gone too, and it became clear that Stryker and his sergeant had ridden away from Hartcliffe of their own volition. Tales of treachery had been whispered after that, naturally. Stryker had been offered a fortune, it was said, to take his skills to London.

Or perhaps he had gone through some religious enlightenment. Maybe it was simply fear of retribution from Colonel Crow. The dragoon was a powerful man, and his enmity was no secret. But Forrester had not bought any of it. He felt sure that another reason would present itself in time, and now, it seemed, it had.

Mowbray was shaking his head firmly. 'He has turned his coat. He is a mercenary, when all is said and done.'

'As am I, sir.' Forrester glanced at his Dutch comrade. 'And Captain Kuyt. And most of us here. But that does not make us traitors.'

Without warning, Mowbray smacked a fist against the earth beside his thigh. 'Enough, Captain Forrester!'

There was silence, a cloud of tension swirling about the party like the smoke from their fire. But as Mowbray looked from face to questioning face, his own taut features seemed to soften, and he bit his lower lip as though he wrestled with his own mind. Eventually he spoke, his voice barely audible. 'Stryker's loyalty is not in question. And I believe Gloucester will *not* surrender.'

'*Ha*!' Forrester beamed. 'I knew it!'

Mowbray threw the captain a menacing stare. 'Breathe a word to anyone, Lancelot, and I shall make a new scabbard out of your hide.'

Forrester swallowed hard, though his smile lingered. 'My lips are sealed.'

It was with a sense of unmitigated relief that Lancelot Forrester joined lieutenants Thomas Hood and Reginald Jays an hour later. Helping himself to a generous portion of the junior officers' meal, he went to perch on the stump of a long-felled tree and crammed a hefty slice of bacon between his lips.

'What news, sir?' Jays asked. He had been a Parliamentarian up until the late spring, when his small unit of infantrymen had stumbled into Forrester's company on the western edge of Dartmoor. He had possessed the advantage of surprise, and had launched a direct assault upon the small Royalist force, holed up as they were in an isolated tavern. But his ambition had been undermined by his inexperience, and a bloody and ignominious defeat had been his only prize. Fortunately for the lieutenant, who had not yet reached fifteen years, his conqueror had taken pity on him, seen some spark of promise in his youthful naivety, and taken him on as his second in command.

'The hope,' Forrester replied, a jet of bacon-laced saliva pulsing from his mouth as he spoke, 'is that Gloucester will give up without a fight.'

'And will they?'

'No.'

Lieutenant Hood had been crouching over a narrow stream that bisected the woodland against which the tents of Mowbray's regiment nestled. He straightened now, pacing back towards their little fire, his face and hair glistening with water droplets. 'Pray the buggers want a fight.'

Forrester twisted to look at him. 'You would storm the city?'

Hood took his new red coat from where it hung limp on a gnarled branch and swung it like a cloak across his shoulders. 'Aye, sir.'

'Even after what you saw at Bristol?'

'I am a soldier, sir.' Hood set his jaw indignantly. 'Every man here knows I am green as goddamned grass.'

The captain regarded Hood wryly. 'And you would remedy that situation.'

'Aye, sir, I would,' Hood replied, his voice a touch strained. 'I need battle experience.'

'It has been a bloody summer, Lieutenant.'

'And I regret that I did not play a part.'

Forrester sighed heavily, removing his hat to scratch at a spot on his sandy-haired scalp. 'Then you're a damned fool. The man who regrets not fighting a battle, proves he has never seen one.'

'But I must show Capt—' Hood began, strangling his own words with a look of embarrassment.

'Captain Stryker?' Forrester asked, suddenly understanding. 'You feel you will earn his respect?'

For a while Hood was silent, but eventually he offered a barely perceptible nod. 'Aye, sir. If ever he returns to us.'

'He will return,' Forrester said firmly. He considered Hood's words. 'You had hoped he might treat you a little differently if you had faced the enemy in battle.' He shook his head, genuinely sorry for the lieutenant's plight. 'Your experience in the field, Tom, is not the captain's foremost concern.'

'I asked him—'

'Asked him what?' Forrester said sharply.

'To tell me of Stratton Fight. I heard it was hard. Terrible.'

'And he was not best pleased with the inquiry?'

'No, sir,' Hood muttered weakly.

Forrester replaced his hat and stood, arching his spine with a deep groan. 'Stratton Fight was indeed hard. We marched up a bloody great hill, and fought a bloody great army that outnumbered our own by three to one. It was at once both horrific and glorious. But we lost a friend there. A young officer who had become like a brother to many. Like a son to Stryker.'

The light of understanding seemed to come into Hood's eyes then. 'And I am his replacement.'

'You have it. He took Burton's death to heart. It was as though the very world had taken up some vendetta against him. He has not been the same since.' Forrester approached Hood, slapping him on the shoulder. 'He does not needle you for your lack of soldierly experience, but for the memories you conjure.'

Hood closed his eyes, tilting his head back to study the clouds that appeared as inky blotches on a grey canvas. 'Christ, but how am I to proceed here, knowing my own captain harbours such resentment?'

'But not for you, Lieutenant,' Forrester replied gently. 'He is angry at the world. At the man who murdered his friend, at the armies of Parliament, and most of all at himself. He will return to us soon enough, and you, my lad, will bear the brunt of his ire to begin with, I dare say. But give it time, Tom. Stryker is not the easiest officer to impress on any given day, that is assured, but you will find him of sound advice and good judgement, despite that scowl. And once you have fought beside him, you will thank God that he is simply on your side, let alone at your very shoulder.'

'I hear he is an accomplished fighter, sir.'

'With sword in hand, young Tom,' Forrester replied with a wolfish expression that made Hood shudder, 'he is the very devil incarnate.'

CHAPTER 8

Gloucester, 9 August 1643

Stryker regained consciousness over the course of what seemed like several hours, though it might have been less for all he could tell. It was simply a period of darkness and light, intermingled, melding from one to the other like clouds drifting across a bright sun. With those clouds came images. Faces of people he knew and those he had long forgotten. Lisette's narrow features peered at him angrily from their frame of tousled gold hair, berating him for abandoning her in London. Forrester would drive her off suddenly, his own round face creased in an expression of hurt, silently asking why Stryker had turned traitor. And then Burton would appear. Young Andrew Burton, shot through the skull by a witch-finder whose real hatred had been for Stryker. Burton's face had no animation at all, his eyes staring lifelessly up at the sky, as they had on the blood-stained hill where he had died, yet Stryker could still see the pain in them; the accusation of betrayal. He heard himself sob.

The dreams ceased for a while, replaced by blackness and the stench of mouldy straw and piss, and Stryker found that he was able to force open his eye. It took a while to prize the lids apart, for they felt as though they had been slapped with a tar brush, and he knew that it was glued with dried blood. Eventually it came free, burning at the skin of the eye socket, and he explored the area with his fingertips, noting the familiar stickiness of a fresh scab. As he strained to see, chinks of blurry light seared through him like a thousand wasp stings, and he slammed the eye shut, terrified that he had been blinded. But when he tried again, the pain had lessened, his eye gradually adjusting, and he realized that he was in a small, gloomy room, lit by a tiny square window through which daylight and a balmy breeze streamed.

He tried to sit up, but a hideous pounding reverberated inside his head and he was forced to slump back on the cold stone floor. He felt wetness at his crotch, touched fingers to his breeches, and knew that the smell of urine came from him.

'Jesu,' he rasped, feeling his lips peel reluctantly from his teeth, the agony in his throat nearly matching that in his head. The thirst was unbearable, and he resolved not to swallow or speak. He became aware of his empty baldric, and a quick, wincing glance to the room's four corners told him that his sword was not near by. Indeed, the chamber was empty, save a large pile of rags dumped just to the side of the door. He slid a tentative hand to his waist, but could not find the hilt of his dirk. He groped, despite the pain, at his boot; again, no dagger. He realized then that he had no weapons at all.

'What,' a deep voice echoed suddenly in the enclosed space, 'in the name of Lucifer's ballocks happened to us?'

Despite the pain, Stryker smiled, for, though he could see nothing, the voice was one he knew as well as his own. 'Your brazen assailant has done for us again, Sergeant Skellen.' He tried again to ease himself up on to his elbow, and was relieved this time when the wave of nausea subsided without flattening him. He took a moment, steadied himself, and opened his eye. 'You are wounded?'

The rag pile shifted in the darkness as though it concealed a nest of rats, before the entire form seemed to levitate. From amid the formless shape, a wan face with deep-set eyes appeared. 'No,' Skellen grunted, thrusting his legs out straight and letting his back slump against the wall. 'Brains smart like buggery, though. That big brag clubbed me right after he got you.'

More confident now that the pounding in his head was bearable, Stryker quickly gave each of his limbs a tentative shake to check for any other injuries, but was happy to find none.

'Musketeer Port,' Skellen growled bitterly, voice echoing in the grey half-light. 'First he stabs me, now this. Me and him are due a serious chat.'

Stryker felt his face again, gritting his teeth as the wound throbbed at his touch. Thankfully the cut – though he could tell it had bled profusely from the caking that had formed past his ear and down as far as his neck – seemed superficial. 'I confess, I did not think we would see him again. He scampered off into the woods at Hartcliffe like a terrified doe. I imagined he would go back to his home, his family. Not enlist here.'

Skellen hawked up a mouthful of phlegm and ejected it loudly. 'And now he has us caged. Must have seen us give Dodd the slip.'

'We fulfilled the Prince's orders, leastwise.'

Skellen brandished a mirthless smile in the gloom. 'And now Massie'll stretch our necks for it.'

Footsteps sounded outside the room; the metallic clunk of a key wrestling with a sticky lock. Skellen shuffled along the wall, shying instinctively away from the threshold. The prisoners exchanged a glance, a shared acknowledgement of impending plight, and waited for their captors to enter. In would stalk Edward Massie, Stryker supposed, incandescent with rage and vowing to make use of the direst consequences at his disposal. Port will have scuttled straight for the governor's headquarters at the Crown Inn, eager to impart what he had learned, and Stryker imagined his damaged arm stretched out in front as the young colonel dropped silver coins in his palm. He imagined, too, the noose being prepared. Measured, tied, and pulled taut, the thick rope creaking like the chatter of demons.

The door groaned open. The figure of a man stood there beneath the lintel, light streaming in from behind to frame him in a cowl of shadow. Stryker stared up, blinking hard despite the pain, so that he could see his captor clearly. He felt his eye strain against the new brightness, ignored the tears that welled like a miniscule flood, and let the man's features rise from the darkness until a face he recognized took shape.

But it was not Governor Massie. Not even Captain Backhouse.

'Good-morrow, Captain,' said Richard Port. 'Trust you slept well?'

London, 9 August 1643

'*Peace!*'

The crowd cheered. They had grown in number and confidence during the course of the day, and now, as the bell in Westminster's ancient clock tower chimed noon, they crowed and brayed and chanted their way through the city and down towards Parliament.

'Give us peace now!' the man bellowed again. He was in the upper floor of a building that had once been a well-frequented brothel. It had been closed down by the Roundheads at the turn of the year, though the fact that he was naked from the waist up seemed to suggest it had opened up again. The surging mob did not appear to care, and they echoed the words as one, the noise reverberating off the tightly packed buildings at either side to make it seem as though a great earthquake was rupturing London's streets.

The crowd swept on, filling the roadways like a flood, pulsing with each new influx of bodies as smaller mobs merged with the main group at every junction. They jostled and shoved, shoulder to shoulder from one side of the street to the other, pushed up to shop fronts and houses on either side, the outermost protesters squeezed until they were forced to spill into the alleyways like rainwater coursing along so many drains. Every now and then the heaving mass would flinch at the sight of a soldier in one of the doorways, peeling away from the threat with one mind like a flock of starlings from a falcon. But when that threat vanished, the soldier sinking with his long musket back into the shadows, the chorus would start in earnest; a smattering of disparate shouts, rising in quick time to a deafening crescendo of anger and defiance.

It was a chant that rang with violence but called for peace. The protesters, mostly women, had had enough of war. Enough of their menfolk taken away to far-off towns, unnamed fields and unmarked graves, bleeding for the great and good of the land. Enough of the taxation needed to pay for this lingering violence. Enough of the gloom-laden reports that seemed to trickle daily from every corner of the nation. Reports that spoke of lost sieges and battles in their bland, official language, but whispered of the horrific reality that each engagement had wrought. They wanted an end to it. Why not now, when the situation might still be resolved? Things were not going well for the rebels, whose cause had been so heartily bolstered by the citizens of the capital. If the Parliament would not negotiate with their all-conquering sovereign now, then a far more terrible resolution might be forced upon them. It was common knowledge what Prince Rupert had done to Cirencester. Everyone had seen the blackened, beleaguered souls who trudged back from the ruin that was Bristol. They would not see London suffer that same fate.

Lisette Gaillard and Christopher Quigg were on King Street, to the north of Westminster Abbey. For once they made no attempt to conceal themselves, for the sheer mass of people assured complete anonymity. Just two more faces in a sea of humanity. Thousands of folk had come to Westminster this day, clogging the streets so that no traffic of any kind could get through, surrounding the abbey and palace, filling the palace yards, Old and New, and lining the Middlesex bank of the Thames right up to Westminster Stairs.

Lisette had wanted to come, wanted to see what incendiary effect the news-sheets had produced, but even she was astonished. It was as if the entire population of London had appeared before the great buildings of Parliament to voice their dissent at the ongoing war. As Quigg had foretold, the city was roused in opposition to the hostilities – hostilities the rebels were losing in all quarters – and the fake diurnals produced in the back room of Henry Greetham's house had added fuel to the flames of discontent.

'You wanted a riot,' Quigg, at Lisette's side, grunted into his sleeve. 'Now you have one.'

Lisette could not suppress a smile, even as she was jostled by the swelling crowd. 'We have done well.'

Quigg nodded. '*Peace!*' he bellowed, joining the growing chant. '*Peace!*'

'*Peace!*' Lisette echoed, eager to appear part of the mob.

Quigg grasped her elbow suddenly. 'Look!'

Lisette strained on to the tips of her toes, craning to see over the shoulder of a man in front. She did not have a great deal of difficulty for he was elderly and stooped, but he waved a long, bone-capped blackthorn in the air in time to the chants, and she had to shift her weight from side to side in order to see beyond it. Eventually, she managed to get a good view of the entrance to New Palace Yard, and there, spreading out along its northern edge, she saw soldiers.

There had been plenty of armed men patrolling during the morning, of course. Since the king's perilously close capture of the capital the previous winter, the city had been a place of cautious martial law, with regular patrols becoming a part of the everyday rhythm. But this, Lisette knew, was different. The protesters swarming about the canopied octagonal fountain in New Palace Yard had hemmed themselves into a natural cage, easily encircled around the open area to the north of Westminster Palace, and the infantrymen were quickly marching on them, leaving men at intervals, to form a hedge of primed muskets. Even from Lisette's position, the upended muskets rose like thin black trees above the heads of their bearers, silent yet, but each a harbinger of something terrible.

'I've a bad feeling.' The strain in Quigg's voice was clear and raw.

Lisette silenced him with a savage glance. 'We have seen enough. Let us be away.'

But the crowd seemed to close in on them just as they went to turn. The people were no longer moving as one, surging instead in all directions, the mob contracting and expanding in sudden, panicked anarchy. Enough eyes had seen the troops' arrival, sensed the new danger, and passed the message back to the rest, so that now the mood had changed. The din of coordinated chants was being replaced by a low murmur of disquiet that quickly swelled to a roar as people shied away from the gunmen. There were no soldiers on King Street, and the crowded bodies there began to move northwards, away from the imminent threat at New Palace Yard. Lisette let herself be carried along, swept upstream with the fleeing protesters like a leaf on a tide, looking back just once. And then it happened.

It sounded like rain at first, or hail dashing the roofs of the tightly packed capital. But in moments her mind had distilled hoofbeats from the chaos, and her heart felt as though it was smashing through her throat and into her mouth.

'*Cavalry!*' she hissed, snatching Quigg's sleeve and dragging him on through the crowd. She wrenched her head left and right, searching for the origin of the sounds, and in seconds saw the glint of a lobster-pot helm. Its wearer perched atop a huge mount at the entrance to one of the alleys to her left, and behind him trotted a dozen more horsemen. She did not stop to look for more, for she knew there would be cavalry units manoeuvring around them, coming, she supposed, from Tothill Fields, where, she had heard, a troop of harquebusiers were billeted.

'Keep moving,' she hissed. 'Keep moving before the bastards charge, damn you!'

Shouts came, sharp and bold, riding the crest of the thundering wave, distinct in their martial tone. She could not hear the individual words, but the bone-chilling rasp of unsheathing swords was unmistakable. The cavalrymen reached the road in short order, but they did not charge, looking instead to the south, where the musketeers had cut off a section of the crowd at New Palace Yard.

Lisette did not hear the order to fire, but she heard the volley right enough. It exploded in a vast, ear-smashing torrent that funnelled its way up through the narrow streets towards the fleeing protesters. And they screamed. Wailed in their terror. Some fell and were trampled by those behind. Others began to fight and claw at their comrades, desperate to be away from the carnage at their backs.

'Christ on His Cross!' Quigg bleated at Lisette's side. 'They're shooting at the crowd! They're shooting at the fucking crowd!' He turned back, staring in utter disbelief at the smoke rising in twisted shapes above New Palace Yard.

'What did you expect?' Lisette snarled mercilessly.

Quigg peered down at her with his blood-shot, bulging gaze. 'Not this. *Christ.*' He looked as though he might weep. 'Christ.'

'We wanted chaos, sir, and we have succeeded.'

Quigg seemed taken aback. 'Chaos, aye, but not this. Not *this*!' His bottom lip was trembling. 'Oh, Christ!'

Lisette led them northwards along King Street, shoving her way ruthlessly through the crowd, thankful with each step that the majority of the mob had been women. Leaving the chaos of Westminster in their wake, they reached the sprawling palace of Whitehall. She could see its guards already leaving their posts, forming ragged units that she guessed would be destined for the protests. It was a brutal sight, proof, if any more were needed, that the leaders of the rebellion had decided they would no longer suffer this kind of dissent. They were going to end it, one way or another. But to Lisette's eyes it meant hope. The hope that perhaps many more of London's soldiers were on their way from all corners of the city, ordered to quell this challenge to Parliament.

They crossed under the arch of the Holbein Gate at a run, its towers already devoid of sentries, and continued north, Lisette leading the way while Quigg gasped and spluttered a short distance behind. And then they were into the cluttered build-ings around Charing Cross, the carefully landscaped expanse of St James's Park away to their left. The road was still busy here, but passable, and they crossed the junction easily enough, the weathered old monument looming over them as though in judgement. They had left a pair of horses at an inn in the shadow of the cross, and now Lisette darted around the side of the building to find the servant-boy who had been charged with their care. By the time she had pressed a small silver coin into his grubby hand, nodded her thanks and led the beasts out on to the roadway, Quigg had finally caught up. He took his mount's reins in one hand, leaving the other braced against a knee as he doubled forward in search of air.

'Let us,' he rasped through heaving breaths, 'be away from this sorry place.'

Lisette was already clambering up into the saddle. She glared down at the red-faced, panting intelligencer and cast him a withering expression. 'Get on then, monsieur.'

St Mary without Bishopsgate, London, 9 August 1643

Major General Erasmus Collings looked down at the girl with a level of disgust that surprised even himself. He did not like women, found them to be shrill and vacuous, and had certainly never felt attracted to one in the base fashion that seemed so readily intoxicating for other men. But this one positively repelled him. She was the kind of wench he despised. Arrogant, stubborn and above all, Royalist.

'You lied to me, Miss Cade,' he said quietly. He was leaning against the wall of the little ground-floor cell that had been his prisoner's most recent home.

Cecily Cade was sitting on a low bench in one of the room's dingy corners. She was wan and gaunt, a result of so many weeks without sunlight, but defiance remained etched on her face. She lifted a hand to push a matted ringlet of black hair behind her ear. 'I did not.'

Collings stepped forwards, pulling down the hem of his sky-blue doublet with an irritated jerk. 'You most certainly did.' He gritted his teeth, scratched at the smooth skin of his bald head with long, manicured fingernails, and stared at his charge. 'And you are lying now. My people wasted an inordinate amount of time in their search.'

She shrugged. 'They should have looked harder.'

'Damn your malignant tongue, woman!' Collings shouted suddenly, pleased to see her flinch. He licked his thin lips slowly. 'I should cut it out myself.'

Cecily shuddered, but met his stare. 'You would not dare, sir.'

Collings leaped forward, grasped a fistful of the girl's filthy dress and hauled her up so that her face was no more than an inch from his. 'Where is the gold?'

'I do not know.'

He let go, thrusting her back on to the bench with enough force to punch the air from her. 'Harlot!' he hissed, the sound cutting through her desperate gasps. 'Where is the gold?'

Her eyes were big and green, speckled with shards of auburn, and they glinted in the dim room. 'Oxford,' she said slowly.

Collings turned away, lest he throttle her there and then. She had taken him for an utter fool, but what could he do? Earlier in the summer he had decided upon a drastic course of action, one that would certainly have paid dividends had events turned in the way he had foreseen. A notorious witch-hunter named Osmyn Hogg had been assigned to use his various techniques – normally employed in the securing of confessions for witchcraft – in the interrogation of Miss Cade. Hogg had been close to breaking her when the great armies of the south-west had come to blows on a hill above Bude, and in the midst of that terrible defeat, Hogg had been cut down in cold blood. Collings had not been unduly concerned either by that twist of fate, or by the defeat itself, for he had taken his prisoner and fled the battle-field. But then the rumours had begun to circulate. Men whispered that Hogg had committed a murder of his own. Had shot dead a Royalist officer in cold blood. And that rumour did not sit well with the rank and file of the Parliamentarian army.

In the weeks that followed, men had visited Collings. Representatives of his friends at the Commons, who had warned him that such associations would no longer be tolerated. That was not a significant problem, of course, for Osmyn Hogg was dead and rotting, except that the implication was clear; Collings could no longer conduct business outside of Parliament's gaze. He would be watched, and that meant his dealings with the infuriating prisoner could not cross the boundaries of decency, however much he wanted them to. No torture could be employed, therefore. No walking or pricking, as Hogg would have done. No swimming the girl till she spluttered the location of her dead father's gold through waterlogged gasps. None of that, for the craven mice at Westminster lacked the stomachs for such work, however expedient, and Collings was left cursing the girl and the spitting-feeble threats that he knew he could not act upon.

'You will languish here for as long as it takes,' he said, after letting the silence linger like a heavy cloud for a minute or two. 'As long as it takes for you to tell me what I want to know.' That, at least, was true. She was his prisoner, and he'd be damned before he handed her to his masters. He would be the one to find the treasure, and he alone. It was for that reason that he had purchased the handful of buildings at this corner of the defunct religious estate.

Cecily glanced at the wooden trencher that sat on the floor between them. It held a jug of weak beer and a small loaf of bread, neither of which had been touched. 'I'll starve first.'

Collings smirked. 'So be it, Miss Cade. The enemy will not have the gold either.' He stepped closer. 'Indeed, you are the last of your line, are you not? Your brother, I fear, was killed at Kineton Fight, and your father shot before your very eyes. The location of Sir Alfred's treasure will die with you. All that he worked for gone; vanished for eternity.'

'You think he would have been happier knowing it was in Parliament's greedy paws?' She spat on the threshing between her feet. 'You clearly did not know my father.'

Collings opened his mouth to speak, but an urgent knocking at the door stayed his words. 'Come!' he barked irritably, turning away from the prisoner.

A heavily bearded sergeant appeared, halberd in hand, beady eyes darting about the room. His gaze loitered on Cecily for just a moment longer than was appropriate, before returning to the major general. 'Sir.'

'Spit it out, man!' Collings snarled.

The soldier snatched off his hat, straightened the white hand-kerchief tied at its crown, and offered an awkward bow, grimacing apologetically. 'Trouble, sir. Down at the Parliament.'

Collings folded his arms, his irritation rising. 'And what, pray, would that have to do with me?'

Lisette Gaillard and Christopher Quigg loosely tied the horses amongst the withered trees outside the old edifice of St Mary without Bishopsgate and advanced to the edge of the thicket. From there, behind the cover of the outermost brush, they had a good view of the priory's side entrance, and, more import-antly, its guards.

'The bastards are not leaving, monsieur.'

Quigg sucked his teeth. 'It was always a risk.'

Lisette stared at him angrily. 'And now we have no more dice to throw.'

The doorway behind which Cecily Cade was supposed to be kept was flanked by two of the blackcoats. Each man clutched a musket, though neither had a lit match, and their eyes raked the land in front.

'Shall we check the other entrances?' Quigg asked.

Lisette shook her head. 'How could we reach her once inside? It would take forever to get through that damned labyrinth.' She slammed her eyes shut, whispering a silent prayer. Collings had not taken the bait.

A commotion erupted away to the west, at a place near the far corner of the compound where a large doorway was set into the flat stone blocks. They had not kept vigil on that particular

door, for it was one of the hospital's chief entrances and consequently the most heavily guarded. Sure enough, the usual
half-dozen musketeers were there now, except that this time
they had been joined by a trio of their black-coated comrades
and the big, bearded commander.

'That is half their total number,' Lisette said, hope beginning
to rise within her. Perhaps they were indeed relaxing the rest
of the pickets. But even as she and Quigg watched the group,
the men began to gesticulate to one another wildly, chattering
in a strangely animated fashion. The spies looked on, too far
away to eavesdrop. Just then, a new figure emerged from the
building.

'Christ,' Quigg muttered, 'it's him.'

The man was of middling height but whip-thin frame. He
wore a suit of light blue, adorned with flourishes of lace and
silver thread that sparkled as he moved. He wore no armour,
save the delicate rapier hanging at his waist, and carried a wide-
brimmed, black-feathered hat in his hand. It was that last detail
that had captured Quigg's attention, for the man's exposed head
was nearly as white as his falling band collar. It was completely
hairless, shining brightly in the afternoon sun like a marble
globe set atop a blue column.

'Collings,' Lisette said. She frowned. 'He is agitated.'

They watched Collings berate his small party of grim
subordinates. He might have been slight of stature, a child's
body compared with the brawny blackcoats, but they gathered
around him nonetheless, nodding and bowing like errant
schoolboys as his skinny arms pointed and waved. Fox-Beard
seemed to be receiving the most vehement tongue-lashing, and
his hairy chin worked frenetically as he babbled a defence.

'Giving a fair account of himself,' Quigg said.

'*Oui*,' Lisette replied, equally surprised. 'A brave man.'

It was then that the burly commander turned on his heel,
pointing away to the west where, beside the crumbling pillars of
the hospital's ancient gateway, another man waited atop a horse.
He was too far away for Lisette to make out his features, but he

was dressed like a soldier, the beast beneath him swinging its head from side to side as it snorted and whinnied.

'A messenger?' suggested Lisette.

Quigg's amphibian eyes swivelled down to her. 'Or an extra guard.'

She looked at him. 'Cavalry to guard a building?' She shook her head, turning back to the horseman. 'Look at his mount. It has been ridden hard.' Quigg made to speak, but she placed a firm hand on his arm. 'Look.'

Collings had pushed through his gaggle of sentries and, with the blackcoats trailing in his wake, stalked across the open ground towards the old gates. The rider kicked his horse gently so that it trotted to meet him, and the rider dismounted as they came close. From a distance, Lisette and Quigg could see that Collings seemed to be reluctant about something, shaking his bald head and lambasting the horseman for whatever it was that he had come to impart, but evidently the newcomer was standing his ground, for the major general cut off the meeting with a curt nod and spun sway, striding back to the building.

And Lisette Gaillard's heart soared, for the musketeers had not followed him this time. Indeed, they were turning away, forming a crude line in the horseman's wake, Fox-Beard shouldering his halberd in the lead. As Lisette and Quigg looked on, the pair of blackcoats at the nearest doorway responded to an enraged bellow from Collings and left their posts, clattering noisily along the paved walkway in the direction of the main entrance.

'God is truly on our side,' Quigg breathed into Lisette's ear. 'Let us get this done, and we'll share a jug o' claret by sundown.'

Lisette returned his smile. 'We'll share it with Master Greetham.'

'Amen to that.'

With that they were on their feet and running. Lisette took the lead, holding her breath as she bolted across the long grass fringing the walkway. Out in the open, the sense of exposure was excruciating, her pulse roaring loudly in her skull so that she felt sure others might hear it. She reached the paved ground in seconds, glancing back to see Quigg blundering behind, and slammed into the smooth stone of the wall. It was strangely warm at her shoulder blades, baked as it was in the August sun. She waited for Quigg. 'Do it.'

Christopher Quigg may have been inept as an intelligencer, clumsy, slow-moving and so ugly that he was unlikely to blend in, but he was as strong as an ox. Lisette watched him approach the door without breaking his stride, suck a great wave of air through his twisted nose, and smash his boot into the wooden timbers. The noise was horrendous, echoing between wall and woodland, but the blow had been struck hard and precise, and the mouldering slats gave way immediately.

Lisette pushed past Quigg as the door swung inwards on rust-clogged hinges, stepping over the splintered debris, her boots unnaturally loud in the gloomy interior. If the exterior proclaimed the church's magnificence, then the interior had been built with frugality in mind. It was plain and pale, just a corridor built in stone, with none of the intricate carvings of the outer walls. There were three doors to choose from, and Lisette opened the first, which was immediately at her left hand. The chamber was completely empty.

'Nothing,' Quigg's voice echoed through the corridor. He had gone beyond her, testing the next door. He closed it with a shake of the head. 'One more to try.'

Lisette darted to the last room, rounding Quigg and pressing her shoulder to the door. It was locked. She looked at her companion. 'You think you can break it?'

In answer, he kicked the door hard. This one, unharmed by harsh winters and scorching summers, held firm, and he recoiled with a yelp and grimace, clutching his kneecap to his chest. They were at the furthest point of the corridor now, where the passage met another conduit running from left to right across its path, and at the place where they formed a junction there were three statues. All had been broken in some way, arms smashed

by Tudor church-breakers or faces mutilated by Puritan icono-
clasts, but only one had been fully decapitated. The head still lay
at the statue's feet.

'Here,' Lisette said, trying to lift the carved stone, 'help me.'

Quigg hobbled over and lifted the heavy stone in one movement. He hefted it in both hands, loped to the door with a
series of guttural grunts, and swung it at the timbers. Wood
and stone crashed, dust billowed in a little, furious cloud, and
Quigg jerked back. He righted himself, scowled at the stubborn
door, and swung again. This time there was a high-pitched
crack and the door shuddered. Quigg's face gleamed with sweat,
the cratered skin contorted with the effort. Cursing under his
breath, he lifted the stone for a third time and swung it in a low
arc with all the strength he could muster. The door exploded
inwards, the metallic remains of its lock in ragged ruins, and he
dropped the head between his feet, the wide eyes staring up at
him in mute affront.

Outside, there were shouts of alarm. They were faint, presumably from the guards down at the main entrance, but Quigg
nodded, moved aside, and Lisette hurried into the chamber.

What she saw was a young woman, perhaps in her early twenties, with a narrow face, hair the colour of Henry Greetham's
ink, and skin as pale as ivory. Her eyes might once have been
beautiful. But now they seemed cast in shadow and strangely
distant.

She gazed up at Lisette from the bench on which she perched.
'Who are you?'

'Cecily Cade?' Lisette asked brusquely.

The girl nodded.

Quigg was beside Lisette. 'We're here to rescue you, miss.'

'Come, girl,' Lisette ordered, holding out her hand, 'we do
not have long.'

But she was wrong. They had no time at all. Because in the
doorway stood a man wearing a black coat and a hat tied with
the white band that denoted his fealty to Erasmus Collings. His
clean-shaven face was alight with triumph, and in his hands he

held a long musket, the muzzle pointed into the room. Her eyes snaked along the barrel to the serpentine, noting the match-cord dangling ominously from its jaws. The tip glowed hot.

Christopher Quigg reacted quickest. 'One shot.'

The musketeer swung his weapon sideways to point directly at Quigg's chest. 'Shut it, you poxy nigit.'

Quigg looked at Lisette instead. 'He has one shot, mademoiselle. One shot.' And with that he strode forwards, chest pressing into the muzzle so that the blackcoat was forced to stagger backwards in shock.

The shot burst about the chamber like the eruption of a volcano. Smoke lurched out from the doorway, filling the room, roiling at the low ceiling, choking Lisette and the girl in a malevolent miasma of grit and sulphur. And from that smoke the body of Christopher Quigg tumbled, flung from his feet by the sheer force of the lead ball as it punched through his chest, flattening to a wide disc as it smashed flesh and ribs, and ripping out through his back.

Lisette did not stop to look. She gripped Cecily's cold hand tightly, dragged her up from the bench and ran into the smoke. They collided with the musketeer somewhere beyond the threshold, and she pulled the dirk from her cloak, jabbing it into the smoke. On the third strike she was rewarded with a scream, followed quickly by the clatter of metal on stone as the musket hit the ground, and she pushed on until they were out in the corridor. She turned to find the blackcoat still there, trying to stand his ground, but his right hand clawed at his left shoulder as fresh blood pulsed between his bare fingers. Lisette did not even pause to think. She released the girl and ran at the guard, stabbing at him again and again. He held up both hands to defend his face, though the wounded arm would not rise above his sternum, and lost two fingers for his trouble. He screamed again, recoiling before his assailant's startling ferocity, but she leaped at him, knowing more men would be here soon, and slashed at his throat and eyes. One of the blows broke though his lacerated palms, nicking his cheek, and he twisted away. She kicked him in the groin, his hands swept low, and she thrust the blade hard into his neck. He went down, not dead but immobile, gasping for air like a trout on a hook, blood pooling unstoppably about him in a crimson halo on the hard stone.

Lisette went back to where the pale-faced girl stood, mouth agape, eyes glistening with horror. She took her hand again, pulled hard so that Cecily stumbled forth, and coaxed her past the prone soldier, blood smearing their shoes to leave macabre footprints in their wake.

They rushed out into the open. Before them, two black-coated musketeers were running up from the main entrance, calling to one another in hoarse voices.

'They'll shoot us!' Cecily's voice was shrill with terror.

'They are too far away, Miss Cade, and they cannot shoot while they're running.' Lisette ushered Cecily out on to the open grassland that divided the former hospital's lands from the copse. 'The horses are in the trees. Can you ride?'

'Of course.'

'Not *do you know how* to ride, Miss Cade.' She cast an appraising gaze from Cecily's shoes to the drawn features of her face. '*Can* you?'

Cecily set her jaw determinedly. 'Aye.'

'*C'est bon*. Follow me, and do not look back.'

CHAPTER 9

The South Gate, Gloucester, 10 August 1643

Nikolas Robbens watched his companions shiver in the chill air. It was less than an hour after midnight, and though the days were sweaty and cloying, the darkness seemed to throw a marrow-numbing shroud over the land. He drew his cloak tighter, not willing to show that he too felt the bite. He wryly observed his new master, the man they called Slager, give a sudden violent shiver, his massive shoulders trembling beneath layers of wool and buff-hide. How a man of such size could feel the cold was a mystery.

The three of them – Robbens, Slager and the crookback, Nobbs – were standing on the bastion that protected the city's southern port. From here they gazed out upon the fields that stretched beyond Gloucester's ramshackle suburbs. Further south was the open land of Tredworth Field, while immediately to their left was the wide expanse of rough heathland known as Gaudy Green.

'Nothing green about it this night,' Slager grunted at Robbens' left side.

'Though perhaps it is a little gaudier than before,' Robbens replied, eliciting a snort of amusement from the huge man. It was a colourful sight, even in the darkness. The tents of thousands of soldiers had been pitched on the heath, clusters of off-white awnings staked to the soil around fires that now guttered manically, the orange glow licking hellishly against the banners of the great men of the land. And those standards, driven into the ground on long poles so that the rebels on Gloucester's feeble walls could see, were harbingers of the terrible price to be paid for defying a king.

'There's more to come,' Slager intoned grimly. 'Many more.' He was sucking a pipe, and he tapped the chewed clay stem against his front teeth before slowly blowing a fragrant funnel of smoke from his wide nostrils. 'I hear the whole royal army's set for this place. Look to the hills at dawn.'

Nobbs was leaning against the parapet and staring down at the Royalist encampment, which seemed to grow by the hour. He straightened suddenly, arching his back, and grimaced as the twisted shoulders clicked. 'And we'll be trapped 'ere.'

Slager looked down at him. 'This is not our fight, Nobbs, remember that. When the city falls, we will surrender with the rest and look to put our plans into action.' He paused to draw again on the pipe, closing his eyes as he breathed in the smoke. When he opened them again, he stared off at the horizon, his face taking on a serene glaze. 'Our destiny lies elsewhere. And for that destiny to come to pass, we must be in Gloucester.'

Robbens watched Slager and marvelled. He had met many like him in the Low Countries, those who would travel to the ends of the earth for their cause, but few had hailed from England. Slager was different to the usual gentlemen adventurers who had sailed across the Channel to seek fame and fortune in the destruction of a continent. Something about him spoke of an inner resolve that would never waver. The name alone spoke volumes to a man like Robbens, who knew what it meant in the Dutch tongue: butcher. He did not wish to discover how Slager had garnered such a name, contenting himself simply with the knowledge that the man was formidably wealthy. And, more importantly, that should this mission succeed, he would pay Robbens' family a lifetime's worth of coin. 'You are certain he will come?'

Slager nodded, jowls quivering. 'Certain as I can be. There was talk the Cavaliers would come here after Bristol. We listened to the talk and travelled here first.'

Robbens nodded. They had vacated their base at Malmesbury as soon as word reached them of the Royalist advance. The king, it appeared, was going to take Gloucester before he looked to London, and that suited Slager just fine. The three had ridden direct to the city, where Slager's reputation had seen them welcomed with open arms, much to Robbens' surprise, and after that they had simply waited. The Dutchman moved his straw-coloured hair from his eyes with a spindly hand, before straightening the ear-string across his left shoulder. 'And now the bastards have come.'

Slager pointed the pipe at the flame-bathed camp. 'Now they have come. The first part of the rumour was right, so I must trust in the second part. He will come and you will kill him.'

'I still can't see—' Nobbs began gingerly. Slager turned to him.

'See what?'

Nobbs swallowed thickly. 'How we'll get close enough.'

Slager stepped up to the rampart, tapping his pipe against the stone. The black dregs fell away to sprinkle the ditch below. 'You leave that to me, Nobbs.'

'And the rest you must leave to me,' Robbens said. This one death was all that was needed to complete his life's dream. And it was hardly a challenge to a man like Nikolas Robbens. He killed without mercy. He was an assassin.

—ɷ—

Stryker had hoped they would kill him quickly. He had looked into Port's gleaming eyes, seen the vengeance within that dark gaze, and known for certain that the musketeer would not let him live. And perhaps he would still be right in that, at least. But quick it was not.

The pain seemed to smoulder. It was as though his body had been dusted with black powder and set alight – as his face had been all those years ago – for the feeling was sickeningly familiar. A relentless burn as muscles flexed and released in grotesque spasm, driven mad by their agonies, beaten to trembling jelly by fists and feet. He felt as though he was a mere shell, crippled and twisted, curled inwards on the stinking floor like a malformed foetus.

It was fully dark now. Stryker wondered what the time was, not that it mattered, and he strained his neck to look up at the window. It told him nothing, though he saw a cluster of tiny pricks of light that he supposed were stars. He peered around the room, suffocated by the oppressive blackness. Where was Skellen? He had been taken hours ago; dragged out backwards after one blow from the man named Bones. The scrape of his boot heels still rung in Stryker's ears. But where had they taken him? Stryker let his head slump. No Skellen. No friends at all. No way out.

Richard Port had not gone running to Massie. Nor did he have any reason to. For it increasingly became clear to Stryker that the musketeer had not seen the Royalist agents make their clandestine signal. He had simply been patrolling the streets, reached the foot of the rampart, and looked up.

'And there you were, like a gift from God Almighty Himself,' Port had said. 'And I knew I had to take my chance. By Christ, I knew it.'

Port, it transpired, had spent a whole day seeking his green-coated comrades after the calamitous ambush outside Bristol, but had found none of them. And so he had walked to Glouces-ter, flinching at the call of every owl and the bark of every fox in the night, clutching his shattered wrist, praying he would not run into soldiers – or worse – and cursing the one-eyed captain of foot whose boot heel had inflicted such unremitting and unwarranted torture.

'And you've turned your coat, *sir*?' Port had sneered as he paced in front of Stryker. The captain and Skellen had moved back against the far wall, immediately beneath the low window, and stared up at their triumphal captor as he revelled in his small victory. 'You're a proper soldier now, are you? A man of the Parliament?'

'Aye, that I am,' Stryker had answered, forcing his trepidation deep down into his guts, lest Port sense it.

'Well that is just grand,' Port had replied jauntily, turning to the pair of bluecoats who had been with him on the rampart, 'ain't that right, Bones?'

The bear-like man who had felled Stryker with the butt end of his musket offered a grin that showed off a set of bizarrely tiny teeth. 'Right you are, Dicky.'

And then the beatings had started. Slow at first. A moment of calm, for Port to posture and crow, before a heavy fist to the midriff from the gargantuan Bones. But as the green-coated ringleader's reserve of self-congratulatory statements began to run dry, he had cut his eager henchmen loose.

'Cut him up, Dicky,' the second bluecoat had said, 'can't we? Chop off his stones, or—'

'All in good time,' had been Port's reply. And then he had gazed down at Stryker with a startling malevolence. 'I do not care what you're doing here, Captain. All I know is that a one-eyed bastard broke my arm. And now he's here. You tortured me, you swaggering goddamned bravo. Out in that forest, when the battle was over and you had me at your mercy, you crushed my fucking arm like it was a twig.'

Even now, in the silence of the night-shrouded room, Stryker could not defend his actions. He had seen Port's injury, had crushed his bones beneath his boot and, though it was painful to admit, he had revelled in the agony it caused. It had been grief, he knew. The loss of Burton had been his fault. Stryker had carried the guilt with him for weeks, finally letting go of his restraint as he inflicted suffering on the prone Richard Port.

A stab of pain pulsed through his guts with sudden venom, and he curled himself more tightly around his knees, spitting a savage oath through the bile that bubbled in his mouth. For a moment he wondered whether Massie would step in to help a fellow gentleman. But he remembered Port's words as Bones' battering-ram fists thumped into his guts.

'Governor Massie is not aware of your current predicament,' the greencoat had said. 'Oh, he thinks you've absconded, sir, aye. For I slipped a groat or three to my old feodary, Mister

Dodd, and it appears he spied you leaping over the lowest part of the wall. Another man was beaten up on the rampart, I hear. They've assumed that was you as well.' Port had grinned broadly, as though meeting an old friend for the first time in years. 'So here we are, Captain—Stryker, was it? I'm sure I heard them call you by that name.'

Stryker had nodded mutely.

'You have no Christian name?'

'None.'

If anything, Port's grin had widened at that. 'No matter. We have time to properly acquaint ourselves. This here is my friend Nelly's house. A private house, you understand? No prying eyes here, Captain, not anyone. You are mine now, Stryker. No one knows you're here. No one is looking for you. You might as well be dead already. And soon, o' course, you'll wish you were.'

They had gone in the early evening, just as the colour had drained from the sky, and Stryker had been dumped like a sack of offal in the centre of the room. There he had remained, racked by waves of pain but thankful to still draw breath. He had dreamed of Lisette again; the smell of her, the taste. When he woke, fitfully and dry-mouthed, he had wondered what tale the army would tell of his disappearance, and how his fellow officers had taken the news. He thought too of Cecily Cade. He did not like the girl, for she had played him for a fool, but she had been his responsibility – his to find. Yet now he was in no better a position than she. He could almost laugh at the absurdity of it all.

He shut his eye tightly, forcing the pain deep into his body, and felt himself slide towards another fitful sleep. He wondered whether this time he would wake.

Outside Gloucester, 10 August 1643

The main army of King Charles reached Gloucester in a blaze of new light as morning reached its zenith, their ensigns fluttering serenely above bristling phalanxes of pike, deep squads of musketeers and snorting, thunderous troops of cavalry. Many of the regiments had arrived the previous day, some during the night, but now almost the whole force was here, descended upon the rebel enclave in a vast dust cloud heralded by the hammering of drums and the shrill, haughty calls of trumpets.

Captain Lancelot Forrester marched at the head of his company of foot, his personal colour of deep red, with four white diamonds in the field, looming at his back. Reginald Jays was with him and, as they rounded the last copse that obscured their view of the defiant town, the young lieutenant let out a soft whistle.

Forrester smiled. 'Not often a man witnesses such a gathering.'

Jays's sharply tapered jaw had flopped open as their field of vision cleared, revealing a great stretch of scrubland that teemed with life. There were tents clustered about the charred remains of fires, men drilling in squads harassed by bawling sergeants and corporals, and vast trains of baggage and artillery, which were still being ushered, cajoled and threatened into their respective positions. It was an army on the march, a bigger army than Jays had ever laid his inexperienced gaze upon, and now it had come to rest before the walls of one of the nation's most ancient cities. Those defences ran across the fringe of Gloucester, forming a protective ring about the bunched houses and the cathedral beyond. But even that structure seemed worthless in the face of such a vast horde. It was as though the entire population of England had gathered in this place.

'I'd guess we've near twenty thousand, give or take,' Forrester continued. 'Six or seven thousand of which we have here and on Tredworth Field. But there are many more out at Barton to the east, Vavasour has four thousand on t'other side of the Severn, and the Prince has a host at Prinknash Park.'

'Hard to fathom we are a part of that,' Jays said as his boots scraped up a miniature dust cloud that rose to merge with all the others.

'An integral part, Lieutenant!' Forrester barked with mock formality. He made a mental note of the flags down on the fields before them, realizing quickly that there were more than he could count in an entire day. 'If we are meant to frighten the young governor into submission, then this should do the trick.'

'If it doesn't?'

Forrester laughed. 'Then you're in trouble, Mister Jays, for I shall be forced to send you over the rampart on a ladder!'

'They say the walls are strongest here, sir,' Jays said tentatively.

'If you are asking why the bulk of our mighty force approaches from the south-east, where the walls are strongest . . .'

'Strongest?' Jays repeated the word incredulously. 'It is the only place they have real walls at all, sir!'

'Very well,' Forrester replied with a sigh. 'If you are asking why we focus upon the only place they have walls, and not some makeshift pile of earth, then the answer is in the terrain.' He broke his stride, stamping his tall boots on the cracked mud of the track worn bare by so many thousand feet. 'The ground here is hard and high. If—*if*—it comes to a siege, we will remain dry, and our ordnance will do well from this position. The land to the north of the city is foul, marshy territory. Not country from where to fire cannon, lest you wish the bloody things to sink into a stinking abyss. Oh, we'll probe from all angles, do not doubt it, but here is where our big guns will wreak the most havoc. And once they've made a nice big hole,' he added wolfishly, 'we shall fall upon the wayward citizens like a host of avenging seraphim.'

Greyfriars, Gloucester, 10 August 1643

Lieutenant Colonel Edward Massie stared at his reflection in the small looking-glass. His face was pale and sorrowful, his large eyes ringed in shadow, lips set tight in a thin line. The strain of the last few days had taken their toll, and that irked him, for was a leader not supposed to be strong and bold, touched by bluff fearlessness rather than worry? He maintained the stare, forcing himself to pout a little so that the tension was not so obvious in his expression, and then, with a deep, lingering breath, he set the mirror down on the oak table, the bone handle rattling against his untouched trencher of food.

He stepped out into the street and nodded to the squad of bluecoats who were to escort him to the cathedral. They set off immediately. The white faces of Gloucester's terrified people were everywhere: a sea of staring eyes, all boring into Massie's skull. He ignored them, looking straight ahead as he strode through, battling to keep the fear from his own face as he went to receive the king's heralds. They had cantered into the city twenty minutes earlier, he had been told, all proud and haughty, chins thrust out, noses pointing at the clouds. They would read a proclamation, it was said. Announce the monarch's terms for all to hear. For King Charles himself had come to Gloucester.

Massie caught his breath as the thought struck him. All the politicking and the preparation; all those hours refurbishing fortifications and constructing new ones; all those sleepless nights. It had now come down to this one moment. Outside was the Royalist army: vast, confident and well supplied. Massie had known they would come eventually, and had done everything in his power to make Gloucester ready for this day. He thought of the loud rebuttal he had given Gerard's messengers just four days earlier, and how he had smuggled out a secret message of his own, couched in the friendliest language he could come up with. That second message had expressed his loyalty to his sovereign. It had hinted that he might yet surrender the town if Charles Stuart himself were to ask it of him. Well the king had called his bluff, and now Massie's wager would be tested. He had hoped to confuse the enemy, cause infighting at the King's Council and convince the Royalists that Gloucester would be an easy nut to crack. He would never know if the strategy had worked, he supposed, but at the very least it seemed to have given them a little extra time before the malignants finally descended. In that time, Massie had mustered nearly fifteen hundred men. He had obtained fifteen cannon and forty barrels of black powder. He had ordered the Vineyard, at Over to the north-west, stripped of its lead in order to make musket-balls, and had captured and bought as many weapons as possible. And now it was time to lay down Gloucester's challenge. If duplicity had afforded a small amount of breathing space in which to make the city ready, then all to the good. But now it was time to show the malignants his true hand.

'God bless you, sir!' someone shouted from the crowd, the sentiment echoed by a handful of others, and Massie waved a pale hand in acknowledgement. The road was busy, but no one seemed to be moving. They all stood stock still, watching.

He saw the square summit of the cathedral above the houses and his pulse quickened along with his step. Twenty paces ahead a group of men waited as had been arranged, and he hailed them in as cheerful a manner as he could.

'Ready, Governor?' a voice, deep and stentorian, rang out in response.

Massie recognized the tone instantly and searched the party as he drew close. Some of the most senior military men were there. He saw young Captain Lieutenant Harcus, nervous with excitement, as ever, and beside him the steady face of Captain Backhouse. But the distinctive voice belonged to neither man, and it was only when an imposing form pushed out from the group that Massie's dour face split in a wide grin. 'Vincent. By God, it *is* you.'

The man was tall and round. He had once been muscular, Massie had been led to believe, but that brawn had run to fat almost as soon as the man had reached his fortieth year. Now he was nearing fifty, and his auburn hair had begun to turn silver and retreat at the temples, his blue eyes cracked at the corners with the lines of age. The big man placed meaty hands on a stomach that hung low over his breeches like a vast fatty apron. 'I sent word, sir.'

Massie nodded. 'And I received it, Vincent, but I hardly dared believe.' He turned to Backhouse and the others. 'Vincent Skaithlocke, gentlemen. A comrade from the wars on the Continent, and a better man never existed.'

Skaithlocke beamed, glancing back at the cathedral. 'Well, sir? *Are* you ready?'

'As ever I shall be,' Massie said seriously enough, though the smile quickly reappeared. 'I am glad to see you, old friend.'

'I heard you needed men, sir.'

'Just so, Vincent. Just so.'

Skaithlocke moved out of Massie's path as the governor resumed his stride, though his booming voice continued at Massie's heel. 'This is your time, sir. I have travelled the length and breadth of England these last few weeks, and the diurnals bleat incessantly of Prince Robber and his vile exploits.'

Massie looked back. 'He is an impressive soldier.'

'He is nothing but a popinjay,' Skaithlocke spat. 'It is time this country had a new hero.'

'Just so,' Massie replied, fighting back the pride from his voice, grateful for the big man's arrival. He thought of Stryker. The enlistment of the famous one-eyed mercenary had been a real coup, and his desertion after such a short time had been hard to stomach. He had not trumpeted the disappearance beyond a trusted few, for such a revelation would destroy the carefully nurtured city morale as sure as any besieging army, but the disappointment was nevertheless keen. At least now he had another hardy professional at his side.

They reached the cathedral. The courtyard beyond was brimming with people from all walks of life. Massie saw many of the soberly dressed town aldermen, muttering like washer-women, no doubt still venting their collective spleen at his governorship. At least three of Gloucester's innkeepers were there, joined by millers, butchers, chandlers and shopkeepers. Men and women whispered while children stared wide-eyed at the two men who stood at the very centre of the courtyard. They were under armed guard, lest they be lynched by the jostling mob, though their faces were calm enough, their bearing confident.

Massie strode up to the king's heralds without delay. 'What have you to say, sirs?'

The first man, in his early thirties, with a clean-shaven face that was narrow and hard-hewn, offered a deep bow, sweeping his wide, red-ribboned hat from his head. The rest of his suit was of a similar rich red, adorned with flashes of golden thread and a long, fine sword. 'I bear a message from King Charles, sir.'

'Then let us hear it, sir.'

The man in red shot his companion an impatient glance and he delved within his coat and brought out a tight scroll. The senior herald took it, broke the wax seal and deftly unravelled the vellum sheet. He cleared his throat noisily, pulled back his shoulders, drew in a huge breath, and looked down.

Tredworth Field, Gloucester, 10 August 1643

The heralds returned to their master soon after they had finished reading out the proclamation. It had been worded in concili-atory terms, though carefully barbed with the threat of what would happen if the order to surrender was refused. And yet now, nearly two hours after their return, His Majesty was still waiting.

'It w–w–won't do. Won't d–d–do at all.' He had not wished to spend the sweltering afternoon outside the upstart town like some young buck waiting by his lover's window for a sign that she might see him. But Massie and Gloucester's puritanical aldermen had evidently decided to play games with his patience, and his mood was souring rapidly. Charles had been staring up at the walls around the south section for the last twenty minutes, imagining the smirks of the tiny guards up on the rampart, but the heat had finally won the battle and sent him in search of shelter. Flanked by a pair of granite-faced musketeers, he stalked into the tent of the Earl of Forth and Brentford, the commander of his forces at Gloucester. 'They m–m–mock me, Patrick!'

The elderly earl, Patrick Ruthven, had been resting in a stout chair that now creaked madly as he sprung forward. 'Your Majesty,' he blurted, blinking the drowsiness away. He rubbed calloused hands into the droopy red lids of his watery eyes. 'Have patience, Your Majesty. If our intelligence is correct, he will be preparing to down arms this very moment.'

'*If* the intelligence is correct.'

The king's small brown eyes shot to a corner of the tent, where another man stood. He was an unassuming fellow, short in height, round across the midriff, with pinched features that made him appear rather mean. He wore a simple brown cloak, the hood arranged in folds around his shoulders so that a head of oiled black hair was exposed. 'I do not know why I s-s-suffer your p-presence, Killigrew.'

Ezra Killigrew offered a slow bow. 'Your nephew sent me, Your Majesty.'

'In one last effort to sway my mind, no doubt.'

Killigrew smiled. 'He would not deny it, Your Majesty, and neither would I.'

'Prince R–R–Rupert,' the king replied, ire suddenly rising, 'sulks with his d-damned cavalry like a whipped ch-ch-child.'

'He is upset, Your Majesty, aye,' Killigrew said. 'He advised an all-out assault, sir.'

'And I refused him, as is my d-d-damned choice. That should have been an end t-to the matter.'

Killigrew winced. 'Would that were so, Your Majesty. But the Prince fears for our lot.'

A slim, middle-aged man of pale complexion and glum countenance, who had been leafing silently through a pile of papers that littered a low table in the large tent's far corner, straightened. 'Ah yes, Killigrew, your own man went in, did he not?'

'He did, my lord Falkland,' Killigrew answered in an acid tone. 'And he reported back that Gloucester would not surrender. Massie's second message was a lie.'

Lucius Carey, Viscount Falkland, Charles' severe secretary of state, gazed down his long nose at Killigrew. 'You trust this fellow?'

'As far as I would trust any man, sir, aye.'

Falkland offered a smile of no warmth. 'And where is your man now?'

Killigrew shifted his weight awkwardly from one foot to the other. 'Alas, sir, he has not come out.'

'*Ha!*' the king cried, the noise sounding unnaturally loud beneath the low awning. 'C–c–convenient, rather, is it not?' He turned to the secretary of state. 'Remind me what it said, Falkland. M–M–Massie's message, that is.'

Falkland smoothed the ends of his thin moustache. 'He told Legge's man that if Your Majesty were to come to the city, in person, then he would not hold the walls against you.'

'You s–see?' Charles said triumphantly. 'He will not hold it.'

'Massie claimed,' Falkland went on, 'that he could not, in all conscience, fight against the person of the King.'

'Forgive me, Your Majesty,' Ezra Killigrew ventured again, 'but my master disagrees. Our man has seen the mood in the city. He tells us the rebels will hold. Ergo, the message to Legge was erroneous, designed to cause just such a rift as has now opened. My master—'

'*Enough!*' King Charles barked with ferocity so abrupt that it made Killigrew take a rearward step. 'Enough of this t–talk. We will consider no assault. The streets will n–not run with blood. Not this time. Your master is a rogue, Mister Killigrew. Tell him I care not what your spy reports. If there is a s–s–spy at all. Tell him he will do as he is t–told. Tell him—'

It was the king's turn to be interrupted, as a stern-looking sentry poked his head through the tent flap.

'What?' Charles snapped, his face red with bluster. 'What is it, man?'

The sentry remembered his helmet, and hurriedly snatched it off, staring at the ground as though diamonds lay between his feet. 'Majesty, the city delegation has arrived. They carry a reply.'

Lancelot Forrester, Reginald Jays and Thomas Hood were engaged in furious sword practice in an open piece of ground between the myriad tents of the Royalist camp. Hood, Stryker's lieutenant, had de facto command of the absent captain's company, but he lacked experience, and Colonel Mowbray had been only too happy to let him gain some valuable know-how by shadowing Forrester whenever possible. Thus, the second and fourth companies of Mowbray's Foot were bivouacked together south of Gloucester, and so they witnessed the rebel delegation being escorted through the South Gate and into the teeming encampment.

'Hold!' Forrester called, as the young lieutenants circled one another with swords drawn.

Neither heard the order, and they surged inwards, meeting almost toe to toe, blades clashing loudly between their heads. They held the pose for a moment, lips peeled back in their efforts, breaths laboured.

'*Hold*!' Forrester snapped, louder this time.

The two men parted with a metallic slice, lowering their weapons. They wiped the sweat from their eyes with gleaming forearms as they strode through the roiling dust cloud – kicked up by their own frenetic movement – to where Forrester sat on an empty barrel.

'You wish to show us how it is done, sir?' Hood asked through panting breaths. He shook his head, a shower of droplets flinging in all directions, and strode with fatigue to the pile of clothes that he had left during the session.

'Alas, Lieutenant. I'd have loved to have shown you both what a real swordsman can do, but we have other matters to which we must attend.'

'He means he's eaten too much bacon again,' Jays muttered under his breath.

Forrester raised his eyebrows. 'You presume a great deal, Mister Jays. I could trounce the both of you blindfolded.' His mouth twitched slightly at the corners. 'Though I am rather full, truth be told.' He stood as the officers pulled on their shirts. 'But, as I have said, we have better ways by which to pass our time. Follow me.'

The delegation comprised two men. One, Forrester would later discover, was city alderman Tobias Jordan, a bookseller by trade, who would represent Gloucester's civilian government. The other was an altogether more grizzled man, of impressive height, tousled grey hair and a face weathered to the bone. His name was Major Marmaduke Pudsey, and he would stand for the city's military element.

The pair strode into the Royalist camp behind a phalanx of pikemen. They were not blindfolded, for the king had decreed that they should see exactly what nature of foe they faced. He would have them take the impression of overwhelming odds back to their rebellious friends, in case that message had not already permeated Gloucester's walls.

Forrester led Hood and Jays through the crowd of officers and men who now gathered around about the garrison messengers. He was pleasantly surprised to note no air of hostility in the camp. More, he supposed, a feeling of curiosity. Just what kind of men would stand up to an army of this size?

The assembly waited in silence for a small party of soldiers and officers to make their way from the largest tent in the temporary canvas town between Gaudy Green and Tredworth Field. They were well dressed in the finest silks and satins, each sporting fashionable whiskers and wide hats adorned with the most flamboyant feathers imaginable.

'It is the King,' Reginald Jays hissed at Forrester's shoulder.

Forrester flapped a hand at him irritably. 'Of course it is.' For at the centre of the party that heralded its own arrival with the jangle of blade and spur, King Charles himself walked.

Hundreds of pairs of eyes descended upon their sovereign. He was probably one of the smallest people in the entire encampment, but the white lace and golden thread that snaked about his garments was regal indeed. His back- and breastplates were blackened and studded with gilt rivets, and his long, black cavalry boots gave him at least some extra height. If the sheer size of this army was meant to intimidate, Forrester mused, then so too was its commander-in-chief.

The courtly group reached the open space where the garrison men were waiting. They halted, leaving the king to advance a further two paces. He did not deign to greet the delegates, but instead cleared his throat daintily, smoothed down the hem of his dazzling emerald and gold coat, and straightened his broad blue scarf. He looked directly at the bookseller, a tiny flicker at the corner of one eye betraying his pleasure at the fellow's failure to hold his gaze. 'Speak.'

The tall soldier, Pudsey, handed his compatriot a scroll fastened with black ribbon. As Jordan took it, his bottom lip shook so hard that he was forced to bite down on it. Laughter rippled through the expectant throng.

'Now, sir,' Forrester whispered loudly enough for his two protégés to heed, 'we will hear you surrender, or I will never eat a Lombard slice as long as I live.'

Tobias Jordan was not an imposing man. He was short and bald, had a grey pallor to his face, a beard that seemed a tad unkempt, and teeth that were visibly crooked. But as Forrester looked on, he saw the man straighten just a fraction, roll and square his shoulders, and whisper a silent prayer.

'Oh, Christ,' Forrester muttered, as his heart began to sink.

'*We the inhabitants, magistrates, officers and soldiers within this garrison of Gloucester,*' Jordan shouted, his voice suddenly as clear as the bells of St Paul's, '*unto His Majesty's gracious message return this humble answer.*' He paused, squinted at the parchment, breathed deeply again. '*That we do keep this city, according to our oaths and allegiance, to and for the use of His Majesty and his royal posterity, and do accordingly conceive ourselves wholly bound to obey the commands of His Majesty.*'

'There,' Jays chirped happily into his captain's ear. 'They give up.'

'*Signified,*' Toby Jordan continued, louder still, a vein of defiance steeling his tone now, '*by both houses of Parliament, and are resolved by God's help to keep this city accordingly.*'

Forrester simply looked down at the youngster, his face sad. 'No, Lieutenant. They do not.'

The East Gate, Gloucester, 10 August 1643

Edward Massie leaned against the edge of the wall, the cool stone welcome against his elbows. His men were down there in the lion's den, brave souls both, where they would be reading the rebellious reply to all who might listen. And even from up high, Massie could see the banner of King Charles, and he knew that the sovereign would be absorbing the words, gritting his teeth and pondering his next move. Because Gloucester was going to fight.

'The dye is cast,' Thomas Pury, one of Gloucester's more powerful aldermen, intoned darkly. Pury was standing beside the governor on the wooden platform that had been placed against the wall. He too gazed down at the sprawling Royalist nest, and he rubbed a hand against the bristles of his rectangular chin. 'They will give us no quarter.'

Massie looked at him. 'Then we must not let them in.'

'And we will not,' another man spoke now. It was Vincent Skaithlocke, a man so obese that the timber walkway groaned ominously as he shifted his weight. Most of the men in Massie's entourage eyed him warily, fearing the entire scaffold would collapse beneath them at any moment.

Massie offered him a wan smile. 'I am grateful you have joined me in this, old friend.'

Skaithlocke inclined his head. 'A pleasure to serve with you again, Colonel, though you were not colonel when last we met.'

'Nor Governor,' Massie said. 'The Lord works in mysterious ways, right enough. And I am convinced he sent you to me.'

'Oh?' Skaithlocke boomed.

'It is nothing,' Massie said dismissively. 'Simply that I lose one experienced man to desertion, and straightway gain another.'

'One of your better men deserted? Would I know the scoundrel, sir?'

'No, Vincent. A Captain, formerly with the enemy, and now, it seems, returned to them.' He shrugged sadly. 'Man named Stryker.'

Skaithlocke's broad face scrunched into a deep frown. 'Stryker?'

Pury cleared his throat suddenly, though his eyes remained fixed on the busy encampment below the walls. 'They return, Colonel.'

Massie looked to the heathland. The delegation was already trudging back towards the city. 'One last gesture, gentlemen, if you please.'

He felt Pury's stern gaze bore into his temple as the alderman turned. 'Governor?'

Massie pursed his slender lips. He was no Puritan zealot like Pury, nor an ideological rebel like Harcus or Backhouse. He was a professional soldier, and for him to excel in life, he needed promotion – and fame. Gloucester, he had decided, would be the making of him. And for that to happen, he needed not only to hold out against the king, but also to create such stories that the people whispered them in every alehouse and marketplace from here to Scotland. His deception of Colonel Legge had been the first step on that journey, and now, he hoped, Toby Jordan and Sergeant Major Pudsey would conjure a myth of their own. He pointed his thin finger at the returning delegation. 'Watch.'

Down below, Jordan and Pudsey had cleared the enemy lines. They were perhaps thirty or forty yards away from the nearest Royalists, and, as they had agreed with their young leader, it was here that they turned back to face the king and his forces. With an ostentatious wave, and the shout of *God and Parliament*, the pair clapped on their hats.

Up on the rampart a great cry of huzzah went up, coursing along Gloucester's battlements in a rippling wave crested by whistles and jeers. For the hats the two men wore were tied with bright orange ribbons.

Thomas Pury gaped first at the men who now ran back to the city gate, and then at Massie.

Massie grinned, facing his entourage and speaking loud enough for all to hear. 'Let there be no doubt, gentlemen. We are for the Parliament! Let His Majesty do his worst!' He turned to Harcus, who seemed to be raised permanently on his toes. 'James, tell the men to fire the suburbs.'

'Aye, sir,' Harcus replied enthusiastically. 'Everything?'

'As we have arranged,' Massie said firmly.

Pury stepped across him, his face hard. 'Is there no other way, Colonel? That is more than two hundred homes.' He wrung his hands in agitation. 'The cost, sir.'

'The cost is nothing,' Massie said, 'if we lose the city. We raze everything outside the walls to clear our lines of fire and to deny the malignants a place in which to shelter as they plot our destruction.' He glanced at Harcus. 'Do it.'

Massie turned away from Pury, even as Harcus bounded down the ladder. He stared at the enemy. 'God preserve you, Your Majesty. But may He keep you from our city.'

CHAPTER 10

Near Chipping Barnet, Hertfordshire, 11 August 1643

Lisette Gaillard and Cecily Cade had ridden northwards, the capital firmly at their backs, until dusk made the roads treacherous. When finally they had eased their heaving mounts to a gentle trot, there were no accompanying hoofbeats from determined pursuers, no shouts of alarm, no warning shots. Taking their chances with the dense woodland at their flanks, they plunged deep into the summer-swollen foliage until they were sure the sound of horses could not be heard from the road. There they made camp.

They hardly spoke that first night, for both were exhausted, and a lack of victuals did nothing to lighten the mood. They sat, knees drawn to their chests, before a pathetic little fire. Cecily chewed a small scrap of salted meat, the only food Lisette had to offer, and nibbled the shredded corner like a rodent.

Lisette watched intently, struck by the girl's fragility, and chided herself for lacking the forethought to bring ample provisions, but events had simply overtaken her and she had been forced to act quickly. The riots in London had escalated beyond her hopes, developed from whispered grumbling to open, ranting dissent, shrouding the capital's streets in powder smoke in a matter of days.

'Who are you?' Cecily had said after a time.

'Lisette Gaillard.'

'But what is your role in all of this?'

'A friend,' Lisette had replied tersely, relenting a touch upon seeing Cecily's arched brow. 'From the Queen.'

'The Queen?' Cecily was stunned.

'She felt my talents would expedite this task.'

Cecily lent forward, her nose breathing into her ragged sleeve, green eyes wider than ever. She had looked up then, staring at Lisette with unconcealed puzzlement. 'But they send a—'

'Woman?' Lisette had interrupted hotly. She looked into the fire, feeling her expression turn sour. 'Aye, well, there were supposed to be others, but they have let us down, mademoiselle. It is just you and me now.'

Cecily had met the Frenchwoman's gaze. 'That poor man.'

'Quigg gave his life to save you.' Lisette decided not to mention the protesters. 'We must not waste his sacrifice.'

The next day a brief scouting expedition found the road teeming with soldiers. Riders, Lisette assumed, sent up from London on a hunt for two women. They stayed in the forest, ignored the complaints from their hungry bellies, and prayed the men would not stray too far from the road.

Now, as morning lit countryside eerily devoid of activity, they set off again.

'Where will we find General Hopton?' Cecily asked as they ventured on to the compacted and cracked earth.

'He is still in the West Country, as far as I am aware,' Lisette replied. She had had no contact with her masters in several weeks. 'We should go to Oxford.'

Cecily shook her head. 'No, Miss Gaillard—'

'Lisette.'

'Lisette. I must speak to Sir Ralph and none other.'

'Not even the King himself?' Lisette said in disbelief.

Cecily tilted her head to one side. 'You can gain me an audience with him?'

Lisette shrugged. 'I imagine he will wish to know where your bloody money is, will he not?'

'But you cannot be sure. I have suffered much to protect the location of my father's wealth.'

'So have many others,' Lisette said caustically, thinking first of Christopher Quigg and then of Andrew Burton. Stryker had passed on the salient facts of it well enough.

'Have I wronged you, Lisette?' Cecily asked.

Lisette stared into the gaunt young woman's eyes for a moment. She was a shadow of the person she must have been when young Burton had first seen her, and Lisette could well imagine the effect such bright eyes and raven hair had had on him. She shook her head. 'No.'

Cecily's intelligent gaze narrowed. 'But you do not like me.'

'I neither like nor dislike you, mademoiselle,' said Lisette bluntly, and that was partly true. The other part of her despised the wealthy, arrogant English gentry, a class to which the Family Cade clearly belonged. Such was the heartache and death on account of this scrawny girl; first to protect her and now to rescue her. And it was all for the much-needed funds she promised to deliver. That, at least, was worth fighting for. But was it worth *this*?

'Before we make our next move,' she said abruptly, 'we must find you some proper clothes.' Cecily looked down at her tattered dress and offered a reluctant nod.

Within the hour, they spotted a dark funnel of smoke meandering skyward above the treetops in an unbroken column, for there was no breeze to diminish or bend it. They took a side track that looked likely to lead them to its base.

The branches hung low about them as they rode. Eventually they were forced to dismount, walking their horses the last fifty or so yards, until the trunks abruptly ceased and the land opened out into a clearing, at the centre of which was a large house. At least, the land had, at one time, been manually cleared of the woodland that encircled it. Now, though, they could see that the grass immediately surrounding the brick-and-flint building was wildly overgrown, and the timber animal pens positioned around the small estate were dilapidated and empty.

Lisette handed her reins to Cecily. 'Stay here,' she said. 'Don't scream if you see a fox.'

Cecily looked as though she might issue a stinging retort, but she nodded silently and stayed near the tree line, while the

Frenchwoman moved quickly across the grass to the house's low wooden doorway. She half expected a cry of alarm to ring out through the trees, but no sound stalled her as she pushed firmly against the door. To her surprise, it yawned inwards without resistance.

A foul smell brought tears to Lisette's eyes as she stepped into the gloomy interior, and she paused to steady herself. The stench of putrefying flesh, enriched by the warm air, was bitter enough to bring bile to the throat, yet it was strangely tainted with a lingering sweetness. She turned back, thinking to leave this sorry place immediately, but the wan visage of Cecily Cade stared out at her from the tree-thrown shadows, and she knew she must press on.

Tentatively, she edged over the threshold. In front of her was a tight spiral staircase, while to her immediate left was a large chamber, the house's main hall, and she could see that a big table dominated the centre, surrounded by four high-backed chairs. To her right was another, similarly proportioned room, though it was a more cluttered affair. There were cooking utensils hanging from hooks along the walls, clay pots of various sizes jumbled on a table and several shelves, and a large bake-oven in one corner. At the bakehouse's far end was another door, and she guessed it would lead to a buttery. She stepped towards it, keeping her breathing shallow to avoid taking in too much of the pervading stink, and wondering if she might lay her hands on some food therein. But her progress was abruptly curtailed by a creaking above her head. She moved silently to the foot of the staircase and drew her knife, squeezing the bone handle harder than was necessary, the cold solidity reassuring as her knuckles turned white. She felt her throat tighten as her heart quickened.

'Who is there?' The voice of an elderly woman echoed down the wooden steps.

Lisette had been utterly still, but now she leaned over the bottom step to call a response. 'I mean you no harm, Goodwife.'

More creaking, louder this time as this woman moved closer to the staircase. 'You speak strangely, lass.'

'I am not from hereabouts.'

'Oh?' The woman paused, evidently picking her next words carefully. 'Do not let those bold-faced Roundheads hear you, for they'll think you a Boglander.'

'Boglander?'

'An Irish,' the woman replied in a nasal tone pitched high through age. 'They'd have you dancin' from the chates afore sundown.'

Lisette was emboldened by that. 'You are for the King, Goodwife?'

'Aye, lass,' the woman called down.

'Then I will tell you that I am French, and for the King also.'

'Then you are welcome, for I despise the rebellion with all my heart.'

Lisette saw a shadow snake across the top of the staircase. A body followed. The woman was indeed old, her face tarnished by deep wrinkles and brown liver spots. A grey shawl was wrapped tight about her shoulders, despite the warmth of the day, and a coif framed her face. But it was none of this that captured Lisette's attention. The woman's eyes were as white as the coif, as though the sockets were brimming of milk. They stared directly out in front, unable to discern the steps down which the woman now descended, simply twitching uselessly in their ancient hollows. 'How could I not, after what they did to my Robert?'

Lisette met the woman halfway down, taking her by the elbow and guiding her the last few steps to the firm safety of the brick floor. 'Robert is your son, perhaps? Wounded in battle?'

Tears welled in the woman's waxen eyes. 'God forgive me, lass, for I wish that were the truth of it.'

Only then did Lisette realize that the awful smell in the house had been stronger on the staircase. She stared up at the ceiling, then back to the blind woman. 'Robert is here, isn't he?'

'He is, lass. My husband.'

'And he is upstairs.'

The woman nodded slowly. 'Though I know I shall see Hell for it, I cannot bury him myself.'

*

Goodwife Hulme had lived in the area all her life. She was either seventy-five or seventy-six, and as wizened as the trees encircling her home. The house was even older than its occupant. It was a yeoman's farmhouse constructed in timber and thatch more than a century earlier and refurbished in flint by her husband in his prime. That husband, Robert Hulme, forester and smallholding farmer, had been in his eightieth year when his skull had been crushed just above the left temple.

'They came near two weeks back,' the elderly woman had said when Lisette returned with Cecily. As soon as cursory introductions had been made, the three women made their way upstairs, Mistress Hulme clutching the Frenchwoman's arm. Now they stood side by side in the doorway of the Hulmes' bedchamber. The old woman gazed sightlessly at the far window, its mullions painted a brilliant white that matched her eyes. Lisette and Cecily stared down at the bloated body.

'Who came?' Lisette asked gently, fighting to keep the disgust from her voice.

'Is it as bad as I imagine?' Goodwife Hulme responded.

Lisette ignored the question. She would not describe the stinking corpse, fat with rot, its skin turned to marbled blue at the face and jet black at the fingers. The wound was the size of a fist, though a fist had not made it. The head had caved inwards, blood pooling where Master Hulme lay, and even through the corruption of decay Lisette could still see the sticky tangle of ragged flesh, shattered bone and matted hair. 'Who came here?'

The wrinkled face screwed into a mask of anguish. 'Parliament men. Four of the knaves.'

'Forgive me, Goody Hulme,' Cecily said, taking her sleeve from her mouth and nose, 'but how could you know?'

'This is Parliament country,' the old woman said simply, unable to see the look exchanged by her guests. 'The men stank of black powder, leather and horse flesh. Their boots clinked with spurs, and they called one Sergeant. They was soldiers.' A frail hand rose to her grey mouth as she let slip a small gasp. 'My poor Robert. He fought 'em off, he did. I did not see the brabble – *could* not – but I heard it all right. All screams and curses, and then silence. They took what coin and plate they could lay their sinful hands on, for that clinked loudly enough, but then nothing. It took me a long while to find Robert's body. And when I finally did, I knew that it would lay there till help came.'

'But none came,' Cecily said.

'We are so secluded here. Robert always said it was a blessing from the Lord. How wrong he was.'

'What of the pens?' Lisette asked. 'Where are your livestock?'

'The Roundheads return on occasion,' Mistress Hulme said bitterly. 'They steal them when their bellies grumble. I hear the piglets squeal as they're dragged away, though one day they were all gone.' She shrugged. 'Now they only come when they need shelter, or to water the horses. We—*I*—have a well.'

'And what do you do when they come?' Cecily asked, appalled.

'I hide up here with Robert. They know I am here, but who would fear a blind woman? I could not even pick them out if they visited for Christ-tide.'

They buried Robert Hulme without much ceremony. It was a grim affair, for dragging a large cadaver down a flight of stairs was difficult enough, let alone one blighted by severe decay, but with Cecily's help they managed to get the corpse out into the clearing. There, having searched the small estate for some tools, the women dug and scraped at the hard turf for the best part of an hour.

'*Merci*,' Lisette said to Cecily as they finally swept the last of the soil on to the grave. The Frenchwoman had done the lion's share of the work, for Cecily was far too weak, but her willing-ness to help did not pass unnoticed.

'What do you need?' Goodwife Hulme asked when they had completed their bleak task.

Cecily looked into her vacant stare. 'Beg pardon, Mistress?'

The old woman smiled sadly. 'You did not come here to bury my poor husband, much as I am grateful for it.'

'We flee the wrath of Parliament.'

'And you came here for—food?'

Lisette stepped close now. 'Food, *oui*, and clothing.' She glanced at Cecily. 'My companion is not suitably attired for our journey.'

Goodwife Hulme reached out suddenly, her bony hands snaking up Cecily's wrists and arms, rounding her shoulders, until they cupped her hollow cheeks. 'My late daughter, God rest her, was of a similar figure. But you are thin, child. And sad.'

'We have little time,' Lisette interrupted, instantly regretting her urgent tone.

But the elderly woman did not seem to take offence. 'I am sorry. Of course.' She turned back to the house. 'Come this way, child. You will find vittles in the buttery. Nothing of extravagance, of course, for the Roundheads took what they wanted, and much of the rest has gone bad. But I still have some salted meats.' She gave a bitter laugh. 'It is what has kept me alive in recent days. And, if we are lucky, the thieves may not have noticed the cheese cratch.'

'You are too kind, Goody Hulme,' Cecily said. 'We will come back for you, take you away to safety, I promise.' She looked at Lisette, setting her jaw defiantly. '*We* promise.'

Lisette rolled her eyes, but took the old woman's arm and guided her back towards the building. They had not gone far when all three were forced to turn on their heels. From somewhere out in the forest, shouts rent the air.

Gloucester, 11 August 1643

Stryker woke with a start. His eye hurt. His head and chest throbbed.

For a moment he did not remember what he was doing on the mouldering floor of this strange, bare chamber, but then the memories pounded him like the petard explosion he had witnessed at Cirencester during the winter. Fear came quickly, too. The vengeful musketeer and his pair of malicious lackeys had visited him in the night hours, kicked his ribs until he could not breathe, and vanished like wraiths. He had survived again, but that did not diminish the horror.

He realized it was light in the room. Too light for a cell with just one little window. *Christ*, but something had woken him. He forced himself to sit up, though the pain seemed to sear along every sinew. With a numbing dread, he saw that the lone door was open. Three men stood before it.

'It's been merry, Captain Stryker,' Richard Port said, 'but I'm afraid our brief association must come to an end. The fucking Pope-turds outside are digging in.'

It took a moment for Port's words to sink into Stryker's mind, but eventually he stared up at the greencoat. 'Digging in? There is to be a siege?'

Port nodded, turning back to close the door. 'The Cavaliers are everywhere. All around us. Smell that?'

Even as Port spoke the words, Stryker realized that the air smelled strongly of smoke. 'There has been a fire?'

Port shook his head. 'Our leaders have burned everything outside the walls.'

To clear the line of fire, Stryker thought, and to deny the Royalists shelter. He wondered if his message had reached Killigrew. Was Prince Rupert preparing for another escalade even now? 'What is to happen to me?'

Port glanced at his companions. 'Clearly we are expected elsewhere, now that the enemy has come. Still,' he added brightly, 'I would very much appreciate one last—*discussion*—before Bones, here, wrings your neck.'

Stryker shuffled back, desperate to put as much space between him and his captors as possible. It was agony to move a single limb, and to shift his entire body in one motion was like white flame against his skin, but he had no choice. For in Port's hand he saw a pair of pliers.

He felt suddenly light-headed, but bit savagely down on the instinct to plead. He shuffled ever rearward, slamming into a stone wall, its coldness screaming of futile entrapment. Even so, he pushed against it, knees and thighs quivering with the strain, as though the stones might sense his desperation and crumble like a wall of dry mud.

Port stepped further into the room brandishing a nasty smile, and handed Nelly the pliers. Nelly lifted the metallic tool, seemingly revelling in its sturdy weight, and slowly licked his cracked lips. But there was nothing slow about Bones. The heavy-set musketeer took off his blue coat, pushed the sleeves of his shirt beyond his elbows, and lumbered up to Stryker. He grasped him by the shoulders in a motion that was surprisingly swift, hauling him to his feet as though he were a rag doll. Stryker cried out, and Bones, suspending him by his filthy collar, snaked a free arm around his neck. Stryker felt the air trap in his throat as his head was locked tight in the crook of the big man's elbow. He felt instant pressure push behind his eye, and wondered if it might burst from his skull.

Nelly moved forwards, holding forth the pliers. Bones had released Stryker's collar, for his entire weight was now hanging from the roof-truss thick arm, and with his spare hand he prized Stryker's jaw apart. Stryker tried to bite, but the strength had all but seeped from his body. He clamped his mouth tight shut instead. But Port was there too, squeezing Stryker's nostrils closed, and the urge to breathe overpowered everything else. Stryker gasped, hands forced their way past his lips, yanked hard in all directions so that his jaw cracked below his ears, and the next second he tasted metal.

'Hold still,' Nelly rasped, his tongue poking from the corner of his mouth as he concentrated, a perverse parody of a schoolboy performing a difficult task.

One of Stryker's teeth clinked as the pliers grasped it. He moaned through the invasive trellis of salty fingers. Then a series of cracks juddered through his jaw and gums and cheeks and skull. It put him in mind of a great tree coming down in a storm, the roots drawn inexorably from their deep beds. But then the pain came, a pulse and a stab and a burning all at once, and he knew it was the roots of his own tooth that were coming away. Tears filled his eye, tumbled down his cheek, as the coppery tang of fresh blood flooded across his tongue. It welled over his bottom lip and across his chin, drenching Bones' vicelike forearm and beading like crimson dew on the dark little hairs.

Next, they let him go. All at once, the throttling grip was gone, the grasping hands had retreated, and he slumped to his knees. A deep, animal groan reverberated around the room, like the lowing of a wounded bullock, and only when it was spent did Stryker realize that it had come from him. He forced himself to look up, unwilling to allow these men to take his dignity as well as his life, and saw the pliers in Nelly's hand. In their bloody jaws a large chunk of white seemed to glow. He stared at the tooth, spat out a thick gobbet of fresh blood, and lifted a hand to press uselessly at his agonized jaw. He noticed the door had opened again.

And then Nelly fell over.

The doorway behind Stryker's torturers had suddenly darkened, as though all the light from the corridor outside had been buried beneath a vast black sheet. Nelly was on the ground, flat on his front, and, as though in some pain-crazed dream, Stryker watched dumbly as Bones and Port followed suit.

He stared, blinking. A man stepped into his vision. He held a musket by its barrel, the heavy stock turned outwards like a club. He was tall and thin, with a head that was bald, teeth that were rotten, and eyes set deep within sepulchral caverns.

'Fuck me, sir,' William Skellen said, 'but you don't look too grand.'

Stryker saw the gash on his sergeant's head. 'Nor do you.'

Skellen sniffed. 'You look worse, sir, trust me. And you sound drunk.'

Stryker was about to respond when the words simply vanished from his mind. He was staring over Skellen's shoulder, at the darkened doorway, his mouth agape. It was the silhouette of a man, a man big enough to fill the space between threshold and lintel. He was striding into the room now, and Stryker saw that he was tall – taller even than Skellen – with heavily muscled arms and legs like twin cannon. The man's hair was tightly curled auburn and grey, and it was receding at the temples, framing a face wide and welcoming. His chest was broad and his stomach hung low in a vast shelf of fat that drooped across his breeches.

'How fair thee, stripling?' the huge man said.

And Innocent Stryker, to his own surprise, felt himself grinning. 'All the better for seeing you, Colonel.'

'Sir?' Skellen's face was a mask of bewilderment.

Stryker laughed. The sound was dry and racking and it hurt his ribs, but he could not help it. 'This, Mister Skellen,' he slurred, pausing briefly to jettison a clot of blood, 'is Vincent Skaithlocke, my first colonel.'

'Colonel?' the fat man said. 'I practically raised you, lad.'

'Aye, sir,' Stryker said. 'I'd say you did.'

Near Chipping Barnet, Hertfordshire, 11 August 1643

The horsemen burst from the tree line and swept into the clearing with a chorus of whoops and jeers. There were four of them, and they wheeled their mounts sharply around – two pulling right, two to the left – and traced its perimeter, trampling the tall grass as they encircled the women. With a whistle from one, the circle became suddenly smaller as they trotted inwards as though corralling sheep.

Lisette studied them, even as she felt the shoulders of Cecily and Goodwife Hulme touch her own. The men were armed with simple straight-bladed swords and each carried a brace of holstered pistols. 'Only four.'

'That is what I told you,' the old woman's fear-laced voice croaked in her ear.

'Indeed,' Lisette replied softly, considering the riders. It had not occurred to her before, but four horsemen roaming the area seemed strange, now that she was confronted by them. A whole troop might be billeted nearby, or a small squad would certainly have ridden through on some errand, but the same four men returning time and again?

The riders tightened their horse-flesh noose, bringing the beasts to within ten paces of the women. They were young men, Lisette saw, guessing none would be older than twenty, yet their faces carried a certain shadow she recognized all too readily. Theirs were faces that did not often smile, eyes that had seen more than was good for the soul. They might have been youthful, but they were hard creatures, joyless.

One of the horses skittered forth suddenly, making the trio of women press harder into one another. It stopped close enough for Lisette to smell the animal's heaving breaths and she noticed its grey flanks were narrow, the hint of a rib showing behind one of the dangling stirrups. The rider slid nimbly down from the saddle. He patted the animal's neck with a gloved palm and the beast, taking the touch as its cue, dipped its head to tear frantically at the long grass. The man placed his left hand at the hilt of his sword and stepped around the jerking muzzle that was now spouting green froth.

'My, my,' he said with a yellow-toothed smirk, 'what have we here?' His gaze raked across both Lisette and Cecily, and he licked his narrow lips. 'A nice pair o' dim-morts, lads.'

The other three horsemen laughed. There was no mirth in the sound; it was a chorus of iron files grating out a tune of menace and malice. Lisette looked from each face to the next, searching for some glimmer of compassion, but these were not compassionate men.

Cecily Cade must have felt it too, for she left the false safety of her companions' backs and addressed the man on foot. 'Please, sir,' she said.

Lisette almost joined in the laughter. If Cecily had hoped to appeal to some misguided notion of soldierly honour, she was gravely deluded, for there was no chivalry here. 'Not even soldiers,' she said aloud.

The man turned to her. He had a bony, thin face that tapered steeply into a stubble-shaded chin as sharp as his long nose. His cheeks were set high, pronounced like twin cliffs beneath eyes of a startling blue. He wore a battered hat on a head framed by long, straw-blond hair, and, though he had no armour, his torso was protected by an ancient-looking buff-coat that was waxy and darkened with the filth of a lifetime. That coat gave him away more than anything else, for the sleeves seemed baggy and the flared skirts hung beyond the knees.

'Summink to say, miss?' he asked, fixing the cold gaze on Lisette.

Lisette did not think it worth dissembling. 'Your coat. It was made for another man. A taller man.'

The fair-haired horseman brandished another smile of crooked, amber-mottled teeth. 'So? I won it at dice.'

'I think not.'

'Bless me.' The horseman glanced over his shoulder. 'Well here's a fiery piece, eh, lads? Funny tongue, too.' He looked back at Lisette. 'Froggy, is it? Long way from home. And you can call me Dan.'

'Well, Dan,' Lisette said, 'it has been pleasant speaking with you, but we really must be leaving.'

'Hold there,' said Dan, holding up a staying hand. 'You're trespassing, and I'm saddened to say such a thing brings with it consequences. Certain taxes, if you will.'

The three remaining men all dismounted. As they approached, Lisette could see that each was as lean and wiry as the next. They led physical lives, probably sleeping rough and eating sparsely.

To her back, Goodwife Hulme spoke. 'These are the men I told you about.' She spat on the grass. 'Cursed Roundheads.'

'They are not Roundheads, Goody Hulme,' Lisette replied.

'But the king's men—'

The king's men would behave in no better a manner than their Parliamentarian counterparts, thought Lisette, but she elected not to pursue that truth. 'They are common brigands. Thieves and murderers.'

The leader, Dan, wrinkled his long nose at that. 'Now, now, lass. Mind that forked tongue, lest I rip it out your head.' His blue eyes searched her again, from her boots to her golden hair. 'Would be a shame, though. Bless me, it would.' He closed the space between them with a quick step that caught Lisette offguard and had his fingers at her cheek before she could react. He left them there, ignoring her expression of revulsion, and wetted his lips as he stroked her skin. 'Lovely. Just lovely.'

'So's this'un, Dan,' another of the brigands said. He was taller, but perhaps a year or two younger, and had greasy brown hair that seemed to sprout in haphazard clumps about a lumpy scalp. He was looking at Cecily with the eyes of a famished man. 'Bet her arse is firm as a new apple.'

Dan smiled. 'We shall have to find out, Cal, bless me we shall.'

'What do you want with us?' Cecily blurted. Lisette shot her a caustic glare.

Dan spoke. 'What do we want? Bless me if this ain't all a bit of a surprise.' He put his hands to his hips as he considered. 'We come here to graze the mounts, find grub, and suchlike. The old bitch don't need all them vittles, after all. But now we find some new friends, and, I must admit, our *wants* are somewhat altered.'

The taller man, Cal, advanced to take Cecily by the waist. She resisted and he slapped her hard. Tears filled her eyes and he grinned. 'Let's swive 'em, Dan. Please!'

Dan pursed his lips as though he weighed the merits of the request, but Lisette knew he was simply toying with them and she began to back away. He already had her face within his grip, and now he squeezed. 'You shall enjoy it, by my word you shall.' He looked across at the whimpering Cecily. 'Relax your bones, lovely. Cal may be a lank sort, but his prick's like a pike stave.'

'*No!*' Goodwife Hulme squealed somewhere behind. The men laughed. One of them strode over to her and knocked her to the ground.

'Do your best, fillies,' Dan hissed as his free hand plunged between the folds of Lisette's cloak. She felt his fingers snake around her breast, dig into the soft flesh, and she pushed him hard in the chest, forcing him to take a step back. 'And if we enjoy it,' he said as he moved in again, 'then we'll have ourselves a nice little earner. Put you sluts up in the house there and bring in a little coin for your services.'

'Get rich with these beauties, won't we, Dan?' the man who still stood over the elderly lady called happily.

Dan's gaze drifted over Lisette's shoulder. 'Rich and fat, Benny. A nice little swiving ken.' He glanced down at the old woman. 'Not you, Goody, bless my soul, not you. But praps you might wash the sheets.' He had Lisette's cloak in his fist again, and he drew her in to him with a strength that shocked her. His face pressed against her ear, the hot air of his breath making her skin crawl. 'They shall need washing, bless me, but they shall.'

'I will not be your whore!' Cecily Cade screamed, still struggling to keep her clothes fastened against Cal's groping attentions.

Dan looked across at her. 'A lot of rich old curmudgeons hereabouts, miss, bless me but there are. All with deep pockets and hard pizzles. War makes 'em rut like boars in spring!'

Cecily bit Cal's hand, and the tall man released her so that she stumbled back. She straightened defiantly as he set himself for another sortie. 'Then they will lose their pizzles as fast as they might wield them.'

All four of the men laughed. '*Ha*!' Dan exclaimed. 'Glib-tongued thing ain't she, lads? Good family, by the sounds of you. We could fetch a pretty price for your royal cunny. A proper gentlemen's curtezan, lads. Try her out for size, Cal, and don't hold back!' He turned back to Lisette, eyes shrunken to slits in his lust-driven resolve. 'Now come here, froggy. I've a burning in my stones. Bless me, but I have.'

Lisette let him come, and she did not resist as he took her shoulders in both hands and lent in to press his cold, glistening lips against hers. He stank of beer, sweat and leather. Tasted of salt and the hint of blood. She let him push up against her, felt the hardness at his groin as he ground his crotch into hers. He closed his eyes and groaned. It was a deep, guttural sound that only changed when she stabbed him.

Dan screamed as he pulled away. He stared down at his breeches. Lisette's eyes followed his. Next to the bulge at his groin there was a new appendage. The hilt of her dirk jutted, bobbing freely in a macabre parody of his still swollen member. A vast red stain bloomed at the place where it vanished into the cloth of his breeches. He was bleeding profusely, and his hands fumbled there, desperately trying to stem the crimson tide but not willing to pull the blade free.

Cal had abandoned Cecily now. He ran over to his friend, staring in dumb horror at the dangling weapon. Lisette did not wait for him to move. She stooped to draw her second knife, the smaller blade concealed at her boot. He turned to her, jaw still lolling open, and she prayed to God that He might give her the power to overcome this new enemy. But in that moment the enemy was gone, clubbed to the ground from behind, and Cecily Cade was looming over him, a hefty chunk of flint cradled within both palms.

The last two bandits reached for their swords, but Lisette held up the wicked little knife.

'Come,' she challenged. 'You will not have us alive, bastards.'

It was Dan who changed things, for the blood had not abated, and now he slumped on to his knees. He groaned again, but this time it was not out of pleasure but the last wisps of air leaving powerless lungs. His heart had given out, and he fell forwards, face thudding into the churned turf without raising a hand to slow his descent.

The other two glanced from Dan to Cal and then at each other. Lisette recognized the expression – a sour concoction of incredulity mixed with indecision and fear – for she had fed off similar moments so many times before, and she strode towards the brigands, unwilling to let the momentum slip. And then she was advancing upon their backs, for they had turned tail, running like confused sheep in the face of a raging mastiff. In less than a minute they were in the saddle, galloping back into the forest. It was over.

CHAPTER 11

Gloucester, 12 August 1643

Stryker woke in a room that was dazzling with daylight. Some-where outside a baby was crying and, further off, a dog yapped madly until a woman's shrill scold cut it off with a yelp. His throat was dry and his face throbbed, and for an awful second he feared he was back in the cell with Port and his confederates. A while later, however, he recalled seeing Skellen flatten his torturers with the butt-end of a musket followed by the surreal visage of the man who had first recruited him into the life of a soldier.

'Can you sit?'

Startled by the voice, Stryker turned his head gingerly to see Vincent Skaithlocke seated in a high-backed chair in the corner of the room. 'I think so.'

'Nasty beating,' Skaithlocke said as Stryker heaved himself first on to his elbows, and then upright.

The movement smarted through every inch of his flesh, but he managed it. 'I'll live.'

Skaithlocke leaned back and cracked his knuckles. 'Aye, you will.'

'Port?'

'Gaol, by order of Colonel Massie.'

'Where is this?'

'The apothecary on Westgate Street. I believe you know it?'

Stryker nodded. They were back where their mission to Gloucester had started. He noticed Skellen entering the room. 'Thank you, Sergeant.'

Skellen shook his head. 'Not me, sir. Colonel Skaithlocke's the one, sir. Sprung me from the room next to yours.'

Stryker stared at Skaithlocke in surprise. 'How did you—?'

'I am advisor to Governor Massie,' Skaithlocke replied, his voice sounding strangely loud in the confined space. 'He mentioned you had been in Gloucester, but that you had deserted. I know you, do not forget. Seemed strange that you would run just when things were getting interesting.' He grinned, and twitched his big shoulders. 'I asked around. Spoke to the man who supposedly saw you leap the wall.'

'Dodd.'

'The same. Turns out he'd been given a fistful of tin to concoct a nice little tale. That didn't mean you hadn't deserted, of course, but there were rumours.'

Stryker frowned. It made his damaged eye socket sting furiously. 'Rumours?'

'Just that a musketeer named Port had some miserable cove locked up. He'd bragged about it to his new blue-coated mates. The story followed that it was an old flame's new swiving chum. Port didn't like it. He knocks around with a musketeer from Stamford's. Harold Nelly, a Gloucester man, has a house in the town, so I knocked on his door. His sister answered, tried to slam it shut in my face, but I—' he paused, and his broad face creased in a wince. 'I heard your voice.'

Stryker felt himself colour with embarrassment. His tongue automatically investigated the gaping maw in his gum where once a large molar had been. 'I can never repay you.'

Skaithlocke dipped his head. 'It is good to see you again.'

Stryker looked at Skellen. 'Will, this man enlisted me when I was barely older than Lieutenant Jays.'

'Caught him picking my pocket,' Skaithlocke grumbled, though his eyes sparkled with the memory, 'the little bastard. Gave him a choice. Join my lads or face the magistrate.'

Skellen grimaced. 'Snout-fair choice.'

Skaithlocke tilted back his head and brayed to the ceiling. 'That it was, Sergeant! That it was!'

Stryker gazed at Skaithlocke, assailed by the memories. He had carried the big man's colour through mud and snow, hardship and horror. They had campaigned across Europe from one incalculable bloodbath to the next, yet those years had been some of the happiest he had known. He smiled through his throbbing gum. 'I chose wisely.'

'Aye, you did,' Skaithlocke agreed. 'And learned quick as a fox. Commanded one of my best companies by thirty two.'

'Thirty-one, sir,' Stryker corrected. 'At Breitenfeld.'

'Well bless me, so you did.' A huge, lingering sigh eased from Skaithlocke's barrel chest. 'How long has it been, Stryker?'

'Nine years, sir. I went to serve the Prince in thirty-four. You've been in the Low Countries all that time?'

'You mean to ask why I did not race back here when war was declared,' Skaithlocke said with a wry smile. 'Aye, well, I might have done, but I was employed by the Dutch. The money was very good.' He spread meaty palms. 'But everything reaches an end, old friend, and my time in the Low Countries was no different. Here I am.'

Stryker canted his head as he searched Skaithlocke's pale eyes. 'With the Parliament.'

'Like you.'

Stryker nodded. 'Like me.'

'Although I hear your choice was only recently made.'

'The King does not pay well,' said Stryker.

That made Skaithlocke grin. 'Spoken like a true soldier of fortune! *Ha*! Well, do not think you will find riches in Gloucester.' He leaned forward earnestly, pointing a fat finger at Stryker's chest. 'But you've made a good choice yet again. The rebellion is in the right of it.'

That threw Stryker and he frowned. 'Spoken like an idealist, sir.'

'Perhaps my mercenary days are behind me.' Skaithlocke leaned back, crossed one foot over the other and folded his arms. 'I believe the monarch has ruined my homeland, and it is time for change.' There was a period of silence as the old comrades regarded one another. 'How fares Lancelot?' Skaith-locke exclaimed in an obvious move to break the awkwardness. 'Still treading the boards? And the beguiling Miss Gaillard?'

'They are well,' Stryker said simply, thinking it best to skirt that subject altogether.

Skaithlocke moved a hand to his left eye, making small circular motions in the air. 'I heard Eli Makepeace was dead.'

Stryker lifted his own hand to the messy scar where once an eye had been. 'That he is. Malachi Bain, too.'

Skaithlocke's eyes widened. 'Pray God by your hand.'

Stryker nodded. 'Autumn last. At Brentford Fight.'

'But were you not on the same side? I heard he had joined the Cavaliers.'

'Their debt to me was older than this war.'

'*Ha!*' Skaithlocke exclaimed happily. 'You are still the man I knew!'

But perhaps you are not, thought Stryker, still considering his friend's uncharacteristically partisan stance. His thought was severed by a deep jolt that rippled through the floorboards, accompanied by a series of disparate shouts and screams from somewhere out in the city. He waited until the vibrations had died before staring at Skellen. 'Ordnance?'

The sergeant nodded. 'It's started, sir.'

Skaithlocke stood, held out his hand for Stryker to grasp. 'Tell me, Stryker. Do you think you can walk?'

Perhaps, Stryker reflected as they made painfully slow progress down to the V-shaped wedge of wall that formed the southern tip of Gloucester's defences, he had been a little optimistic about his ability to walk. The sleep had done him the world of good, that was certainly true, but he still felt as though he had been trampled by a whole troop of cavalry, and Skellen was forced to take his arm in order to support the captain's weight.

But walk he did, and he was soon helped slowly on to the battlements, staring southwards, the two turncoats gazing in unconcealed awe at the sight below. It was a city in a field, a sprawling mass of grubby canvas islands in a sea of green and brown. White-shirted soldiers milled between the tents, bored witless, Stryker knew all too well, as they settled into life as a besieging army. Further off, a troop of cavalry performed their evolutions amid a frenetic cloud of dust, their plated torsos winking through the sandy pall like pearls in a silt-clogged seabed. A block of pikemen drilled in one corner of the camp, their long dark staves rising and falling like the spines of a gigantic hedgehog, while smoke slewed sideways across the front rank of a company of musketeers who were practising in the heat. Either side of the wedge of stone that formed the intersection of the south and east walls, he could see newly constructed artillery batteries. They were stark against the green landscape, dark rectangles of raised earth protected by a shallow ditch and a ring of wicker gabions filled with soil and stone debris. Smoke still wreathed one of the batteries. He looked at Skaithlocke. 'No doubt where the blast came from.'

Skaithlocke nodded grimly. 'They call this point Rignall Stile. The malignants mean to catch the exposed corner of the wall in a vicious crossfire.' He pointed at another spot, this time closer to the defences. 'And when they've made a breach—'

He let his words hang so that Stryker could follow his outstretched finger. Little more than a hundred paces from the defences, running along either side of the road and curving beyond the sharp angle of the city wall, he could see dark lines in the scrubland. They took the form of gigantic zigzags, which were running parallel with the defences in the main, but thrust inwards towards the city at intervals, like huge brown serpents basking in the sweltering afternoon.

'Saps,' Stryker said.

'Aye.'

Stryker stared down at them. Once a breach had been made in the wall, the Royalists would need to bring their assault troops close enough to launch the attack. In order to cover that dangerous ground between camp and wall, they were digging trenches – saps – that would allow those troops to move up in relative safety. They were just over a yard wide, just under two yards deep, and would, in time, extend as far as Gloucester's outer ditch. Once there, Stryker imagined, the Royalist troops would ferry material such as faggots and stout planks along the channels, all the way up to the foremost men, in order to fill the ditch well enough for a crossing to be attempted. They were still some distance from that goal, however, and he could just about discern the occasional helmeted head as a man bobbed up and down behind his timber screen. It was exceedingly dangerous work, for a sapper was a prime target for sharpshooters on Gloucester's wall. Stryker wondered if the man had volunteered for digging duty for the extra pay, or whether he had been placed there as a punishment.

'They're within range,' Skaithlocke said, evidently guessing at Stryker's pattern of thought. 'We line the walls and pelt them with shot, but they seem to draw closer by the hour.' His gaze drifted westward. 'You see the Severn?'

Stryker traced the wide glistening course of the river to the west of the entrenchments. 'It protects the flank.'

'Aye. The Welsh are camped out at the old palace on the far bank. The Vineyard, the locals call it. The river keeps the bastards at bay, thanks be to God.'

Stryker's eye fell upon a group of stone buildings on the near side of the river, some four hundred yards to the south-west of where they stood. More tents, carts, men, horses and oxen could be seen milling about the area and its surrounding fields, which were set within the neat lines of trees. 'An orchard?'

'Llanthony Priory, Stryker. General Ruthven is based there, his troops billeted amongst the apple blossom. There was a tower there until recently, but fortunately the governor had the good sense to pull it down before the buggers could use it to spot their damned ordnance.'

'What is the situation to the north?'

'They are camped up there too, have no doubt. But it is boggy terrain, Stryker, not good for artillery, mine-works or saps. From here, though, Gaudy Green and the Priory, they intend to smash this part of the wall from both sides. If they make a breach, they will crawl up their damned trenches and sweep down through the city with impunity.' He offered a shrug that set his jowls rippling. 'Would you not do the same?'

'I would.'

'Now we should be away from here, for it is not safe,' Skaithlocke said, but even as Stryker registered his warning, the battery on Gaudy Green thundered into life. Bright tongues of orange licked out over the gabions, belching dark smoke as they recoiled on their big wheels, and a dreadful howl shrieked about the blue sky.

'*Jesu*,' Stryker heard Skellen hiss, and all three ducked by sheer instinct.

The iron balls soared past them somewhere to their left, careening into one of the taller houses that were tucked within the tight streets just beyond the wall. A vast smash echoed about the other roofs, swiftly followed by the chaotic din of tumbling tile and masonry. But when he straightened, Stryker saw to his surprise that the cannonade had not served to cow the citizens. Indeed, far from hiding away, the people of Gloucester, alongside Stamford's bluecoats, a smattering of dragoons that had escaped from Bristol, and volunteers from the Town Regiment, had emerged in groups from their temporary places of shelter. They now hurriedly gathered up the splintered rubble, loading it on to wagons or into baskets on their backs, and brought it to the foot of the wall.

'The common folk work alongside the soldiers,' Skaithlocke said proudly. 'They pile the debris into gabions, and place the baskets against the wall. We are also bolstering it with turf to absorb the shock of the guns.'

Stryker looked at Skaithlocke in amazement. 'Turf from where?'

'The north-west. Little Mead.'

Stryker had heard Massie mention Little Mead, and remembered that it was a boggy water meadow. But that would surely now be within range of Vavasour's Welsh marksmen. 'Are they not shot to pieces?'

'No. The women—'

'Women?'

Skaithlocke nodded. 'It is the women in the main. They work in gangs out on the wet soil, cutting and piling the clods, and they bring it to wherever it is needed. Often-times to replace a small breach, but usually to add to the walls hereabouts, where the enemy seem to keep their focus. I wonder if it is the very fact that they are women that stays the malignants in the trenches, for they could take a terrible toll if they so wished.'

Stryker blew out his cheeks, unable – and unwilling – to hide his astonishment at the sheer bravery of the people of this beleaguered city.

Skaithlocke smiled. 'Little Charlie may pound the walls, but we shall plug each gap as it opens, mark my words.'

Stryker thought about that. It was a surprise that the Royalists had chosen this route, given his message to Killigrew. 'If I am honest,' he said, 'I had expected the enemy to storm the place.'

'And that might have worked, I'll admit, for we do not have the manpower to defend every inch of the city against such overwhelming numbers.'

'Then why does Rupert not storm?'

'Because it is not Rupert's decision to make,' Skaithlocke replied with a wry smile. 'We understand the King would not countenance another escalade so soon after Bristol. Rupert and he quarrelled, and the Prince skulked off to be with his villainous horsemen. Overall command is with Ruthven, who now plots the siege.'

So the message did not reach Killigrew, Stryker thought, or it was ignored. He could well imagine Rupert's chagrin at hearing of his uncle's adopted strategy. His eye caught a sudden flurry of movement over towards the huge bastion of the South Gate, and he squinted to see what was happening. Men were gathering at a point below the wall, blue-coated and armed. He indicated the party with a nod. 'A sortie?'

'As I say,' Skaithlocke replied, following Stryker's gaze as he removed a leather-bound perspective glass from a snapsack across his shoulder, 'we plug the holes.' He handed the glass to Stryker. 'But we do not sit back and wait for them to be made.'

Stryker lifted the glass to his solitary eye, and trained it on the bluecoats. They were indeed armed; some with swords, others with muskets, and many more with dirks, carbines, pistols and even hefty wooden staves. 'Who is the officer? A yellow-haired man, by the looks of it.'

'Lieutenant Harcus. Young, brave and mad as a Frenchman. See there, he leads them out.'

Sure enough, Stryker watched as the officer led his squad of bluecoats out through a little sallyport in the wall. They had long, mud-caked siege ladders that, though he could not see from his position on the wall, he guessed would be used to span the defensive ditch on the outer face. He waited, glass fixed on the far side of the ditch, breath held, anticipating the emergence of the courageous sally party. The first man crossed, followed by another, then another, all the men leaping wildly on to the far side of the dry moat. Then the flaxen-haired Harcus was with them, blade glinting as he whirled it above his head.

Muskets fired immediately, blazing forth from the Royalists in the foremost saps. One bluecoat fell, the rest screamed in battle-crazed fury, and Stryker felt his heart batter his ribs as he watched them race like hunted deer across the tattered no-man's-land beyond the ditch, ducking and weaving against the unseen leaden balls that whistled past their ears. They were now at the first brown, zigzagging trench, Harcus still screaming unintelligible oaths, and they launched themselves into the complex labyrinth that the king's men had constructed.

'Fuck me,' Skellen whispered. The sergeant did not have the benefit of the perspective glass, but he could see the smoke rising from the saps well enough, and could hear the gunfire. Louder blasts could be heard now, rocking the rampart at their feet, and they could all see the spray of black mud shoot into the air like an inky fountain. 'Grenadoes.'

Stryker made to speak but found he could not, and merely offered a mute nod. The scrap would be terrible in those stinking trenches, he knew. Mud-calked, bloody and fierce. The bluecoats were there to destroy the saps and kill the sappers, and the Royalists would do whatever it took to rid their hard-dug works of the gnashing, snarling Roundheads. They would be clawing at one another down in that cloying maze, biting and spitting and killing.

A score of people had joined them on the wall. Massie was there, some twenty yards along the rickety walkway, surrounded by his ever-present entourage of soldiers and bureaucrats, while many of the turf-lugging townsfolk had made the climb too. Save the governor, who coolly followed proceedings through his own leather-bound lens, they cheered Harcus and his squad, bellowing abuse at the sappers and calling down God's punishment on the men who would dig too close to their beloved city. It was terrible yet infectiously exhilarating, and Stryker felt a pang of guilt, for part of him wished Harcus' brave bluecoats success. It was reckless, battle-lusting valour at its most desperate, and he could identify with it wholeheartedly, despite his secret allegiance to the men who would strive to bring down Gloucester's patchwork walls.

Stryker bit his lip hard lest he add his own voice to the cheers, flinching as another grenadoe blasted a trench to a fuming morass. But suddenly he saw Skellen, who was braying with the rest, and realized that now was the time to show that their coats truly had been turned, and he took up the shout, bellowing for the king's men to slink back to their masters if they did not wish for more of their blood spilt. Along the wall, he noticed Edward Massie was eyeing him, and he offered a nod that was immediately returned.

'He knows all,' Skaithlocke's stentorian voice broke through the din. 'You are welcome in our ranks.'

'Again, I thank you,' Stryker acknowledged.

'No matter, old friend,' came the reply. 'Now let us see to your recovery, for the governor wants you out leading our sallies as soon as possible.'

Stryker froze. He peered up at Skaithlocke. 'Sir?'

'I told him you were no good to us behind these bloody walls, Stryker,' Skaithlocke said happily. 'Told him you'd be rocking like a bear in a cage if he cooped you up too long.' He shook his head, patting Stryker's shoulder with his great paw. 'No, sir. It is the saps for you, where you can go kill me some fucking Cavaliers!'

St Mary without Bishopsgate, London, 12 August 1643

Major General Erasmus Collings slapped the quill down on the paper as he stood. His chair shot backwards, screeching all the way to the wall. The table juddered against his knees, ink sputtered in all directions, and the cowed soldier stared at the tiled floor.

Collings knew he had hard eyes. His mother had told him so. She was not a kind woman. But a sharp mind and a hard gaze, he had learned, achieved much for a man who was built little sturdier than a young girl, and that, he admitted, was something he could thank the bitch for. It had frightened great and meek men alike, and now it reduced this gruff soldier to ruin.

'You have failed me, Wallis.'

The red-bearded chin seemed to shrink into the soldier's collar, putting Collings in mind of a turtle he had once seen. 'I am sorry, General. Give me more time.'

Collings' glare did not falter. 'You are a disgrace to your coat, sir.'

Wallis let his eyes flicker to his black sleeve. 'I am ever honoured to wear it, sir.'

'And that is a great shame, since you will not be wearing it much longer.' Collings moved from behind the table to pace slowly round its edge and into the room. He kept his steps sharp and hard, so that the crack of his heels sounded loud against the cold tiles, making the soldier flinch. He stopped a pace from Wallis. It was unpleasant, for the fellow's breath stank enough to render a horse unconscious, but the effect of such close proximity was immediate, and Wallis seemed to shrink further into his shirt. 'I fund this regiment.'

'Yes, sir,' Wallis muttered meekly.

'From my own pocket. Your coats and breeches, the shirts on your lice-ridden backs, and the hats on your empty skulls. I pay for your vittles and weapons, your shoes, your ale and your damned powder ration.'

'Aye, sir, and we are grateful for such generous—'

'And in return,' Collings continued unabated, 'I expect my men to do their duty.' He reached out and flicked a speck of dust from the black wool at Wallis' otherwise pristine breast. The soldier almost stepped back at the touch, which was most gratifying. 'You lost my prisoner.'

'But the riots, sir—'

Collings slapped the bearded cheek as hard as he could. Wallis' head jerked to the side, his skin below the left eye glowing as red as his wiry hair. 'I will hear no more of the damnable riots!' He spun away, seething, voice coarse through gritted teeth. 'Curse me, I will not. Your attention faltered, and that is the nub of it. You lost a valuable asset to the rebellion, and you have failed to retrieve her.'

'It is impossible, General, I swear!' Wallis bleated in sudden desperation. 'The roads are full of soldiers and provisions. Of folk fleeing one town, and others rushing to another. Carts full of supplies clog the highways, brigands infest the fields and ditches. My men know not where to look.'

Collings turned on his heel. He felt his breathing surge with the growing rage, and fought hard to control it. He stalked back to his desk, battling to push every muscle in his face back into a neutral position that would present the cold expression he had taken so many years to cultivate. Christ, but he needed to find Cecily Cade. She had been whisked away from under his nose, and he would be a laughing stock if the news reached Westminster. Worse: he might be accused of incompetence, or even collusion. Tried for treason by the dour grey-faces of the Commons. His blackcoats were loyal as any soldiers in the land,

and they were sworn to secrecy, but these things, he knew, had a way of getting out, and it was only a matter of time before his error was made public.

He stared at Wallis, narrowing his beady eyes to black slits. 'It is imperative you find the girl. No blunders.'

'But, sir—'

'Two women were seen heading north on the Barnet road.'

Wallis wrinkled his flat nose. 'Two women does not mean—'

'Two women on horseback, one fair of hair, the other dark. One dressed all in black, the other in blue.'

Wallis' eyes widened. 'When were they seen, sir?'

'Days ago. They will be long gone by now.' Perhaps, he thought with a wave of dread, they were already supping claret with the king in Oxford. But he could not entertain that thought. Not yet. 'But it is a start, is it not? Take your men and find the King's whores, Mister Wallis. Bring them back to me.'

Leighton Buzzard, Bedfordshire, 12 August 1643

The cart rumbled gently over the compacted earth of the road. The cracks were deep, dark wounds cleaved into the mud by relentless heat and feeble rain, but the wheels negotiated them with admirable robustness. The narrow track had proven a blessing since they had elected to plunge along the canopy-smothered route, for it had been empty of both soldiers and bandits, and now, mercifully in time for dusk, they could see the first buildings of civilization.

Lisette Gaillard twisted in her hard seat, feeling her buttocks sear against the wooden slats, but forced a smile on to her lips. 'How fare you, Goody Hulme?'

From back in the cart, the old woman wafted a hand that was as airy and translucent as goose down. 'Well, thank you.' She was leaning against the rearmost upright timbers, shoulders bouncing gently against the wood as the wagon traversed the uneven ground. The vehicle was empty save her skeletal frame.

Her face betrayed a deep sorrow. 'But now that I am away from that place, I cannot wrest my thoughts from Robert.' A tear tumbled across the wrinkles of her cheek like a waterfall over a craggy cliff face. 'Those murderous—'

'Times force men to unholy acts,' Lisette responded. She had seen far worse as a child in France, and she had quickly learned that to dwell upon grief was to let it devour you.

'And they were not soldiers? You're certain?'

'Not soldiers any longer, though perhaps they were at one time.' She shrugged. 'Deserters most probably. Broke camp in the dead of night for fear of battle or plague.'

'And now fallen to evil,' Goodwife Hulme said bitterly.

'Hunger will drive any person to dark places.'

'As will lust,' Cecily Cade added from her seat beside Lisette. She was more sensibly clothed now, having been free to choose from whatever garments she could find in the Hulme house. Like Lisette, she was dressed in the garments of a man, with breeches and hose, a simple shirt and brown coat. She had taken a long, grey riding coat that had been Robert Hulme's prized possession, for his elderly wife claimed she had no use of it any longer.

Lisette nodded. 'Lust too.' She tried to brighten. 'But they are well behind us, and well forgotten.'

Their elderly cargo worried at her coif with calloused fingertips. 'I am a burden.'

'Aye,' Cecily said cheerfully. 'But a welcome one.'

Lisette could not help but smile. Stryker had warned her to expect a pompous, outspoken example of the most irritating woman imaginable. He had been angry with the girl when he had told Lisette of the horrifying ordeal on the summit of a bleak Dartmoor tor. Freely admitted that the vengeful cavalryman, Gabriel Wild, and his witch-hunting lackey, Osmyn Hogg, had laid siege to the place in order to flay the skin from Stryker's bones. But he had also told of a second design. Erasmus Collings' determination to capture Cecily Cade and learn the whereabouts of her dead father's fortune. The torments to which Stryker's loyal men had been subjected were, in no small part, the fault of Miss Cade. Moreover, and worse still, the beautiful heiress had seduced young Andrew Burton in order to escape Stryker's protection and make her own way through the moor. She had failed, of course, but it was her eventual spurning of Burton that had led him to his demise.

Yet now, as she looked across at the gaunt face beside her, she felt only admiration. Cecily Cade might have trifled with poor Burton's naive emotions, but she had proven her worth time and again since London. Her own trials at the hands of Erasmus Collings would have been hard for any woman – or man – to bear, and the manner of the escape from the capital had taken a great deal of courage. The journey since had hardly been a Sunday stroll, and she had shown no fear at all. And then there was the lonely house in the woods, where they had almost been raped. How could Lisette resent one who had saved her life, crushing her attacker's skull with a rock? This was no ordinary young woman.

'Look there,' Cecily said, causing Lisette to follow her outstretched finger. 'Houses. See? Through the trees.'

Lisette squinted to discern the pale shapes of whitewashed walls and flint beyond the greens and browns that danced to obscure them. 'You're right, praise God.'

Lisette had insisted they leave the Hulme smallholding immediately, for they had neither the time nor the fortitude to bury two more souls in that blood-soaked turf, and that meant the pair of craven thieves would doubtless return to find their fedaries stinking in the sun. Such a sight could only breed a hunger for vengeance, however timid the men were by nature, and they would not be so easily bested a second time. Thus the women had released their own horses, for they were tired and one was already holding its hoof gingerly on the root-rutted paths, and taken the two mares ridden by the unfortunate Dan and Cal instead. Those beasts were ill-fed and skinny, but they were big and seemed robust enough. The sticking point had been the old woman. They had initially agreed to leave her, but that was before the brigands had waylaid their journey, and now, Cecily had argued, they would surely vent their anger upon poor Goodwife Hulme upon their return. Lisette had protested, but Cecily refused to move without their new companion. Goody Hulme could not ride, of course, so the mares were harnessed to the only road-worthy vehicle her late husband had owned, and then they had set off northwards. The younger women still failed to agree on a final destination, for Lisette saw Oxford as the only viable target, while Cecily yet clung to the notion of meeting General Hopton at one of the West Country garrisons. But the westward road was fraught with danger, making either plan unworkable. The Thames Valley divided the two capitals – rebel London and Royalist Oxford – and it seethed with Parliamentarian troops, and so it was agreed that they would strike north initially, only turning west once they had crossed the chalk heights of the Chilterns. Any uncertainty was laid to rest when the old woman mentioned that she had family at one of the settlements on their circuitous route.

It had taken the rest of the previous day, and all of this, to reach their destination: Leighton Buzzard. A dusty-faced, shoeless lad driving a herd of goats along the road during the first hours since dawn had told them that the bridleway would take them down into the small town, and that, so far as he knew, no soldiers of either persuasion held sway there. They could not know whether to trust him, but Lisette had decided they would trundle down from the hills and put their fate in the Lord.

The Black Sheep was the first inn they reached. On the town's outskirts, its gable end facing out on to the surrounding fields that formed an arable buffer between civilization and the wilderness of the Chiltern Hills, it was a substantial building of timber frame and steeply pitched roof.

Lisette glanced up at the dark thatch as she and Cecily left the cart out on the road with its grieving passenger, and carefully eased open the door. The interior was better kept than she had expected, with clean floors of compacted chalk and straw, and a brick hearth painted with red and yellow stripes.

'Ladies,' a surprised voice greeted them from further into the chamber, which smelled strongly of wood smoke.

Lisette laid eyes on a man of middling height and frame, with long, black hair and a beard that fell all the way to his sternum in a sharp point. 'You are—'

Cecily's hand went out to grasp Lisette's elbow, cutting her off. 'You are master here?'

Lisette glared at Cecily, but she gave an almost imperceptible shake of her head.

'Aye, tapster in this fair place,' the man said. He sounded gruff, as though he had not used his voice for a while, but not impolite. He waited in the shadows, regarding the newcomers with glinting eyes. 'Two pretty women alone.' He clicked his tongue softly. 'These are dangerous times.'

Cecily stepped forward, rounding her shoulders. 'Listen to me, Master Tapster. We have money, and will pay you well if you agree to let us rest our heads here for the night. But be sure that we work for the highest authority in the land, and will not suffer any kind of hindrance lightly. Do I make myself clear?'

Lisette looked from the innkeeper to Cecily and back again, and for the first time she saw the real quality in the girl. Now, though, as the man casually stroked his pointed beard, she could see that he heard the same streak of authority ring like the clash of steel in her patrician tone.

Eventually he nodded. 'Aye, mistress, and I think I have a room that'll serve.' As he walked across the room, Lisette heard the sound of straw rustling and glanced down to see that the tapster dragged his right leg awkwardly. He patted it with a vein-threaded hand. 'Shot through the thigh at Newburn.'

'You fought the Scots?' Cecily asked.

'I did. Much good it did me.'

'And now?'

The tapster shrugged. 'Now I pour ale and serve food.'

So he did not wish to speak of politics, Lisette thought. That would suit them just fine. She looked at Cecily, as the latter spoke again. 'Are there soldiers hereabouts, sir?'

The tapster said that there were not. 'Parliament men most recently, but they're out to the west, pressin' the Oxford garrison.' He folded his arms above a tight paunch of a belly. 'Now let us see to your room.'

Cecily dipped her head. 'Thank you, sir.' She shot him a coquettish half-smile. 'And needless to say, there will be more coin, so long as we receive no—unwanted—attention.'

The man brandished a mouth full of chipped, rodent-sharp teeth. 'Soul of discretion, mistress.'

They helped Goodwife Hulme to the house on Lake Street. The kin she had mentioned was a short, stooped man, probably in his sixties, with a grey moustache, grey hair and grey skin. They did not speak to him, for another man knowing their business was a risk too far, but they waited beyond the corner of a house across the street, carefully watching for his reaction at finding his milk-eyed kinswoman at the door. With relief, they saw only recognition and joy on that dour face, their guilt at leaving her lessened by the man's welcoming embrace.

They went quickly back to their little room in the roof of the Black Sheep, careful not to tarry any longer than was required, and soon they were perched on the edge of their respective straw palliasses, staring at the floor and listening to the murmur of the men in the taproom below.

'You would like to be down there?' Cecily said.

Lisette looked up. 'I am used to rough men. I have lived and worked with soldiers all my life. They have kinder souls than you might expect.' She closed her eyes, thinking of the nights she had spent in warm, dark taverns with Stryker, held tight in his arm while his pipe smoke swirled in pungent halos about them.

'Oh, I do not doubt it,' Cecily replied. 'I spent some time with a company of foot before my capture. They were kind in their own way.' She yawned, stretching her hands high above her head. 'You forgive my interruption before?'

'*Naturellement*. It was right for you to step in. My accent is no help to us.'

Cecily regarded Lisette, her head cocked to one side. Eventually Lisette shifted her rump irritably. 'What is it?'

'Tell me, Lisette, do you have a man?'

'Sometimes.'

Cecily's dark eyebrows shot up. 'Sometimes?'

'My duty does not allow me a typical life.' She waved the younger woman away. 'But you would not understand.'

Cecily gave a rueful bark of laughter. 'I have spent the past months hounded, threatened for my father's money. Do not think to belittle me so.'

Lisette saw that Cecily was serious, and decided to relent. 'My man is a soldier.'

'Oh? A dashing Cavalier, I'll wager.'

'Not really.' She leaned back on her elbows, the surface of the straw mattress feeling coarse against her skin. 'A Royalist officer, *oui*, but perhaps not as you might imagine. He is with the infantry. Pike and shot.'

Cecily seemed intrigued. 'And what does he think to your work?'

Lisette snorted. 'He can think what he likes.' But as soon as the words passed her lips, she regretted them. She was angry at Stryker, but Cecily did not deserve such a response. She sighed. 'He does not care for it, in truth. I think he would have me with the goddamned baggage train if he could. Washing his bloody britches.'

Cecily grinned, and Lisette saw a flash of beauty. 'But you laugh at such a wish, I'd wager.'

Lisette nodded. 'He knows me well enough. Knows I would die in such a life. It is no life at all. I was born into war, and I will die at war.' There was an awkward silence as Cecily searched for an adequate reply, and Lisette felt badly for it. 'What of you?'

'Men?' Cecily shook her head. 'None.'

Lisette wondered if she even knew what her casual dismissal of Lieutenant Burton had caused, but she did not wish to dwell on that subject for now. 'None at all?'

'I think of a man from time to time,' said Cecily after a lingering heartbeat. 'An officer, like your *amour*.'

'Oh?' this threw Lisette somewhat, for Stryker had not mentioned this aspect of Miss Cade. Perhaps he had not known, but one might expect such things to be discussed during their time shared on that lonely hilltop.

'It is nothing. I knew him once, that is all.' She gnawed her lower lip. 'He was not the kind of man I had ever thought I would think of in *that* way.'

'But?'

'He was kind to me. Clever, strong, frightening for all that, but—'

Lisette smiled. 'Exciting.'

Cecily returned the expression. 'Yes, exciting.'

'Handsome?'

Cecily seemed to consider that question carefully. 'In his own way.'

The words reminded Lisette of Stryker, the man who had been so handsome once. Even damaged as he was, he was yet still able to draw her to him with that quicksilver gaze and blazing temper. 'I understand.'

'It was nothing, as I have said. A moment of attraction, perhaps, but I let him slip away. The fault was mine.'

Lisette pushed herself up from the palliasse and padded across the warm floorboards to a small table beside their single, unglazed window. The gentle fluttering of paper had caught her eye, lifted daintily by the breeze. She looked down at what she now recognized as a news-sheet. The parchment was well handled, its edges frayed and smudged by many a hand, and for an amused second she thought it might have been one of the pamphlets she had commissioned from Henry Greetham. But quickly she saw that it was one of the Parliamentarian diurnals, with stark black words emblazoned at its head. She read it aloud, '*An account of the fight at Lansdown.*' She read on silently for a short while, until her eyes fixed on a point halfway down the page. She swore viciously.

Cecily was staring at her from the other side of the room. 'Lansdown? What of it? I heard the king's men triumphed.'

'*Oui*,' Lisette said, turning slowly back to return Cecily's gaze. 'But there were casualties.'

'Aren't there always?'

Lisette crossed back to the palliasse and handed her companion the paper. 'See for yourself. On the morrow, I think you'll agree, we ride direct for Oxford.'

CHAPTER 12

Near the South Gate, Gloucester, 14 August 1643

Stryker was on the wall near the bastion, a position he had begun to take by force of habit as he waited for his injuries to heal. From there he could see the square batteries that the besieging force had constructed against this vulnerable corner of the defences. Two had been placed on either side of the sharp intersection of the south and east walls – dark, gabion-hedged mounds blighting Gaudy Green like buboes – and the other a little way round to his left, directly facing the East Gate.

'I saw it,' William Skellen's voice droned from somewhere behind.

Stryker turned to see his old friend struggle up to the parapet. There was no longer a wooden scaffold at this place, for the earthen buttress that Massie's volunteers had been constructing was now as tall as the wall itself, and as deep as five feet in places. A man, therefore, could simply scramble up the new slope if he wished to view the sprawling Royalist encampment. Down below, the teams of townsfolk laboured with their clods, hauling them down from the water meadows by the wobbling cartload to slap on to the compacted face of the ever-growing mound.

'Where?' Stryker said.

Skellen pointed to the east. Beyond the ever more complex system of saps that had grown from the ruins of the burnt-out suburbs before the East Gate, another large concentration of tents had sprouted like a colony of toadstools. 'In amongst that lot.'

They waited while a desultory volley of musketry rippled along the rampart down towards the corner of the wall at the Rignall Stile. Return fire crackled back almost immediately from the men down in the Royalist saps.

'With Astley then,' Stryker said when the musketeers had paused to reload. He fixed his gaze upon the tall pole from which the colour of Sir Jacob Astley hung lifeless in the sun. There were other flags around the camp, reds and yellows and blues, and Stryker searched for the standard that Skellen claimed to have seen. 'You're sure?'

'Aye,' Skellen said simply. 'It was Mowbray's all right. And they'll be first in if they make a breach.'

'Jesu.' Stryker's wounds were healing well, though they seemed to throb with more vigour at the dread thought.

'Sir,' said Skellen, leaning against the stone rampart and waiting for his captain to look up at him. 'You know I'd march into hell if you told me to, sir.'

'But you'll not fight the King.'

Skellen snorted. 'Fuck the King, sir.' He stared out at Astley's encampment. 'I'll not fight my mates.'

'You'll fight who I bloody tell you to,' Stryker retorted, though without conviction.

'What are we going to do, sir?'

'I don't know.'

The sergeant made a growling noise and deposited a gelatinous globule of phlegm over the side of the wall. He watched it plummet into the ditch below. The digging of the man-made ravine had tapped into scores of natural springs that threaded through the soil on which Gloucester had been built, and already the ditch was beginning to resemble a moat. Skellen watched ripples pulse out as his spittle touched the stinking mire. 'Can't believe they ain't stormed.'

'They would have, had Rupert taken command.'

'Bet he's raging about that,' Skellen said with the ghost of a smile. 'Forth's a doddering old palliard.'

Stryker shrugged. 'Did well enough at Brentford.'

'Should've stormed,' Skellen repeated the opinion as he gazed out at the king's army.

'They've decided upon bombardment, and they must live with it,' Stryker said, even as he noticed a flurry of activity around the shielded emplacement nearest their position. He could not see the detail, but he knew gunners and their mattrosses were readying the ordnance for another volley. It was a formidable battery. A pair of 24-pounder demi-cannon, the heaviest guns at Forth's disposal by Stryker's reckoning, together with a 12-pounder were gaping up at this section of the wall. They had thundered since late morning the previous day, attempting to soften walls and morale. The hastily piled earth on the inside of the stonework had cushioned the effect to an impressive degree, but that did not mean the guns were impotent.

Stryker looked left and right, cupping hands at his mouth. 'Down!' he bellowed at the musketeers lining the walls. 'Down!'

The battery lit up before Stryker could turn, rippling light glaring at the back of his eye even though he had clamped it shut. He crouched; he was half running, half rolling down the turf buttress as the world shook to its very essence. He had never felt an earthquake, but some of the Italian engineers he had known would often speak of them, and he guessed this was just what it was like. It was not simply the boom and the howl of the iron shot as it cut a hot trail through the air, but the wall behind him was shuddering as though it would collapse into the ditch. Stryker found himself on his back, two-thirds of the way down the muddy slope, gazing up at the rampart. It did not fall, but he could see the pall of stone splinters shower the air like a great grey rain cloud. One man was already screaming, and Stryker caught sight of him at the top of the wall, wheeling away with a bloody hand clamped at his neck. Stryker watched the bluecoat as he rocked forward suddenly, thighs hitting the stonework, and toppled into the abyss beyond, his scream cut dead by the splash of his body as it met the quagmire below.

Rough hands were at Stryker's shoulders. He saw Skellen's face, grim and professional. 'Thank you.'

Skellen nodded as he hauled his captain to his feet. 'Careful, sir.'

Stryker's old bruises smarted all the more now, but he managed to find his footing in the loose soil. A young man, perhaps not yet into his teens, was prostrate a short way up the slope, blinking dumbly at the darkening sky. Stryker scrambled across to help, dragging the lad upright as Skellen had helped him. 'Slowly, son, slowly.'

'Am I dead, sir?'

Stryker grinned at the stunned boy. 'No such luck.'

'They'll break through, won't they, sir?' the boy said in a feeble voice. His red hair was matted with the mud of the buttress and his freckled face streaked with tear-carved valleys. 'They'll kill us all.'

'No, son, they won't.' He ruffled the lad's hair. 'I won't let them.' From the corner of his eye, he caught Skellen's arched brow. 'Now let's get you up, eh?'

The boy stood on trembling legs. All around them stunned defenders were scrabbling to climb the earthwork again, desperate to take stock of the damage, and, with a final pat of the boy's shoulder, Stryker led Skellen to the summit.

'Curious promise,' Skellen rasped under his breath, 'seeing as they're the enemy, an' all.'

Stryker ignored him.

'Christ above!' someone exclaimed from further towards the rampart. They looked to where he was standing just as the wall began to sag. The smooth blocks were crumbling away, caving outwards into the moat, and in their wake slid the earth that had been nestled against them.

'They've done it! Jesus save us, they've done it!' another shouted, peering over the rampart so that he could see the lower face of the wall. The man, a corporal, twisted back, his face distraught. 'Fetch the Governor!'

Captain Lancelot Forrester climbed out of the trench and kicked the mud from his boots against the solid wheel of a filth-spattered dog cart. An engineer, encased from head to foot in thick, unwieldy metal, gave him a shout of warning as he strode past, a long shovel resting across his shoulder, but he waved the man away. He judged himself far enough out of range that only the very best shot might hope to reach him. He had been inspecting the work some of his musketeers had been about this past day. They had dug in, made themselves as comfortable as possible behind the wicker screens, and set about exchanging fire with the jeering rebels on the wall. Similar rivalries would be going on all around the city, Royalist sharpshooters trying to pick off the defenders, while the motley assortment of Parliamentarians within the city would spit as much lead back at the saps as they could muster. Now, though, something had changed. The huge barrage from the Gaudy Green battery had shaken the very base of the trench, which in itself was nothing new, but the cheer that spread through the king's lines like wildfire had compelled him to take a look.

Forrester leaned on a damaged gabion at the edge of a trench that had been abandoned after a Parliamentarian raid had reduced it to a fuming ruin. Much of the basket's stone innards had been pilfered for use elsewhere, but it still retained enough solidity to hold him as he let it take his weight while he packed his pipe. He stared across at the pair of still smoking demi-cannon. He watched the smoke drift lazily away from the battery and drew heavily on the smouldering sotweed, gnawing the worn pipe stem between his front teeth and adding his own pungent smog to the evil air. He peered through it with bleary eyes, from exultant gunners to the mud-caked sappers in the trenches that now touched the flooded ditch, and up to the men who had reappeared on their confounded rampart. 'Stuck a hole in it, Reginald, see there.'

Lieutenant Jays clambered out of the trench and came to stand beside his commanding officer. He followed Forrester's outstretched arm, the pipe used as a smoking pointer. 'Praise God, sir.'

Forrester nodded, and removed his hat. 'And praise Prince Rupert, for he spent the night out here, sighting the damned cannon himself.' He stared at the small breach that had opened at this beleaguered corner of the wall. The larger stone blocks from the ancient construction had collapsed outwards into the ditch, followed from within the city by a miniature landslide of soil that formed a small glacis on the outer face. 'My God, they've done well. That's a lot of turf to lug. The Prince wagered they'd bolstered the inner face, for our lads at the Vineyard watch them cut the turfs. But I think even he would be impressed. No wonder our damned artillery have struggled so.'

'When will we attack, sir?'

A musket-shot interrupted Forrester, and both officers were startled to see a ball thump into the gabion against which they stood. It bounced off like a pebble shied at a tree-trunk, for much of its power had dissipated over the distance, but Forrester beckoned Jays to retreat all the same. 'I cannot say,' he said as they moved to a safer distance. 'Now that our saps have reached their blasted moat, the engineers'll drain it and, God willing, we'll be unleashed to do our work.' He turned back to assess the dark tongue of crumbled stone and fallen earth. 'It is not a large breach, by any standard, but if we might fill the ditch enough for us to cross quickly, we have plenty of good men to force a way through.'

Jays swallowed hard. 'I hope they do not stand, sir.'

'You and me both, Reginald,' Forrester said, turning away to stare at the black clouds gathering to the east. 'You and me both.'

Near Oxford, 14 August 1643

The droplets were fat and strangely warm. They bounced mercilessly on the surface of the hardened road and in amongst the green canopy overhead, causing a fine spray to obscure everything in Lisette's vision.

She dipped her head against the rain, pressing her chin into her chest, and whispered encouragement to her bony mare. They were close now – she recognized this part of the county from her time in Oxford – and Lisette thanked the Holy Mother for it. Progress had been slow indeed since leaving Leighton Buzzard the previous morning. Though they had donated the wagon to the tapster at the Black Sheep in thanks for his discretion, their speed on the two horses had not been as good as she had hoped. The road teemed with soldiers. She had expected as much, but presumed that, this close to the new Royalist capital, any martial forces would be loyal to the king. Not so. She had bitten her lip and held her breath more than once as they waited in the forest for roving Parliamentarian patrols to pass. To make matters worse, most of the troops seemed to carry field signs with which she was not familiar, forcing her to hide from even those men she suspected of being allies.

And then it had rained. It started with grey skies and a few desultory gusts of wind, but quickly developed into a full-scale storm that compelled them to slow to a pathetic walk rather than the glorious, homecoming gallop she had envisaged.

'Bloody English summer,' she mumbled.

'You miss France?' Cecily Cade asked as she drew her black horse alongside Lisette's bay.

'Sometimes,' Lisette admitted. 'The weather.' She shrugged. 'The hills, and the forests and the rivers and mountains. But France was not kind to me. Now I go where I am told to go. You? Do you miss your home?'

Cecily sighed. 'We had many homes, always travelling from one to the next as my father looked in on his interests. Now the memory of each place is like a knife to my heart. Though I suppose there was one place.' She looked across at the Frenchwoman. 'You know the Isles of Scilly?'

Lisette nodded. 'In the ocean off Cornwall?'

'That's right. We had a place there, a small place, built in thick stone against the wind. I would play outside, gaze out to sea.' She smiled. 'Father would shout if I strayed too near the cliffs.'

'It sounds nice.'

'It was. I miss it.' Cecily gritted her teeth in sudden anger. 'I still cannot believe it. Hopton burnt, blinded?'

Lisette shrugged. They had been through this discussion many times, and she was beginning to tire of it. 'Believe it.'

'Perhaps it is mere rumour,' Cecily continued unabated, 'spread by the Parliament to frighten us.'

Lisette reflected again on the news-sheet and its claim that, despite a Royalist victory at Lansdown Fight, the king's men had lost two of their foremost leaders. '*One great Cavalier dead, the other barely alive.*' According to the exultant report, Sir Bevil Grenville had been slain during the battle itself, while General Hopton had been caught in an explosion later in the day. 'I fear it is too easily proven to be false.'

'I had thought—' Cecily went on unhappily.

'You had thought to speak with Hopton,' Lisette said, feeling irritation rise. 'I know, Cecily.' She looked across at her companion. 'But he might have perished by now, for all we know. His injuries were severe by that paper's account. We must go direct for the King and Queen. I am known to Her Majesty. She will grant me an audience.'

Cecily eased her mount to a halt, the rain dashing against the grey hood of the riding coat given to her by Widow Hulme. 'What if she does not? I have spent too long keeping this knowledge to myself. Resisted those who would claim to pass it direct to the King. Hopton and Grenville were the only men I could trust, and now they are gone.'

Lisette turned her mount to face Cecily. She peered into the girl's eyes, so dark in that sepulchral hood. 'Trust me.'

'But I—'

'Not with the gold, Cecily. I do not wish to know where your cursed treasure is.' It had already cost too many lives. Lisette ran a hand along the horse's pricked ear, wringing water from the tip. 'And you are right, you have suffered too much to give it up to just any fool. Trust me to bring you safe to King Charles.'

Cecily's almost translucent face smiled from within its sodden cave. 'King Charles.'

'King Charles,' echoed Lisette, turning the horse back to face the road.

The men blocking their path wore grey coats and breeches. They had emerged from the bend about fifty paces ahead, mud caking their legs from shoes to knees, and marched behind a huge square of grey taffeta, hoisted high at the end of a long pole. Lisette and Cecily stared open-mouthed. Perhaps the drums had been smothered by the roar of the rain, or perhaps there were no drums at all, but that mattered little. They were facing an entire company of foot, arrayed in alternating blocks of pike and musket, and the foremost dozen men were already running towards them.

Cecily turned to Lisette. 'Do we run?'

'No.'

'But they have no horses. We can get away!'

'They have muskets.'

'It is raining,' Cecily protested.

'Stay where you are!' Lisette stared at the flapping colour.

Cecily shook her head. 'Then it is over? After we have come so far? How could you give up so easily?'

Lisette spurred forwards suddenly, twisting back to wink. 'Because they're king's men! We've made it!'

'Down, Waller! Down, I say! Now where was I?'

Lisette shot Cecily a quick smirk as they watched the little mongrel, Waller, run rings round its master's horse. The hooves slid frantically in the sticky terrain as the liver-chestnut gelding tried to kick out at the yapping canine, but the dog simply skipped out of range. 'You were explaining your business here, sir,' Lisette prompted, trying not to laugh.

Major Titus Greening, company commander in Colonel Thomas Pinchbeck's Regiment of Foot, leaned across the saddle and shook his fist at the dog. In reply, the wire-haired, pot-bellied creature scampered over to the nearest tree, cocked its leg at the exposed roots for a few moments, and scuttled off down the line of marching infantrymen. Greening straightened with a long-suffering sigh. 'Yes indeed! We are – that is to say – we *were* en route to Aylesbury. Patrol, you understand. Checking for rebels. Got to keep the lice off the coat, eh?'

The women had been welcomed heartily by the Royalist officer. Lisette suspected he would have swallowed any tale that meant he could turn his rain-lashed recruits about and go home to the warm fires of Oxford. Now they were making steady, if slow, time in the ankle-deep morass that would lead them to the king's new capital. The women rode at the head of the column either side of Major Greening, but the sixty or so men at the rear trudged in sour-faced silence through the mire.

Cecily cleared her throat as they filed past a gap in the thick trees that signified the mouth of an ancient bridleway. 'Thank you again for your assistance, Major,' she said sweetly.

Titus Greening was a plump fellow in his mid thirties, with long hair that had already turned as grey as his coat, and a clean-shaven complexion. His eyes were kind, his nose long and pointed, and his lips full. He wore a broad grey hat topped with a red feather and a voluminous crimson scarf tied diagonally about his torso. 'Not a bit of it, madam. Glad to be of help.' The dog raced past them again, and this time its shrill barking made Cecily's horse shake its head irritably. Greening screwed up his face in embarrassment. 'My apologies. Waller is a great nuisance.'

'Why do you not give him away?' Cecily asked.

'Or shoot him,' Lisette added mischievously.

'Shoot him?' Greening repeated with unconcealed shock. 'He is our talisman, madam. Joined us shortly after our first taste of a brabble, and followed our ranks ever since.'

'Waller?' Cecily said.

'After the dastardly rebel general, of course,' Greening said impishly. 'Short, fat and ugly.'

Lisette watched the dog splash through a water-filled rut, mud splattering up its scruffy flanks. 'I am surprised he can follow so well on the march, Major, for his legs seem so short.'

Greening guffawed. 'Aye, well he'd surprise you, I'm certain. Besides, it has been a while since we campaigned, so to speak.'

'Oh?'

'We are part of the Oxford garrison. We stay in the city and guard it.' He swept his hand back at the men. 'Save for the odd patrol, naturally. And these lads are raw. They're new recruits in the main, not the hardy scrappers we've sent down to Gloucester.'

Lisette looked across at him. 'Gloucester?'

Greening nodded. 'Why, surely you are aware of the great siege now undertaken there? The King has gone himself to see our brave forces reduce that crucible of revolution to dust.'

'The King?' Lisette echoed. She glanced at Cecily. 'In person?'

'It is the last great stronghold in those parts,' Greening said. 'He would see it smashed before he looks to London.'

Cecily drew her mount to a standstill. 'He is not at Oxford, Lisette. After all this, he is not there.'

Greening reined in his gelding too, his lieutenant issuing orders that rippled down the column to bring the company juddered to a gangling halt. 'Does it matter, ladies? I will escort you to Oxford where you will be safe, I promise.'

Lisette had been slightly ahead, and now she wheeled back to them. 'There are more spies in Oxford than anywhere else outside of London.'

Halfway down the line, Waller was barking into the rain. His hackles were up, teeth bared at some unseen foe. The men ignored him.

'Then you agree with me?' Cecily said.

'That we should make for Gloucester instead?'

Cecily's stare was intense. 'Aye.'

Lisette thought of the risks of being on the road any longer than was necessary. It was not a pleasant thought, but Oxford, though militarily safe for the king's supporters, was a seething nest of agents and double-agents, and Collings' reach would most certainly extend beyond its new fortifications. She nodded. 'If King Charles is at Gloucester, then that is where we must go.'

Cecily mouthed her thanks, while Greening shook his head in exasperation. He made to speak, but whatever he meant to say was drowned out by the rain, and almost immediately by the shrill scream that drifted up from the rear of the column. They peered back over the heads of the men, but their view was obscured by the forest of pikes that brushed the overhanging leaves.

There was another scream, followed fast by a wail of utter despair that rose like a sudden ocean swell to an ear-shredding din. More men turned now, squinting back down the line as an anxious murmur rumbled up from the ranks. And then it was clear, for the ground was vibrating and more men were shouting. The branches at the side of the road towards the column's rearmost tail were rustling louder than the rain, as they were thrust roughly aside. Huge shadows moved there, pushing through the woodland on both flanks. Whinnies and snorts pulsed on the wind, a wave of sounds crested by the shouts of men and the scrape of metal, and Lisette turned her horse in a tight circle as she gazed at the unfolding horror that was already sweeping up from the back of the company.

Horsemen. Lots of horsemen. Snarling and stabbing, slashing and cursing. They were under attack.

The south wall, Gloucester, 14 August 1643

'It is imperative we block that hole.'

Edward Massie stood at ground level, his hands planted firmly on hips, peering up at the damage to his southernmost defences. He was surrounded by a flock of blustering garrison men and politicians, though he seemed to notice none but an elder sergeant, who kept his distance, his tired bones draped nonchalantly against a black-staved halberd. 'See to it immediately, Sergeant Clements.'

Clements straightened, doffed his cap and covered his mouth as he yawned. 'The volunteers are exhausted, sir.'

For the briefest moment, Massie's cool facade appeared to slip and his pale face tightened, but a slow breath in and out of his lean nose seemed to calm his ire. 'Then put some damned soldiers to the task.' He pointed a narrow finger at the top of the rampart. This section of wall was the best part of fifteen feet high, and, at the breach, it had been sheared of six, the turf spewing out into the ditch on the far side. 'More soil, stone, gabions, woolsacks, I care not what. But get it closed.'

The sergeant bowed. 'Right away, sir.'

Massie nodded sharply. 'And get an artillery piece over here. I want it pointed straight at the breach, loaded with case shot. If any man appears in that hole, you flay the flesh from his bones, understood?' He turned away before Clements could respond. 'Stryker, you are recovering I trust?'

Stryker and Skellen had already joined the crew attempting to patch up the breach when Massie and his entourage appeared. 'I am, Governor,' he replied as brightly as he could, though his tongue immediately snaked its way back to the shattered ruin of his missing tooth.

'Good.' Massie offered his hand for Stryker to shake. 'I had hoped to speak with you again. I was very sorry to hear what happened. Colonel Skaithlocke explained it to me. The black-guard Port and his men will be dealt with, I can assure you.'

'Thank you, Governor.' Vincent Skaithlocke loomed from the crowd to stand with Massie, and Stryker smiled a greeting. 'I owe the colonel my life.'

Massie glanced between the two men. 'I understand you are old comrades.'

Skaithlocke nodded happily. 'Brothers of the blade, sir.'

'I enlisted with Skaithlocke's Foot in twenty-nine, sir,' Stryker said. 'My first command was given me by the colonel.'

'Breitenfeld,' said Skaithlocke.

The governor was clearly impressed. 'Before my time, I'm afraid to say, but a bloody day by all accounts.'

'We served with the Swedes,' said Stryker. 'A marvellous victory, but bloody indeed. Near fifteen thousand dead.'

'A rare baptism of fire, sir,' Massie said. He blew out his white cheeks. A gust of wind funnelled between the wall and the houses, and slammed rain into their bodies in a spiteful blanket. He drew his cloak tighter about his thin body. 'I am glad men such as you serve with us. You are content to be with us at our time of need, Captain?'

'Aye, sir, that I am,' Stryker replied, and, for the first time, did not feel as though he was lying.

'Sir!' a voice bellowed from up on the rampart, a short way along from the breach. 'Colonel Massie, sir!'

Massie's eyes betrayed a flicker of fear, and Stryker knew he must be expecting an escalade at any moment. 'What is it, man?'

The bluecoat moved off the wall, turning sideways on the muddy crest, and let his boots slide a few yards down the slope. 'The trenches, sir, they're full o' water! They're collapsing!'

The governor bolted on to the mound, immediately sinking in the loose soil, but he jerked his boots free and clawed his way up to the crest. Others followed close behind, and they lined the walls around the breach, staring down at the Royalist saps.

Stryker found himself leaning on a loose slab of masonry, squinting from the black band of the moat to the labyrinthine siege-works that stretched all the way out to the gun emplacements. From within that new-dug warren emerged soldiers with their long muskets and sappers with picks, shovels and a myriad of other tools. Like rats fleeing a blazing ship, they slogged back to the main camp as their works began to disintegrate.

'They've hit the springs!' someone on the wall shouted in delight.

'Not all,' Massie said, tempering the excitement. 'The ones closest the moat.'

Stryker realized that he was right. The initial report had been an overstatement. The saps had not filled with water as if suddenly becoming tributaries of the nearby Severn, but like the city ditch, the gullies had reached deep enough to disturb the subterranean springs. Gradually, over a matter of hours and days, the water had seeped into the walls of the saps so that now, heavy with saturation, they were beginning to cave inwards.

The people of Gloucester cheered. They fired their weapons at the retreating Royalists and the king's men fired back. The garrison and citizens lined the walls to witness the miraculous sight. Men and women balled fists, whooping at the heavens and jeering at the ground.

Stryker scanned the dark lines below. In truth, only a tiny fraction of saps had become saturated enough to make them collapse, and the soggy interlude would do nothing to delay the king's men in the long term, but to the people of the surrounded city this was nothing short of a sign from God, and he could hardly begrudge them that.

An engineer in full body armour slithered out of one of the closest trenches, rolling on to his back like a flipped stag beetle. He wallowed there for a moment while the rebels howled their delight. Eventually he managed to turn on to his front, and, sliding like a drunk on an iced lake, made it to his feet. It was a ridiculous sight, and the folk at Stryker's flanks poured scorn on the slithering man, who looked like he might be off to joust in his heavy helm. He ran from their taunts and they brayed into the sky. Stryker found himself laughing with them, infected with their joy and sharing their relief.

'Sir?'

Stryker turned to see Skellen at his side. 'What is it, Will?' he said with a grin.

The tall man spoke into his collar. 'That's our lads down there, sir.'

Stryker's mirth shattered. He cleared his throat awkwardly. 'Not necessarily, Sergeant.'

'Even so.'

All Stryker could do was turn away. Skellen was right, of course. They had come here on a mission for Prince Rupert, yet already he was feeling drawn to the iron-hard rebels. He would not admit this to Skellen, but his pleasure at seeing the sap collapse had been as genuine as that of any other soul on Gloucester's pockmarked walls. The guilt hurt more than his wounds.

Near Oxford, 14 August 1643

They were like a flock of ravens, all black, with razor beaks that glinted like steel. Except these predators did not fly, but rode out of the trees on the backs of horses. Lisette counted at least a score, and though it was a small enough force, the element of surprise had proven deadly for Titus Greening's ill-prepared recruits.

The black-coated cavalrymen kept coming, bursting through the scrub like four-legged demons, white-eyed mounts snorting and gnashing and stamping their way into the column. The rear half of the line was hopelessly enveloped, even as the sergeants began bawling orders to charge pikes for horse. It was all too late. The road boiled. Steel and armour, helmeted harquebusiers with tawny scarves and flashing blades, anguished faces and snarled oaths, all seething in manic chaos. Pistols discharged at no range at all punched into the chests and faces of men encumbered by their great pike staffs. And those fearsome staves toppled like rotten boughs in a storm, for they were no use in such a close fight. The enemy was already inside the killing range.

'Lisette!'

It was Cecily. Lisette turned to her. 'Stay with me!'

Along the road, the black-coated Parliament men were hammering at the feeble Royalist line. They destroyed the musketeer units first, keen to deny the company time to prime their weapons, and most of those stricken men were already dead or had scattered into the forest. The greycoats were not fighters, they were shopkeepers, labourers and clerks. They took up arms because civil war had overrun their lives and

they yearned only for peace. The men in black were of a different breed entirely. They were professionals, trained in war and
paid well by one of the most feared men of the rebellion. Lisette
searched the line, praying to see some means of escape, for she
knew the Royalist position was utterly futile.

'Are they—?' Cecily's words died on her lips.

Lisette followed her gaze. At the end of the line, coming last
from the darkened bridleway, rode a young cornet of horse. He
wore russet breast- and backplates over a buff-coat, the tawny
scarf of the Earl of Essex at his waist, a billowing black riding
coat and a wide, black hat. In his hand he gripped a short staff,
atop which fluttered a simple black colour adorned with the
profile of a white raptor in mid-flight. She had not seen the
device before, but the white band at the man's hat told her
enough. 'Oui,' she said simply. 'They are Collings' men.'

'What do we do?' Cecily shrieked, her delicate features made
haggard by terror.

'Stay alive.'

Lisette vaulted from the saddle, her boots sinking to her ankles
in the hoof-churned mire, and ran to Cecily, dragging the
younger woman from the horse. Cecily yelped, but let Lisette
take her arm and steer her into the midst of a group of greycoats
who had yet to be engaged by the tide of harquebusiers. The
corporal in charge had had the presence of mind to move his
panicked squad into space and get their pikes charged for horse.
There were only a dozen men, but they made a formidable
defensive ring, with their tapered staves thrust out at an angle,
butt-end braced against the instep of the rearmost foot, bladed
tip wavering in the air at the height of a horse's muzzle.

The cavalrymen reached them in seconds. The first to come
took a wide swipe at the tip of one of the pikes, his horse wheeling expertly with the movement, but the shaft of ash had steel
cheeks riveted for two feet below the point, and the sword
bounced harmlessly clear. Another of the pikemen crouched,
jabbing low so that his weapon pricked the horse's flank. It
whinnied in anguish, reared, and threw its rider.

'*No!*' Lisette screamed, but her voice went unheeded in the melee. The greycoats broke ranks, as she knew they would, and descended upon the fallen Parliamentarian with discarded pikes and naked swords. But now the rest of the black-coated killers were amongst them, and they turned back, eager to regain their defensive ring. They were too slow, and found themselves hopelessly cut off. The hedge of ash and steel had been broken, the horsemen now commanding the space and felling the naive greycoats where they stood.

Lisette hauled Cecily savagely away, almost pulling her from her feet. She made for the trees, followed by a lone infantryman whose hands gripped a rusty sword, his face streaked with tears. They forged on, holding cowls tight over their heads as they scrambled through the snagging brambles and wet bracken, hoping the blackcoats had not noticed them amid the chaos. But the crashing of foliage at their backs continued. They turned to see one of the harquebusiers. His skewbald destrier was big enough to smash its way through the tangled forest floor with little difficulty, and he had soon closed the ground between them.

The horseman shouted a challenge and Lisette looked over her shoulder, her long hair billowing out over her shoulders as her hood fell.

The greycoat turned. He held up his tuck, tip trembling in unsteady hands, and the horseman grinned like a gargoyle, wrenching at his mount's taut reins so that the beast veered to the left. As the horse flanked the infantryman, its rider's sword was free in a blinding flash. Lisette and Cecily had stopped dead now, transfixed by the spectacle. Metal winked at the Parliamentarian's boot, and Lisette caught sight of the bright spur as the horse snorted and lurched forwards with a sudden burst of speed that caught the greycoat flat-footed. In a heartbeat the long cavalry sword was above him, scything down in a heavy arc to cleave at his head. He went down without a sound, a scarlet curtain drawn across his face.

The blackcoat surged on without respite, letting his mount's hooves maul the body as he spurred it through the brush. He let it circle round, finishing only when the women were trapped between him and the road. He offered a smart bow, even as more of his comrades cantered along the pathway his skewbald beast had beaten.

Cecily turned to Lisette with pleading eyes, but the French-woman could only shake her head. 'It is over.'

CHAPTER 13

Near the cathedral, Gloucester, 15 August 1643

Nikolas Robbens glanced at himself in the looking glass. His skin was utterly smooth, shaven down to nothing along his angular jaw, while his golden hair shimmered in the sunlight as he lent against the frame of the large window. He noticed that the coloured silken strands of his ear-string had become twisted during the night's exertions, and he took a moment to smooth them out, draping them across the bony surface of his naked shoulder. Happy with the result, he set the glass down on the wooden sill and padded back to the palliasse, where, sprawled on her front across his straw mattress, a woman waited.

She twisted slightly to look up at him, her long hair fanning over the pillow like a mousy halo. 'Why are you here?'

Robbens scratched at his flaccid member. 'Because English tavern girls have the tightest cunnies in all Christendom.'

She pushed herself on to her elbows. 'No, Nikolas,' she complained, though her pout betrayed the hint of a smile as she noticed his eyes shift to where her pale breasts hung invitingly above the sheet. She turned on to her side, showing him more. 'Why are you in Gloucester?'

Robbens felt himself stiffen, and he moved to stand over her. 'To fight your tyrannical king, of course.'

An argument broke out on the road outside, four or five different voices haranguing one another over the destination of a cartload of wool sacks bound for the defences, and she waited for them to finish with a roll of her eyes. 'Don't they have tyrants in France?'

'I am Dutch, Molly,' he chided. 'From Holland.'

She wrinkled her nose to show that she cared little for his provenance. 'Don't they have tyrants there?'

'Oh, they do, Molly. That they do.' A stink of powder smoke and scorched flesh invaded his nostrils, and he had to fight the sensorial memory that returned him to a quivering child. He had been born into the struggle against the Habsburg Empire, a revolt that had laid waste to his beloved homeland in a manner so brutal that this pathetic English squabble almost made him laugh. An image of his disembowelled father ghosted across his mind, as it so often did, and he swallowed back the bile as he remembered his mother frantically clawing at the sticky mess between her legs after the Spanish soldiers had had their fill of her. They had left her with a swollen belly and a broken heart, and she had taken a blade to her own wrists. He blinked hard and stared down at Molly. 'How old are you?'

'Eighteen.'

'Then you are too young to know enough of life. I am thirty.'

She stroked his hairless thigh. 'Old man.'

He ignored her. 'And I have learned that every nation has its tyrant.'

'Then why do you not fight in Holland?'

He often asked himself that question. Was it simply the money? After all those years honing his skills on the throats and hearts and flesh of Europe's Catholics, he had established a reputation that made him wealthier than he had ever thought possible. His work had kept him away from his home, for the contracts had been in France and Spain, Bohemia and now England. But would he ever have returned to the place of such grief? He offered a weak shrug, for it no longer mattered. This would be his final adventure. 'Your king is particularly bad, and my business is to punish him.'

'What business?'

He ran his gaze across the exquisite twin hills of her rump, between the two dimples at the small of her back, and up to the fragile shoulder blades across which her long, brittle hair cascaded. He reached out to stroke some loose strands away from her dark eyes. 'Never you mind.'

She frowned. 'Soldierly business.'

'Soldierly business, aye,' he said with a nod, though his thoughts had drifted to the tiny balestrino crossbow adorned with images of prancing stags that lay under the floorboards beneath the bed. He could hear the creak of the straining bowstring in his head; the music of death. It would play soon enough, and a man would die, and Robbens' employer, the one they called the Butcher, would achieve his goal. He forced a smile. 'Business that has brought me to fair Gloucester.'

'And are you pleased you came?' She did not take her eyes off his, but her hand snaked out to reach between his legs, making him gasp. She began gently to massage him, her dextrous fingers working faster as he swelled in her grip.

Robbens flexed his thighs, arched his back, and tilted his head to the beams above. 'Oh yes, my love.' He staggered backwards suddenly as the heat built in his loins, breaking from her damp palm. When he had gathered himself, steadied his breathing, he went to her again, this time pushing her on to her back. She squealed as he moved between her legs, bit her lip as he entered her, and clamped her eyes tight shut as he began to move. Robbens dropped his head and rasped into her ear, 'Very pleased indeed.'

The East Gate, Gloucester, 15 August 1643

The tour of the walls was a grim affair. Though the bombardment seemed to have abated, the ramshackle defences still inspired little confidence. Edward Massie, joined by his usual group of senior officers, save Captain Lieutenant Harcus, who was leading a small sortie down towards the Rignall Stile, was pleased enough with the work on the small breach, for it was now filled almost to its previous height with wool sacks, timber and earth. But no one could be so blinkered as to think a concerted assault by the vast numbers of enemy troops would result in anything but defeat.

'We must keep at them, Stryker,' Massie said as he stared down from the East Gate at what had once been a vibrant suburb of the city. Now it was a vision of hell, of homes reduced to rubble, abandoned trenches and crow-pecked corpses, twisted and blanched in the sun. The soil was sodden, the water lying beneath the dry surface of the fields having been freed by the Royalists' digging, and bloody pools gleamed where once grass grew. Further back, beyond the enemy lines, pits were piled daily with the besieging dead, killed by raiding parties, sharp-shooters on the ramparts or Gloucester's numerous small cannon. 'If they attack from all sides, we are finished. We must keep the buggers busy. Raid their saps and kill their men, though God knows it is costly enough for us to undertake.'

Stryker had deemed himself well enough to join the tour, though Skellen shadowed his every move. He peered down at one cadaver through the glass handed to him by the governor. It was half-naked, its eyes long plucked out by carrion birds, and its skin mottled blue. The face was permanently frozen in a parody of a grinning jester, lips draw back over black teeth and gums. One of the man's hands seemed to reach out to him, clawing the air, and he looked quickly away. 'How long can we hold out?'

Massie closed his owlish eyes. 'God only knows. The Parliament must know of our plight by now. I pray reinforcements are already on the road.'

Vincent Skaithlocke was, as ever, at Massie's side, and he cleared his throat loudly. 'There is a raid planned for the morrow, Stryker. Do you think you are well enough to join it? We need your expertise if you are able to give it.'

Massie turned to look down on the city, at a wagon-load of sodden turfs being dragged against the sticky glacis below, and

Stryker took the opportunity to deflect the question. 'More for the walls, sir?'

Massie nodded. 'Naturally. I intend to line the drawbridge at the South Gate with earth. Make it cannon-proof. I would also bolster the bastions at the North Gate and Friar's Barn. We must do whatever we can.' He looked down at the cumbersome wagon. 'Would you take this for me, Stryker? I have other business to which I must attend.'

Stryker nodded, relieved. 'Gladly, sir.' He looked at Skellen, who slid away down the slope with a nod.

The party moved on, slipping along the earthen battlements a little way down from the bullet-riddled rampart. Skaithlocke paused to shake Stryker's hand. 'Glad to see you're well,' he boomed. 'Though you look damned awful.'

'Bruising is all,' Stryker said with a smile. 'I shall be black and blue a long time yet, but it is no serious matter.'

'All is well, then,' Skaithlocke said happily. He seemed to study Stryker for a time. 'What we have been through, you and I, eh? Do you remember that citadel we garrisoned in thirty-two?'

Stryker nodded. 'How could I not? Held it against the Imperial troops for a month.'

'On our guts alone,' Skaithlocke grinned. 'We raided their damned lines a dozen times, killed a score and pushed them back with each and every sally.' He slapped Stryker's back. 'Was a good life, in its own way, eh?'

Stryker laughed. 'Good, sir? I recall almost getting killed many a time holding that blasted fort.'

'But we won!' Skaithlocke said. His eyes narrowed a touch. 'Though, as I recall, you were near blown to kingdom come by a petard.'

'I was, sir. Ears were ringing for a week.'

'And who was it dragged you free of the rubble with his own bare hands?'

Stryker remembered the darkness, the stink of burning flesh, and the taste of blood on his tongue. He vaguely recalled being hoisted from that fuming chaos and thrown like a rag doll across muscular shoulders, jolted to the safety of their craggy enclave on the back of his burly leader. 'You, sir. It was you.'

Skaithlocke nodded slowly. 'To fight an empire, eh?' He looked out upon the Royalist siege lines. 'King Charles is like the Emperor, old friend. He has grown to view himself as a god. And just like the Emperor, it is left to the likes of you and me to see he's brought back down to *terra firma*.'

Stryker stared at the first man he had truly respected. His muscle had mostly turned to fat, and the auburn curls were fading to grey, but that same sparkle lit his eyes as ever it had. 'You really believe in Parliament's cause, Colonel?'

'Truly. I am no longer a soldier of fortune, Stryker. But a man who can see his homeland for what it is.'

'And what is that?'

Skaithlocke rubbed his cheeks with thick fingers, breathed out heavily through his nose. 'England is like a fallen woman. Beautiful but corrupt. We must exorcise her demons. Cleanse her.'

'I've heard other men speak as you, sir,' Stryker said cautiously.

'I am not other men.' Skaithlocke scrambled up to the parapet, leaning his great bulk against a spiked storm pole. It rocked, but held him all the same. 'Listen to me, Captain, it is a grand thing that you have joined the Parliament's cause, for we need men like you and your brave sergeant, but you must truly believe in it, as I do.'

'And what does John think?' Stryker said, and immediately regretted the question, for the shutters came down upon Skaithlocke's face.

'John—' Skaithlocke's voice was barely higher than a whisper. He let his eyes fall to his boots, where they stayed for what seemed an age. 'He is dead, Stryker.'

'*Jesu!*' Stryker let his own gaze fall. John Skaithlocke, his comrade from so long ago, had been wise beyond his years and as hard as steel. 'How?'

'Musket-ball,' said Skaithlocke, and his hand went to his thick neck. 'Here. Killed him outright, thank God.' Tears welled in the red hammocks of his lower eyelids, and he let them tumble over his cheeks without shame. 'Near three winters gone and still it pains me to speak of him.'

'I am sorry, Colonel, truly.'

Skaithlocke sniffed, shook his head. 'No matter.' He stepped closer, planting a heavy hand on Stryker's shoulder and capturing the lone grey eye in the crossfire of his own. 'I have another son, do I not, Innocent?'

Innocent. Stryker wondered how many men might call him by his Christian name with such easy confidence. He could think of none. 'Aye, sir, you do.'

Skaithlocke beamed, wiping away his tears. 'We'll fight together again soon enough, eh?' He turned to follow Massie's party, only glancing back to shout, 'Brothers of the blade, you and I! Never forget that!'

'Close with the colonel, sir.'

William Skellen was standing at the foot of the man-made escarpment, hands on narrow hips, as he surveyed his little domain. About him the team of sweaty volunteers grunted and groaned as they hefted the turf into place.

Stryker went to him. 'Is that a question, Sergeant, or a statement?'

'Whichever you prefer, sir,' Skellen said wryly.

'Vincent Skaithlocke rescued me, Will. Saved me from myself. I was roaming the streets. Picking pockets, robbing homes. He took me under his wing. Put me on a ship to the Low Countries, gave me a sword. I already knew how to kill, but he showed me how to fight.'

Skellen kicked an errant clump of soil into place. 'Bit of a bed-presser now though, ain't he?'

'Don't let that fool you. He's as good with a sword as any I've seen. Strong as an ox, too.'

'You owe him a lot.'

Stryker remembered the explosion at the citadel all those years ago. It was just one incident out of many. 'I owe him my life.'

Skellen sniffed to show he was unconcerned with the answer, though when he spoke his eyes searched Stryker's face. 'Your loyalty?'

'What are you asking?'

Skellen stooped to pick up a large shovel. He banged it against the ground a few times to shed its skin of dried grime, and stooped to scrape at the loose soil at the edge of the mound. 'Your men are out there, sir,' he said without looking up, 'and you've made no move to escape.'

'The bluecoats watch the walls,' Stryker said. 'They watch *us*. We'd be shot as soon as we even thought upon it.'

'That's as maybe, sir, but I wondered if you were thinkin' to renew old acquaintances, so to speak. Reminisce a bit more with the colonel, like.' He evidently sensed that he had gone too far, for he stood suddenly, taking a small rearward step. 'Don't mistake me, sir. I ain't saying you've turned your coat. But our lads are outside the walls, waitin' to break in. Who will you fight for when they come?'

Stryker felt his jaw tighten. 'Have a care, Sergeant.'

Skellen propped the shovel across his shoulder and in a long-cultivated pose, stared into the near distance somewhere to the side of his captain's head. 'Beggin' your pardon, Captain, of course.' He paused, fishing some stubborn scrap of food from between his teeth. 'But you said before that he was like a father to you, sir. That's a powerful pull. And now he's saved you again.' He shrugged. 'I don't know. Just seems a big debt to me.'

That was more than Stryker could suffer and he stalked forward. 'I told you—'

'*Sir*! Captain Stryker, sir!'

Stryker stopped in his tracks and turned to face the man who had hailed him from amongst the nearest houses. It was a chance for Skellen to retreat to the safety of the work team, who were now lighting pipes and chattering like birds in a rookery. The newcomer was of short, meagre build, with greasy brown hair, sallow face and eyes saddled with drooping grey bags. 'Mister Buck?'

''Tis I, sir,' Buck said, his own surprise matching Stryker's. 'And good it is to see you. There was a rumour you had been grievous wounded.'

Stryker shook the spy's hand. 'Recovered, thank God.'

'Well met,' Skellen greeted Ezra Killigrew's unassuming intelligencer as he stepped up to rejoin his captain.

James Buck stepped closer, dropping his voice. 'And your—task?'

'Completed.'

Buck grinned conspiratorially. 'Mine too, I am happy to say. I am clerk to Alderman Pury, a happy position providing access to a great many documents of interest.'

'You have gathered what your master requires?'

Buck nodded like a pecking sparrow. 'One more commission to execute, as it were, and I am done.'

'Then godspeed you,' Stryker said.

Buck looked away. 'Quite.' He frowned suddenly. 'Though they have sealed the city now. I cannot break out.'

Stryker glanced around to check there were no flapping ears close by. The city volunteers were gathered in their own discussion, absently drinking their pungent smoke. 'We must ride out this siege, whatever it may bring.'

'Indeed,' Buck agreed. 'May we speak?'

'Certainly.'

Buck glanced at Skellen. 'In private.'

'My sergeant,' Stryker said firmly, 'is party to our loyalties, Mister Buck, as well you know.'

Buck's face split in an oleaginous smile. 'Aye, sir, but what I must impart is for your ears only.'

'Mister Skellen risks his life as we do, sir, and no less. He may hear whatever it is you have to say.'

Buck seemed more pained by that response than was necessary, and he wrung his childlike hands in desperation. 'Please, sir. I beg of you. I must see you alone.'

Stryker sighed, glancing at Skellen, who shrugged with typical nonchalance. 'Very well.'

They went to walk away, Buck leading Stryker towards a spot at the gable end of one of the nearest dwellings. Its tiled roof had been smashed by a cannonball, its chimney stack reduced to a pile of clay-coloured rubble that was already being plundered by the folk working on the walls.

'Here, sir,' Buck beckoned with a wave of his hand. He pointed towards the end of the building, meaning to conceal their meeting beyond the corner.

Christ, Stryker thought, but what further perils did the confounded Ezra Killigrew wish to plunge him into by way of this new order? He followed with a growing sense of trepidation.

'Blast your ballocks, yer bliddy beef-brained fool!' The shout came from back towards the walls.

'Hold,' Stryker told Buck. He strode back to the earthworks to find two of the volunteers barking at one another like rabid dogs. Skellen was in the midst of the melee, parting the men with his long, sinewy arms. 'Sergeant?'

'Toppled cart is all, sir,' Skellen replied smartly. 'Not to worry.'

Stryker saw the cart beyond the group of growling locals. It lay on its side, bounty spilled across the bottom of the slope, one wheel spinning in the warm air. Evidently someone had lugged it across the city, only to have another member of the team flip it over in a display of clumsiness that had enraged the rest of the group.

'David Young, you're a dull-witted bastard if ever there was one,' the aggrieved man complained.

At Skellen's far side, another man, face red with embarrassment, called back, 'Shove it up yer arse, Uriah. You always was a whinin' ol' donkey!'

Stryker went to stand between them, resting a hand on the hilt of his ornate sword with deliberate slowness. The group fell silent. 'That'll be enough. Sergeant Skellen is in charge. Do as he damn well says, pick that cart up and get back to work.'

'Permission to clobber the next man to speak, sir,' Skellen said in his blank-faced drone.

'Granted.' Stryker turned away and strode back to the corner of the cannon-battered house. But when he reached the shadows, James Buck was nowhere to be seen.

The London road, near High Wycombe, 15 August 1643

The dog, Waller, followed the small cavalry detachment at a distance. He knew better than to approach the big horses or their glowering riders, for a single kick from one of the mud-calked destriers would crush him like a rotten apple beneath a blacksmith's hammer, but his occasional yap reminded them of his continued presence.

'He has nowhere else to go,' Cecily Cade said as one such bark reached them from a hundred paces back. 'The poor thing saw his master killed. They were his pack, the greycoats, and he watched them die. What must he think now?'

'Think?' Lisette said sourly. 'It is a dog.'

'Do they not think?'

'I do not know, or care. His fortunes are better than ours.'

Cecily bunched her reins in one hand and rubbed her other hand across her grimy face. The pale skin had been spattered in mud and soaked by rain. Now that the sky was clear, the water-cut valleys had dried on her cheeks to form pale streaks in the filth. 'Some of Greening's men escaped into the woods. Do you think they will send help?'

'No,' said Lisette. 'They will run home. Greening is dead, and that is what matters.'

'Quiet there!' the harquebusier at the front of the squad snarled over his shoulder. 'Save your gossip for Major General Collings!'

The blackcoats, it transpired, had been tracking the women ever since they fled London. It had not been an easy task, Wallis, the Parliamentarian commander, had admitted. But these were Collings' private troops, paid with his own coin, furnished with the best weapons and the fleetest mounts, accountable to him alone. They had scoured the countryside from Wingrave to Aylesbury, finally risking Royalist heartland around Thame and Wheatley, and were almost ready to abort their mission when they had stumbled into the column of infantry in the dark woods.

'You were spotted first near Barnet,' Wallis had gloated as they made camp the previous evening, 'and again at Leighton Buzzard.'

He had not known the women were with the detachment from Thomas Pinchbeck's regiment when they attacked, but God, Wallis had bragged, was clearly on their side, for He had offered the fugitives – and the ill-prepared recruits – to Wallis on a platter.

Now they were on the move. The rain had turned the roads to sucking bog in the hours after the skirmish, and their precious horses had struggled and fretted as darkness descended, so Wallis had ordered they spend the night in an abandoned farm complex in the fields near a place called Stokenchurch. Every single roof had been black and exposed, beams turned to brittle shards by the fire of one malicious army or another, but they found enough shelter to pass the night. Thankfully, at least as far as Wallis was concerned, this new morning had brought blue sky and warmth, and already the ground was dry enough to make good speed away from one capital city and towards another.

'You've upset the General,' Wallis said as he rode beside the stony-faced captives. His thick red beard, like a fox pelt across his chin, jerked upwards as he smiled. 'By Satan's teeth, you have. Black mood, he's in, an' no mistake.'

Cecily stared across at him. 'Collings is a vile little man.'

Wallis' face darkened. 'Have a care, woman. General Collings has the ear of Pym.'

Lisette interrupted with a derisive laugh. 'That is no ear at all. John Pym is ailing. He'll be dead by the new year.'

'A pox on your forked tongue,' Wallis spat suddenly. 'Foreign witch.' He looked past Lisette at the wan Englishwoman. 'You consort with this Popish slut and you'll burn in hell.'

'She is no more evil than your poisonous leader,' Cecily replied levelly.

Wallis ignored her, returning his malevolent gaze to Lisette. 'You'll swing, lovey. The General says so. And what he says goes.'

'Pretty thing, though,' one of the nearest blackcoats chirped.

Wallis nodded. 'Aye. Too skinny for my taste, but I'd wager she swives like her life depends on it.' He licked his lips, winked at Lisette. 'Which, of course, it does.'

Lisette spat at him. 'Come near me with your rotten pizzle and I'll cut it off.'

Wallis brayed like a mule. 'Yes, my lovey, I dare say you'd try! Perhaps we'll truss you up, nice and tight. You'll get to meet each one o' my good men, and each will turn your sweet soil till his plough goes soft!'

Lisette spat again, the phlegm flinging past Cecily to catch in Wallis' russet whiskers. 'Bastard.'

Wallis wiped the dangling spittle on the back of his glove. 'And then Collings will pull all the nails off your dainty fingers and toes while he asks you a few little questions. And after that we'll have your neck stretched for a froggy spy, or for a Romish witch.'

'*Sir*!'

The call came in urgent tones from the quartet of scouts up ahead. They had been riding in an advanced position some half a mile ahead, but now bolted back along the road, great clods of mud showering the air in their wake.

'Look,' Lisette whispered.

She and Cecily watched silently as Wallis kicked forward, breaking a few yards from the head of the column in a jangle of spurs and weaponry. 'Speak!'

The first scout overshot his leader in his urgency, and wheeled back in a tight circle. 'Horse, sir,' he said breathlessly. 'Up on the hill.'

Lisette and Cecily exchanged a glance that fairly blazed with hope.

Wallis stared in the direction in which the scout was pointing, though he could not see the hill through the trees that smothered this part of the road. 'Ours?'

'Theirs.'

'Certain?'

'Red scarves and hat bands, sir, clear as day.'

'Strength?'

'Four score, at the least, sir.'

Wallis hissed a caustic oath. 'How far away?'

The scout sucked his front teeth as he considered. 'Couple of miles, sir, no more. They're on the crest, but looks as though they're following a track down to the road.'

Wallis turned to look past his charges, as though considering whether to ride back the way they had come.

'You would flee towards Oxford?' Lisette mocked. 'Why thank you, sir.'

'Shut your fucking mouth, whore!' Wallis snarled, though she could see the indecision in his eyes. To forge eastwards in the hope of reaching safety, knowing that a huge Royalist force might cut him off, or turn tail and run, all the while riding back towards the enemy capital from whence they had come. Eventually he stood in his stirrups to address the men. 'Dismount! Into the trees!'

It took another twenty minutes for the Royalist cavalry to come. As the scout had feared, they cantered down from the hill and on to the road, and there they had turned west, cutting off Wallis' route back to London. The scouts, positioned nearest the tree line at the highway's flank, passed back the detail through a chain of strained whispers. They counted seventy-two harquebusiers, all well armed and riding good mounts. The cornet carried a colour that was predominantly blue, with yellow trim, though they did not recognize it. But that did not matter, for the scarves at their waists and ribbons in their filth-spattered hats were as red as the blood that had spilled from Titus Greening's ill-fated greycoats. This was a large, dangerous force, and Wallis knew better than to engage it.

'Any man speaks,' the black-coated commander hissed, 'I'll run him through myself.' His men inched as close to the ground as they might, trying to keep their long scabbards clear of bent knees and tangled roots, each one peering through the foliage with apple-eyed concern.

The time it took for the new arrivals to come down from the hill had been well spent. Wallis had led his troop, less the four scouts, deep into the surrounding woodland until he was certain the horses would not be heard from the road. He had ordered them tied to sturdy trunks with loose knots in case a swift departure was required, and then they had paced out into the thick veil of summer-swollen bracken and boughs laden with the broadest leaves. The prisoners stayed close to Wallis, driven like sheep at dagger point by sullen soldiers made all the more resentful by the nature of this most ignominious concealment.

Wallis, crouching beside a fallen log, fixed the women with a slit-eyed stare. He covered his mouth with one hand, patted the hilt of his sword with the other. Cecily looked away. Lisette sneered, but stayed silent.

They watched and waited. Birds burst from the highest branches, startled by some perceived danger, and the rustle of the breeze was soon overwhelmed by the noise of the enemy troop as it clattered through the forest. Lisette listened intently, ever surprised by the sheer din that soldiers made. Thudding hooves and creaking saddles, chains and straps, sword-hilts and spurs, stirrups and whinnies and laughter. She glimpsed them through the trees, but the distance Wallis had put between his party and the highway meant that the Royalists appeared like wraiths gliding through chinks of light in dense undergrowth. She prayed that they would leave the road, flood into the wood and descend upon Wallis and his black-backed ghouls, but the very nature of their cacophonous progress told her that they were completely unaware of the rebel force lurking in the brush. This was a big, confident troop who knew their own strength, trusted in it, despite their proximity to land that was in the stranglehold of Parliament. They were arrogant and oblivious, and she knew that this rare, God-sent opportunity would slip like water through her fingers. Wallis would kill her if she ran, but if she did not, she would be hanged as a spy by Erasmus Collings. There was no choice to be made.

She stood. It was as if the world slowed. Wallis was peering up at her in terror-fuelled rage, Cecily's green eyes were widening in shock, and then she was sucking air into her lungs, turning to face the highway and the unwitting friends who rode there. Now or never.

The pain ripped through the rear of her knee, pushed by immense, inexorable force, and she collapsed helplessly backwards, even as her lips were working to bellow for help. The air punched ruthlessly from her chest, she could make no sound, and instead fell down and down until her back hit a dull hardness that seemed to sear along her spine. She stared up at the sky through shimmering branches, and the next moment a man loomed over her, casting a shroud across her eyes, and she squinted mutely up, wondering what had happened. Movement flashed in her face, like an adder's strike, then all was night.

CHAPTER 14

The Outer North Gate, Gloucester, 16 August 1643

The sun was sinking behind the western hills as the party gathered before the Outer North Gate. Captain Peter Crisp, a flaxen-haired man in his early twenties, was to command the one hundred and fifty musketeers of Stamford's blue-coated regiment, and he removed his hat as he faced the milling mob. They were hard men. Many of them were veterans of other campaigns, and that had set them in good stead, but now each had suffered the trials of this siege and had tasted the successes and failures of Massie's policy of continual sallies against the creeping Royalist entrenchments. They knew what to expect, knew what was expected of them, and that made them grim-faced and dead-eyed as they prepared their bristling array of weaponry. Muskets, swords, pistols, hatchets, clubs, axes, knives, grenades. Every blade had been honed to a zinging edge, each musket-ball kissed, each powder flask filled.

Crisp paced before his silent raiders. He wore the blue of his regiment beneath a sleeveless buff-coat. His hands were gloved, his lean face carried a fresh livid scar that ran vertically between his left eye and the corner of his narrow mouth, and his eyes were dark blue. He waved the hat at his men as he spoke, though his other palm gripped the hilt of his sword. 'You all know what we're about. They've extended their damned warren from the East Gate towards Friar's Barn. The Governor, God keep him safe, is determined the malignants pay dear for their boldness.' He forced a grin that did not touch his eyes. 'We have the honour of collecting that debt.' He drew his sword slowly, held it aloft and nodded to the men who guarded the hatch adjacent to the huge bastion.

Stryker was a short way back, in amongst the files of anxious rebels. He and Skellen could not avoid the storming parties any longer, lest they draw unwanted suspicion, and now had come their chance to show Massie where their loyalties lay. It was an ambitious plan by the young colonel, he conceded. A huge gamble to risk so many of his best fighters in the destruction of the Royalist positions, but the big siege guns had been quiet for two days now, and that had encouraged Massie to take the fight to the enemy. Rumours within the city spoke of a lack of powder, or a shortage of courage, or some divine deliverance that had spiked the cannon in retribution for the king's continued persecution of his people. Stryker was more circumspect. Though he did not speak his thoughts, he knew that the bombardment of Bristol, not yet a month past, had consumed a vast amount of howling round shot, and the first days of Gloucester's tribulation had seen the same. He guessed the Earl of Forth had simply run out of cannonballs. But whatever the reason for the cessation of the hitherto lethal pounding, the need to destroy the encroaching saps had not diminished.

Beside Stryker, a young boy of no more than thirteen checked his dirk, flicking the cutting edge with a black fingernail. 'What are you doing here?' he asked.

The boy's freckled face blushed hotly as he looked up at the man who must have seemed like something from his nightmares, with his hideous burns, puffy blue-black bruising and single grey eye that glinted like quicksilver. 'I wish to run the malignants through, sir. Every last one of 'em.'

Stryker shook his head at the show of bravado. 'There's nothing noble in killing, lad.'

The boy looked away, his eyes suddenly glassy. 'In truth, sir, I've no choice. Pa was killed by the cannon, sir. M' brother, Geoffrey, died with poor Mister Harcus. No one left to fight for our home. No one 'cept me, sir.'

246

Stryker stared down at him, appalled and impressed in equal measure. He was an enemy of this rebel city, sworn to defeat it for the king's cause, and yet these people had a courage that tore mercilessly at his loyalties. 'Godspeed, then.'

'And to you, sir,' the boy said.

The timbers and stone-filled bushels plugging the little sally-port were pulled away piece by piece to expose the studded door that would lead them to the slop bottomed ditch that served as Gloucester's moat. Stryker shuffled forwards with the rest, jostled by blue-coated shoulders and moving his head at awkward angles to avoid the jutting muzzles of muskets as the men were corralled into line. He carried no firearm of his own, save a pistol thrust into his belt, for he wished to avoid killing the Royalist sappers if at all possible, but he patted the swirling basket hilt of his sword as a matter of instinct, finding comfort in the solidity of the Toledo steel. He glanced up at the rampart. Some hundred yards to the south, looming above the area they planned to attack, a drake had been positioned. The small cannon had been brought up to pulverize the trenches and the sappers who dug them in advance of the main raid, and he hoped it would do its job well. Otherwise, he thought fearfully, all its black-mouthed presence achieved was to alert the Royalists that a sally was imminent.

Crisp was ordering a team of a dozen men forward. They carried the ladders that would span the moat. They moved to the port and, as soon as the door was thrust open for the first of them – the pioneers – to scurry out into the exposed world beyond, the drake began to fire.

'May the Romish bastards hide while our brave lads go to work!' Crisp called stoically above the boom at their heads. He moved to the sallyport himself, replacing his hat, and lifted his sword in salute to the men who were about to follow. 'For Captain Lieutenant Harcus!'

'Harcus!' the men echoed.

Skellen, clutching a halberd, was at Stryker's side. 'What about him?'

Stryker grimaced. 'Lobbed a grenade from the wall down into one of the nearer trenches. Got himself shot while he admired the result.'

'Hell's bells,' Skellen muttered.

Peter Crisp disappeared through the hatch and the musketeers followed in a tide of blue coats and curses. They bolted across the ditch, the long ladders bowing hazardously beneath them, and on to the devastated land that had once flanked the main highway to the east. They were like an army of demons, screaming threats and prayers, shrieking their hatred to the dimming sky. The ground to the east was as torn and potted as the violated acres to the south, old homes smashed and burned by the rebels to clear their line of sight and now enveloped by the besieging army's advancing trenches, made into breastworks behind which the king's men might fire up at the city.

The raiding party skirted crumbling walls and tumbledown, blackened roof beams. They leapt over the first trenches without resistance, for these had become sodden and duly abandoned. The sappers, encased in their suits of protective iron, were in the next row of trenches. They were desperately trying to climb out and away before the bluecoats reached them, all the while replaced by a scrambling file of musketeers. Massie had told Stryker that this part of the enemy camp was occupied by Darcy's Northern Brigade. They were a good fighting unit. The scrap would be hard-fought and bitter.

The Royalists crouched behind upended dog carts and slithered into some of the more robust ditches, fishing for musket-balls in their leather pouches and blowing frantically on smouldering match-cords. In a matter of seconds, the firing began.

'On! On! On!' Captain Crisp screamed, ducking instinctively as a musket-ball whistled past his head. He turned back to see the large force swarming in his wake, and he twirled his blade high so that it winked in the orange light. A man to his left flew back, punched in the chest by a ball fired at devilishly close range, and he collapsed in a bloody heap, staring lifelessly at the dusky ether.

Stryker was there, running with the men as though they were a herd of maddened oxen willing to trample anything that dared block their path. He drew his sword as he reached a trench, leapt down into it, his boots plunging into the sticky morass that had already crept up through the cracks between the timbers lining its base. He lost his footing for a moment, steadying himself against an upturned and empty gabion, and twisted round to see a metal-clad engineer charge at him, pick axe in his big hands. The attack came swift and heavy, and Stryker barely managed to shift his weight to the side to avoid a certain killing blow. The axe point ploughed a deep cleft in the trench wall, sticking there, as the saturated mud would not relinquish its new prize. Stryker felt the urge to kill the man as he tried in vain to yank the weapon free, but he knew the thick body armour the engineers wore would only damage his blade, so he shouldered his way past. He ran along the sap, faintly registering Skellen's foul-mouthed war cry somewhere behind, and reached a lone musketeer. The man had been cut off, for already the bluecoats had overrun this ditch and were swarming into the next, but his musket was primed to fire and he pulled the trigger. The ball whipped wildly to the side, holing a wicker basket to Stryker's right, and he charged into the acrid plume of smoke that had belched around the musketeer. The man had already reversed the long-arm, putting it to use as a club, and he thrust it powerfully forth, hoping to smash the butt end into Stryker's face. But the captain pivoted away, wise to the move, and battered the bewildered Royalist's cheek with his sword-hilt. The man fell, dazed but not seriously hurt, and Stryker left him to wallow in the filth.

He climbed out of the sap, sprawled in the mud, and charged on. The air had turned thick with powder smoke. Somewhere cannon fired, though he could not tell from which side it had come. A pair of corpses lay ahead, one dressed in Stamford's blue, the other in yellow, tangled together in a raging embrace that had killed them both. Stryker vaulted them, his boot clipping one of the outstretched arms, and he stumbled all the way to the next trench. He virtually fell into the sap, hit the bottom hard, feeling all the beatings at the hands of Richard Port come back to taunt him, but Skellen was there as ever, hauling him up in defiance of the pulsing agony. They saw that this trench had already been purged, bodies scattered all the way along its length, and Skellen swung his long legs up and over, dragging Stryker up in turn.

Musket-balls whined about their heads as they ran on. The clang of steel rang out ahead and they knew they were close to where the bulk of Crisp's bluecoats must be. They pushed through more drifting, sulphurous smog, and, like an unfolding dream, the battle spread out before them. The rebel raiding party was flooding the next two saps, where a concerted effort to repel them was underway. Musketeers and sappers of various Royalist units were joining the fray with every passing second, sent into the trench system from Darcy's encampment further back along the road. They would soon overwhelm Crisp and his men, but there appeared to be no sign of a retreat.

Stryker and Skellen tumbled into the trench with the rest. Along its snaking length personal duels were being played out amid the screams of the living and the dying. The shovels of terrified sappers scythed the air in crushing arcs, while their guards fired muskets and stabbed with their tucks, desperate to rid the carefully constructed works of this baying rebel mob. Blood sprayed in great gouts, spouting into the gory mud from split skulls and lacerated throats, mixing with the guts of belly-slashed men and the vomit of those for whom the sheer sight had rendered them quivering wrecks.

A man burst from the rabid melee up ahead. He was tall and thick-set, and he knocked Stryker aside with a contemptuous blow of an upturned musket. Stryker went sprawling, tasting the coppery tang of soil laced with blood, and wrenched himself away, rolling out of range of a follow-up blow. But the big man had advanced beyond him, determined to fell Skellen, and he swung the musket butt again, clubbing it at the sergeant's head. Stryker watched helplessly as Skellen parried the blow with his halberd, stepped back a pace, and swiped his pole-arm low. The halberd blade was made up of a sharp point, a bill-hook, and an axe, and it was that latter facet that cleaved through his attacker's knee, chopping him to the bone so that he bellowed like a gelded bullock as he dropped into the mire.

Stryker had recovered his wits and his feet, and he was ready as another man came on. The Northern Brigader hefted a fierce-looking partizan, and Stryker slashed the air between them with his sword, caught nothing, and was forced to duck low to avoid the irresistible arc of the partizan's heavy riposte. He retreated a fraction, set his stance again, and realized that he was grinning; madly, wickedly grinning at the man who was trying to kill him in this sticky pit. Because this was what he lived for, what he craved: battle and chaos and carnage. Blood pulsed in his ears, the song of rage that played its tune when fear and exhilaration mingled in visceral harmony, and he knew that he should be ashamed. These were his comrades, his own army, but he did not fight for Parliament. He fought for the approval of a man he had not seen for half a lifetime, yet who still commanded his utmost respect.

Skellen was at his side again, and together they forced their shared foe back until the Northern Brigader tripped on a body and went sprawling. Stryker lurched across him, stabbed him in the shoulder so that he dropped his weapon, and the pair surged on along the sap. They were with the main body of bluecoats again now. The raiders, it seemed, had reached an impasse, for the next few rows of trenches were brimming with Royalist reinforcements, who were shooting back with increasing regularity. Captain Crisp was in the midst of his men, urging them on, but even he could see that the day was done, and he called for the squad of bluecoats who had stayed with him during the sally, unused thus far. Stryker saw that each of them clutched a small sack that bulged as though it might carry turnips, but he knew well enough what nestled within the embrace of the cloth.

'Get 'em over there, men!' Crisp bawled. 'Give 'em hell! *Hell!*'

The squad lined the trench wall, covered by the fire of their musket-toting comrades, and produced clay spheres from their sacks. Each ball had a fuse jutting from its smooth surface, and the men lit them with the glowing matches carried by the musketeers. They fizzed into life for a second, and then they were airborne, lobbed by the raiding party into the saps beyond.

Stryker ducked, pressing his back against the muddy side as the explosions ripped the evening apart. His ears rang, his head swam, and yet more of the powder-brimming vessels were prepared, lit and thrown. The ground shook, screams rose above the blasts, distinct in their shrillness, and a shower of soil and blood and flesh and gristle descended from the heavens like a biblical plague. Limbs slapped the wet earth, a scorched head landed just a few feet from Skellen to stare accusingly up at him. He kicked it quickly away, swearing as gelatinous ooze splattered his boot.

One more round of grenades was hurled, one more swelling blast tore the Royalist trenches to smithereens, leaving them in seething, gory tatters for the crows and kites to squabble over, and then Captain Crisp was ordering the retreat and they were running, scrambling, clawing their way back towards the safety of the North Gate, vengeful musketry snapping at their backs, fallen friends left to rot in the August sun.

The eastern trenches, Gloucester, 17 August 1643

The fragrant smoke from Captain Lancelot Forrester's pipe billowed out over the shattered network of saps to mingle with the rotten-egg stench still lingering after the previous evening's skirmish.

'God's teeth,' he muttered on a fuming outbreath, blinking through the rising pall, and clamped the clay stem firmly between his teeth.

'Quite,' a muffled voice came from his side.

Forrester turned to the man who had spoken. He was tall, at least six foot, but that was all that was discernable through his jangling cage of siege armour. It was enormously heavy, Forrester knew, with thick plates at back and breast, more hanging across the thighs and a death's-head burgonet that completely encompassed the man's skull. All this was necessary, of course, for the man's occupation made him a target for every musket-wielding man and woman on Gloucester's walls.

'I'm looking for Mister Sang,' Forrester said. 'Chief engineer for this sector.'

'I am he,' came the muffled answer. The engineer carried a long-handled shovel, and he trudged laboriously across to a cluster of stone-filled gabions and leaned it against one so that he could lift his visor.

Forrester followed, upending his pipe and dropping it into the snapsack hanging from his shoulder. 'What's the bill looking like?'

Sang's face was deeply pitted, ravaged by some childhood disease, and his eyes were watery and red. He blew out his cheeks. 'Twenty-four of theirs.'

Forrester's brow shot up. 'Jesu, he must be running out of men at this rate. Ours?'

'Nearly as many.' Sang turned to survey the saps destroyed by the rebel sally. Rebuilding work had not yet started, and the teams of sappers in their mud-encrusted leather aprons stood around in small groups, unwilling and unable to return to their little valleys while the wicker screens were not in place. 'But it is the trench-works that matter.'

'And?'

'The damage is extensive. We lost quite a few tools and weapons, and the buggers detonated grenadoes all along this section. They came from the north, so I'm told.' He glanced at the looming edifice of Gloucester's East Gate. 'Swept down into the trenches all around here. It was ambitious, I'll give them that.'

'Though this be madness, yet there is method in't.'

'What's that?' Sang said. 'Marlow?'

'Shakespeare,' Forrester replied in a slightly admonishing tone. '*Hamlet*, Act 2, scene 2. And who could say it better? These raids seem mad enough, for Massie cannot have the manpower or ammunition to keep them up. Yet they play havoc with our lads' morale. I suppose that's the point of 'em.'

'And we must press on regardless,' Sang said, scanning the fallen screens that littered the ground beside each collapsed sap. 'Might I presume you're here to guard us, sir?'

'Indeed we are,' said Forrester. He looked back at the files of red-coated musketeers who waited a short way back from the trenches with Lieutenant Jays. He nodded to Jays, who began to bring them forward. 'The merry men of Mowbray's Foot.'

'From where do you hail, sir? Local?'

Forrester shook his head. 'Rather a hotchpotch, if I'm honest. Our colonel's estates are – *were* – in Hampshire, though God only knows what Puritan zealot owns 'em now. We began with men from thereabouts, as you'd imagine. But as the war's rolled on, we've recruited from whichever town we've been billeted. And, of course, a good many of us are veterans.'

Sang stared up at the gate and the figures of those who perched so defiantly upon it. 'How does this compare, sir?'

Forrester took a moment to think upon that, recalling the bloody battles and bitter sieges that had punctuated his formative years. 'Smaller in scale,' he said eventually, 'but harder on the heart.'

The engineer grasped his shovel. 'I'll set the men to work, sir.'

'You do that.'

Sang lowered his visor and hauled his right boot out of the mud, then the left, and repeated the process until he had achieved enough momentum to walk towards the siegeworks, his weighty armour making each movement painfully slow. The sappers saw him coming and began to stretch, grumble, and stoop to collect picks and hatchets or fasten filthy pads to their knees. Some went to fetch the wooden sledges they would use to drag away the excavated turf, while others waited in order to discuss covering fire with the advancing musketeers.

Forrester remained beside his gabion screen. The East Gate was well protected, the walls shored up by earth and incorporating some of the more robust houses built immediately adjacent to it, but it was still viewed as a weak point in the ring of defences, for it had not been afforded the formidable bastions of some of the ancient city's other great entrances. Yet success had been limited even here, the Royalist attacks repelled with scarcely fathomable ease, while audacious raids by the Parliamentarian garrison had pecked away at the will of the king's seemingly unstoppable force. Forrester wondered whether it was the reluctance to storm the city that had proven so costly, or perhaps the decision to award the ageing Earl of Forth overall command. He thought of Stratton, of the silent march of the Cornish troops, a move even bolder than anything Massie had conjured, and imagined what those mad-eyed men of Kernow might have done if they had been sent into the breach.

Well, that was all irrelevant for now. The grand Oxford Army and their Welsh allies would have to deal with the impudent folk of Gloucester in their own way. He watched the rampart as a sudden flurry of activity made it appear like a disturbed hive of bees. He noticed there was an artillery piece, a drake or something similar, mounted on the palisade, and men were scuttling about it. He shielded his eyes with a flattened palm and squinted against the sun, watching the animated bluecoats go about their business. Did they know what consternation they had caused in the Royalist encampment? He gave a rueful laugh. They probably had no idea. The senior officers seemed to be more jittery than ever this morning, as though the lack of progress had been highlighted to a nerve-shredding point by the night's daring sally. It was openly bandied about that Massie's stubborn force must surely be running low on powder and shot, but Forrester suspected that the Royalist provisions were hardly in rude health either. They had exhausted all the ammunition for the bigger cannon, which meant, until more could be sent from Oxford, they had no hope of opening another breach. Moreover, Lieutenant Colonel Baxter had muttered over dawn's bacon and eggs that he had heard the latest consignment of powder consisted of just five barrels. They had ordered fifty. He had not seen it for himself, but rumour was that Gilby's musketeers, recently up from Bristol, had been issued with six-shot bandoliers instead of the usual dozen, which proved the point well enough. Forrester wondered how long it would be before Mowbray's men felt the same austerity measures bite. And what would that do for morale?

'Christ, but we need to get in there soon,' Forrester muttered aloud. He suspected the engineers would begin undermining the walls as soon as the saps could reach them. Blow the whole thing sky-high as they had at Lichfield. As far as he was concerned, it could not happen soon enough. Gloucester was battered and bruised, but by no means beaten.

He was startled by a sharp cough from the walls, followed immediately by a scream that grew in pitch and intensity. An expanding ball of smoke raced out from the top of the enemy palisade like a gigantic mushroom, and Forrester felt himself duck, his legs buckling as a matter of instinct. He thrust himself against the gabion. All around, men did the same, dropping tools and scrambling for shelter, but not all could clear the slippery ground in time, and they scattered in all directions like hens before a fox. The scream became louder, and Forrester tasted blood as he bit the inside of his mouth.

The whining ball caught one of the sappers straight between the shoulders. It burst through him as though he were a pillar of butter, careening through spine and sinew in a shower of gore, ripping a tattered path through his shirt and apron. It seemed to lift him for a heartbeat, carry him away as though he had sprouted wings, and he flew the best part of ten yards before dropping into one of the saps, head down, legs splayed and upright, shoes thrust above the muddy bank like twin flag poles. They shook for a few seconds, beating the air while the man's blood and innards seeped into the shallow ditch. There were others in the sap, hiding from the murderous iron shot, and they stared, dumbstruck and horrified, at the man who had been snuffed out like a candle flame in a storm.

It fell silent, save for the jeers from the men up on the wall. They waved and whistled, slashed their blades in wide arcs that caught the sun, or shook their muskets like trophies above their heads. One man scampered along the rampart, arms out at his sides for balance as he danced a mocking jig.

In the trenches all was silent. Forrester stood. 'Get him out to the pit, lads!' He cast his gaze about at the nearest saps and their white-faced occupants. 'And get back to work!'

No indeed. Gloucester was far from beaten.

Near the North Wall, Gloucester, 17 August 1643

By two in the afternoon the sun was at its searing height, pulsing down upon the patchwork walls and cannon-pocked rooftops, driving most folk indoors to seek shelter. The rattle of musketry continued from all corners of the city, regulars and volunteers alike taking desultory pot shots at the engineers and diggers down in the trenches or at the soldiers making abortive approaches at various points in the sprawling encirclement. From the fortified camp – the leaguer – at Llanthony Priory, at the Rignall Stile, up at the Alvin Gate or across the water meadows to the north, the king's regiments came, but their efforts were singular, isolated affairs, each swatted away by defenders allocated to the most vulnerable points, immediately redistributed to quell the next attack when the last was at an end. The king's force was a vast beast with many heads, but instead of attacking with all its jaws at once, the Royalist hydra sent each to snap and harry in turn. Massie's bedraggled garrison cut off each head as it came.

As the gunfire crackled, a reed-thin man in a suit of black, with pale blue eyes and a thatch of blond hair poking chaotically from beneath a black hat, strode into one of the alleys not far from the earthen rampart to the north-west of the city. A distant burst of fire from a small artillery piece made him flinch and he cursed softly. Nikolas Robbens was a patient man, it came with his profession, but he had come to loathe Gloucester. Brought here for this most lucrative mission, he had been prepared to wait out the siege, which his employer claimed would swiftly end. Even when the situation had developed along a rather alarming tangent, he had made the most of the good supplies of food and ale, and the small but willing group of whores who frequented the taverns, but now things were becoming desperate. The rebels hereabouts were a stubborn bunch, it seemed, and the king's army appeared only to grow in size beyond the walls. Robbens feared things would end bloodily, and he did not like it.

He stalked along the alleyway, glancing left and right at the doors on either side of the stuffy path, checking all were tight shut, and stopped only when he reached the very middle. Out of the darkest shadows came the man he had been expecting; a huge fellow whose meaty frame had once been impressively muscular but which had run mostly to fat with advancing years. They exchanged a nod, waiting silently in the shade of the bow-framed houses for the third man to arrive. That man came in less than a minute, scuttling from the far end of the narrow walkway, his profound limp and twisted spine making him grimace as he moved. He looked up at the biggest of the three. 'All clear, Slager.'

The leader of the furtive trio nodded. 'Good.' He was tall as well as broad, with a vast slab of flesh hanging like a bulging sack over his belt, and he rested massive palms on it as he spoke. 'I have called this meeting because I would show you something.'

'You said I would get an opportunity, Slager,' Robbens cut in. His face was clean-shaven and blemish free, but the anxiety was etched deep into the lines at the corners of his mouth. 'A clear shot.'

Slager peered down at him over wiry auburn whiskers. 'And you will, Nikolas. You will.'

'When?' Robbens pressed. His ice-blue eyes met Slager's defiantly. 'This city will fall any day now.'

'Oh?' Slager chuckled in deep tones. 'Have you seen the mess they have made of their cursed siege?'

'I have seen how little powder the garrison has left.'

'And have the king's men fared any better? Their small cannon do nothing to our walls, and the big ones have been silent these two days. They've run out of shot, I'd wager, so now they must sit and stare at us.' Slager spat derisively. 'The malignants are pathetic. Ten thousand flies on a bullock's rump.'

Robbens lifted a hand to fiddle with the silken strands at his earlobe. 'What if you're wrong?'

'Then I will guarantee your protection, as I have this last month. If Massie loses his nerve, I will ensure we three are exchanged with the rest of the high-rankers.' Slager planted a hand on Robbens' shoulder. It felt like an anvil had been dropped on him. 'Trust me, Nikolas. Have I not ensured your safety before? Did I not kill Jonas Crick with my own hands when he threatened to betray us?'

The man with the crooked back and awkward gait shuffled forward. 'That you did, Slager. Taught the bugger a—'

'Hush, Nobbs,' Slager hissed, rounding on the much smaller man with a face like thunder. 'Keep quiet, damn you, or you'll find yourself in the moat.'

Nobbs clamped shut his lips with a shivering nod.

'When will I get the shot, Slager?' Robbens asked under his breath. 'When? First you said Massie would surrender and I'd get my chance when they negotiated terms. Then you claimed he would not surrender, but it did not matter, because the King would parley in person.' He squinted up and down the alley, dropping his voice further. 'Now we are trapped here like rats in a fucking barrel.'

Slager glowered. 'What concern is it of yours, Nikolas? The successful conclusion of this mission will see your death.'

'And my death will secure my brothers' future.'

Slager stepped closer to the Dutchman so that Robbens could smell the tang of small beer on his breath. 'Listen to me. You are mine. I am paying you a fortune to do a job and I expect you to do it without question. Understand?'

'Then let me do it,' Robbens implored. 'That is all I ask.'

As if for answer, Slager pushed past him, forcing him against the wall of the nearest house with his lumbering bulk. Robbens and Nobbs followed in his wake, half in curiosity, half in frustration. They went north, out of the alleyway and into the open ground between the homes and the hastily piled defences. There were musketeers on the slope, some lying back in the warm sun, ostensibly loading their muskets, though most were tamping pipes and basking in the beating rays. A more diligent few were nestled against the wicker blinds protruding from the palisade, aiming their weapons across at an enemy who offered but sporadic fire in return.

'They will not parley,' Slager said as he acknowledged a couple of the bluecoats. He began to scale the gently sloping earthwork. It was not as steep as the works to the south that buttressed the high stone wall, and Robbens followed him easily. 'The King is embarrassed by his failure here, so he cannot be seen to show weakness, while Massie is simply too stubborn to surrender.' He reached the summit, staring down at the low-lying land that fringed this part of Gloucester. 'But you can still get close.'

'What you talkin' about, Slager?' Nobbs panted. It had been a difficult ascent for him, and he stretched out his upper torso with a chorus of sickening crunches. 'The whole point o' this plan was cos we couldn't get close enough. That's why we've been traipsin' across the country waiting for the bugger to come to us.'

Slager inspected the flat terrain. Immediately outside the wall was the eastward limb of the River Severn, splitting the city from the waterlogged meadow of Little Mead. That meadow appeared like a gigantic chessboard, large swathes appearing almost black where the courageous women had cut away the turf, all within range of Vavasour's men. Some patches remained green, though they were shorn to stubble by the city's cattle, which grazed on the site. Immediately north of Little Mead were the rambling enemy lines, stretching off towards Kingsholm in the east and Over to the west. It was a wonder that the beasts had not been killed or rustled by the surrounding Royalists.

Slager peered over the protective blind to follow the course of the river, as it glimmered against the outer glacis. 'That was necessary before.'

Nobbs screwed up his narrow face. 'Before what?'

'Before we became trusted members of this garrison.' Slager's voice was as sure as ever, but his eyes seemed lost in the progress of the Severn, mesmerized by the glimmering surface and the gurgled whisper. 'It is not wide here,' he said. 'Nor so fast-flowing.'

'He's lost it,' Nobbs muttered.

Slager looked up abruptly. 'Shut your mouth, Nobbs, or I'll shut it for you.' He turned back to stare down into the city. 'I know every inch of this place. Cannon placements, fighting numbers, powder reserves.'

Robbens frowned. 'So?'

'So I will tell it all to you.'

'And what will I do with it?' the assassin asked, nonplussed.

The fat man went back to the blind and studied the river once more, his eyes transfixed as though he counted the very pebbles on its silted bed. 'You, Nikolas? You will go and tell good King Charles.'

CHAPTER 15

West of London, 18 August 1643

The cell was dank and dark, lit only by the chinks of light breaking through below the sturdy door. Its walls were made of stone, which, mercifully, kept it cool despite the raging sun outside, and in places tentacles of slime spread from ceiling to floor.

Lisette Gaillard woke in a panic, failing to remember where she was, but soon the stagnant air kicked her senses like an angry cob and she swore softly. She was sitting on the brick floor, legs crossed and shoulders pressed against the wall. She scraped her cheek gingerly with the tips of her fingers. It throbbed at the contact and she winced.

'Still painful?'

Lisette peered through the gloom to where her fellow captive sat. '*Oui.*'

'You dream of your *amour*?' Cecily Cade asked.

That was a shrewd thrust. Lisette was rendered mute for a moment. 'I—'

'You spoke in your sleep.'

Lisette was glad it was too dark for Cecily to see her blush. 'What did I say?'

'I know not. You spoke French. The hint lay in the tone, more than the words.'

Lisette thought of the dream. The swirling images of a man dressed in black, with a wide hat that concealed a once handsome face, long since ravaged by the world's wickedness. Stryker. She leaned forwards, hugging knees to her chest. 'You would think me a fool. *I* think me a fool. All this time, I had hope of him coming for us. For me.' She forced herself to laugh, though a deep ache pulsed at her ribs. 'Foolish nonsense. And what of your man?'

'I told you, Lisette,' Cecily said dismissively. 'His was a tryst that never took place. A near dalliance that I let fizzle out like wet powder, all for my hubris. We are both fools, you and I.' Minutes slipped past before Cecily spoke again. 'He'll come for us, won't he?'

'Collings? Eventually, though he might make us sweat in here for a while.'

'I wonder where we are.'

Lisette remembered what they had been told when first they had been unceremoniously incarcerated in this modest stone building. 'To the west of the capital, the bastard Wallis said.' She peered at the door and the ceiling in turn. 'Though I feel I have been here before. Strange.' She thought of the blow that had felled her in her moment of escape. Of the bearded fiend looming over her, knocking her into a silent abyss. 'I would like to flay the skin off his bones.'

'He might have killed you, Lisette,' Cecily chided gently. 'You are lucky he did not.'

Lisette snorted derisively. 'Lucky? To be saved so that the bloody rebels can stretch my neck is not what I consider lucky.' She touched the bruise again. It smarted but would heal well enough. The Royalist troop, so close to saving them, had, according to Cecily, trotted straight past the secreted blackcoats, completely unaware of Collings' personal militiamen. The chance had drifted by as Lisette lay sprawled in the leaves. She looked up, making out Cecily's undefined silhouette. 'Does the gold really exist?'

'Yes,' said Cecily.

'How much is there?'

'Hard to say. It is plate, mostly. Difficult to value.'

Lisette imagined a gleaming horde of wide plates and intricate salvers, of golden decanters and bejewelled ornaments. A welcome contrast in this murky hole. 'But a lot?'

Cecily's silhouette bobbed. 'A lot.'

What could such riches secure for the Royalist war effort, Lisette wondered? She had once seen a vast ordnance piece in Paris. It was said that such a beast weighed eight thousand pounds and could fling a 64-pound shot nearly a mile. It was a castle-killer. 'Enough to buy a Cannon Royal?'

Cecily sniffed to show that she did not much care for the type or value of large siege cannon. 'Enough to buy as many of those as the King would like, I'm sure.'

For the first time, the real possibility of such wealth manifested itself in Lisette's mind's eye. It could change the course of the war. 'No wonder Collings wants it.' She leaned forwards eagerly. 'Where is it, Cecily? Where is the treasure?'

'My father died to protect it, Lisette,' Cecily said firmly, 'and I will do the same if necessary. The King will hear me speak of it, and none other.'

Lisette grunted and slumped back against the wall to sulk, but her thoughts only gathered pace. They led her to a room full of glowing gold and winking jewels, of plate that could be melted to coin and of sturdy chests brimful of possibility. Sir Alfred Cade's treasure verily shone amid the darkness of the cell. One thing was clear; she had to get Cecily to the Royalist lines. Whatever the cost.

Near the Alvin Gate, Gloucester, 18 August 1643

The dawn tour of the walls ended in the north, where Edward Massie reviewed a restless mob of over four hundred musketeers clustered in muttering excitement by the Alvin Gate.

The young governor paced slowly, nodding to any who might catch his eye, offering his blessing on their forthcoming enterprise, but his mind was elsewhere. His thoughts were of tumbling, bewildering numbers. He calculated the city's food supplies and tussled with the needs of the rapidly growing housing crisis. He considered the ever depleting stores of powder at the modest little church of St Mary de Crypt on Southgate Street, which had been commandeered for use as the garrison magazine, versus the reserves of ammunition, and wondered how best to man the walls when more men died every day. It was getting desperate, and with the enemy saps creeping ever closer like a spreading canker, it would not be long before a more concerted assault came. He thanked God that the huge demi-cannon out on Gaudy Green had been rendered mute, but surely even that unlikely miracle could not last. They were into the ninth day of the siege, far longer than any had imagined they would survive, and that was something of which the people of Gloucester could be immensely proud. The tactic of disrupting the enemy engineering work, continual vigilance against artillery bombardment, and the occasional raid against the Royalist lines had proven more fruitful than any dared hope, but how many more weeks could they endure? They had plentiful enough water, for God had kept the wells full despite the Royalists having cut off the main supply conduits at the springs on Robinswood Hill, but that was almost an irrelevance. What Massie needed – what he prayed for with every passing hour – was an army. Messages had been sent days ago, yet no relief force had appeared. No host of avengers marched over the eastern hills behind the banners of Essex or Waller. But what could he expect? The most recent reports placed Waller back in London, scratching around for men to replace the army that had been shattered up on Roundway Down. The Earl of Essex at least had an army, but it was laid low by some pestis that refused to relent, forcing him to stay put, festering uselessly in the Thames Valley. The situation seemed as hopeless as ever, and yet here they were. Massie breathed in and out slowly, letting the chill air settle his nerves as he paced before the heavily armed throng. He had taken a risk by refusing to surrender the city, one that would make his name, however the outcome. The die had been well and truly cast, and he must hold Gloucester with as much vigour and ingenuity as he could summon. The morning's raid would be the biggest yet, and with any luck the enemy would know that the end was far from nigh.

'God with you, men!' Massie shouted over the heads of the bristling multitude.

They gave a cheer made half-hearted by tension, and turned as one to their commander for the dawn enterprise.

Major Marmaduke Pudsey stepped out from the side of the party. He was tall and lean, with straggly iron-grey hair and a face weathered to a leathery toughness. He stared hard at the largest body of men the city had yet mustered for a single operation, and nodded in satisfaction. 'You'll do.'

The men grinned. 'Let us at 'em, Major!' a voice piped from the back.

Edward Massie shared the smiles, for he was fond of these tough men, turned to diamond-hard veterans in such a short time. He bowed to Pudsey, a man who had had his utmost esteem ever since volunteering to take the initial declaration of defiance to the king, and left him to his duty.

Massie and his entourage, made smaller today by the need to post extra eyes down on the south and east walls because many of the regular defenders had been diverted to where they now stood, strode to the Alvin Gate bastion and climbed to its summit. From there he swept his perspective glass from right to left, perusing the dark tentacles of the Royalist works, the eagle-eyed musketeers in amongst the ruined northern suburbs and the new artillery pieces brought downstream from Worcester to reinforce Vavasour's Welshmen. It was those cannon that would be the target.

Massie lowered the glass. He glanced to his right. 'Captain?'

A tall man dressed in black turned to him. He was lean, but moved with a predatory confidence that spoke of innate strength. His face was narrow, coloured in places by the blue and yellow wisps of barely healed bruises, and a huge, mottled patch of scar tissue obscured the place where his left eye should have been. His right eye, though puffy from recent damage, seemed to dance with a silvery shimmer as he moved in the new sun. 'Governor?'

'Would you be kind enough to tell Lieutenant Pincock that Pudsey is ready?'

'Aye, sir.'

'Just so, Captain. Just so.'

Stryker moved from the bastion down to ground level, and found one of Massie's runners. 'Lieutenant Pincock is out towards the West Gate?'

The runner nodded. 'He is, sir, aye.'

'Tell him to make his move.'

'Now, sir?'

'Now.'

The boy scampered off along the line of the northern earthworks while Stryker returned to the Alvin Gate. His injuries still hurt, some of them terribly, but the recent action had gone a long way to reinvigorating him. A new energy coursed through his veins, and he welcomed it. It made him feel alive. Made him feel useful. But for whom was this usefulness employed? A pang of guilt hit him as he walked, knotting his guts so that his stride faltered.

'What are you doing?' he whispered at his boots. 'What in God's name are you doing?'

Up high, Massie and the others had seen him, and they were gesticulating for him to return. Evidently, Pudsey's daring sally was underway. He quickened his pace, eager to witness the raid, though the realization that he truly wished the bold manoeuvre success made him feel all the more guilty.

What *was* he doing? At every turn he had consoled his troubled conscience with the fact that he could hardly claim to have turned rebel and then refuse to fight. And who had sent him into the damned town in the first place, but Prince Rupert and his creature, Killigrew. The fault, he told himself – the treachery – was theirs.

He could honestly say that he had no new-found love for the Parliamentarian cause. But the people of Gloucester needed men who knew how to fight, and part of him offered

267

that knowledge freely in return for the admiration he had gained for them during his time behind their battered walls. More compelling still was the presence of Vincent Skaithlocke. There had been a time when Stryker would have followed the colonel through hell's inferno, if it had been asked of him. He had thought such blinkered loyalty had faded with the passing of so many years, replaced by world-weary cynicism nurtured by a life where death and cruelty had become commonplace. Yet now, confronted by his old tutor, *rescued* by him, no less, from torture and certain death, that long-forgotten compulsion had renewed its pull in a way that he found difficult to deny.

He reached the summit, clattered along the fire-step behind the staked palisade, and joined the governor's party to watch the unfolding skirmish. Lieutenant Pincock, they were told, was advancing as planned. The young officer, finding himself with more responsibility since James Harcus' death, had taken fifty musketeers across the Little Mead in a diversionary attack, and, though they could not yet see his progress from this position, the noise of frantic musketry was already pummelling the dawn.

Below them, Pudsey's much larger force was moving swiftly northwards. They ran, swarming through the tumbledown brickwork of the flattened suburbs, smashing the protective screens and overwhelming the Royalist trenches. Stryker watched in astonishment as the king's men buckled against the surging tide. The feint to the north-west had taken the besiegers' focus away from the Alvin Gate, but the sheer size of the sally party simply overwhelmed them. They turned tail, scattering in all directions like rats before a terrier, all the while harassed and bloodied by Pudsey's musketeers. The rebels fired in teams, loosing their musket-balls, not bothering to pause to reload but reversing the weapons to use as clubs. They tossed grenadoes in high arcs to clear the sticky saps, leaping through the smoke clouds to take the next obstacle, snatching up tools and weapons where they found them. In moments they had overrun the first of Vavasour's two batteries. A single, black-mouthed cannon had been placed directly before the Alvin Gate, and enough of Pudsey's men turned to wave up at the watching garrison for Stryker to know that the big gun had been successfully spiked.

Major Pudsey did not stop there. He took his men on, charging up the old road towards the village of Kingsholm, where a new, larger battery had been constructed. This one held three cannon, and the bluecoats found that the Welsh infantrymen based there had, like their compatriots, been duped by the diversion at Little Mead. They reached the battery with surprising ease, slaughtering those gunners foolish enough to stand and fight, and Stryker knew that they would be hurriedly driving nails into the touch-holes of the forbidding pieces, rendering them impotent for hours to come.

The battle grew louder suddenly, as more muskets were fired and more smoke slewed sideways across the fields, and it was clear that Vavasour's men had finally managed to regroup and go on the offensive. They pushed out of their lines at Kingsholm, shooting and snarling their way southwards as one of Pudsey's trumpeters gave the shrill call to retreat. The fight was nasty, men fell on both sides, but from up high Stryker could see that Pudsey's men had had the best of it. They were falling back towards the walls now, though blue-coated bodies still slumped to the ground, and the folk all along Gloucester's rampart bellowed their encouragement, beckoning them to safety.

Massie was beaming. He was a reserved character to Stryker's mind, pensive and quiet, but even he pumped the air with a fist and openly gave his thanks to God. The others on the bastion, a couple of officers, Alderman Pury and Colonel Skaithlocke, patted him on the back and shook hands with one another. Marmaduke Pudsey would come back a hero, Massie had forged yet another inroad into the Royalist siegeworks, and the city could breathe easy for a few more precious hours.

Stryker realized that he too was grinning. It had been a marvel to watch. He was no Parliamentarian, but perhaps, he silently conceded, he was a rebel.

The eastern trenches, Gloucester, 19 August 1643

Prince Rupert of the Rhine stalked through the trench, the glow of the lantern making his eyes glint like an owl on the hunt. Night had not come quick enough on a day that had been catastrophic for his uncle's great army.

'Will we be out here long, sir?'

Rupert stopped abruptly, turning on his heels to glower down at the man who had to run to keep up with his long stride. 'All night, Killigrew, so get used to it.'

Ezra Killigrew grimaced, his sharp teeth unnaturally white behind the lantern he held at arm's length to light his master's way. 'It is dangerous, General. They'll shoot at you.'

Rupert cast him a withering look. 'It is midnight, Killigrew. They cannot bloody see me.' He motioned that they should continue their progress, and the dumpy aide scurried to keep up once more. 'We gave ourselves ten days.'

'Highness?' Killigrew chirped.

Rupert did not stop this time. 'Ten days to complete this damnable siege. It is almost up.'

'They've been stubborn,' Killigrew offered unhelpfully.

'We have been incompetent, Ezra.' He spat at the side of the trench. 'Feeble.'

'But Forth is in charge, Highness,' Killigrew said.

'*Ha!*' Rupert barked without mirth. 'It is all of us who risk our reputations, and you know it. Forth, aye, but me also. Astley, Vavasour, Falkland. Even the King himself will lose face.'

'You wanted to storm at the very beginning, Highness. It was you who told them not to sit and wait.'

'But I did not get my wish, Killigrew,' Rupert replied, his faint accent thickened by his brooding, 'and now my argument will be conveniently forgotten. It was I who sued for the taking of Gloucester, that is what will be whispered by the Queen's faction. The manner of the taking will not feature in their poisonous games.'

'What will you do?'

'I would still launch an escalade, but it is forbidden,' Rupert said morosely. 'The Council have decided to increase the bombardment.'

'Increase?' Killigrew echoed incredulously. 'But we are low on powder, and our larger cannon have no ammunition at all.'

Rupert stepped over a basket full of tools of various shapes and sizes. A sapper had been sitting nearby, and he rose quickly, doffing his cap. Rupert nodded to him, oblivious of the way the man shrank beneath his hawkish stare. 'We have enough powder and shot for the smaller pieces. We will concentrate our efforts around those, hammering the walls for as long as it takes.'

'To what end?'

'It is hoped Massie will be intimidated into surrender. And if not,' he added before Killigrew could question the strategy, 'we will be making every effort to bridge their cursed moat with faggots. The bombardment will provide covering fire.'

'We pulverize the city with the design to force surrender,' Killigrew said. 'All the while filling the ditch for an assault if the cannons fail.'

'Correct,' the prince confirmed.

'And why are we slopping through the saps, Highness?'

Now Rupert stopped. 'Because we construct a new battery during the night, ready for the bombardment in the morning. I would see it sighted properly. And our men in these trenches need to see me. They need encouragement. I will not skulk at Prinknash Park when I should be showing the scrofulous rebels that I am not afraid of them.'

A stone hit Prince Rupert on the side of the head, denting his helmet and plopping into the mud between his boots. He reeled sideways, thrusting a hand out against the wall of the trench to steady himself, mud oozing between the fingers of his exquisite kid–skin gloves. He straightened quickly, face creased in boiling fury, and stared up at the walls. From the rampart came the unmistakable sound of laughter.

Near the Cross, Gloucester, 19 August 1643

The bombardment had only been underway for an hour when Stryker met Skaithlocke in the centre of the city, yet he felt as though his ears would bleed at any moment. The Royalist gunners had been unleashed for a morning of sport, and their evil iron had smashed at the walls and at the rooftops and at the minds of Gloucester's people.

'Where are these men, sir?' he called above the din of cannon fire and falling masonry. The Royalists had evidently decided to mount their biggest artillery offensive yet, the small six, twelve and fifteen pounders rattling away to the east and south. They still apparently lacked ammunition for the demi–cannon, for that seemed the only reasonable explanation for the silence of the only guns capable of breaching the walls, but the sporadic fire shook Gloucester's introverted world, nevertheless.

Vincent Skaithlocke strode out from under the lintel of a stooped old bakery. He pointed to a range of buildings located across the road. A pair of bluecoats waited outside. 'Over there.'

Massie had dispersed the garrison into eighteen different posts, and one such unit, of 120 men, was permanently stationed at the very core of Gloucester to ensure, as Skaithlocke now wryly observed, that its rebel heart still beat.

'He said he wished to learn the state of their morale,' Stryker said, walking beside his former commanding officer.

'Aye,' Skaithlocke's huge head bobbed, the thick rolls of flesh at the back of his neck squashing against one another like dough being kneaded. 'It is important for a leader to know such things, is it not?'

Stryker flinched as a cannonball whistled overhead to pluck a chimney pot from its roof. A woman screamed near by, though the shot did nothing more than topple bricks, which would straightway be put to good use elsewhere. 'I sense the mood is positive.'

'And it is, generally speaking,' Skaithlocke agreed. 'But logic would say it cannot hold indefinitely. We are surviving for now, son, but how can a city last with no hope of relief? Eventually it must run out of food or powder or lead or water. Some will pre empt that inevitability and try to escape.'

'How?' Stryker asked, fighting to keep his tone neutral, though his mind was tumbling. Skellen had accused him of a reluctance to escape, and he had denied it, citing a lack of credible chances. He had been genuinely angry when his sergeant had questioned the stance, but perhaps Skellen had been right. Had he truly considered all the opportunities?

As if in answer, Skaithlocke looked back at him with a rueful chuckle. 'Men always find a way out of their predicaments, Innocent. If they want it badly enough.'

The bluecoats stationed around the Cross were not the kind Massie needed to worry about. They filed out of their makeshift billets, weapons clean and ready for action, and gathered in tight files for inspection. Their leader, a fresh-faced captain in his early twenties, proudly put them through some cursory drills to prove the reliability and competence of his charges, and bowed when Skaithlocke commended his diligence.

The howl reached them long before they saw it, and all eyes jerked skyward, fingers cupped as shields against the sun. The company disintegrated as rapidly as it had come together, the front ranks backing away, the rear ranks shunting forwards, as the screeching wail grew inexorably louder. There were old men, too frail to volunteer for active service, walking by, as were women and children, and everyone twisted round, craning their heads to the clear sky. Stryker scrunched up his scarred face to ward off the blinding rays, as he searched for the harbinger of King Charles' fury. And there it was; a black fleck against the blue. It grew with every second, like a tick gorging itself on blood, and still the noise increased.

'*Mortar*!' someone shouted, and the call immediately echoed throughout the streets.

Stryker took up the call, walking backwards, never taking his eye from the incoming projectile. Mortar shells were worse than cannonballs in a siege. The latter were primarily used for breaching walls, perhaps blowing a few holes in the houses beyond for good measure, but once they had reached their target, the terror was over. But a mortar was a wicked thing, designed to cause maximum carnage and horror. Its sole purpose was to lob explosive shells from a high trajectory into the midst of beleaguered garrisons in order to set buildings ablaze and shred morale. Stryker had faced the wide guns, like squat black toads, many times, most recently at Lichfield. There, he had set teams to discover the shells before they exploded and dowse the maniacal fuse with water. But even as this newest shell dropped into the city, he knew he would be too late. It would fall too far away, and nothing could be done. He bellowed for folk to take cover, for the musketeers to retreat to their stone-built quarters, but it all happened so quickly.

The mortar struck the street some fifty paces away. It bounced, but most of its force had been cushioned by the mud, and it rolled a few feet. The nearest people scattered, diving for shelter anywhere they might. For a second it seemed as though the shell would lay dormant, its fuse damaged by the impact, but then an almighty explosion ripped through the centre of the city. A vast gout of black smoke roiled up, spreading down every road and alley in the vicinity, and molten hot metal fragments cartwheeled in all directions.

A moment's silence followed, save the hissing of the boiling roadway. Heads poked gingerly over walls and round door frames, between window shutters and through interlaced fingers. Stryker had not found safety and was curled in a ball near the Cross. Skaithlocke was with him, and both men unfurled their limbs with cautious slowness and stood. Before Skaithlocke could finish his prayer of thanks, a terrible scream sang out. This time it was not fear that gave the woman her voice, but pain, and heads turned to the mouth of one of the alleyways.

Stryker ran to the source of the noise. A large woman in a threadbare shawl lay on her back. One of her scarlet-coated hands was clawing at her chest, and it was clear that she had been hit by a metal shard. It had spun from the shell, part of the thick casing, and carved a large hole above her sternum. Already her shawl and the garments beneath were blooming with the rose-petal redness of fresh blood. It pumped freely, unstoppably, and, though Stryker made a show of tearing her shawl to strips and pushing them against the wound, he knew that she would bleed out in, quite literally, a matter of heartbeats. A young girl knelt over her, squeezing the injured woman's hand in both of her own and rocking back and forth like a Tom o' Bedlam.

The woman gasped suddenly, opened her eyes wide, then visibly relaxed. The air seeped from her body in a gentle hiss, and her mouth lolled open. Stryker knelt with the girl.

'I am sorry,' he said awkwardly, and reached out to ease the lifeless eyes shut.

Skaithlocke was with them now, and he placed big hands on his fleshy hips. 'See to this, men!' he boomed at the emerging bluecoats. 'Get her out of here!'

It struck Stryker as a callous response, but Skaithlocke was a professional and should not be expected to behave in a weakly compassionate way. He got the job done, as he always had, and already the soldiers, dazed though they were, had come running to do his bidding.

Stryker stood, staring down at the torn flesh that glistened at the poor woman's chest. 'Jesu.'

Skaithlocke turned away with a shrug. '*C'est la vie*, as your Lisette would say.'

Stryker felt his jaw drop. 'Colonel?'

'Losses are a fact of war, son.'

'Fact of war?' Stryker repeated, baffled by the big man's nonchalance. 'A civilian had her lungs ripped open by a lump of mortar shell, sir.'

Skaithlocke stopped, his brow rising as he looked back. 'Civilian? There are no real civilians, Innocent. No real innocents,' he added with an impish smirk.

Stryker grasped his friend's elbow, tugging him back. 'You are a man of the rebellion, Colonel. Not just for the money, but for your conscience, too. You said so yourself.'

Skaithlocke shook him off easily. His bright eyes were darker somehow, his mouth set in a thin line. 'Let us simply say that the fortunes of this cursed little town are not high on my agenda.'

'You are not a rebel?' Stryker blurted in disbelief. 'After all, you—'

'Oh, I am for the Parliament, son,' Skaithlocke interrupted. 'More than you know.'

'More than I know? You're making no sense, sir.'

Skaithlocke stared down at him for a lingering moment, rubbing a grubby hand across his auburn beard. 'Perhaps it is time.'

Stryker shook his head in bewilderment. 'Time? Time for what?'

Skaithlocke rolled back his shoulders, bringing himself to his full, daunting height, and clicked his tongue against his teeth. 'No. You are not ready. Not yet.' He walked away, long strides carrying him quickly across the debris-strewn ground.

Stryker followed for a futile ten paces. 'Sir?' he shouted in the bulky mercenary's wake. 'I don't understand.'

'No, son, you do not,' Skaithlocke boomed in response. He glanced over his shoulder. 'But you will. In time, you will know all, I promise.'

The city centre, Gloucester, 19 August 1643

Nikolas Robbens loved his hair. It was thick, lustrous and as beautiful as spun gold. The ladies, he reflected, always loved it too. He ran a hand through it, luxuriating in its thick strength.

'Must I really go?' the girl grumbled at the closed door.

Robbens shook himself from his reverie. 'Yes, my love, I have work to do.'

'What work?'

She was a red-headed firebrand, this one, who had sat on his lap in the tavern and not moved, even when he had made to stand. Robbens had thought it churlish to toss her to the rushes, so he had thrust his hands beneath her rump and carried her up to his chamber. Such was her lithe energy that it had been a vigorous night's work. The downside, he now reflected, was that she was not as easy to shed as the others.

He rolled his eyes. 'What is it about the women of this bloody town? They ask questions with every breath they draw.'

The redhead glowered. 'Women? There haven't been others have there, Nikolas?'

Robbens brandished a broad, white-toothed smile. 'Of course not, Tilda, my radiant buttercup.'

Tilda folded her arms. 'Then why?'

The Dutchman was barefoot, and he moved silently to the doorway. He slid both hands through the curtain of her copper fringe and cupped her cheeks. 'An expression is all,' he said, tilting her face up to meet his. 'Just a manner of speaking from my homeland.' He leaned in, and she did not resist, so he let his lips close with hers. He lingered there for long enough to know that her ire had ebbed, before parting wetly. 'Now be gone.'

Tilda pouted. 'And you'll come find me later?'

'After dark, Tilda,' he promised, 'you have my oath.'

Robbens watched her leave, drinking in the sway of her hips as she padded along the landing and disappeared down the spiral staircase. Shutting the door, he stalked back to the palliasse and sat down to pull on his boots. Pausing briefly to wiggle his toes, he stood up, ran a hand through his hair again, and went to the windowsill where he kept his looking glass. He took it up in one hand, drawing a small, fine blade from his waistband with the other. He walked back across the echoing floorboards to a deep basin of water, and stooped so that his head was entirely submerged. The coldness sent shockwaves through his body and he juddered involuntarily. Straightening, he tossed back his head, showering his voluminous shirt and the waxed floorboards in a hundred droplets, and lifted the glass. There it was as ever. His proud, handsome face, framed in gold. He sighed heavily, cursed quietly as he raised the knife, and began to shave his head.

CHAPTER 16

The Palace of Westminster, London, 20 August 1643

Erasmus Collings kept a brisk pace along the gloomy corridor. It was six in the evening, still light outside, though one would never know it in Westminster's coney warren of candlelit passages and wood-panelled chambers. He hated it here, where there were the low whispers in every corner and where every hallway pattered with clerks scurrying about their worthless lives like so many rats; where abounded the mumblings of assiduous grey-beards who now ran things in this new, monarch-less society. Collings was not one of those dour bastards; he was no Puritanical hypocrite hiding behind prayer as he slaughtered his way to power. In truth, he was a product of the old ways, of a nation led by kings and a valued elite. But trade had made him truly wealthy, and it was trade that suffered from the current king's overreaching policies. Charles, therefore, would have to be removed.

He found a clerk he recognized at the end of the corridor and ordered the stooped old palliard to show him to the correct room. The man muttered something begrudging but shuffled off nevertheless. Collings made a mental note. The fellow and his kin would pay for his rudeness.

'Here, sir,' the clerk said as he stopped by one door in a row of half a dozen. 'He has company.'

Collings gave a nasty smirk. 'Company? Some thick-thighed slattern, eh?'

The clerk covered his lips with an ink-stained hand. 'Of course not, sir.'

Collings laughed and pushed open the door, leaving the outraged servant in his wake. He strode across the echoing floorboards to stand before a paper-strewn table beneath the room's only window. There he nodded casually to the two men seated behind, each with a stack of reports and lists and orders to examine. 'Gentlemen.'

One of the men looked up. 'One day you will regret your brash arrogance, Collings.'

'Sir,' Collings replied coolly. He doubted the warning very much. John Pym could admonish him all he liked, but the old man was dying, and everybody knew it.

'Marriage between our cousins does not make us familiar.' Pym was as soberly dressed as ever, the very reflection of a good Puritan. But even in the few weeks since last they had met, the nominal leader of Parliament had become gaunt and frail, the skin of his face appearing even more pale than usual against the dark bristles of his beard and whiskers. He slowly moved his head to indicate the man seated at his right hand. 'You know Sir Henry Vane?'

Collings bowed. 'Your servant, sir.' He looked back at Pym. 'I see the hurly-burly is quelled.'

Pym sat back, letting the creaking frame of the chair take what little weight he now had. 'If you mean the peace riots, aye. They were dealt with.'

Ever the one for understatement, Collings thought. The orderly little man was not known as King Pym for nothing. He was a political genius, a calculated mover in a world of treachery and deceit, and the chief architect of the Stuart dynasty's imminent downfall. Any challenge to the authority of the Parliament will have been swiftly and brutally crushed, whatever careful description Pym might attach to it. Collings smiled. 'Glad to hear it. Can't have an army of dirty sluts calling your word into question, can we, sir?'

'Enough chatter,' Vane rumbled at Pym's side. 'What news?'

Collings let his gaze drift away from Pym. Vane was another steeped in intrigue and politics, and weaned on the stabbing of backs. He was a powerful man, had once even served as the king's secretary of state before choosing the Parliament's side at the outbreak of war. Collings was not as familiar with Vane as he was with Pym, and he chose to tread a more respectful path. 'I have her,' he said triumphantly.

'What, sir?' Vane, in his early fifties, was still an imposing figure, with thick greying hair, a brush of a moustache and a burly frame. He folded his arms, digging big hands into the black folds of his slashed doublet, and peered up at Collings, jaw set belligerently. 'Do you expect congratulations, Major General Collings? Some kind of reward, perhaps?' He thrust out an accusatory finger. 'When it was you who lost her?'

Collings returned Vane's unpleasant stare. ' I lost her amid a riot caused by the lowly drabs of London. People who should have been under your control.'

'Enough,' Pym ordered. His voice was soft, cracking pitifully, but the antagonists fell silent all the same. The most powerful cog in the rebellion's machine scrutinized Collings' face. 'She is properly secure this time?'

'She is, sir, though I doubt I will get anything useful from her.'

'Oh?'

Collings spread his delicate palms. 'Refuses to speak.' He shrugged. 'You know what course I would take, sir.'

Pym shook his head. 'No torture.'

'But—'

Pym held up a hand to intercept. 'We have danced this reel many a time, General Collings, and the answer is the same. You will not torture women.'

Women of gentle birth, at any rate, Collings thought bitterly. If the bitch had been a peasant, he would have been authorized to flay the skin off her spine without so much as a moment's hesitation. 'She will starve herself to death.'

Pym's round eyes narrowed. 'You will not torture her, sir. Bring her back to the capital. I would speak with her. Gentle persuasion may be the key that will turn this particular lock.'

You'll be dead before she breathes a word, Collings thought. 'Very well,' he grunted, deciding it best not to tell the stuffy old God-botherers about the second woman in his charge. The French spy could spread her legs for Wallis and his men, and have her neck stretched for the privilege.

'Besides,' Pym went on, 'your talents are required elsewhere.'

Collings shifted his feet and linked his hands behind his back. 'Elsewhere?'

'You've heard of Gloucester?'

Collings smiled. 'A city in the West Country, sir.'

Pym sighed in exasperation. 'A razor wit as ever, Major General. Have you heard the news?'

'Plenty,' Collings nodded, 'though what is true is at best debatable. They say the governor, little more than a stripling, holds out against the best the King has to offer. I heard one rumour that he fuelled his fighters with strong drink, another that his entire garrison is comprised only of women and children.' He recalled the Royalist news-book he had read that very day. '*Mercurius Aulicus* claims his stubbornness has cost the city hundreds of souls, while our own sheets proclaim his fighters have killed more than two thousand malignants in what has, it is suggested, become rather a dog's breakfast for our stammering sovereign and his lackeys.'

Sir Henry Vane slammed his broad palm on the table top. 'Have a care, sir!'

Pym placed a placating hand on the bigger man's elbow, but addressed Collings. 'King Charles is misguided and misinformed, General. But he is still king.'

Collings bowed obediently. Goddamned hypocrites. 'Then what is the truth of it, sir?'

'The siege continues,' Pym said calmly. 'Young Massie has achieved what Fiennes could not, and the city gates are firmly shut.' The corner of his blue-lipped mouth trembled. 'And your rather crass analogy is not far from the truth. If not a dog's meal, then perhaps Gloucester is best described as a thorn in the enemy's flesh. They would dearly like to pluck it out.'

'And you would dearly like to stop them.' As ever, it had come down to political machination. The siege had been under-way for days, predicted in some quarters for weeks, and yet the Commons had not lifted a finger to help. But now the winds of opinion had changed.

'The people want it,' Pym said, confirming Collings' suspicion. 'They feel a compassion for their fellow rebels at Gloucester. It would serve morale no end to see the city survive. The assump-tion has been that Gloucester will fall quickly. She has poor defences and a small garrison. But the most recent news is encouraging.'

And the Parliament needs a distraction from the seemingly unending chorus of bad news, Collings thought. A quick win to give the people a hero and shut the peace protesters up for good. He frowned at a new consideration. 'But His Excellency's army ails, does it not?'

'My Lord Essex,' Vane responded as Pym burst into a fitful bout of racking coughs, 'cannot rely on his main force, you are right. Not to mount a credible challenge to the Oxford Army.'

'So?'

'So,' Pym managed to splutter, 'we must build him an army.'

'Out of what, sir?' Collings responded in surprise. 'Thin air?'

Pym had regained control now, and he sat back, dabbing the corners of his mouth with a small handkerchief. He rolled his eyes. 'Come now, Major General, you think more of me than that, I hope. The City of London will provide the funds for our enterprise. Fresh horses for a cavalry contingent are being found even now, and we have authorized conscription of four thou-sand recruits to the infantry.'

Collings scoffed derisively. 'Pressed men are worthless.'

'And that,' Pym said, tucking the fabric into the sleeve of his coat, 'is why the earl will march with the Trained Bands.'

'Surely not,' Collings replied in sceptically. The Bands had been raised for the defence of London, not for traipsing across enemy country to engage a large, experienced field army. 'They'll never agree to it.'

Sir Henry Vane leant forwards on his elbows, peering at Collings through watery eyes. 'This is a sensitive issue, Major General Collings, so you will not breathe a word of this conversation beyond these four walls on pain of death.'

Collings assented with a tilt of his bald head, though he glanced at Pym.

John Pym made a steeple of his fingers as he spoke. 'I am negotiating with the Militia Committee even now, General. Public opinion compels me to do so, and that same opinion will compel the Committee to see things from my perspective.'

That was a bold assertion, but Collings supposed the attitude of the mob was not something to be ignored, even by the most obstinate of the capital's thick-skulled militia leaders. 'How many regiments do you look to gain?'

'Six,' said Pym.

Collings whistled. 'Best part of eight thousand men.'

'And fifteen hundred cavalry.'

'They're not good, sir,' Collings warned. 'Not real soldiers.'

Pym nodded, conceding the observation. 'But they'll give Essex a fighting chance. If we can lift the siege, then our people will be heartened a hundredfold. The groundswell of support for the struggle will be truly wondrous.' He glanced at the beams above their heads. 'God willing, it might even turn the tide of this war.'

'Well,' Collings mused, 'this is all very interesting, I'm sure. And I wish you luck with it, gentlemen. But where do I come in?'

Pym drew in a deep breath, letting it out slowly through his wide nostrils. 'You have influence within the Militia Committee, do you not?'

'It has been said.'

Vane slapped the table again. 'Do not play coy with us, General, lest you wish to spend the night in the Tower.'

Collings fixed the politician with an acid stare, but suspected it would not be wise to call the bullish oaf's bluff. 'I have the ear of one or two of their number, sir, aye.'

Pym sat back, a look of genuine relief washing across his features. 'Good, good. Bend those ears for me, General Collings.'

'And if I refuse?' Collings ventured, sniffing an opportunity.

'Then the Tower awaits,' Vane threatened.

Pym restrained his colleague again, patting his sleeve. 'Make them do as I ask,' he said to Collings, 'and perhaps we will revisit the question of Cecily Cade.'

Erasmus Collings grinned. 'I will visit them tonight, sir.'

Friar's Orchard, Gloucester, 20 August 1643

'Put your backs into it, lads!' Sergeant William Skellen bawled at the men who scraped the mud, bare torsos calked in grime.

One of the shovel-wielding musketeers under his watchful eye straightened, rubbing the small of his back. 'Couldn't lend a hand, could you, Sergeant?'

'I'm busy overseeing your good endeavours, Barrow,' Skellen drawled in reply.

'But it's past nine of the clock,' Barrow complained. 'It's practically dark.'

'Better get the candles lit then, m' good man.'

'You'd treat blackamoor slaves better.'

Skellen cocked his head to the side. 'Fancy diggin' the latrines, Barrow?' The other men laughed.

'Not likely, Mister Skellen.' He turned back to his work.

'Thought not, Barrow. Thought not.'

Friar's Orchard was a wedge of open ground behind the intersection of the south and east walls. It was across the breadth of this ragged terrain that Massie had ordered the newest obstacle constructed, for this would be the first place through which any Royalist assault troops would swarm.

The barrage had ended six hours after it first shook the city's foundations, and, in truth, it had barely dented Gloucester's walls, or its resolve. But an attack had been made during the night, a sizeable force bridging the moat with ladders, and though they had been spotted quickly enough, driven away by fire from the rampart, it had served as a timely reminder that an effort to scale the wall did not necessarily depend upon the presence of a breach.

The breastwork now supervised by Skellen was nearly as high as a man's head and rose above a ditch first begun during the previous night, as soon as the Royalist bombardment had ended. The digging crews had changed every hour since, Massie insisting on keeping the men fresh and alert, and had pressed on during the course of the afternoon. Now, as the summer sun finally conceded the day above a cooling breeze, this new line of defence was beginning to look as though it might actually prove useful.

Skellen hefted his borrowed halberd with easy strength, gripping the end in one hand as though the heavy weapon weighed no more than a brittle twig. One of the men made a ribald jest, upon which the grunting workers brayed like mules, and he found himself laughing along with them. He glanced across the orchard to where his commanding officer leant casually against the wheel of a cart, a flaming torch glowing behind him in a makeshift embrasure that had been set in a crumbling wall. Stryker was puffing on a short pipe, and he lifted it in acknowledgement. Skellen nodded back, pleased with the way the new breastwork was progressing, and proud of the men who laboured to scour it out of the earth when the very real danger of a renewed bombardment still hung heavily over them.

'Shite,' he muttered, chiding himself for the feeling. He had been uneasy with the whole affair since their clandestine flight from Bristol. First fearing doom at the hands of Killigrew's slithery meddling, then witnessing with horror the change in Stryker's attitude. But now? He had dared to tell Stryker that he would not fight Mowbray's men if it came to it, and that sentiment had not altered one bit. Yet he had to admit that the rebel cause in this cannon-ravaged city had been inspiring in the extreme. The bravery of each and every citizen was something that he could not help but respect and admire. And what did that make him? 'A paper-skulled fool, that's what,' he said aloud.

He looked again at Stryker. An imposingly tall man wearing a coat that strained to hold in his bulbous midriff had joined the captain by the cart. Skellen grimaced in distaste. 'But you're the real trouble, ain't you, Colonel Skafflock? You're the real reason his head's turned. Thinks he owes you, the silly bugger.' He spat, turning angrily back to the party digging the ditch and piling the breastwork. He wondered if things would be different if they had never encountered the greencoats in the wood at Hartcliffe. Never run into bloody Richard Port.

'Coming along nicely,' Vincent Skaithlocke said as he produced his own pipe from a snapsack that seemed like a tiny purse in his massive hand. He had a lighted scrap of match-cord and braced it between his lips, the smouldering tip lolling like a fiery tongue as he fished a plug of dark sotweed from somewhere in the voluminous folds of his coat.

'Aye,' Stryker reflected, 'they're working well. If the king's men come over the wall here, they'll run straight into it. Not that you'd be concerned about that,' he added pointedly.

Skaithlocke winced. 'A fair accusation,' he hissed, the match forcing him to speak through the corner of his mouth. He crumbled the tobacco deftly into the pipe bowl and plucked the match free from the embrace of his lips. 'Perhaps, then, it is time for you to come into my circle of trust.'

A gout of smoke tumbled around Stryker. 'No more games, sir, please.'

'It is no game, Innocent.' The colonel dipped the match's hot end into the bowl as he sucked hard upon the bone-white stem. Soon his bearded face was obscured by the pungent cloud, and he snuffed out the match between thumb and forefinger. 'I have misled you a little, I think, though I pray you will forgive me when you learn of my reasons.'

Stryker watched the black shapes of the digging crew as they bustled around the breastwork. 'Go on.'

'Gloucester is a means to an end. Indeed, the same can be said for the entire conflict.' He stared down at Stryker through the twisting grey tentacles. 'There are greater issues at stake than this pathetic war, son. You remember the horrors of the Low Countries as well as I.'

'We've spoken of it many times, Colonel,' Stryker said. The nightmares still haunted him. Screams of dying men, the fearful faces of families caught in the path of a marauding army, the laughter of men for whom life was cheap. The sickly sweet stink of scorched flesh had become ingrained in his nostrils, he felt sure; an ever-present reminder of a youth spent in hell. 'You know I could never forget our years there. No man could.'

Skaithlocke seemed to pause, letting his billowing outbreath linger for a time. 'What if I were to tell you,' he finally said, 'that my years fighting for the Provinces have not yet reached an end?'

Stryker did not try to conceal his bafflement at this new line of discussion. 'You said you had come home to save England from a tyrant.'

'And I have,' Skaithlocke nodded, 'in a way. The real tyrant is Ferdinand.'

'Ferdinand? The Emperor? But he is dead.'

'Not our old enemy, Stryker. His son; Ferdinand the Third.' Skaithlocke slammed a fist into his solid palm as he spoke. 'Unholy Roman Emperor, King of Hungary, Germany and Bohemia. Archduke of Austria. Murderer.'

The titles hit Stryker like case shot, throwing his mind into an uncontrollable spin, and he let it tumble away, forgotten places and long-dead faces pushing their way from misty obscurity to sudden sharpness. Comrades who would now be nothing but bones piled with so many others in pits around the desolate continent raced up to glower at him. Men who had been courageous or craven, amusing or dull, hawk-witted or foolish. So many faces; so many names. Yet one returned to him again and again; a man who had been around the same age as Stryker, trained as a killer by the enormous soldier who towered above him in this most unlikely place.

'This has something to do with your son, doesn't it?' he said abruptly, focussing on Skaithlocke's intense gaze.

Skaithlocke took his time emptying the charred contents of the pipe with seemingly deliberate slowness. 'What I told you about John was true, Stryker,' he said when the clay stem was safely secreted about his person. 'He was shot.' His eyes became distant, then suddenly glassy, sparkling in the warm torchlight. 'But it was at dawn, by a Papist squad of villains who refused to offer quarter.'

Stryker's throat tightened as he imagined the fear his friend would have felt that day. It was one thing taking a ball or blade in the heat of a fight, quite another to know one's own fate in advance. Even so, he told himself, such things happened. 'But, Colonel, it is a brutal war,' he said, careful to choose his words wisely. 'John was a soldier.'

'And he should have expected death?'

Stryker shrugged. 'Men who live by the gun tend to die by it eventually.'

Skaithlocke rounded on him with a ferocity Stryker had almost forgotten the big man possessed. His right arm jabbed against the captain's chest, jolting him into a stumbled retreat. 'Should he have expected the bastards to poke out his eyes too?'

'Jesu,' Stryker blurted, reeling from the human storm cloud. 'They did that?'

But Skaithlocke was not listening. His eyes were blank and his mind elsewhere, lost in some blood-stained German field, replaying his deepest horror as if in his own personal torture chamber. 'Should he have laughed merrily as they sliced off his stones, Stryker? As they crammed them into his screaming mouth?' He was crying now, sobbing, his broad face distorted like that of a gargoyle with the anguish of the moment. 'Aye, he was a soldier, and soldiers expect death every day. But not like that.' He stopped, let his mortar-barrel arms drop as though the bones had dissolved from the inside, and blinked in utter bewilderment as if the last seconds had been lost on him. 'Not my son,' he said in something akin to a sigh. 'Not like that.'

Stryker went to pick up the pipe he had dropped in the sudden outburst. 'Christ, Vincent, I am sorry. Truly I am.' He felt his own eye prickle, even as John Skaithlocke's terrified face changed in his mind into that of Lieutenant Burton. He blinked hard. 'Why are you here?'

'To alter the war,' Skaithlocke said, his voice still drifting in the distance.

'Which war?'

Skaithlocke looked at him, his pupils contracting in the guttering half-light to focus on his face. 'The only war that matters. The war against my son's murderers.' He raised an arm again, though this time the fist was uncurled, beseeching. 'Come with me, Innocent. We will take the fight to the Papists like no man since Adolphus, with the united English army at our backs.'

Stryker could not stifle a low chuckle. 'And how do you expect to arrange such a thing? It is absurd!'

'By killing a man.'

'*A* man?' Stryker echoed incredulously. 'Who?'

The north wall, Gloucester, 20 August 1643

The bluecoats walked away at precisely the right time, showing their backs as had been prearranged. They were on the fire-step at the summit of the earthwork that formed the north wall, posted here to patrol the area for an attack across the Little Mead, but now, and for the next five minutes, they would be looking elsewhere.

'Very impressive,' Nikolas Robbens said in a small voice. He was pressed up against a pile of masonry some twenty paces from the rampart. It had been plundered, he assumed, from one of the houses destroyed by the previous day's bombardment, and would be destined to plug any gaps in the dilapidated walls. Not yet, though. Tonight it served as the first marker on his night-shrouded adventure. He watched as the bluecoats moved further away from the next marker, the spot on the northern rampart where Slager had told him to cross. The place he had made sure would be empty.

Now was the time, Robbens knew, for the soldiers would soon be back. He stooped to gather the snapsack at his feet. It was reassuringly heavy, and he felt the contents briefly; one final ritual before the off. Satisfied, he absently smoothed out the silken ear-string at his left lobe, hoisted the sack on to his shoulder, and made his move.

The earthwork was not steep here, for Massie had concentrated all his efforts in strengthening the south and east walls in response to the clear Royalist intent in that area, and Robbens scrambled up the glacis with ease. At the summit, he scrambled over the palisade and slid sideways down the outer face, knees slightly bent, legs braced, and plummeted into the ditch. This was not the formidably deep barrier that lined the wall to the south, and he negotiated it without difficulty. Massie had no need to create a moat here, for he already had one, and Robbens now stood at its bank. The River Severn split into two limbs further west, the earthworks of the West Gate cradled in its fork, and one limb ran all the way along the north wall, providing a natural, fast-flowing moat to keep the Welsh infantrymen camped this side of the city at bay.

Nikolas Robbens stared into the black abyss as the water rushed by. It was not a furious current, for the river saved its most dangerous power for the time when it swelled with autumn rains, but it looked vigorous nonetheless, and the assassin had to breathe deeply to calm his nerves. He jerked his shoulder so that the snapsack slipped free, and reslung it so that it was tied tightly around his neck.

Someone shouted up on the rampart. Robbens swore ferociously as he kicked off his shoes. The bluecoats were returning. He said a short prayer, asking God to forgive him his wrongs and to welcome him into His house when he departed this life. Judgement would be terrifyingly soon, and the thought made his guts twist. He shook his head violently, chasing away the doubts. He would commit his last murder, and in return

Slager would make his beloved brothers rich. Ruud and Marc had been little more than babies when they had witnessed their parents die, and Nikolas, the eldest, had not been able to protect them from that awful sight. Now, finally, he could set matters straight. He, of course, would die, slaughtered where he stood, but his brothers would be lifted out of poverty at a single stroke. And that, without doubt, was worth a hundred martyrdoms.

He patted his hands against the perfectly bald expanse of his pate, and cracked his elbows. When a second cry of alarm broke across the sound of the water, he knew he could stall no longer, lest he wished a leaden ball in the back. Nikolas Robbens took a huge gulp of air so that his lungs burned, and hurled himself into the river.

Near the cathedral, Gloucester, 20 August 1643

'The King?' Stryker blurted in astonishment. 'You mean to assassinate the King?'

Colonel Vincent Skaithlocke bobbed his massive head. 'King Charles will die, my friend. He will die, and the Parliament will win, and the war will be over.'

They had left Friar's Orchard with all its flapping ears and prying eyes, Skaithlocke leading his puzzled protégé to the rooms set in the middle of a row of sagging oak-framed hovels that he used as his quarters. Now, seated on a three-legged stool beside the empty fireplace, Stryker gazed up at Skaithlocke as he tried to make sense of the night's revelations. 'You mean to take us into the fight on the Continent? How, Colonel? There would be no stomach for such an enterprise.'

Skaithlocke was pacing back and forth across the middle of the room, and he wagged a reproachful finger as he replied. 'That is where you are quite wrong, son. There are plenty in the Commons who would see the defence of the Protestant Union as a calling from God. A new crusade.' He shut his eyes, tilting his chin upwards as if sniffing the air. 'Just imagine it. Dream it, as I have. England united by a Protestant Parliament, its gaze turning to a Europe on the brink of annihilation at the hands of Romish evil-doers.' He looked back down at Stryker, his eyes narrow, drilling through the space between them. 'Austria and Spain are strong. The Swedes and Dutch and their allies cannot turn the tide on their own. Not after so many years of carnage.'

Stryker rubbed his eye, suddenly feeling exhausted. 'I cannot believe the Parliament would countenance such a thing.'

'But what if an army of Englishmen sailed to their aid?' Skaithlocke went on. It was clear that he had not heard what Stryker had said. 'Our men are no longer green as grass, are they? They're veterans now. Forged in the fire and blood of Kineton and Adwalton. Roundway, Stratton, Lansdown, Bristol.' He clapped his wide hands together in a sound that echoed about the ceiling like a thunderbolt. 'Just imagine it, Innocent. All those battles, all that experience. Bring those hard men together under a single banner. Send them to the Low Countries in an armada. Trust me, Stryker. We can achieve this. We can avenge John and all the others.'

'Does Massie know about this? Is he part of the plot?'

Skaithlocke waved a dismissive hand. 'Of course not. He cares only for his precious city, for he believes it will make his name. Besides, there is no stomach for such a plan, not even in the most ardent Roundhead. They would win their war, but they would not commit regicide.' He shrugged. 'So I must do it for them. Take the dirty work away and leave only logic.'

Stryker did not know what to say. The scheme was mad. And yet Skaithlocke seemed entirely committed to it. Had he lost all reason? His eyes blazed with a zeal Stryker had encountered before in the stare of other men. Dangerous men. 'How will you kill the King?' he managed to ask.

Skaithlocke beamed, though his hands were beginning to tremble, and he thrust them behind his back. 'I have a man already in the Royalist camp. A deadly man of such skill with weapons that you and I could only marvel.'

'Who is he?'

'An irrelevance,' the big man replied dismissively. 'A tool.' He laughed, an unnatural, high-pitched sound amid this new fervour. 'He is a self-important knave with an eye for the ladies, a love of his golden locks, and a penchant for dandyish bloody ear-strings. But, by God, he can kill.'

'Vincent,' was all Stryker could say. He rocked forward, propping elbows on his knees, and put his head in his hands. 'What has happened to you?'

'Happened to me?' Skaithlocke replied in a tone that suggested Stryker was a dullard. 'I have told you already.'

Stryker rubbed his face hard, hoping he would look up to find this was all some morbid dream. But he knew it was not. Indeed, he could understand Skaithlocke's reasoning, for he too had been afflicted by the same madness these last weeks. He thought of the woods around Hartcliffe and swore softly. He had crushed a frightened man's wrist when intoxicated with the heady concoction of grief and guilt. It was a poisonous brew.

Skaithlocke was close now, his shadow creeping over Stryker. 'You're with me, aren't you, son? One brother avenging the death of another, eh? *Exitus acta probat.*'

Stryker looked up. 'I—'

Footsteps sounded in the doorway. 'You've told him, then.'

Stryker looked up sharply as Skaithlocke spun on his heels. The newcomer was a weedy man with greasy hair and pockmarked cheeks, one of which flickered uncontrollably. He came into the room, and Stryker saw that his gait was severely lopsided, made so by a dramatically twisted upper back.

'Ezekiel Nobbs,' Stryker said, his eye flicking down to the pistol in the man's hand. 'Still alive, I see.'

Nobbs took a moment to take in Stryker's ravaged features. His chuckle was teeth-gratingly nasal. 'And well, which is more'n can be said for you, by the looks of things.'

'You always were a charitable soul, Ezekiel.'

'And you always were a sanctimonious prick,' Nobbs hissed.

Stryker stood slowly, scanning the room for a chance to escape. The pistol quivered slightly in Nobbs' grip. 'Where's

Jonas? You and he were inseparable, scuttling about like a pair of rats to do the colonel's bidding.'

'Mister Crick is dead,' Skaithlocke said, his deep voice echoing loudly. 'The less said about him the better.' He moved between the two men. 'Stryker is with us, Nobbs, do not doubt it.'

Nobbs' secretive eyes shrank further into his skull. 'Sure about that, are yer, Slager?'

Stryker frowned. 'Slager?'

Skaithlocke's lips twitched. 'It is what the Dutch call me. A friendly name.'

'Friendly, sir?' Stryker said, unconvinced. 'It is not the kind of name a man is given. He earns it by his deeds.'

'Admiring, then,' Skaithlocke muttered testily. 'I have conducted things – *conducted myself* – rather differently since John was ripped from me.'

'And now they call you Butcher?' Stryker asked, wondering what horrors had been inflicted upon this man's enemies already in the years following John's death. 'My God, Vincent.'

Skaithlocke's jaw quivered as he gritted his teeth. 'Enough of this, Innocent! Enough, I say! You are with us, and that is what matters. Comrades in arms again, as God intended. King Charles will soon be rotting in the ground, and we will lead our new crusade against the Lord's foes.'

'Sir,' Stryker said weakly, thinking how best to penetrate the colonel's feverish mind. But just to look into Skaithlocke's eyes was to know that he was not for turning. 'Aye, sir. I am with you.'

The fat man grinned in blissful triumph, patting Stryker hard on the shoulder, and only turning away when the shuffle of a dragging leg sounded close at his back. Nobbs, it seemed, could see what the colonel could not, for he had levelled the pistol directly at Stryker. He shook his head as he limped into the room. 'He's lying, Slager.'

Skaithlocke went to intercept him. 'Do not be a fool, Nobbs. You heard my son.'

'He ain't your son, Slager. He's a fucking liar. Look at his face. He thinks you're a Bedlamite.'

Skaithlocke seemed confused for a moment, rotating his head between the two men. 'You are mistaken,' he murmured.

Nobbs came closer, keeping the cocked pistol steady, its black muzzle gaping at Stryker. 'Look at 'im, Slager. He's makin' you look a right bumpkin.'

Stryker raised his hands in supplication. 'He's the liar, Vincent. He's jealous.'

'Jealous?' Nobbs grinned nastily, exposing sharp teeth that jutted from festering gums like a row of fangs. 'He thinks you're mad, Slager. But he can't tell you so, cos he knows you'd have to kill 'im, now that he knows what we're about.' He shook the pistol. 'Why don't you let me do it?'

Vincent Skaithlocke's hands were around Ezekiel Nobbs' throat before the small man could react. The pistol fired, smoke jetted outwards to fill the chamber, but the ball slammed harmlessly into the floorboards. Nobbs dropped it, his hands clawing desperately at the great paws that now crushed his windpipe. He scratched and kicked, but he was too weak to fight off Skaithlocke.

Stryker stood, but could do nothing to prevent the attack. He had seen bears maul ban-dogs many times, and this was not so far removed. Skaithlocke lifted Nobbs off the floor, the smaller man's toes helplessly scraping the boards for some kind of purchase. But the colonel was too big, too strong, and he shook Nobbs like a rag doll, throttling the life out of him until the whites of Nobbs' eyes filled with blood and his tongue pushed its way out between blue lips like a pink slug, dangling there in a coating of foam turned crimson by gnashing teeth.

And then it was over. Nobbs hung limp like a puppet in Skaithlocke's vicelike grip. The colonel released him, let the corpse collapse to the floor, lifeless limbs resting in strange positions, as twisted as his deformed spine.

'Colonel?' Stryker ventured.

Skaithlocke looked up, turning slowly to his old friend, blinking blearily as though he woke from a strange dream. 'He did not believe,' he said.

'Is that what happened to Jonas Crick?' Stryker ventured.

Skaithlocke nodded. 'They only wanted the money I'd promised. They were not like you and me, my son. Not like us.'

'Not like us,' Stryker replied.

CHAPTER 17

Beside the east wall, Gloucester, 21 August 1643

Stryker walked the walls in the hour or two after midnight.
He paced alone, his hand twisting around the shark-skin
sword grip, tension tightening every muscle. His mind, it
seemed, had been consigned to an invisible rack, where it had
been stretched to breaking point. They had hidden Nobbs' body
in the cellar of Skaithlocke's temporary residence, a pathetic
bundle of rags and limp flesh stuffed face down in a barrel. It
would be found before long, but neither man could think
beyond their immediate futures. They spoke instead of the
daring soldiers they had fought with and against, of the things
they had seen and the tribulations they had suffered and survived.
They remembered poor John, of course, toasted his memory.
Finally, though, Stryker had had to depart, for he was due to
take part in the next instalment in Massie's schedule of disrup-
tion and audacity. He had left the man he revered above all
others staring at the walls as he continued his obsessive plotting.
And now Stryker paced because he needed the fresh air, and
because he knew he must put space between himself and the
troubled colonel; because he needed to consider his next move.

He crossed Friar's Orchard and made his way towards the East
Gate. Moving beyond the ancient city entrance, he continued
towards the earthworks around Whitefriars Barn at the corner
of the old section of medieval fortifications. Adjacent to those
works was a terrace of single-storey wooden huts, all pressed
together and rotting as one. He scanned them quickly as he

skirted the hovels, looking to see what life still remained in this part of the city. Nothing stirred. Perhaps the locals had had the good sense to leave, given the crumbling buildings' proximity to the battered walls.

When he turned, the man behind him was so startled that he did not even try to hide. Instead, he stood stock still, seemingly frozen to the debris-strewn road. 'Captain.'

Stryker nodded. 'James Buck.'

'Surprised to see me?'

'Surprised to see a clerk abroad at this time.' He raised his brow. 'Surprised to see that you're spying on me.'

Buck's perpetually sad eyes creased at the corners. 'Not spying, sir.'

'Then why do you follow me? Incidentally,' he added, 'you are not very good at it. I've been listening to your heavy feet since Friar's Orchard.'

'You were at the quarters of Mister Skaithlocke, were you not?' Buck asked. 'The governor's advisor.'

Stryker thought about that. 'Did Killigrew send you here?'

Buck wrinkled his nose to suggest Stryker might be stupid. 'You know he did.'

'To watch me.'

'Not a bit of it.'

'Did he not trust me to carry out the task, is that it?'

'No, sir. You are wrong.'

Stryker searched Buck's sallow face for a trace of guile, but something in the intelligencer's confident tone made him believable. 'Then what is your business here? You say you were sent to infiltrate the rebels, just as I was, and tried to arrange a clandestine meeting with me some days ago. But when I was distracted, you vanished.' He paused to listen for sounds of anyone approaching, but all was still. 'Now I find you have decided to act as my shadow. It is strange behaviour, Mister Buck.'

Buck lifted a hand to ruffle his lank chestnut hair. He blew out his cheeks and stepped closer so that they were only an arm's length apart. 'I am Ezra Killigrew's man,' he said in barely a whisper. 'And I was sent into Gloucester to gather intelligence, only to find I have no reasonable way out.'

'But?'

When the blow came it felt as though Stryker's guts had been bludgeoned with a musket stock. He doubled over, helplessly winded, and spewed a thin stream of stinking yellow vomit on to his boots. Buck stepped casually away, and Stryker saw the dark shaft of a cudgel in his white-knuckled hand.

'But,' the intelligencer said, 'my sister is wife to a man named Triggs, and he, you will be pleased to learn, is a dragooner.' He waited for Stryker to straighten, though the captain staggered uneasily, hands pressed tight to his midriff. 'A dragooner in a yellow coat.'

Stryker spat sour residue from his mouth. 'Crow.'

Buck lifted the cudgel menacingly. 'My brother-in-law is one of Colonel Crow's men, aye. He asked me to see what influence I might wield, and, you will again be pleased to learn, I wield quite a bit. At least enough to know that Mister Killigrew had asked you to carry out your own little mission. I was due to come to Gloucester at a later date, but it seemed logical enough to inveigle myself into Killigrew's plans. So here we are.' He slapped the hefty club into the palm of his free hand. 'And you shall die knowing that you've been a walking corpse since the day you crossed Artemas Crow.'

Stryker's stomach lurched again and it took all his strength to keep another torrent of vomit down. 'He's tried to kill me before,' he hissed through clenched teeth.

Buck grinned maliciously. 'Well, he won't need to try again.'

Stryker went for his sword, but Buck was faster than he had anticipated. His would-be assassin struck in two swift motions, wrapping the knuckles of his hand before he could get them behind the hilt guard, and then bringing the weapon up to clatter against his chin. Stryker pitched backwards, biting his tongue as he went, and tripped on a pile of stone scraps. He landed on his rump, the metallic zing of blood filling his mouth.

'Silly,' Buck said, stepping over the loose shards and drawing a dirk from his waist.

Stryker knew he had to stall for time. 'You're no mere clerk,' he said, recalling the well-worn sword Buck had carried on their journey from Bristol. It was not the weapon of a man who spent his time shuffling paper. 'Massie saw right through you when first we met him.'

'Almost,' Buck admitted. 'Fortunately, you helped me convince him. But you're right, of course. I have carried out one or two of Killigrew's more *ugly* assignments in my time.'

'Why not kill me on the road?'

'Before Gloucester?' Buck replied, taken aback at the question. 'I could hardly prevent you from doing your duty, Stryker. I am a loyal subject, whatever antipathy my kinsman may feel towards you. I considered denouncing you as the spy that you are, but I dare say you'd have returned the favour. So it has been a game of watching and waiting.'

'The other day?' Stryker said, remembering the meeting that had been so abruptly cut short.

Buck nodded. 'I'd have stuck you there and then, but your gangling shadow was too close for comfort.'

'Skellen,' said Stryker. 'Doesn't trust anyone.'

'Probably a good way to be, considering the circumstances.' Buck sucked his teeth. 'But all's well that ends well. Now it is just the moon and the stars and you and me.' The knife came up for the killing blow. 'No phlegmatic sergeants to get in the way.'

'There's nothin' wrong with my phlegm,' Sergeant William Skellen grunted as his left arm snaked round Buck's neck, hoisting him to the tips of his toes. Buck's mouth dropped open but no sound followed, save a small gurgle at the back of his throat. Skellen let him go, jerking his own knife free from Buck's back, and the intelligencer collapsed on to his face. 'And I ain't ganglin'.'

Stryker rolled to all fours and spat a rich gobbet of blood on to the mud beside the twisted body. Slowly he rose to his feet, his guts still griping as if he had eaten a surfeit of rotten meat. 'Thank you, Will.'

'He's not your only follower, sir,' Skellen replied, wiping the dirk on his sleeve and prizing the other from Buck's clawlike grip. He thrust one into each boot. 'Saw you went into Skafflock's place. Thought I'd wait outside for a bit. You looked a tad—' he pursed his lips, searching for the right word, '*strange*, when you came out, so I thought I'd keep with you, check you was well.'

'I'm glad you did,' said Stryker. 'And no, I'm not well. Not really. We've much to discuss.'

'We're due at the muster point in less than an hour, sir. You can tell me on the way.'

Gaudy Green, Gloucester, 21 August 1643

Two companies from Sir Edmund Mowbray's Regiment of Foot had been assigned to Gaudy Green as soon as the pre-dawn barrage thundered across Gloucestershire's black skies. The Royalist commanders had roused their men at points all around the city, for the suspicion had been that a rebel sally was in the offing.

'What say you, Tom?'

Lieutenant Thomas Hood, de facto leader of the regiment's second company while his captain was away, cocked his head to the side as he listened to the distant crackle of gunfire. It was louder than usual, not the ubiquitous coughs from individual muskets as the opposing sentries chipped away at one other from the walls and saps, but a wave of sound that rattled like a thousand spurs in the grey half-light. 'Skirmish, Mister Forrester. Down at the Priory, by my reckoning.'

Captain Lancelot Forrester was standing at the head of his company, amid the desolate ruin that had once been the community around Bristol Road, the blocks of pike and shot waiting patiently for the order to move. He followed Hood's gaze. 'I think you're right. Forth's camp is not half a mile from here. Let us see whether they require assistance.'

The redcoats marched. Within the space of five minutes they could see the smoke rising from the land around Severn Street and Llanthony Priory, the great river writhing like a black snake beyond. The sun was only just shedding light across the eastern horizon, and yet a major firefight was already underway.

'We'll make for the main artillery redoubt,' Forrester said as they marched.

Hood looked across at him nervously. 'You think they intend to take it?'

'Absolutely. Even if Massie's entire force had come out of the city, they could not rout Forth's men. They must have a target, and I'd wager it is the battery.' He saw the strain on the young officer's face. 'You've done well these past days, sir. Stepped into the breach, if you pardon the expression.'

Hood forced a smile. 'Thank you, sir.'

Forrester glanced back at the long line of redcoats. 'You have their loyalty, Lieutenant, and that should stand you in good stead.' He lowered his voice. 'Keep Barkworth by your side and you'll be just fine. He may look like a dwarf, but he fights like a demon.'

Hood nodded rapidly. 'I will, sir.'

Forrester reached across and slapped Hood's shoulder. 'That's the spirit! We few, we happy few, we band of brothers.'

'*Henry the Fifth*, sir?'

'You'll do just fine, Tom!' Forrester exclaimed in genuine delight. 'Now, let's go and kill some Roundheads!'

Below the South Wall, Gloucester, 21 August 1643

The fight had already started by the time Stryker and Skellen's boat slid on to the bank of the River Severn. The two men waited for it to judder up the smooth slope alongside the rest of the craft, and jumped out to join the sally party, wading the last few feet through the frothing water. The raid was Massie's most ambitious enterprise yet. It was a two-pronged attack, designed to spike the Royalist guns in front of both the south and east walls, the first part of which would see a large detachment of

Stamford's bluecoats take to the river and land between the strong enemy leaguer at Llanthony and the Severn Street artillery position. So far the plan was working, for they had made it to dry land under the Earl of Forth's nose, but the leading groups, under Captains Blunt and White, had now run into resistance somewhere in the direction of the battery.

'Think they've reached the guns?' Skellen asked as he and Stryker rushed north-eastwards with the rest of the bluecoats. Neither had muskets, but Skellen's halberd seemed all the more fearsome in the gloom.

Stryker had been thinking about James Buck, his body tipped over the side of the wall to rot in the filthy moat, and looked up, startled. 'Sergeant?'

'The cannon, sir.'

'If they have,' Stryker said, 'then we need to hurry. The plan is to roll up the sap system until we meet the others at the East Gate. If we don't join Blunt and White soon, they'll overreach themselves and be cut off.'

The group forged on, running across the muddy ground until they reached the redoubt. The advance party was there, and at first Stryker thought one of the cannon had exploded, such was the devastation. Corpses lay strewn about, including that of one high-ranking Royalist officer, to judge by his gold-fringed scarf, but it was quickly apparent that the ordnance had not even been fired. Blunt and White had taken the battery unawares, storming it with speed and brutality. Now their men set about spiking the iron barrels as the sally party regrouped.

'Captain Lieutenant Stevenson,' the dour-faced Blunt shouted, 'leads two hundred of our lads out of the North Gate. They will sweep down to the East Gate, immobilize the artillery, and destroy the trenches. We will move towards them, meeting on Gaudy Green. We will destroy what we can before the enemy can muster a proper response. Understood?'

Stevenson saluted in agreement, and the blue-coated force marched to the east.

*

Forrester and Hood took their companies to one of the old roads that ran between Severn Street and Bristol Road. There had been a vibrant neighbourhood here before the siege, but the houses, mostly timber-framed and thatched, were among those Massie had ordered to be destroyed lest they offer protection for the king's men. Now this whole area was a wasteland. A few walls persisted, the crumbling and blackened remains of those buildings built in stone, but they simply jutted up from the muddy morass like gigantic tombstones, a sad reminder of a once lively area.

'We'll hold them here!' Forrester bellowed. A terrified and bloodied gunner's assistant had come sprinting through the shredded streets, bolting straight into the red-coated ranks. He had told of a large amphibious raid coming from the west that had already overrun his redoubt. Many had been slaughtered in the skirmish, the mattross claimed through racking sobs, including the battery commander, Major Wells, and now they were headed this way. Forrester drew his sword and held it high, thrusting the tip out towards his great standard. It was getting lighter now, and the men would be able to see the red flag with its quartet of white diamonds. 'Keep your ranks!' He caught the eye of his second in command, Reginald Jays. 'You take the pikes to the rear, Lieutenant.'

Jays' face sagged. 'But, sir, I would fight.'

'Christ's robes, Lieutenant, do as you're damn well told! They'll have muskets. How much good will men carrying long poles be in a firefight?'

Jays flushed. 'Not a lot, sir.'

'Not a lot,' Forrester said witheringly. 'Get them into the saps. You'll protect them if the enemy gets through us. Living storm poles, eh?'

Jays turned to his work. 'Understood, sir.'

Forrester looked along the red line to find Hood. 'Are your men ready, Thomas?'

Hood's own sword was drawn. 'They are, Captain. Pikes in the trenches, muskets with me.'

'Mowbray's Foot, have a care!' Forrester shouted again. 'There's a parcel o' bluecoats heading this way, and I mean to stop 'em!'

The men cheered, though the anxiety was stark in their collective voice, and Forrester turned to face the west. To the left was Llanthony Priory, and he could already see a swarm of men mustering around its ramshackle buildings. But, though Forth had made his camp there and would have a huge number of men at his disposal, they were taking an age to organize. Behind him, back at Gaudy Green, there were more Royalist troops, but they had been ordered to stay put to guard the main batteries, while further east at Barton the bulk of Astley's brigade would be doubtless readying for deployment. But none of them would reach Forrester's position before the rebel sally, and he arranged his men for volley fire.

Somewhere away to the north, more musketry ripped apart the dawn. It whipped up like a sudden squall, furious and dense, and he had the vague notion that perhaps the rebels were attacking on two fronts. 'Jesu,' he muttered, stepping briskly to the side of his seasoned fighters. 'Prepare to give fire, boys!'

'You should have killed him.'

Stryker, marching in time with the fast pace set by Captain Blunt, glanced across at Skellen. 'I didn't need to. Your dirk in his lungs did the job well enough.'

They had subtly found their way to the rear of the column so that they would have the best chance of avoiding king's men when the surprised Royalists regained the front foot, but Skellen nonetheless kept his voice quiet. 'Not Buck, sir.'

'I considered it,' Stryker said, knowing full well who Skellen had meant.

'Then why didn't you?'

'Partly because he would probably have killed me first.'

'And the other part?'

Stryker waited for a barrage of cannon fire to blast down from the bastion on Gloucester's southern wall. Massie was keeping his vow to soften the enemy entrenchments in advance of the raid. 'When I said he was like a father to me,' he said when the ringing in his ears had begun to subside, 'I meant it.'

They had reached a point along the road where the remains of buildings were more substantial, the occasional stone wall or tottering gable having resisted the blaze that had consumed the neighbouring streets. The column was slowing, the men at its head becoming more cautious now that the Royalists could employ those shattered gable ends as makeshift breastworks. 'But he means to murder the King, sir.'

'Would you kill the man who raised you, Sergeant?'

'I did, sir,' Skellen replied.

The volley took them by surprise. It roared out from the ruins of a line of charred homes fifty paces to their right, and the entire sally party disintegrated as they scattered in search of shelter. The head of the column bore the brunt of the storm, and blue-coated casualties littered the road in their wake. Stryker and Skellen were far enough back to escape the shower of lead, and they kept low, scrambling behind a cart that had been flipped on to its side by a shot from the defenders' cannon.

Stryker peered over the side of the cart. A large body of men had stepped out from the rubble. Their front rank was still obscured by the smoke from their volley, drifting lazily sideways to roil like an army of spirits amongst the crumbling suburb, and he could hear orders screamed by unseen sergeants and corporals, preparing the second rank to fire. Already the bluecoats along this side of the road were offering sporadic shots in return, but theirs was a desultory affair, the disunity of the sudden retreat having spread their ranks too thinly for Blunt and White to organize.

'What now?' Skellen growled, wincing as a musket-ball clipped the cart's wheel, sending it into a mad spin in the air before them.

'We wait,' Stryker said. After all, they had no muskets with which to enter the fray. He hoped one side would withdraw soon, for he did not wish to be compelled to fight the Royalists, but that did not seem likely. It was only when the two bodies seemed to be settling into their positions, both groups pressing up against the jagged walls, neither willing to break cover, that he saw it. 'Oh Christ,' he said in a whisper.

Skellen looked across at him. 'Sir?'

Stryker jerked his chin to indicate a point along the Royalist line. 'See it?'

Skellen gingerly poked his head above the splintered dog cart. 'Shite.'

And from up on Gloucester's walls, trumpets sounded.

The East Gate, Gloucester, 21 August 1643

Edward Massie leant against the stone rampart. 'Sound it again.'

'Sir?' a teenager from the Town Regiment called from a little way along the wall.

Massie rounded on him. 'I said sound the retreat again, damn you! Get them back before we lose them all!'

The youngster raised his battered instrument to his lips and sounded out the notes as powerfully as he could.

Vincent Skaithlocke stood with Massie. 'Should we position another of the drakes to the north, sir?'

Massie shook his head. 'Not enough time, Colonel. They'll have to fight their way out.' He lifted his perspective glass again. Messengers scuttled up and down the earthworks to bring him news of the amphibious landing down on Severn Street, and things, it seemed, were beginning to stall. But those men were bluecoats, Stamford's veterans, and he did not worry unduly for them. From up here he had hoped to watch the second squad make their way down from the North Gate and spike the cannon at the battery immediately below his position, but something had gone horribly wrong. The men, drawn from Stephens' inexperienced regiment, with only a small group of Devereux's more seasoned dragoons as support, had taken a wrong turn in the darkness and now, as the sun illuminated the ambitious attack, it was clear that they had become woefully lost. Instead of engaging the battery close to the walls, they had stumbled along the streets further north, eventually wandering into the vast encampment of Darcy's brigade out on Barton Street. The element of surprise had given them a fighting chance, and they had initially sent the king's men into startled retreat, killing a score of musketeers in the process, but the enemy had quickly regrouped, pushed back with impossibly superior numbers, and now Massie's audacious plan lay in tatters.

'Stryker is down there, sir,' Skaithlocke said, staring out over the smoking trenches.

Massie shook his head. 'He is with the blues to the south.'

'They're in a fight of their own.'

'But they do not have far to go. They'll pull back to the South Gate under covering fire from the barbican.' He looked up at the huge man. 'Worry not, sir. I know he is a particular friend of yours, but they will be safe enough.'

Skaithlocke nodded and went to watch proceedings from the South Gate. Massie noticed he muttered a prayer as he walked.

Below the South Gate, Gloucester, 21 August 1643

Captains Blunt and White ordered their units to move gradually northwards. They could not very well retreat to the boats in which they had come, for by now the riverbank would be teeming with Forth's enraged soldiers, seeking revenge for the audacious landing and subsequent spiking of cannon right under their collective noses. But the South Gate towered above their position, and from it the small artillery pieces belched down at the suburbs, forcing the Royalist infantry companies to stay hidden within their labyrinth of pockmarked rubble screens.

'What do you reckon happened?' Skellen asked as the trumpets repeated the order to abort.

They were still crouched behind the dog cart. Stryker shook his head. 'I don't know. We might have made more ground with the ordnance support.'

'Which means Stevenson's lot have made a ballocks of it.'

'Perhaps.'

'Still, I'm glad we'll be out of it, sir,' Skellen said, raising his voice above the din as a cannonade from the city pounded the infantrymen on the far side of the road. 'Can't say I like fighting for the crop-heads.'

Stryker looked at him, his brow furrowed. 'They're all English, Will.'

Skellen chewed the inside of his mouth. 'Can I speak plain, sir?'

'Do you ever speak otherwise?'

'Were you truly thinkin' of chucking your lot in with the rebels?'

'No, Sergeant, I was not,' Stryker lied. 'But I admired them. Their courage. That lad who fought with Captain Crisp's raid, just a child really. The common folk rebuilding the walls. The women cutting the turf within musket range. They're a rare breed.' In truth, he had experienced moments of doubt. He had not wished to fight his comrades in Mowbray's regiment, but beyond that? Did he care for the king any more than for Parliament? Not especially, he inwardly conceded. But his place was with the red-coated ranks, and his heart was with Lisette Gaillard, and she was the most ardent Royalist he had ever met. For her alone, he would never have really turned his coat. He had known it for days, but part of him wanted to stay in Gloucester simply to fight for its people. They had come so far that it seemed cruel to abandon them. But then he had learned of Vincent Skaithlocke's plans and known that he must leave. He might feel no love for King Charles, but he was still the sovereign, and Stryker would be damned before he would let an assassin reign.

'Mad breed,' sniffed Skellen.

Stryker grinned. 'Aye, that too.' He sheathed his sword and watched the pockets of garrison men creep through the smashed

310

buildings towards the big bastion and the safety it promised. Only he and Skellen were left in this part of the suburb and the Royalist infantrymen were no longer firing on their position, preferring to harass the retreating bluecoats. He stood. 'Are you ready?'

Skellen stood too. 'As ever, sir.'

The iron ball from a booming drake punched into the wall, demolishing the top layer of bricks. Lieutenant Thomas Hood ducked as low as he could, his scabbard becoming stuck between his legs and making him stumble. He swore, grasped the wall, and dragged himself upright. Someone called to his right, decrying their faltering defence.

'Just hold!' he shouted back. 'We can't run into their bloody guns!'

In truth it was infuriatingly frustrating, for they had caught the advancing bluecoats with a stout couple of good volleys that might have halted the attack long enough for reinforcements to come from Llanthony Priory and squeeze the rebels from behind. But the retreat had been trumpeted too soon, the covering fire from the barbican had pinned the redcoats down, and though they had lost only one man in the iron rain, they could not risk a chase. Thus, they were reduced to shooting at the backs of the sally party while they watched the brazen Parliamentarians stroll away. Hood flinched again as another plume of smoke billowed out from the city and a heavy crack signalled the imminent arrival of another lump of deadly shot. The ball found more masonry out to his right, and he chided himself for cringing like a whipped dog.

'Keep at them, men!' he bellowed, knowing the gesture was utterly superfluous, for no more fire came back at them from the sally party. Indeed, the scurrying activity on the looming bastion seemed to have ceased as well, and he wondered if the garrison had decided to save their powder and ammunition now that the dawn raiders had made it back to safety.

He moved out from the cover of the wall, confident that the bluecoats were now well out of musket range. Scanning the surrounding area, he was happy to see that they had suffered no more casualties and the saps had been successfully protected. Away to the north, he could see Captain Forrester corralling his sooty charges with blade still drawn. He smiled, pleased to see the officer had come through the skirmish unscathed.

It was only then that Hood caught the movement in the corner of his eye. Ensign Chase was with him, the giant red square of taffeta hoisted high and proud in his strong grip, and he saw the men too, for he nodded towards the upended dog cart on the opposite side of what once had been a busy street. Hood nodded, drew his sword, and called for a pair of musketeers to join him. They marched quickly across the road that had so recently been a thoroughfare for flying lead, and intercepted the pair of soldiers in dark clothing who now skirted round the side of the cart with hands raised high in surrender.

It was Chase who spoke first, and it was with an astonished oath that he broke the silence. 'You seeing what I'm seeing, sir?'

Lieutenant Thomas Hood squinted at the rebels' faces. He looked again at Ensign Chase, then back at the men beside the cart. 'Good God.'

Near Barton, Gloucester, 21 August 1643

Sir Edmund Mowbray had a tent out to the east, on the periphery of Astley's main encampment, and it was here that Stryker and Skellen were taken. They had requested that Hood convey them direct to Ezra Killigrew, but he was apparently down in Bristol on some business for Prince Rupert.

Hood had not known how to react when he had taken custody of the pair of soldiers who had emerged sheepishly from the temporary rebel lines. He and the other officers in Mowbray's regiment had been aware that Stryker was on a clandestine mission for the prince, but it was still a shock for them to come face to face in the aftermath of such a bitter fight, and he had ordered his men to escort them back into the midst of the waiting redcoats at the end of primed muskets.

But any doubts were quickly erased by the men themselves. The company might have been commanded by Hood these past weeks, but it belonged to Stryker, and they converged on him and their talismanic sergeant with nothing but astonished cheers.

Forrester's force joined them quickly, marching together out of range of the city's cannon with a chorus of huzzahs. 'We might have bloody killed you, you pair of bee-headed fools!' the captain had said as they left the carnage of the abortive sally in their wake. But then he had grinned broadly, thanked God for his friends' return, and boasted that he knew all along that they would never truly desert. Stryker and Skellen had exchanged a sharp glance, but both men kept their peace.

'I am thankful you took your colours to the battle,' Stryker said as they marched, eager to steer the subject on a different course.

Forrester feigned offence. 'I cannot believe you might think otherwise, Stryker.'

'You might have lost them in a little skirmish,' Stryker chided.

'It is right that the enemy sees who we are,' Forrester said. 'Puts the fear of God into 'em.'

'Well I am thankful for it. Without the ensigns I might not have recognized who you were.'

'And if it hadn't been us?' Forrester asked pointedly. 'What then?'

'We'd have thrown ourselves on the mercy of whichever unit it was,' Stryker replied firmly, but he was far from certain. He had already decided to break back to the Royalist lines, but would he have done it in that moment? He doubted it. A secret part of him had wanted to see the ambitious sally succeed, for the men – and their innovative governor – deserved it.

'We had expected you back earlier, Captain,' Sir Edmund Mowbray said as he paced back and forth in the musky gloom of his tent.

Stryker, standing in the centre of the makeshift room, nodded. 'That was the intention, sir. But we were trapped. We encountered the greencoat who escaped at Hartcliffe.'

'S'blood, Captain!' Mowbray exclaimed. 'The very same man?' He looked at Skellen. 'The man who stabbed the sergeant?'

Stryker said that it was. 'And he made life difficult. By the time we were rid of him, the king's army were camped outside. We could not get out.'

'And how did they treat you?'

'Very well, sir. We joined the garrison.'

Mowbray's russet brows shot up. 'Stryker?'

Stryker felt prickly heat rise along the skin of his neck, and he forced himself to stare hard at a point just above Mowbray's shoulder. 'Prince Rupert instructed us to turn our coats for the good of the mission, sir, and that is what we did. We had to do it to make the signal for Killigrew.'

Mowbray rubbed his red-rimmed eyes with balled fists. 'Well at least you were not forced to fight for the buggers, eh?'

'Quite, sir,' Stryker said, ignoring the sound of Skellen's shifting feet.

'And you say this Buck intended to kill you?'

'Yes, sir. He'd nearly succeeded when Sergeant Skellen intervened.'

Mowbray looked at Skellen, slightly behind and to the side of Stryker, before whistling softly at the awning above. 'Zounds. And you're certain he was Crow's man?'

'Oh yes, sir,' Stryker confirmed. 'Quite certain. He was working for Killigrew as well, but had not been due to infiltrate the city until a day or two later. In the light of Crow's request, it seems, he arranged to couple his mission with my own.'

Mowbray's eyes narrowed. 'And Killigrew? Was he involved somehow?'

Stryker wrinkled his nose. 'I doubt he had the first inkling of Buck's association with Colonel Crow, sir.'

'That villain,' Mowbray muttered, setting his jaw as his voice grew in volume. 'That damnable villain.'

'He wants me dead, sir. He's never pretended otherwise.'

'Why, I shall—'

'Beg pardon, Colonel,' Stryker cut in, 'but I urge you to tread carefully. He is powerful.'

Mowbray teased the bristles of his moustache between thumb and forefinger. 'That he is.'

'I am alive,' Stryker said. 'Buck is dead. We may have to settle for that.'

Mowbray sighed unhappily. 'And what of this murderer?'

Stryker grimaced, knowing he should have tried harder to gain more information from Skaithlocke. The reality was that the details he retained from that shocking night were sparse. 'The plan was revealed to me only in part, sir. A man – a professional assassin – has broken out of the city with the express purpose of killing His Majesty.'

'Name?'

'I do not have one, sir. He is golden-haired, and is an expert marksman.' He shrugged apologetically. 'That is all I know.'

'That is a start, I suppose. I will petition the King. Beseech him to leave.'

'Will he agree?'

'I doubt it. You must speak with the Prince also.'

'Me, sir?'

'You were in Gloucester on his business, Captain. He will wish to see you, I should imagine. Mention this killer to him. Perhaps His Majesty will listen to his favourite nephew.'

Perhaps, thought Stryker. And if not, then he would make his own search. Somewhere in the Royalist camp an assassin roamed, and Stryker intended to hunt him down.

CHAPTER 18

Llanthony Priory, Gloucester, 22 August 1643

'And you say your mother was Dutch, Mister Hatton?' Alexander Beak studied the deserter over the wire rim of his spectacles as he leaned back in his chair. He rocked absently on the rear legs as the man standing at the other side of his desk stared implacably at the wall above his head.

'She was,' Hatton said in accented English. 'From The Hague. My father was from York. I grew up in Holland but came here when war broke out.'

Beak held a major's commission, but his duties encompassed a wide range of tasks. One of which was the processing of the Earl of Forth's prisoners. It was a thankless task, for they were invariably a rabble, not fit to clean his boots, but occasionally he encountered one marginally more intriguing than the rest. 'To join the wrong side, sir.'

Hatton sniffed. 'And I am eternally sorry for that. But I think I showed my true colours when I risked the river, did I not?'

Beak removed the spectacles, wiping the lenses in a circular motion against his sleeve. They were in one of the priory's larger buildings, the arches of its high monastic ceiling echoing each word spoken. Outside they could hear a non-commissioned officer berating his fumbling charges, who were presumably attempting musket drill. Beak waited patiently for the fellow to draw breath. 'It must have been a difficult swim.'

Hatton risked meeting the major's gaze with eyes that were blue as sea ice and just as cold. 'It was. The Severn is fast and chilling.' He rounded his shoulders and puffed out his chest a little. 'But I was willing to make the sacrifice for my liege lord, sir.'

Alexander Beak let the chair drop forwards on to all four legs. He replaced the spectacles, clipping them to the bridge of his lean nose above a lump where once it had been broken. 'And are you certain you're quite recovered, Mister Hatton?'

'Almost, sir, thank you. I would simply request a few days' recuperation before I enlist with the royal forces hereabouts.'

'Fight against your former allies?' Beak asked wryly. It was not uncommon, he conceded. Indeed, the battered and frightened soldiery of this bitter war often turned their coats to save their skins. But this man did not seem the usual sort of cowed dullard, which is why the major had felt it prudent to speak with him just one more time.

'Gloucester is holding out against all the odds,' Hatton said. 'Why would I run if I did not truly believe in the King's cause?'

Beak nodded thoughtfully. The man had a point; desertion was very rare from this defiant city. And to have negotiated the Severn in the dead of night was no mean feat. It smacked of a man determined to fight for his king. Albeit a little late in the day. 'You are a gunner, yes?' He waited for Hatton to nod before sifting through a dog-eared stack of papers under his long nose. '*Ah-ha*! Here we are. We lost two gunners and three mattrosses in yesterday morning's raid. The posts are not yet filled.'

'I will do my duty, as soon as I am able,' Hatton said, before doubling over with a wet-sounding cough that made him moan in pain.

Beak looked up, dubious as to the deserter's fitness. 'Rest a few days, Mister Hatton. I will make the arrangements for your new posting, but, for God's sake, be at your ease. We would not want you dying of some ague before you can show us your skill with ordnance.'

Hatton had composed himself and he smiled his thanks. 'I will make His Majesty proud to have me in his ranks, sir.'

'Oh, I think you've already achieved that,' Beak replied. Outside, the musket drill had started up again, and Beak rapped thin fingers on the table as he looked for another lull. 'Your information was vital,' he said at a suitable juncture. 'We will reconsider our efforts now that we have such a thorough assessment of their defences.' He offered a tight smile. 'The King may wish to thank you personally.'

That seemed to thaw the ice in the gunner's veins, for he gave a white-toothed grin. 'I should very much like that. I was wrong to join the rebels, sir, for which I would beg forgiveness of His Majesty.'

'Forgiveness?' Alexander Beak said, mildly amused. 'Your sentiments are touching, naturally, but an experienced gunner is always welcome in our ranks. Especially one who would bring such intimate details of Governor Massie and his vermin.'

'I would only do what is right, sir.'

'Quite.' Beak considered the only man who had successfully deserted the rebel garrison in several days. There was something about him that set him apart from the bleating sheep Beak usually had to process. But his information had certainly been useful, and his determination to break with the Roundheads was admirable enough. He decided to ignore his instinct for the greater good. 'You are dismissed, Hatton. I will arrange a billet for you while you wait to join your new regiment.'

'Thank you, Major.'

'We may have more questions in the coming days.'

Hatton clasped his hands at his midriff and gave a slow blink, putting Beak in mind of a pious monk. 'I will tell you whatever I know, you may count on that, sir.' The Dutch artilleryman pursed his lips. 'And when might I see the King?'

Beak leaned back again, rocking gently. 'Oh, do not presume it will ever come to pass, Hatton. He is mighty busy, as you are no doubt aware. But he has made mention of gracing you with an audience.' He picked up the top page in the paper stack and examined it to show that he was done with the besieging army's newest recruit. 'Have patience.'

'I will, sir,' Hatton replied as he turned towards the door, the light from the windows shining against his perfectly bald head. 'I am a patient man.'

St Mary de Crypt, Gloucester, 22 August 1643

The inside of the small church was cool, offering welcome relief to the party who ducked into her shadowy inner sanctum.

Colonel Vincent Skaithlocke suffered from the heat more than most, and he drew a large handkerchief as soon as he was out of Southgate Street's balmy air, mopping the glistening sheen from his jowls with hurried dabs. 'How bad is it?'

Lieutenant Colonel Edward Massie, the twenty-three-year-old Governor of Gloucester, rapped his long fingers against his breastplate. 'Bad.'

Massie led Skaithlocke and four other officers along the nave and down into the chambers of the crypt. They were small and secure, thick walls of stone penetrated only by stout oaken doors. Once upon a time they had been the private tombs of priests, but Massie, ever the pragmatist, had found a better use for them. He ordered one door open, and a red-haired sentry produced a jangling set of keys, with which he obliged.

'I see what you mean,' Skaithlocke rumbled as he peered over the governor's slim shoulder.

Massie stared down at the barrels in the corner of the room. The magazine had been full at the outset of the siege, but now there were just a handful left. 'We must rein in our attacks.'

'Is that wise?' It was Alderman Pury who had spoken, and Massie, for all his sombre misgivings, was not oblivious to the irony of the words. It had not been that long since the leader of the city's Puritan elite had publicly berated him for his daring and, as Pury saw it, profligate tactics. Now, at least, he had come round to the wisdom of raiding, harassing and bombarding the Royalist lines in order to disrupt the enemy and keep them from storming the walls with any cohesion. Yet just as Massie seemed to be galvanizing the whole of Gloucester behind the rebel cause, it was apparent that those very tactics had consumed more powder than he could afford.

Massie nodded glumly. 'The mills produce three new barrels a week.'

Pury's high forehead wrinkled. 'Will that suffice?'

'It is the equivalent of five rounds per man,' Massie replied. 'Six at a pinch. Even if we cease to engage the enemy directly, wait behind the walls for them to make their move, it would not be enough to see us through the inevitable battle.' He felt suddenly sick. The last sally had been his most ambitious yet. It had almost been the most costly and the most disastrous.

Massie indicated that they should leave, waiting while the rest of the group filed up into the nave. When Skaithlocke reached the stairway, filling it completely with his vast bulk, he paused as if wishing to speak. 'What is it, Colonel?'

'I have not heard from Captain Stryker, sir. Not since the sally against the southern redoubts.'

Massie sighed, not particularly wishing to discuss the calamity. 'Missing, I'm sorry to say. Didn't return with either Blunt or White.' He shrugged. 'Presumed killed.'

Skaithlocke's thick fingers slid over his mouth, his brown eyes glistening. 'God, no,' he intoned in a muffled voice. He exhaled slowly. 'What of his sergeant?'

'Him too,' Massie said, leaving the crypt as Skaithlocke stepped aside.

As the door to the magazine clanked shut behind them, Skaithlocke caught up with the governor halfway up the steps. 'They were both killed?'

'Or captured, aye.' Massie halted suddenly, remembering the time the big colonel had spent walking the walls with Stryker. 'My apologies, Skaithlocke. I know you were close.' He offered a wan smile. 'A tragedy, for they were good soldiers both.'

Matson House, Gloucester, 22 August 1643

Stryker had spent the best part of the previous day walking the encampment in the vain hope of catching the would-be assassin, but as night fell he knew the situation was futile. What was he looking for? Some red-eyed monster with horns and a tail? Perhaps a soldier with the face of a grizzled veteran, carrying a long fowling piece with which he could shoot the king from a great distance? The fact was, he did not know. All he had to go on was the knowledge that the man was blond, and that he was at large in the Royalist camp. In the end he had relented, catching up on the sleep so cruelly denied to men on the inside of a besieged city, and decided to wait for the next morning.

'Even if you knew precisely what he looked like,' Colonel Sir Edmund Mowbray said as they waited by the stone porch, 'the camp is so large now, we'd never be able to search it all.'

They were in a line of generally very well-upholstered gentlemen, queuing for an audience with members of the royalist hierarchy. King Charles had made the Tudor-built Matson House his headquarters and quickly it had become the centre of his itinerant court. Old Patrick Ruthven, the Earl of Forth and, more recently, Brentford, was officially in command of the army, and his fortified leaguer was at the crumbling priory, but everyone knew that this place, two miles south-east of Gloucester, was the real hub of Royalist operations.

The big door jolted open, the smell of perfume, wood smoke and beeswax gusting out from the hallway beyond, and an official-looking fellow in a salmon-coloured coat appeared at the threshold. He beckoned a number of people inside, reading from a list draped across his forearm, and plunged back into the building with an impatient wave to the chosen few.

'Onwards,' Mowbray said quietly, leading Stryker into the house-cum-court. Along with a dragoon captain and a major of cuirassiers, they made their way down a narrow passageway at the smart pace set by the courtier.

'Are the princes here?' the cuirassier said, jangling like a sack of coins as he walked. He had removed his helmet but still wore the full body armour of his creed, menacing in its gleaming coat of black enamel. Stryker had seen Arthur Haselrig's Roundhead cuirassiers, known to the Royalists as the Lobsters, at

Roundway Down. They had been shattered on those bloody slopes, and now that he saw their Royalist equivalent up close, he could see why. The encumbrance of such armour, though doubtless protective against steel and small arms fire, would have made them terribly susceptible to outflanking by the lighter, faster harquebusiers favoured by Prince Rupert.

The courtier did not look round. 'They are, sir, but we try to keep them at bay for their own good. Wouldn't want 'em trampled by horses and suchlike. They're generally shut up in a chamber on the second floor.'

'Must be at their wits end,' the cuirassier muttered.

'Indeed,' the courtier agreed. 'They spend a deal of time carving grooves in the stone window ledges with their knives.' He halted at a side door. 'Captain Stryker?'

Stryker stepped forth, ignoring the expression that twisted the salmon-backed official's tired face. It was a mixture of horror and distaste; something to which he had grown inured over the years.

The courtier cleared his throat uncomfortably. 'Knock and enter, Captain.' He looked at the others. 'If the rest of you would be kind enough to follow me?'

Stryker did as he was told, while listening to the muffling of the metallic clatter of the cuirassier as the party disappeared round a corner. Alone, he stepped into the room.

'Stryker! Good God, man, it is a grand thing to see you.'

Prince Rupert of the Rhine crossed the tiled floor, spurs ringing out each step, and waved Stryker's bow dismissively away. He offered his hand for the captain to shake.

'It is good to be back with the army, sir,' Stryker said, feeling more comfortable now that the sentiment was beginning to feel like the truth. The short time he had spent with his regiment had served to give him some perspective, despite his affinity with Gloucester's spirited citizens. 'Took a while to find a way out.'

Rupert pushed a clump of tangled black curls behind his left ear and walked back to the chair he had evidently been warming before Stryker's arrival. He was different, somehow. His clothes were as martial as ever – silver-threaded buff-coat and breeches, black riding boots and a broad scarf of red silk fastened at his back in an enormous knot – but he seemed jittery, less certain of himself than he had been after Bristol. 'Events have played out as I feared,' he said, as though he could see the questions dancing in Stryker's grey eye.

'Your Highness?' Stryker eyed the little table near Rupert on which perched a decanter.

'This interminable siege, Captain.' Rupert folded his arms sulkily, apparently failing to register Stryker's interest in the richly dark wine. Beside him a white rug suddenly moved and Boye, the prince's poodle, stared up with brown eyes, twitching his glistening black nose for a moment, before returning to flinching slumber. 'I planned to storm the city, did I not? I warned a siege would cause us difficulty.'

Stryker could not tell if he was being criticized. 'I made the signal, General. On my honour, I made it.'

'Oh, we know you did,' another voice broke in.

Stryker's head snapped round to see the diminutive form of a man he knew well. 'I advised that Massie would not surrender, and I was in the right of it,' he said flatly. Ezra Killigrew had not lost his air of easy superiority, and he crossed one foot over the other as he leaned back against the cold wall. His beady eyes studied Stryker with interest. 'I saw the signal, noted it well, reported back to His Highness.'

'Then why not storm?' Stryker asked, looking at Rupert, who glowered at the hearth in the far wall, stewing in his own frustration.

'Because,' Killigrew answered for the irascible young Cavalier, 'the Prince was overruled by malicious elements who would undermine him at court.' He straightened and walked casually into the room. 'His Majesty would not risk a costly escalade, and here, as they say, we are. A messy business, whichever way one looks at it. The rebel news-books make merry with our lack of progress, as you can imagine, I'm sure.' He flashed his rodent-like teeth. 'But I thank you for your service, Captain, as does His Highness.'

'Yes,' Rupert said, looking up as if waking from a dream. 'Yes, I do. You've served me well again, Stryker, and I'll not forget it.'

'Incidentally,' Killigrew asked, 'did you not think to bring my man out of the city?'

Stryker felt heat burn his cheeks. 'Mister Buck did not wish to risk his skin in the raiding party,' he said, feeling certain the shrewd little aide would sense the awkwardness in his voice.

'But you've seen him?' Killigrew asked.

'Oh yes, Mister Killigrew,' Stryker replied as casually as he could manage. 'I've seen him all right.'

Killigrew nodded. 'Good. I look forward to his report when finally he makes his bid for freedom.'

'Or when Gloucester falls,' Stryker added, receiving a withering glance for his troubles.

'Now, Captain, what is it you wished to see us about?' Killigrew said. 'While we appreciate the report, it was you who requested the audience, I believe.'

I asked to see the Prince, not you, Stryker thought. 'I have grave news to impart.'

Killigrew's puffy eyes widened at that. 'Oh?'

Stryker noticed Rupert had taken notice as well, and he made a point of addressing the king's nephew. 'There is a killer in our camp, Your Highness.'

'Are we not all killers, Stryker?' Rupert grumbled.

'A murderer, then. An assassin. Sent here to kill His Majesty.'

'How do you know this?' Killigrew interjected.

'I was told by one of the rebels.'

Rupert stood suddenly, toppling his chair noisily. 'The rebels? Those spavined villains! Those bastardly gullions!' He rounded on Killigrew. 'Did I not say it all along? Did I not warn my uncle never to treat with those foul-hearted black-blooded villainous traitors? Jesu, but I'll slaughter the lot of them! The whole goddamned lot of them! To mutter discontent is enough to stomach, but to plot regicide—'

'Sir,' Stryker said, but saw he had not been heeded. 'General, please!'

Rupert turned. 'What? What is it, man? Spit it out!'

'I heard it from *one* of the rebels within the city, sir, but it is not a plan devised by the Parliament. Nor by Massie. He is operating alone, this man.'

Rupert snorted. '*Pah*! One man? Poppycock. A mere rumour put about to scare us.'

Stryker looked at Killigrew. 'Has anyone come into the camp in the last two days?'

Killigrew nodded while the prince paced like a caged lion. 'One Hatton, swam the river to the north. Spluttered into the Welsh near Kingsholm. I'm amazed they didn't chop him up there and then, truth be told.'

'Hatton? That was his name?'

'Aye. He is – he *was* – a gunner from the Town Regiment, but his feet, as they say, were growing ever cold, and now he has joined us.'

'A gunner,' Stryker said. 'You're certain?'

'Of course I'm certain,' Killigrew said irritably. 'It was I who spoke first with him before he was shipped off to Llanthony. Christ, but he knew the place inside out. Told us the rebels grow short of victuals, and, more importantly, powder. More-over, he has given a rather in-depth assessment of the defences, which should help no end.'

'You spoke with him? Did he have golden hair?'

Killigrew shook his head. 'No, Captain, he was bald. Bald as an egg.'

Hounslow Heath, near London, 22 August 1643

It was chaos. Large convoys of wagons overladen with musket-balls, blades, armour, victuals, tools, clothing and the officers' baggage trundled on to the heath. Spinning-wheeled artillery pieces followed, dragged by loping oxen and whickering nags, their traces and chains rattling like hail on a slate roof. The rough turf quickly turned into a morass, the muck exacerbated by human piss and animal dung, which was ploughed to sticky ruts by the steps of thousands of soldiers and their chattering kin.

Whole families had walked from the metropolis in their hundreds like a biblical exodus, streaming along the Great West Road to flood the wide heath in a noisome throng, and they mixed with the recruits gathering in tight ranks behind bright banners and grim sergeants. Spirits were ebullient; women and children laughed and joked, sang songs, played games and echoed the regimental chants of 'God and Parliament.'

The throng had come to see their husbands and sons march to war, but this time, so different from all those other sombre musters, the atmosphere was already one of triumph. The barks of officers rang out sharply over the trumpet calls and booming drums; it was a warlike orchestra that played for London's citizens. And those people cheered the players in turn, clapping the snorting cavalry and waving happily to the rows and rows of pikemen and musketeers who filed past to form great bristling blocks on the coarse terrain.

Lisette Gaillard looked on with a mixture of scorn and awe. She knew in her heart that the core of this cacophonous mob was the disease-ridden Edgehill army, its withered ranks bolstered by the disgraced Bristol men who had wandered into the capital like a column of scarecrows after their ignominious defeat just a few weeks before. And yet, though these men were hardly modern-day Spartans, their bearing was undeniably proud and their clanging armour and precise drills gave rise to an air of invincibility that she could not ignore.

'The news-books have them whipped up,' Major General Erasmus Collings said, seeing the expression on Lisette's face. 'They've all heard the tales from Gloucester.'

That morning, Lisette and Cecily had been taken from their cell in an abandoned farmhouse and conveyed here under heavy guard. It had been a westward journey along the teeming London road, and she again recognized the area. She asked the wagon driver, who confirmed that they had been held in a village called Brentford End. The place meant nothing to Cecily, but for Lisette it brought back a flood of memories.

They had waited for the best part of an hour, watching in stunned silence as the heath filled with soldiers and citizens, until Collings arrived in a gilt carriage with several dour-looking staff officers. He had brought the women to a large cart, from where they had observed the muster in all its pomp.

Lisette looked across at Collings. 'What tales?'

Collings was resplendent in a suit of purple, the tawny scarf of the Earl of Essex tied diagonally across his chest. He took off his purple-plumed hat and used it to fan his face. 'Your beloved king has failed. His grand army sits where it has sat for days, festering outside the walls of Gloucester. They have barely made a dent in the walls, and the garrison jeer them at every turn.'

'You lie,' Lisette said sourly.

'Why?' Collings replied in amusement as a powder wagon rolled by with an escort of firelocks. 'Why would I bother?'

Cecily Cade leant against the side of the cart, staring out into the sea of humanity that milled on this vast muster ground. 'Men have tried this trick before, sir,' she said, not taking her eyes off the remarkable scene. 'Chudleigh brought me to Stratton Hill to watch his supposed triumph, and look where that got him.'

'Chudleigh is a headstrong fool. I am not.' Collings replaced his hat, pointing a bony finger out at the gathering. 'You can see as well as I, ladies. Do they look as though they fear for their lives? This is a triumphal gathering. The King has entrusted his forces to that drunken Scot, Ruthven, and now they are in grave trouble, I assure you, confounded and humbled by our young hero, Governor Massie. This,' he swept his hand out front to indicate the massing companies, 'is to be his reward. Essex marches to Gloucester's relief.'

Cecily turned to him. 'So you did bring us here to gloat.'

Collings smiled, his black eyes shining like a jackdaw's. 'I would merely encourage you to see sense. Essex's force no longer languishes in feverish stupor. It rises from its ills, all the stronger, and will punish the King for his failures. Indeed, while you have enjoyed our hospitality these past days, I have been hard at work. I have arranged for the London Trained Bands to march with the men you see here.' He shrugged. 'I wanted my pretty pair of doves to witness the genesis of our triumph.'

While Cecily wrinkled her nose in disgust, Lisette's mind whirled with the news. 'The militia go to Gloucester?' she said doubtfully. 'I do not believe you.'

Collings broke into a cold chuckle. 'Believe what you like, Miss Gaillard. I care not a jot. The Trained Bands, for what it's worth, muster on the morrow, and will join the relief force. It will be a fearsome sight. Imagine it, ladies. Essex will arrive in Gloucester in a matter of days with an army the malignants will never be expecting. Indeed, it is an army that we did not even possess when first the King began his pathetic siege. It will be a coup on a grand scale. We will chase away the Oxford Army and its allies, spring the brave garrison from its cage, and trumpet our success throughout the land.' His eyes were bright and hard, and Lisette believed him, despite herself. 'This is what we've been waiting for. *This*,' he slammed a fist into his palm, 'is the turning of the tide.'

The drums left their irregular beat, moving into a more precise rhythm, and like a bristling monster shaking itself to laborious life, the newly created army began to shift, troopers steering their mounts into long columns, infantry units wheeling about in their jangling blocks.

Erasmus Collings looked on, his white face rigid with suppressed excitement. 'Things have gone badly for the rebellion,' he said suddenly. 'Chudleigh's humiliation at Stratton, Waller on Roundway Down, Fiennes at Bristol.' He shook his head slowly at the thought of it. 'Even the Fairfaxes took a battering in the north.'

'Then what is the meaning of this?' Lisette asked, thrusting out an arm to wave scornfully at the lumbering army.

Collings tore his black-pebble gaze from the churning heath to stare down at her. 'Gloucester has held out against all probability, Miss Gaillard. Amid all our setbacks and tribulations, one lonely garrison has managed to resist the combined might of Prince Robber, the vermin Welsh, old Forth, Astley and the rest. It has become a talisman for the whole rebellion. An example for Essex and Fairfax and Waller and Cromwell to follow. Rebel hopes hang upon Edward Massie and his men. If they can keep the king's men from their walls, it will be a clear sign that God is truly on our side.'

Lisette laughed. 'You don't believe that, General.'

'No, I don't,' Collings admitted. 'But I believe in the power of public opinion. Of the rabid, ranting mob. If Parliament can successfully relieve the city, then the support of the mob will be with us. And that is worth a hundred Prince Ruperts, I can assure you. Just take a look for yourself. See the smiles and hear the cheers. The people believe in Essex's new venture, for they know that we are all doomed if he fails. They cannot believe in anything else.'

Lisette and Cecily watched for a while longer as the soldiers followed the flapping ensigns to the west. They would march overnight to Colnbrook, according to Collings, and then on to Gloucester, the Trained Bands moving in their wake. Lisette imagined the besiegers camped all around the rebel city, watching its walls while a new, vast army crept up behind. Would they see it coming in time? Was there a chance they would be trapped between Essex's excitable brigades and Massie's artillery, hammered on both sides and toppled into the Severn? She feared for Prince Rupert. Christ, but it could prove more dramatic than even Collings predicted. If the Roundheads could capture the Teutonic Cavalier, then it would prove more than a mere turning point; the entire war effort would falter. And what of Stryker? Was he there, languishing in the siege lines, blissfully unaware of the threat that now lumbered towards him?

The cart rocked gently as Collings walked across the slats to the far side. He jumped nimbly down, holding out a hand for each of the women to take. 'But sadly we three shall not witness that great day,' he said, the black-coated men of his personal troop immediately flanking him. 'I have learned from my mistakes, and will take far greater care of you both from now on.'

Lisette dropped down from the side of the wagon, ignoring the general's proffered hand. 'Meaning?'

'Meaning you will return to your lodgings at Brentford End, while I attend to the rest of my business with the militia,' Collings replied. 'And then we will make our way east to the capital. Miss Cade is bound for the Tower until such time as she wishes to speak properly with us, and you, Miss Gaillard.' He tutted softly. 'You, I am desperately saddened to say, are bound for Tyburn Tree.'

Near Barton, Gloucester, 22 August 1643

Evening was drawing in as Stryker returned to Mowbray's camp. He had made no progress in his quest to catch Skaithlocke's deadly emissary. He had travelled out to the Earl of Forth's base at Llanthony Priory during the afternoon in order to find the gunner, Hatton, although Killigrew had assured him this could not be his man.

'Not here, Stryker,' Major Beak had said. 'He passed through during the morning, but all was in order and I sent him on his way.'

Stryker had badgered the major for more information, but what could Beak really say? What, after all, did an assassin look like?

'He had no papers,' Beak had explained with growing impatience, 'but then the poor fellow *had* just swum the Severn and braved walking into our lines.'

'Did he carry any weapons?'

Beak had slumped back in his chair and plucked the round lenses from his narrow face in obvious annoyance. 'I repeat,

Captain. He jumped into the River Severn in order to desert. He arrived with nothing, save his shirt, britches and a bloody nasty cough.'

So Stryker had left the priory buildings in the shadow of the decapitated tower with a growing sense of frustration. Hatton was considered a hero, and an ailing one at that, and Alexander Beak seemed extremely reluctant to allow a ranting, ruin faced officer the chance to harass him during his well-earned convalescence. But with the mention of Rupert's involvement – though Stryker had to exaggerate the surly prince's interest – Beak had relented, digging through a well-thumbed ledger to locate the place to which he had assigned the deserter.

'Kingsholm?' Colonel Mowbray repeated incredulously when Stryker had finished his tale.

They were in Mowbray's tent, sipping ale from pewter cups. Stryker wiped his mouth with his sleeve. 'No more exact than that, I'm afraid.'

'I suppose you found nothing.'

Stryker took another swig and shook his head. Kingsholm was a village to the north of the city, turned into a town by the four thousand soldiers in Vavasour's brigade. Apart from the streets, taverns and houses he had been obliged to search, Stryker had been compelled to trawl the fields, which were lined with tents, and the patchy woodland, where some of the more hardened Welsh forces slept out in the open. 'No one's seen him,' he said, recalling with frustration the afternoon's fruitless wandering. 'He's melted into Kingsholm with licence to find a billet and lay low for a few days.'

Mowbray set his cup down on a neatly arranged table and stretched, straining his shoulder blades back with a groan. 'And in fact,' he said with the voice of exasperation, 'we may be thinking of the wrong man altogether.'

That was true enough, Stryker thought. Hatton did not fit Skaithlocke's brief description of the assassin, not least because the first thing he had done was take a detailed assessment of Gloucester's defences to the Royalist high command. And the lack of any weapons made the connection even less likely.

'And how the devil,' Mowbray went on, 'would he carry out this mission, even if he wanted to? A mere gunner is too lowly a rank to gain access to the King, so a blade is out of the question. He'll be working with our ordnance, of course, but the cannon point at the walls. He could hardly coerce an entire artillery team to turn one round, and then successfully aim the thing directly at His Majesty.' He twirled his neatly waxed moustache around his little finger. 'Which leaves a musket?'

'It's the only long-range weapon he'd really have access to,' Stryker agreed. 'But it is hardly the tool of the professional. Far too inaccurate to guarantee a hit, let alone a kill.'

Mowbray blew out his narrow cheeks. 'So is it this Hatton? Really?'

Stryker shrugged, for he knew it to be tenuous. 'I would say not, sir, except he is the only deserter for some time. The only credible candidate.'

'Keep looking, Captain,' Mowbray said with a heavy sigh, 'but be vigilant. It does not look likely to be him. What did the Prince say?'

'Much the same. He is distracted, sir.'

'The siege does not go well,' Mowbray reflected. 'He takes a great deal of criticism from some quarters.'

'But he did not wish to sit outside the city, sir. He advised an escalade.'

Mowbray's small head bobbed in agreement. 'But that is easily forgotten. The fact is, a move on Gloucester was part of his strategy. Those that wished to march straight upon London are calling for his head on a platter.'

'The Queen?'

Mowbray nodded. 'His beloved aunt is not best pleased, by all accounts.' He filled their cups from a frothy blackjack. 'The King was not particularly helpful, either.'

Mowbray had had an audience with the monarch while Stryker was speaking with Rupert. 'He was unconcerned by the assassin?' he asked, surprised.

'We do not have the evidence to prove anything, Stryker. And if the siege goes ill for our General of Horse, then it goes positively rotten for His Majesty. He is angry, embarrassed, and talking of a grand, final attack. They are mining the walls as we speak, I understand, and a Doctor Chillingworth is busy constructing some fantastical engines for our forces to traverse their damned moat. Unless Skaithlocke's man marches into Matson House with a barrel full of powder strapped to his back and a lighted match 'twixt his teeth, I fear the King will ignore the threat.'

CHAPTER 19

Beside the East Gate, Gloucester, 24 August 1643

Stryker assumed command of his company as soon as he had broken his fast, sending Lieutenant Hood to Kingsholm during the morning to search for the gunner, Hatton. It had only been a matter of days since leaving them at Hartcliffe, but the manner in which he and Skellen had departed, and the conflicting loyalties he had felt during his time with the rebels, made him keen to renew their old camaraderie.

Orders for the morning were to escort a team of engineers into the saps before the city's east wall, and to protect them as they dragged a thick-planked gallery into place. Massie's daring raids seemed to have become less ambitious since the ill-fated sortie during which Stryker and Skellen had switched sides, and the frenetic activity in the trenches had taken on a sense of calm. In response, it had been deemed time to move upon the crumbling stone walls with more gusto, and the Royalist command had embarked upon a four-pronged plan. Two teams of engineers – one working on the south face, the other the east – protected by wooden galleries, would fill the moat with debris, thereby building bridges that would take them right up to the base of the old and, it was wagered, vulnerable walls. There they would lay surface mines in order to open huge breaches through which assault troops could pour. The third prong involved excavating all the way under moat. A mining crew was already busily scouring out the soil further back, unseen by rebel eyes, and would slowly tunnel underneath the waterlogged ditch to undermine the East Gate from below ground. All the while, a group of carpenters were scurrying about their makeshift workshops in Llanthony Priory building the siege engines Mowbray had told him about. The churchman and mathematician Doctor Chillingworth, it was said, ranted and raved at the harassed party, making sure his ingenious vehicles, set on great wheels with inbuilt drawbridges to span the defensive breastwork, were just as he envisaged. But they were far from complete, and the trio of mines were to press ahead regardless.

'Can't say I'd want to be in one o' them,' Skellen muttered as the company fanned out along the sticky saps to give covering fire. They pelted the enemy rampart with lead, forcing the defenders back while the wooden shell was pushed by half a dozen men up to the edge of the deep ditch. Already the occasional shot spat down at the engineers, but the musket-balls bounced harmlessly off the gallery's stout planks.

'They'll be fine,' Stryker said as the men disappeared under the shield. 'It is shot-proof.'

'Not for cannon,' Skellen argued.

'They're inside a cannon's range, Will,' Stryker said. 'Too close. They can hardly point a muzzle straight down.'

A cart full of soil and wooden faggots had been pushed up to the rear of the gallery, and the men under the thick roof began bringing the material inside. From his position in the trenches, Stryker could not see what they did after that, but he knew they would be tossing everything into the moat. They would gradually fill it in, enabling the teams of fire-workers to cross safely with their high explosives.

'Fire!' a croaking voice screamed a little way along the sap. Sporadic shots rang out from the red-coated ranks crouching against the muddy trench walls. 'Shoot, yer English bastards! Shoot!'

Stryker rocked back to look along the line of musketeers. Sure enough, there was Simeon Barkworth, his yellow eyes gleaming like a cat's against the dark earth. Ensign Chase was near him, as were the twins, Jack and Harry Trowbridge. They were all here; his men.

'Good to be home, sir.'

Stryker saw Skellen grinning at him. He nodded. 'Aye, Sergeant, it is.'

He picked up a musket that had been propped against the slick earthen slope. It had been a while since he had fired one, and he was surprised by the reassurance he felt just by gripping the wooden stock. When Skellen gave him a scrap of glowing match-cord, he held it between his teeth and carefully loaded the weapon, revelling in each methodical step, until he was ready to fire. He fixed the cord into the serpentine's cold jaws, easing back the trigger to check that the hot tip would touch the centre of the cover guarding his priming pan. It did, and he swivelled the cover back, exposing the pan's charge. He leaned forward, resting the butt against his shoulder and his left elbow on the mud at ground level. Finally he brought the barrel up, training it on a point above the East Gate and dragging it to the left, patches of rubble, timber, gabion and woolsack whirring across his vision as he scanned the much repaired rampart. His dark muzzle eventually rested upon the form of a blue-coated musketeer who brazenly paced the wall, charging his own long-arm ready to shoot down at the engineers before the wall. For a moment Stryker felt a wave of guilt. Had he known this man? Commanded him on a sally? Helped him pile the inner glacis? He swallowed hard. He had made his bed, and now he would damn well lie in it. He pulled the trigger. When the plume of bitter smoke had cleared, the man was no longer there.

The Cob and Saddle, near Barton, Gloucester, 24 August 1643

'He's done well, Stryker,' Captain Lancelot Forrester said when some of the regiment's officers met at one of the more salubrious taphouses frequented by the besieging army. He was red-eyed like the rest of his peers, sooty of face and black of fingernail, but he seemed in good spirits now that his friends had returned to the fold. 'Since you upped and left, he stepped into your boots manfully.'

'I was too hard on him,' Stryker said, glum at the thought. He had ridden out from the main camp with spirits high, not least because the reunion with Vos had been marked by an exhilarating gallop up the churned road, which served to clear his head a deal. But he had entered the crowded tavern with a tentative step, half expecting someone might materialize from the noisy fug wielding an accusatory finger and condemning tale. A prisoner who had turned his coat, perhaps. One who remembered all too vividly Stryker's involvement with the defences and raiding parties. He could deny it all, of course. Rightly claim that he could hardly have refused service with the rebels when he had been ordered by Prince Rupert to join them. But who would believe that? Could he prove it before he was lynched? The likelihood of such a meeting was minimal, but that did not assuage the tension in his limbs and chest.

'Yes, you bloody were,' Forrester replied, the guttering candle flame throwing crazed shapes on his round face. They were in a corner, nestled away in the muggy building's inner sanctum, as night turned the encampment dark. Captains Kuyt and Bottomley had joined them, casually playing dice on the circular table's far side, while some of the more junior of Mowbray's officers milled out in the adjoining corridor, laughing and swilling claret and beer. Lieutenant Thomas Hood was with the latter group, chatting loudly, and both men watched him. Forrester dragged at his pipe, blowing smoke rings around Stryker. When the last had drifted lazily away, collapsing into a score of ghostly tendrils, he leaned in. ''Tis one thing to harangue a young buck in order to keep him from killing his men through stupidity,' he said in a low voice. 'Quite another when that poor bastard has done nothing but replace a lost comrade.'

'I know,' Stryker said weakly, still looking at the men in the passageway. He had hoped to speak to Hood since the lieutenant had returned empty-handed from his errand to Kingsholm, but duties had not provided the opportunity. 'And I will speak with him.'

'Two fives, Aad, my old feodary!' Job Bottomley exclaimed suddenly, juddering the table with a chubby fist.

Aad Kuyt's blue eyes narrowed. 'We shall play again. Give me chance to win back my stake, yes?'

Bottomley, the regiment's third captain, peered at the Dutchman through the miasma. His eyes were saddled with heavy yellow bags, sagging like plague boils on his milky skin, and he blinked rapidly as he considered the request. He pushed a greasy strand of coke-black hair from his ear and sat back, patting his vast belly with both palms. 'I suppose I can afford another pie if I take more of your money, Captain. Let's play.'

As Kuyt scooped up the bone pieces, Stryker looked back at his friend. 'I have seen much of grief, Forry.'

'Haven't we all?'

'These last weeks,' Stryker said. 'In there. The best of it, and the worst.'

Forrester nodded. 'It can poison the hardiest chap if allowed to take hold.'

Stryker thought of Skaithlocke's mind, once so unruffled, now melted by white-hot grief. When he had seen Hood in Gloucester's shattered suburbs, he had realized that he too dallied with that path. It terrified him. 'That it can.'

'What happened in there, old man?' Forrester asked abruptly.

They had not had time to speak properly since Stryker and Skellen stumbled into the skirmish outside the south wall, and he had known his friend's interrogation would come. Even so, it was difficult to know where to begin. 'Too much to tell all at once.'

Forrester rolled his eyes. 'What's he like, young Massie? We are told he forces his men to imbibe strong drink before they fight.'

Stryker laughed. 'Is that what they're putting about?' He shook his head as he lit his own pipe. 'No, he is clever. A good soldier.'

Through the newly billowing sotweed cloud, he saw Forrester's round face crease suspiciously. 'You sound rather like you admire him.'

'I do,' Stryker said, deciding there was little point in denying it. 'But there is something else.' He took another pull on the clay stem, letting the fragrant smoke warm his lungs, and exhaled slowly. 'Skaithlocke is in Gloucester.'

As he expected, Forrester's eyes bulged. 'Skaithlocke? *Colonel* Skaithlocke?' He sat back blowing a gust of air out through pursed lips. Eventually he shook his head. 'Well, I shouldn't be surprised, I suppose. If the Parliament could pay him more than us, then he was bound to throw in his lot with the rebels.'

'No, Forry, that's just it. He's with them for conviction.'

Forrester paused, carefully examining Stryker's face, before the corners of his mouth curled upwards. '*Ha!*' He slapped Stryker's shoulder. 'A fine jest. Almost had me.'

'I'm serious, Forry.'

This time Forrester could see that Stryker meant it, and he rubbed his tired eyes in bewilderment. 'Turned Puritan, has he? Well I never thought I'd see the day.'

'John died,' Stryker continued. He felt bad for the way in which he broke the news, for Forrester had known the younger Skaithlocke just as well as he had, but he could think of no kinder way than the simple telling of it.

'Jesu,' Forrester said, the redness flushing from his sweaty jowls.

'He was killed by imperial forces some time ago.' Stryker leaned in. 'They tortured him first, Forry. Horribly so. It has—' He had removed his hat when they sat down, and now he stared at its mangled feathers, for he could not meet Forrester's drilling gaze. 'It has changed the colonel. Christ, the Dutch call him Slager now!'

Forrester scrunched up his face as his brain considered the foreign tongue. 'Baker?'

Captain Kuyt's head snapped up from his game. 'Butcher.'

Forrester's eyes widened. 'Butcher? They call him the *Butcher*? Now that doesn't sound too chirpy, does it?'

Stryker shook his head as Forrester took a lingering draught of claret, which spilled in tiny trickles down his chin. 'He is not in Gloucester to fight for the rebels per se, but because he thought it would give him the greatest chance of killing the King.'

'Killing—' Forrester echoed, almost spitting out his wine. He looked around furtively, dropping his voice to an earnest whimper. 'Killing the King? Is he mad? Even the most ardent bloody Roundheads don't want that! Christ on His Cross, Stryker, but the Parliament would have him jigging the morris just as we would.'

'But it won't be him directly,' said Stryker.

'Zounds, man,' Forrester said suddenly, the light of understanding appearing across his face. 'I know you'd warned Sir Edmund there was an assassin on the loose, but not that he was working for my old commanding bloody officer. What does the King say?'

'Mowbray spoke with him, but he thinks it a hoax.'

Forrester nodded. 'And things have gone too far awry here, I suppose. He won't abandon the siege and risk the criticism. Not for mere conjecture, leastwise. But you're quite sure? Skaithlocke is really behind this?'

'He means to plunge England into war with the Papists.'

'And it is worth the murder of his king?'

'*Exitus acta probat*,' Stryker repeated Skaithlocke's declaration. 'That's what he said.'

'The end justifies the deed,' Forrester said softly. He began to gnaw at his bottom lip.

'Remember Ezekiel Nobbs?' Stryker said.

'How could I not? A vile rodent, if ever there was one. Skaithlocke's toadying aide. Foul and fawning, if I recall.'

'I watched the colonel strangle him when he thought his grand plan might be at risk.' Stryker's face was grim. 'Wrung his neck like a chicken.'

'God's most precious and holy blood,' Lancelot Forrester muttered, before knocking back the remainder of his wine with an audible gulp. He slammed the battered goblet on the table. 'Grief really did send him mad.'

'It can happen easily enough,' Stryker said as he pushed himself to his feet. 'And that is why I must speak with Lieutenant Hood forthwith.'

He found Hood outside talking merrily with one of the taphouse's serving-girls. He smiled to himself as he approached, but felt instantly bad as the young man shooed her away, evidently fearing another tongue-lashing from his irascible commander.

'Hell, Tom, am I that fearsome?' he said, keeping his voice light.

'S-sorry, sir,' Hood muttered, glaring at the flagstones of the courtyard. Above them the inn's sign swung back and forth, its crude painting of a small horse screeching on rusty hinges like some night-time banshee.

Stryker crammed his hat back atop his head and rested his left hand on the garnet-set pommel of his sword. 'Captain Forrester informs me of your good work in commanding the company, Lieutenant.'

Hood's neck convulsed as though he swallowed a ball of feathers. 'He flatters me, sir.'

'He gives you praise, Tom, and that is not idly given. Well done.'

'Sir.'

There passed a moment of extreme awkwardness as captain fumbled for something to say and lieutenant stared at the rail where their horses had been tethered, as though he considered whether to make a run for it. Stryker finally cleared his throat. 'I would apologize to you, Mister Hood.'

341

Hood seemed even more embarrassed. 'Come now, sir, I—'

'Let me speak,' interrupted Stryker. He sighed deeply, forcing himself to think upon events he would rather have let rest. 'You once asked me about Stratton Fight.'

Hood looked up with a pained expression. 'A childish question, sir. Nothing more. I have learned much of late, not least the ability to keep my peace.'

'It was a bitter one, that is for certain,' Stryker said, determining that he would tell the story regardless, now that it had bubbled to the surface of his memories. 'The men of Cornwall and Devon are not friendly in peacetime, let alone war.'

'But you won, sir,' Hood said. 'Cut your way to the summit and put the rebels to the sword.'

Stryker nodded. 'True enough, Lieutenant, but it was a terrible sight, believe me. It was not the dead that stuck with me, so much as the living.'

'Sir?'

Stryker remembered the carpet of mangled corpses atop the flat summit of the ancient hill fort. Interspersed between the twisted, shocked faces were the pitiful bodies of those unfortunate enough to be left alive. He could not suppress a slight shudder. 'There were so many wounded that the whole ground looked as though it crawled. Like a nest of maggots.' He stared hard at Hood. 'There is nothing noble in killing. Nothing.' He saw the haunting image again; a young man's face, obliterated by a tiny sphere of lead. 'It was there that your predecessor died.'

'Captain Forrester told me, sir.'

'He was my officer, and I should have protected him,' said Stryker. 'I failed, and he died.'

'You blame yourself?'

'I always will,' Stryker said, and felt as though it was the only solid truth he had told for many days. He forced a smile, wondering if the gesture looked more demon than human in the orange glow of the tavern's windows. 'But that does not mean I should punish you for my failures. Burton was a good man, an excellent soldier, and he was my friend. I have no doubt you will do him proud, Mister Hood.'

'Thank you, sir,' Hood said, offering a slight bow that Stryker waved quickly away.

'Now will my second in command allow me to buy him a drink?'

Hood beamed. 'I will, sir.'

By Little Mead, Gloucester, 24 August 1643

The cattle had been coaxed back into the city by a team of nervous musketeers, whose match-tips danced like the eyes of nocturnal beasts as they slapped and prodded the braying animals over the ramshackle bridge of ladders spanning the ditch.

Nikolas Robbens had watched from the Royalist lines on the northern side of the meadow as the Welsh and Worcester men of Vavasour's brigade took a few lacklustre pot shots at the plaintiff cows, but, though there were nearly two hundred to choose from, they apparently hit nothing. Quickly they abandoned their sport, laying back to look up at the scudding smears of charcoal-grey that were smothering the stars, apparently not considering the harassment of the garrison to be worth the minute or two it took to load a musket. Robbens was astounded by their attitude; ten-score cattle and at least thirty unprotected rebels had been well within musket range, and yet the men had not been bothered to make any concerted attempt to rustle or injure either. But then this was his over-riding impression of the sprawling Royalist army. One of low morale and steadily creeping lethargy. The king's men were relatively disease free, had plentiful supplies of food, and new consignments of powder and ammunition had been trund-ling in from mills and foundries at regular intervals. But still the men were not happy. It was simply taking too long, Robbens supposed. The siege had settled into a rhythm of attrition, and, while common sense dictated that eventually

Gloucester would fall, the men gathered outside the city had grown bored.

This kind of inept lassitude would never have been permitted on the Continent, Robbens thought, as he paced the well-trodden grass between two of the besiegers' wicker breastworks. The Royalist commanders would have been marched out of their pampered quarters at dawn and served lead for breakfast if they had been accountable to any of the grand European chiefs. But this kind of thing, he had quickly learned, seemed to be the English way. A nation of hard, disagreeable scrappers, the common sort made undeniably excellent soldiers, but they were so often led by bungling fops or doddering old palliards, and as a result their good intentions would rapidly descend into farce. Still, at least the incompetent machinations of this grim island's politicians and warriors would not be his concern for much longer. He patted his new snapsack, issued to him with a new set of clothes at Llanthony Priory. Inside, along with a plug of tobacco, a pipe, tinderbox, wooden bowl and spoon, there was a square of folded paper. It was signed and sealed by Major Alexander Beak, and gave him leave to recuperate in peace for five days. He had used the pass to secure lodgings in a small house on the Kingsholm road, and, though he shared the space with fifteen truculent and barely intelligible Welsh pikemen, it had served him well. He simply had to remember to cough occasionally, so that the fever-fearing soldiers would steer a wide berth.

'Hatton!' a man called out as Robbens reached the base of an ancient, bowing oak.

Robbens turned to see a musketeer in a brown coat and breeches sidle up with a gaping yawn. He shook the man's gloved hand and stared out over the Little Mead and the city beyond. 'A good day's hunting, Gilliatt?'

Gilliatt, one of the mattrosses down from Worcester, shook his head and picked at a spot beneath his Montero cap. 'Barely a scratch made.' He had been chewing tobacco, for his teeth and gums looked as though he had been feasting on tar, and he sent a jet of brown liquid through the gap in his front teeth. 'The balls are swallowed by their earthen banks. You? How's that chest?'

Robbens gave a little cough for effect. 'Not there yet. Another day or two.'

'Then into the redoubts.'

'Then into the redoubts,' Robbens echoed.

Gilliatt deposited the masticated remains of his sotweed on to the root-webbed ground and pulled his coat tighter, though the cloud cover had made this night warmer than the rest. He whistled the same jaunty tune as he had on the other occasions the pair had met, and Robbens tried to keep the irritation from his face. The oak was where the Dutchman had come on both nights since his arrival, watching and waiting, and both times the gunnery assistant had wandered over. It was irksome to say the least, but he suffered the infernal man's insipid chatter and mind-melting whistles for the good of the mission. It would all be over soon, he consoled himself.

Gilliatt sniffed the air. 'Rain.'

Robbens glanced again at the clouds. 'Indeed.'

'Not good. They'll fuck up our saps better 'an the crop'ead cannon.'

As if God had been eavesdropping on their conversation, a rustling sound began to climb above the gentle murmur of the breeze and the distant bellow of cattle now safely ensconced beyond Gloucester's north wall. The noise grew quickly, building to a substantial rush, like sand being blown across a stone floor, and both men looked up to see the oak leaves shivering madly on their branches.

'Told yer,' Gilliatt said proudly, as the fat raindrops finally penetrated the canopy. He shifted his cap to make sure it covered his fleshy earlobes.

Nikolas Robbens had been issued with a skull-hugging Monmouth cap, knitted deliberately tight to fit beneath a helmet, and he pulled it down hard. His head felt the cold more keenly now that it no longer had its golden thatch, and he expected a dense bout of rain to be even less enjoyable. 'It is heavy,' he said, noting the puddles already forming out on Little Mead. 'Never mind the saps, what of the mines? And the moat will fill.'

Gilliatt fished for some more tobacco in his snapsack and popped it past sore, red lips. 'We'll be here till second coming at this rate.'

They peered out through the downpour a while longer, slanted sheets of rain lashing all along the earthwork. This part of the defences sat between the two arms of the River Severn, and Robbens imagined the black torrent swelling against its banks on both sides, threatening to engulf the entire area. He was glad he had not waited till tonight to cross it. Some fool along the wicker screen to his right fired a hopeful shot at one of the sentries on the city rampart, but his powder was wet and the musket gave a feeble-sounding belch as the charge failed to properly ignite. Laughter rose up from the shadows around him.

Gilliatt was looking up at the dripping, swaying boughs. He shifted his feet from side to side, testing the firmness of the terrain, and gave a shuddering snort. 'Sinkin' here.'

'Back to camp?' Robbens said.

The mattross nodded. 'Got these latchets off a dragooner at cards. Daft bugger. Anyway, they're the best shoes I've owned, and I'll be damned if I'm to ruin 'em for a bit o' rain.' He touched a hand to his temple and picked his way back towards the lanterns, which marked the encampment amid the squall. 'Praps tomorrow night, Hatton!' he called back.

'I look forward to it!' Nikolas Robbens called through the driving droplets, waving him off with a cheery hand. But there was no cheer in his heart, only pounding anxiety that made his jaw feel tight and his skin crawl. After waiting for two nights, the opportunity had finally presented itself. The storm had driven Gilliatt back to the pungent warmth of his company's inn, and that was useful, but it had also served to force the pockets of musketeers back from the most advanced lines. All around him, with lanterns swinging in the blackness, the men of Wales and Worcester were withdrawing from the screens and trenches, evidently deciding that more shelter could be found further back. A couple of eagle-eyed bluecoats up on the wall fired down at their backs, but other than providing an example of how to keep one's powder dry, they achieved nothing, and soon the front line was mercifully empty.

Robbens knew that this was his chance. He had come to this spot north-east of the rebel West Gate on that first night, hoping to retrieve the sack that he had dumped in the bushes flanking Little Mead. But he had been confounded, for the place he had chosen had been impossible to access without being seen by the musketeers dug into the fields. The second night had been the same frustrating waste of time, and he had genuinely begun to despair. The Royalist pickets had stridden out to accost him as soon as he had spluttered his way up on to the bank of the Severn, as it curved eastwards to form a natural moat for the north wall, and he had been forced to act quickly to avoid being found with the sodden bag. He had known then that it would be a devil of a task to find it without causing suspicion.

Now, though, the glittering eyes that had lined Vavasour's extensive breastworks were gone. There was no one to question the motives of a supposed gunner who wished to take a stroll across Little Mead for no apparent reason.

Robbens left the safety of the oak, and the rain felt instantly harder. He uncurled a balled hand, noting the pain where his nails had cleaved into the flesh of his palm, and lifted it to shield his eyes from the vengeful water. He glanced quickly over his shoulder. Seeing no interested heads above the Royalist works, he decided to press on, and plunged into the squally blackness of the squelching meadow. The grass was already rutted and torn by the city's grazing herd, but now great swathes of it shone like shattered glass in the feeble moonlight as puddles distended into rippling pools, water collecting in the places where the city women had torn away the turf for their walls.

He ran a few paces, slowed to look back, ran again, all the while cringing as cold water crept up through his standard-issue shoes. They were cheaply made, straight-lasted so that they could be worn on either foot, and far too big, and the saturated material slapped wetly against his sodden hose. Soon he was at the cluster of vicious gorse bushes he remembered, a crescent-moon-shaped scar on the green pasture, and he dived behind the first of them, gritting his teeth and praying no shots rang out to greet him.

Nothing. He was twenty paces from the river as it swept along the face of the north earthwork, but no sentries seemed to be walking the rampart. They were there, of course, for he knew the garrison well enough to be certain of their vigilance, but he guessed they must be sheltering further back on the fire-step, waxy coats drawn high and tight to provide a canopy for heads, priming pans and bandoliers. No one on the wall would be look-ing directly down at the river, for they would have seen the Welshmen fall back, and would not be fearing an assault from down on the Little Mead in the midst of this filthy tempest. All to the good, Robbens thought, as he slumped on to hands and knees, hissing a murderous oath as his thin fingers sank in turf that now had a consistency akin to the dung that littered the meadow.

He scrabbled in the darkness, cursing as his fingers snagged on the wicked needles of the gorse, and feeling numbness seep through his limbs. A call came from above, and his heart froze as he winced up at the looming city, but no inquisitive faces or hostile muskets greeted his stare. He looked back at the ground, blinking away the rain that had pelted his eyes, and groped the space before him. His fingers touched upon something in the murk. There it was. *There it was.* He grabbed at the sack, revel-ling in the coarse material as he drew it to his breast. He sat back on his haunches, forgetting the rain at once, and pulled open the string-tightened throat. He thrust his hand inside without delay, delving frantically like a starving man rumma-ging through a bread basket, and immediately his probing fingers hit upon their prize.

Relaxing a little, he opened the sack properly now that he was satisfied that the bow was there. He peered into the black innards, but could see nothing discernible, so he let his hand snake gently around the steel stock, the curved limbs, the trigger and the taut string itself. She was all there, waiting for him in one exquisite piece. He slung the sack across his back, looking left and right, back up at the piled earth that served as Gloucester's north wall, then behind at the foremost Royalist lines. Still no one braved the storm, so he thanked God and made his move. Back to Kingsholm. Back to King Charles' sprawling army. He was ready to change the world.

Barton, Gloucester, 24 August 1643

Stryker staggered out of the Cob and Saddle near midnight, the rain slashing the roads and fields so heavily that he wondered if they shouldn't abandon the siegeworks and build an ark. He was alone, for Mowbray's units were not scheduled to work in the saps the following day, and most of his fellow carousers had decided to wait out the storm in the warmth of the tavern. But Stryker had had enough for one night, his befuddled head swimming with thoughts of Skaithlocke and his scheme.

He walked sideways across the courtyard, lurching away from the taphouse's screeching sign as his shoulder clipped the sturdy upright. He swore, stumbling haphazardly over to the open-fronted stable where Vos was waiting beneath a leaky awning. He grasped the wooden rail to steady himself, and the big stallion shook its head, snorting impatiently. 'There there,' he whispered, patting the animal's copper neck, a puff of dust rolling out at the impact. 'Missed you, boy.'

When he had untied the reins, he clambered gracelessly into the saddle and coaxed the patient beast into the night. They clopped across the smooth stones of the yard and on to a cinder path turned to bog by the rain. Stryker looked up at the trees, which seemed to sing amid the downpour. Their branches swayed and shook, the motion making his guts turn, and he vomited the ale-stinking contents of his stomach on to the black cinders. He swore again as he noticed the spatters on his boots and stirrup. Then he froze as he heard the distinct whicker of another horse.

There were three riders on the path, walking small mounts in single file. They were at least thirty paces away, and the rain, the low-hanging canopy, and his alcoholic stupor made it near impossible to discern their faces, but the way they kicked hard when they saw him made him ignore the churning of his innards. He tore at Vos's reins, wrenching the stallion round in a tight circle, and kicked hard, aiming to return to the taphouse and his friends within, but already he could hear the thunder of the hooves at his back.

He pulled left, guiding the horse out through a gap in the fencing and on to the main road, safe in the knowledge that Vos could comfortably outrun the poor palfreys of his hunters. But Vos slipped, his hoof flailing as the slick roadway shredded beneath his iron shoes, and for a brief, heart-stopping moment Stryker feared they would collapse in a crashing, mud-caked heap. His steed somehow regained its balance, pulling itself upright and spurring onwards with a shrill whinny, but the chasing pack was on them now, and Stryker steered Vos back to face the pursuers, taking the straps with his left hand and drawing his sword with his right.

Immediately, one of the riders came at him. The man, a thick-set brute with black hair and beard, bushy eyebrows and a deep scar across his right cheek, jabbed at his face with a straight hanger. Stryker parried it easily enough, for it was an obvious move, but he felt terribly vulnerable, having imbibed so much strong drink. His face felt warm, his empty eye socket throbbed, and everything seemed slow. He blinked hard when the attacker had ridden past to wheel back, screwing shut his eye as if he could purge the alcohol from his body, but when he opened it again nothing had changed.

The second of the trio came on. An older man with grey hair and beard, face half-shadowed beneath a wide felt hat, he seemed more thoughtful in his approach, skirting Stryker for a split second as if feinting to the captain's left. With a deft flick of the reins, he brought his white palfrey lunging in, raising and striking his silver blade in a blurry arc that sliced the air before Stryker's face. Stryker blocked it, letting his own sword slide the length of his opponent's to clang against the hilt. The force was enough for the cutting edge to bounce off the protective guard, clipping the grey haired rider's forearm. It was not a severe blow, but the rider's buff-coat was sleeveless, and Stryker felt his sword cut through wool and flesh. The attacker hissed in pain, ripping himself and his mount away, his face contorted demonically in the feeble light. Stryker exploded in a guttural roar for the confident trio seemed suddenly unsure. His head was still addled, his guts griping madly, but something in the cool of the rain and the heat of the fight had honed his senses like a whetstone against steel.

Yet he knew he could not win this fight, and already the three were circling like sharks. If they came at him together, he would be cut to ribbons in seconds. So Stryker charged. He dropped the reins, crouched low, hooked his left arm about Vos's granite-hard neck, and raked his spurs viciously along the stallion's flanks. Vos reared angrily, as Stryker knew he would, but he did not throw his master. Instead, he powered forwards like a shot from a cannon royal. Stryker still had his sword, and he thrust it out in front like a lance, hoping the steel would make the men shy away, but it was all down to Vos now.

A cry of warning came from one of the assailants as they panicked. They tried to move, to bring their blades down at horse and man, but Vos was too fast, and he galloped straight at the white palfrey. The smaller horse's eyes became huge, pushing from its long face like white toadstools, but its rider was wounded and seemed to list like a holed ship, and Vos smashed home. The palfrey skittered backwards with a terrified whinny, lost its footing and tripped over its own flailing hooves in a juddering, screaming mass of man and fetlock.

Stryker bolted. He regained the reins and thrust home his sword, kissing the garnet in its pommel and whooping at the pregnant clouds that smudged the stars and drenched the earth. He slapped Vos hard on his rain-soaked coat of glistening copper, and did not bother to look back.

CHAPTER 20

Brentford End, west of London, 27 August 1643

The chapel was on the easternmost fringe of the village, perched against the bridge over the River Brent. On the opposite side lay New Brentford, with the older conurbation further east. The small but heavily armed cavalcade had left the farmhouse that morning with no intention of making fast progress back to the capital, for it was a Sunday, and Collings had ordered that they would pause to hear the local priest's sermon. And yet the time it had taken to travel the short distance had surprised even him. The road was choked with men and munitions, all headed out of the city, bound for the Earl of Essex's slowly marching army and its quest to relieve Gloucester. Thus Collings's black-coated band, with a wagon carrying two women at its tail, pushed against the tide, compelled to weave in and out of the Gloucester-bound traffic, which was struggling to make the rendezvous for His Grace's brand new army at a place called Brackley.

'Everyone in,' Collings ordered as he slid down from his piebald mare.

Wallis, the red-bearded man who commanded the personal guard of Erasmus Collings, bellowed in snappy tones that had the blackcoats dismounting with smart precision. The soldier driving the cart brought his vehicle to a jangling halt up close to the chapel.

'You stop to pray, General?' Lisette Gaillard shouted towards the front of the short column.

Collings handed his reins to a subordinate and waved back over the heads of his thirty men. 'Naturally. It is Sunday.'

'You do not have a pious bone in your body!' Lisette goaded.

While his men were tethering their animals to a fence at the side of the chapel, Collings strode along the road until he reached the side of the cart. 'But most of my men do,' he said, concealing the words under his breath, 'and morale is everything, wouldn't you agree?'

She nodded. 'Right enough. Though I'll not step in that heretical place.'

Collings laughed, looking back at the house of God. It was a square-shaped affair of whitewashed walls and simple decoration. 'A Puritan chapel if ever there was one.' He fixed Lisette with a twinkling eye. 'You expect me to leave you out here while we pray?'

'I am of the true faith, General. I would be damned if I sat in your foul little hovel. You say I am soon to die. Let me at least know where my soul will fly.'

Collings laughed again. 'Have it your way, my Romish dove, though I doubt it will be heaven-bound.' He summoned half a dozen blackcoats. 'Stay with her.'

Lisette looked from Collings to the men and back again. 'Do they not wish to hear the sermon?'

Collings' eye flashed in a conspiratorial wink. 'I said *most* of my men were pious.' He caught Lisette's sour expression and patted the side of the vehicle. 'Come now, mademoiselle, do not tell me you had hoped you'd be left unguarded?'

Cecily Cade clambered down from the cart, her breeches snagging on a jagged timber, opening a small hole at the top of her thigh that elicited a chorus of bawdy sniggers. She pointedly ignored them, filing into the church as though she were at the chapel on her family's estate. Lisette watched in grim silence as the party vanished within the stone depths, the preacher's raving voice beginning to echo out through the chapel windows, damning Royalists, Catholics, the Irish and anyone else who opposed the Parliamentarian cause. She wondered if the ranter had decided to put extra venom in his ire this morning, in order to impress his martial congregation.

'Papist 'ore,' one of the guards muttered.

Lisette shot him a glance dripping with disdain. 'No whore you'll ever touch.'

The man was thin and ashen-faced, with gums that sagged open, each rotten tooth set into a crimson sore. He wiped his long nose on his sleeve. 'See about that, won't we?'

She turned her head away scornfully. The men laughed cruelly. One spat a jet of brown tobacco juice at the wagon so that it spattered her cloak.

The sermon went on, half an hour becoming an hour. She waited and watched, stared at the rushing flow of the Brent, considered how she might make a break for freedom, but knew there was no way she could feasibly outrun six men on horse-back. Occasionally she would eye the dark recesses of the distant forests, imagining herself plunging into the depths, where horses would struggle to follow. But she knew this area all too well, knew that the land between the road and the hills was open and split only by hedges, and that the horsemen would eat the distance up in no time. Besides, Cecily was inside the chapel, rendering any attempt pointless. She had come too far to leave her now.

'I need to go,' she said, making to stand.

'Hark at that, lads!' the thin-faced blackcoat said with an amused cackle. 'She needs to go! Shall we let her, seein' as she asked so nicely, like?'

'Not go away,' Lisette spat, 'you ox-brained bloody fool. *Piss*. In the bushes.'

Slowly the blackcoat's thick eyebrows climbed to the top of his forehead. 'Oh, I see. Call o' nature, is it?' He licked his lips. 'Well, I'll have to accompany you.'

Lisette shook her head. 'No you damn well won't, you lecherous bastard.' She looked across at the faces of the others. All made her shudder, such was the hopeful lust in their eyes, but one seemed more shocked than aroused by the thought of a lady urinating in the undergrowth. 'Him. He can escort me.'

'Oh yeah?' Thin Face asked. 'Young Stee, eh? Think I'm stupid?'

'I do not know what you mean.'

Thin Face excavated one of his nostrils with a grimy finger-nail, a gelatinous blob of green mucus coming tackily away. He inspected it as though the answer to some great conundrum could be divined therein. 'The trooper is a stripling. You think you can outsmart him.' He deposited the slime on the tip of his sharp tongue and used the finger to indicate a small copse beyond, a little way along the riverbank. 'Lead him off into the trees and blind 'im with yer juicy little paps. And while his muzzle blows, you'll hop off like a hare in spring.'

'Stupid bastard,' Lisette hissed, gripping her stomach. 'I *must* go now. You would deny a lady?'

'You're no lady, French bitch,' Thin Face snarled. He nodded towards the chapel. 'Go inside.'

'I'll not take a step into that demon den. Not even to piss.'

Thin Face seemed to appreciate that, and his lips peeled back from his rotten mouth in a crooked smirk. 'Take the boy. But if he comes back walking like he's spewed his britches—'

'You'll be angry,' Lisette said as she jumped down.

'I'll be wantin' a turn,' said Thin Face wolfishly.

Lisette swore at him in her native tongue, and waited for the man he had named as Stee to dismount. He had a sword sheathed at his waist, and a pistol that he immediately cocked. She walked swiftly past the chapel and up to the west side of the bridge. The River Brent pounded below them, swollen by recent rains, and she turned left to follow its course rather than cross it. The trooper followed at a careful distance, one hand planted on his sword-hilt, the other holding the pistol out in front. Her eyes darted about as a matter of instinct, for it was unnatural for her to be a prisoner and not seek a way out, yet she saw that she was hemmed in by waterway and building, with rolling fields beyond the copse. There was nowhere to go.

'How far you goin'?'

She looked over her shoulder. 'Just there. The nearest trees.'

'Do anythin' stupid and I'll stick a bullet in your back. Don't think I won't.'

Lisette saw that Stee's face, though unblemished in its youth, was taut with either determination or fear. Regardless, she knew that this was not a man to trifle with, for the result would be a dangerous trigger finger, and she nodded assent.

'Wait here,' she said as she pushed past the drooping bough of a withered beech. It was Stee's turn to nod.

It was more of a grove than a copse, with a ring of trees and dense shrubs encircling a grassy clearing. Lisette found a quiet spot at the edge of the open ground and took off her cloak, tossing it to the long turf in a dark bundle as she unfastened the pewter buttons at her breeches. She squatted without tarrying, unwilling to give Stee cause to come looking.

The trooper called out to her, his voice drifting through the shielding canopy, and she replied loudly to reassure him that she had not betrayed his trust. She stood, pulled up the breeches quickly, and made to leave. Only then did she notice the flat, grey rock in the centre of the clearing. On its smooth surface something moved.

The sermon ended not long after Lisette and Stee had returned to the wagon. Their arrival prompted a bevy of vulgar jeers; Thin Face and the rest of the guards taking turns to guess what lewd acts had been committed out of sight. Stee blushed, Lisette ignored them, and they all fell silent when Collings emerged from the chapel to take his mare in hand.

'Hot gospeller,' the general muttered, spurring the snorting piebald past the wagon as it trundled over the bridge and into New Brentford. 'I do believe we are all destined for Lucifer's flames.' He shrugged. 'At least it'll be warm.'

'He was certainly bitter,' Cecily said. 'Why do you inflict it upon the men?'

'Soldiers are simple creatures, Miss Cade,' replied Collings. 'They fight, eat and copulate, then pray against all three. I make sure they are well trained, well fed and have coin enough for the third. That makes them loyal. But if I make provision for their faith, too, I can ensure the afterlife is taken care of.'

'And so,' Lisette said sardonically, as she arranged the folds of her bundled cloak between her boots, 'they will be happy to die for you.'

He kicked the animal gently. It blew a gust of foam-flecked air through flared nostrils, but increased its speed obediently enough. Collings twisted back briefly to lift his purple hat in mock salute, and went to the head of his small column.

The traffic only worsened now that they were in the more densely populated heart of Brentford's three areas, and the blackcoats found it tiresome to have to beat a path through the throng. They ground to an almost complete stop as the road curved down towards a much broader expanse of water.

'The Thames,' Lisette observed.

Cecily leaned against the side of the cart, squinting to the south, between the houses, to see the glistening river. 'Really?'

Lisette nodded, looking up at the large steeple of another church that nestled in the wedge of land where the mighty river met its tributary, the Brent. 'St Lawrence's. See the holes?'

Cecily followed the Frenchwoman's outstretched finger to gaze up at the impressive stone walls, which loomed over the road in a demonstration of High Church power. She looked back at Lisette in surprise. 'Bullets?'

'I have been here before,' said Lisette as they hit a bump that made them jolt against the hard slats of the wagon. Her bundled cloak unfurled slightly between her legs, and she shifted her feet to pin it firmly in place. 'There was a great battle fought along this very road.'

'You saw it?'

Lisette almost laughed at the understatement. '*Oui*,' she said, staring beyond the black cavalrymen, at the houses lining the road. Swirling images of gun smoke and steel flashed before her eyes, the sounds of bellowing officers and the screams of the dying drifting like distant thunder in her mind. 'I was captured here, imprisoned for a time.'

'By the Parliament?'

She shook her head. 'By an evil bastard named Eli Makepeace. His creature, a sergeant called Bain, almost raped me.'

'My Lord, Lisette!' Cecily's green eyes widened.

'They are both dead,' Lisette said bluntly.

'And it was here?'

Lisette nodded. 'The king's men won. Now look at it. Stinking rebel nest.'

'How did you escape?'

Lisette's mind whirled back to the moment when Bain had his pistol at her temple. It was only then that she thought about the role played by a young officer. 'Lieutenant Burton drew Bain's attention, that was how he injured his shoulder. Though he was an ensign then, of course.'

'Burton?' Cecily gaped. 'Andrew Burton? You know him?'

'Knew him, *oui*. He died at Stratton.'

Cecily slid a hand across her full lips. 'Dead?'

Lisette remembered the terrible agony on Stryker's face as he had told her, and that same pain now flared again as she looked at her pale companion. 'Do not pretend you care, Cecily, for you played your part in it.'

The corners of Cecily's mouth drooped in a mixture of bewilderment and horror. 'Played my part? I do not know what you are talking about.'

'You seduced him,' Lisette went on mercilessly. She had grown to like Cecily Cade, but now, faced with too many memories and riled by the girl's bare-faced denials, she could not stem her anger. 'Do not think I do not know what happened.'

'Where has this come from, Lisette?' Cecily blurted. 'Who have you been speaking to?'

'You deny he loved you?'

'Burton?' Cecily plunged her face into her hands in astonishment. 'Not at all. It was perfectly obvious, but that is not any fault of mine.'

'You deny you seduced him?'

'Absolutely!'

'You led him on, Cecily, so that you could escape the tor.' Lisette spoke coldly.

Cecily leaned forward. 'Who the devil have you been talking to, Lisette?' she hissed. 'I did not lead him on, as you put it. I swear it!'

'Quiet there!' the trooper, Thin Face, called from behind the wagon. He and Stee rode side by side at the very rear of the troop.

Cecily set her mouth in a tight line and sat back. 'I did try to seduce a man on that ghastly tor, I admit it, but not the lieutenant.' She looked out at the houses as they rumbled past. 'Why would I take aim at the second in command?'

Now it was Lisette's jaw that lolled open. 'Stryker?'

Cecily shook her head, utterly nonplussed. 'How do you know these people?'

'He is my man, Miss Cade,' Lisette said, her tone laced with venom. '*My* man, you goddamned—'

'Nothing happ—'

Lisette laughed bitterly, cutting her off. 'Now you deny it?'

'I told you I felt drawn to an officer,' Cecily said, trying to remain calm. 'But I also told you that it did not amount to anything. I did attempt to seduce him, Lisette, but the attempt failed. He said he had another woman.' She smiled ruefully. 'Now I know who.'

They sat in stunned silence for the better part of half an hour, by which time the frustrated convoy had made it through to the eastern fringe of Old Brentford. At the head of the black-coated line, Major General Collings could be heard berating a quartermaster who had blocked the road with four cartloads of coats bound for the Earl of Essex's men. One of his oxen was lame, and his drivers had vanished, doubtless decamped to one of the taverns that hedged the busy highway.

Collings's nasal whine penetrated the sounds of man and beast as he ordered his troopers to dismount and shift the wagons themselves. Lisette caught a few moans of dissent, but the cavalrymen ultimately did as they were told.

'All this time?' Cecily said quietly.

Lisette looked back at Thin Face and Stee, who had both remained beside the vehicle. 'What?'

'All this time you knew the men on the tor. The redcoats. You knew Stryker, but said nothing.'

Lisette bent to rummage with her cloak. 'Burton and Stryker quarrelled because of you,' she said. 'They were like father and son, but they broke with one another, and that is what caused Andrew's death.' She looked up. 'I did not wish to speak to you about any of it.'

Cecily stared back, her eyes boring into the pale blue of Lisette's. 'Lest you find yourself with a knife in your hand?'

That was a perceptive comment, and Lisette could not stifle a rueful smile. She gathered a fistful of her balled cloak and lifted it a little way off the ground, the lowest part of the material hanging low, scraping the weathered boards. 'Something like that.'

Cecily sighed. 'I am sorry about Lieutenant Burton. Truly. But what I've told you is the truth. Did Stryker really say I seduced Burton?'

Lisette considered the question for a moment. 'Not in so many words,' she said eventually. 'But he told me you tried to shy away from his protection by using your – *wiles* – and that Burton broke with him because of you. I suppose I did not consider that it might have been Stryker you were involved with.'

'I was not involved with him,' Cecily protested.

Lisette held up her free hand for silence. 'It does not matter.' She cast a glance back over her shoulder at the melee on the road. The blackcoats grunted and groaned as they heaved the quartermaster's inert carts aside. 'Look.'

'What of it?'

'They've left their horses unattended.'

Cecily shook her head rapidly, tensing her jaw as she bit down hard. 'Do not do anything foolish.'

Lisette stood suddenly, lifting her cloak so that it hung like a sack at her hip. 'I told you I knew this place.'

Thin Face kicked his sweaty bay forwards at her movement. 'Si'down you jumpy bitch!'

Lisette peered down at him defiantly. 'Keep your rotten mouth shut, you crapulous numskull.'

Thin Face's gloved hand fell to his sword. 'Now that's plain discourteous, froggy drab. Sit down afore I chop you in two.'

Lisette grinned, and paused as an anxious-looking Stee urged his own horse closer. She threw her arm out hard so that the elbow snapped forth, her cloak unfurling like a flag in a gale.

At first the blackcoats merely swayed back in their saddles, but as they caught sight of the dark object circling towards them, a look of pure horror crawled over their features. It looked like a length of black and green rope as it twirled to the hoof-ploughed mud between the two horses, but the animals knew instantly what it was, and they reared and bucked in instant terror.

Lisette kept hold of her cloak, thrust it under an armpit, and vaulted over the wagon's shaking side. She did not need to urge Cecily to follow, and the pair raced over to the nearest empty mounts. Lisette clambered up on to a dappled grey, and Cecily swung her leg up to straddle a black beast that skittered uneasily at the feel of a new rider but did not resist as she urged it into a gallop.

'Follow me!' Lisette called.

'*No!*' Thin Face's high-pitched bellow rang out behind them.

'Now, Cecily! I know the way out of here!'

Thin Face's blood-shot eyes seemed to bulge like an insect as he watched them go. 'Get back 'ere you fuckin' pair o' sluts!' But his horse had lost its mind as the hissing, darting adder writhed at its fetlocks. Thin Face and Stee wrestled with their mounts as the white-eyed beasts pulverized the earth with their frantic hooves, desperately trying to stamp on the snake that had been tossed into their midst. 'Sir!' Thin Face screamed. 'General, sir! They've gone!'

But Collings was shouting himself, berating the quarter-master and his brow-beaten men, who were now trudging out of one of the inns at the tips of the blackcoats' blades. He did not turn, did not even glance round, and Thin Face and Stee were left to bully and snarl at their frenzied horses, all the while cursing the women who raced into the sunlit fields without looking back.

Beside the East Gate, Gloucester, 28 August 1643

The new week began for Lieutenant Colonel Edward Massie with a habitual tour of the walls, the sun carving bright shafts into the eastern horizon. He paced with his hands clasped tightly behind his back. He did so to give the impression of calm professionalism, of a man who knew what he was about, simply wishing to walk the perimeter of his domain, safe in the knowledge that it would remain his domain for the foreseeable future. In reality, his hands trembled. Not uncontrollably, but enough to be visible, and that, Massie had concluded, would be as bad for morale as any assault by Rupert and his demons. It was exhaustion, he understood. Sheer, red-eyed tiredness that sucked the strength from a man's bones and, in the governor's case at least, made his thin fingers quiver like feathers in a spring breeze. And so he pushed them together at the small of his back, laced the fingers in a tight ball, and held them there.

Someone up on the gate called down to him, shouting a rebel slogan Massie could not quite hear, but he nodded back never-theless, grateful that the inhabitants of the war-worn city were still with him. He could not help but wonder what would happen when the walls were finally breached. They had all heard tales of other towns. Bristol had been drenched in blood, poor Cirencester had been sacked for three days by the rabid Royalist assault troops. He could not help but reflect upon his own decisions these past weeks. His policy of offensive defence, of disrupting the enemy lines, of bolstering the walls and of outright, audacious disobedience had kept the king's men at bay for longer than any might have hoped, but it must also have enraged the common musketeers, who were forced to drag their comrades' corpses out of those grisly, rat-infested trenches almost every day. And his tactic of subversion and duplicity had been a success too, with the king evidently dithering in his method of attack. But what had such deviousness actually gained? A few extra days and a sovereign with a grudge? He closed his eyes, revelling in the stinging sensation that only came with exhaustion, and prayed that his own hubris had not doomed this brave city to a sacking from which it would never recover.

But the facts were clear and simple. For all the garrison's stoical defiance, the vast Royalist army was still camped at their gates and Gloucester's powder and ammunition were now running seriously low, forcing him to curtail the sallies that had been so effective. Meanwhile, the two efforts to bridge the moat, one at the south wall and another at the east, were creeping ever closer. God had intervened, of course, for the downpour two nights before had raised the water level and made the work painfully slow, but Massie did not doubt the objective was to place large petards against the stone as soon as the moat had been spanned, and that, for certain, would see the end of the rebellion in Gloucester.

'No word from Warwick,' he said as his advisers caught up. Two men, sent out to seek word of Parliament's plans for the city, had penetrated the Royalist lines forty-eight hours earlier. 'I had hoped they would be back by now.'

Vincent Skaithlocke offered a smile of encouragement. 'They'll come.'

'They'll make it back through the lines?'

The corpulent mercenary lifted and dropped his huge shoulders in a manner that made his jowls quiver. 'They managed it once, didn't they?'

Massie rubbed his chin slowly. 'Even if they return to us, what then? If Parliament is able to raise a relief force, how strong would it really be? Enough to oust the Oxford Army?'

'It doesn't matter what I believe,' Skaithlocke said, evidently abandoning the tactic of bluff reassurance. They all knew the situation well enough.

'I had hoped—' Massie began, about to embark on another theoretical discussion as to the unlikely possibility of rescue. He had noticed something that stole his breath.

Skaithlocke frowned. 'What? What is it?'

Massie pointed towards one of the traps he had set. They were essentially small cups of water, placed atop drums that had been positioned at intervals all along the vulnerable south and east walls. Every day, morning and afternoon, he checked them, and every day they had remained serene and flat. But now this one, just inside the foot of the East Gate, was not flat at all. 'It trembles.'

Slowly the implication dawned. Skaithlocke took off his hat to scratch at his auburn curls; the others gazed nervously at one another.

'They're beneath us,' a youthful captain muttered with a hard gulp. 'Dear God—'

'No,' Massie said firmly, careful to intervene lest panic set in. 'The ripples are only slight. They're not here yet, but they're close.' He stared at the walls to his right, buttressed by the earthen slope, then dragged his eyes to the left, taking in the huge gatehouse with its tiled roof, now bullet-riddled and cannon-holed. All this time he had been worrying for the wall; yet now the truth dawned on him that the Royalist design was more ambitious than that. 'Jesu, but they mean to undermine the East Gate.'

A fair-haired major ventured to step from the group. 'Their contraptions are bullet-proof, Governor, but we're creating a port in the wall from which we can fire a saker 'pon their gallery. The timbers are stout, but they'll not stand that.'

Massie shook his head. 'I am not referring to their bridge, Major.' He pointed at the ground between them. 'They tunnel under the moat. *Under* it, do you understand? They mean to blow the gate itself.'

The major's jaw lolled. 'What do we do, sir?'

'Pray,' Skaithlocke said unhelpfully.

Massie thought for a moment. They could combat a land-borne assault with shot and steel, and soon, with the help of the new gun port, they would be able to slow up the engineers beneath their protective wooden shells. But how could they fight off what they could not see? 'We dig our own tunnels, gentlemen,' he said as the assembled officers stared at him expectantly. He looked at the major. 'Begin countermines at once. Two, straight under the gate. We'll flood them out, or collapse them entirely, but their mine must not reach the foundations.'

The major nodded. 'Sir.'

'Just so.' Edward Massie turned away. If the water was rippling, then the drums were transmitting tremors that, though deep underground, were frighteningly close. Perhaps they were too late already.

Kingsholm, Gloucester, 28 August 1643

Nikolas Robbens sat on the edge of his bed. With steady fingers, he took up the three silken strands, dangling them in front of his face as he inspected their quality. Beautiful, he decided. One green, one red and one white, unblemished and smooth to the touch. Carefully he moved them to his left earlobe and threaded them through the small hole, tugging on them to ensure that they hung evenly.

Happy with the ear-string, he stared down at the crossbow in his lap. He had stayed in his room since retrieving it from the Little Mead, for the king, it was said, had gone to Oxford with his headstrong nephew. Rumours of a gathering Parliamentarian relief expedition were rife in the camp, spreading from Kingsholm to Over, down through Barton, Gaudy Green and Llanthony Priory like a bout of French Welcome in a swiving shop. The senior officers denied it, naturally, letting it be known that the enemy could never have raised enough men in such a short space of time, but Charles and Rupert had gone to the Royalist capital anyway, so Robbens was unconvinced. Either way, his regal target was not in Gloucester, so there seemed little point in showing his face unnecessarily.

The bow had been soaked by the downpour, of course, and that had given Robbens pause for concern, but the steel weapon did not suffer the same ill-effects of saturation as its wooden cousin might have. Now, dry, clean and gleaming, Robbens found that he spent a great deal of time simply stroking the beautifully crafted stock as he might a lover's thigh. The etched stags on either side of the grip seemed to prance for him alone, as though the bow somehow knew what great work he would soon put it to. He traced one of the delicate grooves that represented an antler. 'Soon, I promise.'

'Look lively, you flea-bit pack o' mongrels! He'll be here before you knows it, so sort your damned shirts and fasten your coats!'

The shout had come from out on the road below his lodgings. Robbens carefully placed the miniature crossbow on his palliasse, covering it with a sheet, and padded to the window. He was on the first floor, and he thrust open the shutter and leaned out. Soldiers milled down below; something was afoot.

'Ho, friend!'

The man he had hailed, a sturdily built corporal with ink-black stubble and narrow, suspicious eyes, peered up at him from beneath a filthy Monmouth cap.

'What is happening?' Robbens asked, adding a cough for authenticity.

The corporal backed away and scratched at the paunch of his belly, which strained against the pale blue material of his coat. 'Gen'ral o' Horse visits us,' he said, adding, 'for our sins.'

Robbens felt his throat tighten a touch. 'General of Horse? You mean Prince Rupert?'

'No, chum,' the corporal replied, 'I mean Gustavus Adolphus. Of course I means the Prince!'

'He has returned from Oxford?'

'Well, he'll struggle to inspect the army if he hasn't!' the corporal boomed. His men laughed.

'And the King?'

The corporal was already walking away, but he glanced up at the window one last time. 'That'd be my guess, chum! Won't have rid 'ere on his own, will he?'

Nikolas Robbens shouted his thanks and slid back inside. He had to breathe deeply to regain his composure. So they were back, he thought, walking to the bed and its fatal prize. Praise God, they were back.

Near Oxford, 28 August 1643

The capital city of King Charles shone like a gemstone in the grey dusk. Its citizens had lighted their candles and lamps for the creeping night, making every street and building glow, while the soldiers out on the band of rapidly progressing defensive works had lit a string of small fires, which marked Oxford's new limits. It was a beacon among the surrounding hills, a guiding light for pilgrims and fugitives alike.

Two such fugitives eased their shattered mounts to a grunting halt on one of the hills above the metropolis. The beasts snorted and shivered, their flanks caulked in sweat and mud, as their riders patted their exhausted, twitching necks and begged for two more miles of effort. The horses seemed to understand, for they moved forwards, negotiating the edge of the escarpment, which would lead them down into Oxford.

Lisette Gaillard pulled gently at the pricked ear of her mare, its grey coat almost glowing in the gathering moonlight. 'Nearly there. Nearly there.'

She had led Cecily Cade on a mad, terrible gallop through New Brentford the previous day. They had weaved in and out of carts and horses, oxen, children, dogs and soldiers. They had crouched in their saddles and hugged the horses' huge necks, willing them on as the beasts bolted through the stunned crowd, clattered over the bridge that took them across the River Brent, and pushed on into Brentford End. Lisette had veered right, easing them off the London road and into the fields to the north. She knew the area, had marched through it with Stryker when the folk of rebel London had chased the king's grand army from Turnham Green, Brentford and Hounslow, and she remembered the old farming tracks many of the infantry regiments had traversed when the high road had been turned to a morass by melting snow. They had pressed the horses hard, always fearing the sound of chasing hooves at their backs, but the blackcoats had not come. Erasmus Collings would not have abandoned the search, they knew. But there were many routes to take to Oxford, and perhaps, by the grace of God, his malevolent flock of ravens had chosen the wrong ones.

They moved down the hill, trees flanking them like Titans, and trotted in silence. The flickering orange city beckoned them home.

CHAPTER 21

Beside the East Gate, Gloucester, 29 August 1643

'And that's it? They just ran?'
'No, Forry, they didn't run, *I* did.'

It had been nearly five days since the attack outside the Cob and Saddle, and Stryker had had plenty of time, while he guarded sappers and kept a lookout for Skaithlocke's vanished assassin, to ponder just how close he had come to dying on the wet path beside the courtyard. He had not seen Forrester since parting amid the tavern's warm fug, for their respective companies had been posted to different parts of the siegeworks, but his friend had heard about the close call on the army rumour mill, and set to interrogating Stryker as soon as the pair greeted one another in the wicker-screened musket emplacements to which their sharpshooters had been assigned.

'Details, old man,' Forrester said dismissively. He gazed out over the breastwork at the sodden saps. 'The men whisper of a large army marching out from London.'

Stryker followed his gaze. A metal-clad engineer slopped out from one of the trenches like an armoured monster rising from the underworld. A shot immediately rang out from the city, followed by a ripple of cheers as the whistling ball clanged against the man's encased chest, knocking him on to his back. He writhed there for a few seconds, flailing like a flipped beetle on a vast dung pile, before two more similarly armoured creatures appeared like steel rabbits from their burrows, scuttling out to drag him clear, vanishing just as quickly. 'The Parliament could not muster enough men to challenge us.'

Forrester blew out his red cheeks, adjusting his wide hat so that it sat at a suitably rakish angle. 'Still, this is all rather sluggish, wouldn't you say?'

They stared in silence at the ravaged land before them – a flood plain of shimmering pools and black filth. The whole area was waterlogged and had become a cloying, foot numbing morass. It had been wet from the start; dry, flaky mud turning to thick glue as the sappers unleashed spring after spring in the excavation of their man-sized badger set. But it was the rain that had taken the worst toll. The downpour, now just a memory beneath clear blue skies, had filled the moat and trenches, saturated the earth and made the rivers swell. Men stank worse than usual, for their feet were beginning to rot inside shoes and socks they could not get dry, while the mining work had become a lesson in sheer toil. The work beneath the bullet-proof galleries crept on, but the moat was proving impossible to fill as water continued to seep up from below. In addition, the resources dedicated to them had been diverted to the subterranean attack. But that clandestine enterprise, the daring, ingenious mine that reached deep below the ground, sweeping beneath the moat and up to the gatehouse, had taken far longer to dig than even the most pessimistic of the Earl of Forth's engineers could have imagined. The soaking tunnels were difficult to clear and collapsed all too often, trapping good men inside. They were being pulled out hours later as blue-lipped corpses.

'They've brought in a crew of Welsh miners this very morning,' Stryker said after a while. 'I hear they're experts in this kind of thing.'

'I saw them,' Forrester said.

'It is expected they'll lend speed to the whole affair.'

'God willing,' replied Forrester, 'but the undeniable fact is it that our clever mining expedition, the main plank in our current strategy, is simply taking too long.' He looked at Stryker, his face tense and serious. 'If the Roundheads have managed to scrape an army together, I fear our spirits are not high enough to challenge them, despite our numbers.'

Stryker stared back at the East Gate, imagining the frenetic activity of the digging teams beneath its foundations. 'Then let us hope our Welsh friends can prove their worth.'

'But you've no idea who it was?' Forrester asked, suddenly returning to the earlier topic.

'The attack? Oh, I've ideas.'

'Coat colours? Field words? What?'

'None of that. They weren't that foolish.'

'So you do think it was premeditated,' Forrester mused. 'Not just a gaggle of copper-nosed routers out for sport?'

Stryker thought back. He had been drunk, and the details were blurred, but he remembered enough to keep his suspicions alive. 'That's just it. They hadn't been drinking, not that I could tell, leastwise. And they were determined to kill me.' He shook his head. 'It was no chance robbery.'

Forrester screwed up his face in frustration. 'And that's all you have to go on?'

'I managed to escape because their mounts were poor. Just palfreys. And they fought well enough, skilled in the saddle, like cavalry, but dressed like you or me.'

'Infantrymen on horseback.' Forrester was silent for a moment as he absorbed the information. A new light flickered across his eyes. 'Dragooners!' he exclaimed, swotting the wickerwork with a gloved backhand.

'That is what I wondered,' Stryker said. A flurry of musketry crackled up on the walls, and the pair ducked back behind the screen. Stryker met his friend's gaze when the volley was spent. 'Is Crow in camp?'

Forrester spread his palms, indicating that he did not know. 'It is a very big army, old man.'

The musket squall had evidently been intended as a precursor to a larger action, for a bombardment by cannon began to shake the ground at their feet. Iron shot whistled away to batter the eastern trenches, fired from somewhere behind the walls.

'But it is unlikely he'll have spotted you amongst the throng,' Forrester said, having to raise his voice above the artillery fire, ''specially if you haven't seen him. He's a mad-eyed loon in a yellow coat. With all due respect, Stryker, you're just another filth-clothed plodder wading about this delightful quagmire like some sword-swinging mudlark.'

'I suppose you're right.' Stryker could see that the chances did seem slim, and he had to admit that Crow was not necessarily behind the attack. He had plenty of enemies, after all.

'But we must keep our eyes peeled,' Forrester added. The corner of his thin mouth twitched slightly. 'Obviously just the one eye in your case, old man.'

Jesus College, Oxford, 29 August 1643

Lisette Gaillard and Cecily Cade sat in the antechamber for three hours before they were permitted entry. A stooped servant in a dark-blue tabard shuffled through a groaning door and mumbled for them to follow. They stood, stretched, and did as they were told. On the far side was another room, bigger and more lavishly appointed, with richly panelled walls and an ornately carved ceiling.

'About time,' Lisette grumbled. She was not given to waiting, let alone in musty old offices for mouldy old men, and it was a struggle to keep her temper in check.

The servant snorted softly into his white whiskers. 'You must be patient in this place.'

'So we have learned,' Cecily said, cutting off a reply from her French companion that was destined to be acerbic.

Tetchy and tired, they had been in the Royalist capital for a night and a morning, and already the swarming city felt like a great weight about their necks. The king's court had consolidated here after his failure to take London the previous November. Believing it the only city wholeheartedly loyal to his cause, Charles had reconvened his court and administrative machine in the sprawling university buildings, and had begun defensive outworks to ensure its safety. But with the court had come an army of clerks. Black-fingered scribes and watery-eyed paper-shufflers who were necessary to keep the cogs of administration turning, but who also guaranteed the place would be tightly bound by bureaucratic inertia. The women, so joyful as they had galloped into the capital's outlying pickets, had run headlong into Oxford's indolent chains almost immediately. They were escorted by a small troop of cavalry to a stable block on the outskirts of the city, and had been questioned during the night. And though they were eventually given lodgings and promised access to a more senior official, that meeting had not taken place until dawn. The man, a lawyer turned staff officer, had done nothing more than forward them on through another layer of bureaucracy, sending them to the ostentatious rooms in a corner of Jesus College to wait in line for yet another audience. At least now they were on the move, but the entire process was akin to wading through molasses.

'His Majesty is through here?' Lisette asked as they left the room through a far door and filed along a dark passageway hung with tapestries.

The servant's white eyebrows lifted in surprise. 'His Majesty?' His face cracked in a half-smile, but he said nothing more until they turned a corner into a warmly lit reception area, at the centre of which stood a tall, willowy man with wiry copper hair and a severe squint.

'Delighted, I'm sure,' the tall man said after the servant introduced him as Enoch Ferre. He turned quickly on his heels, his brown cloak swirling in his wake. 'Walk with me?'

'French?' Lisette said as they followed.

Ferre glanced back as he led the way. 'I was born in Wallingford, I'm afraid,' he said, 'but the name is Protestant Huguenot in origin, yes.'

Lisette wrinkled her nose in distaste but chose to leave the subject well alone. 'Who are we going to see now? The King's bloody farrier? The Queen's dressmaker?'

'I am sorry to say,' Ferre replied, seemingly amused by her irritability, 'that you are here to see me.'

Lisette stopped, causing the others to halt too. 'A clerk?' She looked at Cecily. 'Another bloody clerk?'

Ferre smiled benevolently. 'I am sorry to disappoint, Mademoiselle Gaillard, but I assure you that I am, dare I say it, a rather influential clerk. If you'll follow me?'

Lisette muttered angrily as they walked the last few yards to a studded door flanked by a pair of menacing sentries bearing crossed halberds. The weapons sang of their sharpness as they were pulled smartly aside at the merest nod from Enoch Ferre, and he strode into the room beyond.

'You've enjoyed your stay so far, I trust?' Ferre asked as he went to a huge table at the back of the room. It was strewn with maps and papers, which he now loomed over to shuffle with inky fingers. 'It is a strange sort of place to the outsider, I grant you that. As if some great leviathan had swallowed up Whitehall and vomited it all over Oxford University!' He guffawed, and sat down in a large, comfortable-looking chair, indicating that his guests should take the seats on the table's far side. 'Now let me see. We have the King's residence at Christ Church, along with the new Parliament, of course.' He counted the elements on his fingers. 'Privy Council convene at Oriel College. Members of His Majesty's inner circle, officers of state, senior soldiers and the like, are quartered here at Jesus College, and at Pembroke and St John's too. The arsenal is kept at All Souls, the powder magazine at New College.'

'Everything a capital city needs,' Cecily said graciously.

'Oh, very much so,' Ferre agreed with an extra-narrow squint. 'And that's not all. We have a mint running here, a newspaper, and everything else you'd have found in that hive of villainy, London.'

'Impressive,' Lisette said.

Ferre smiled wickedly. 'Just do not approach any person with a wet-sounding cough. It is more than likely *morbus campestris*, a nasty fever that strikes us now and again.' He shrugged, his sharp collarbones protruding like twin hillocks from beneath his cloak. 'The lot of garrison life, I'm afraid. We must content ourselves with what we have.'

Lisette looked around the room. It was tastefully furnished, with deep rugs softening the floorboards and an exquisitely crafted lantern clock on the wall behind the copper-haired official. Clearly Enoch Ferre was no mere clerk. 'Mister Ferre,' she said, shifting her seat forwards a fraction, 'I would speak with the King urgently.'

Ferre responded with a tight smile. 'I am well aware of your *situation*, please be assured of that. And would do what I can to help, naturally.'

'Then?'

He crossed his hands, the long, stained fingers weaving together on the desk in front. 'My apologies, mademoiselle. He is not here.'

'Not here?' Lisette repeated incredulously as Cecily shut her eyes in despair. 'What do you mean? We were conveyed to our lodgings by a sergeant-at-arms who told us His Majesty had returned to Oxford.'

'And indeed he had,' Ferre said calmly. 'But he has already gone; returned to Gloucester with the Prince.'

Lisette considered the implication, the snide bragging of Erasmus Collings pounding inside her skull like cannon fire. 'The King himself is at Gloucester?'

'That is what I said. Rode thither yesterday.'

'But there is an army on its way,' Lisette said, hearing the urgency inflect her tone. 'I must warn him.'

Ferre leaned back nonchalantly. 'He knows, Mistress. Our scouts watch them day and night. Why do you think he came back to his capital? Feared my lord Essex had designs upon Oxford.'

'Does he?' Cecily asked.

Ferre gnawed at the inside of his mouth as he considered the question. 'It does not appear that way. Though nothing is certain. You'll have noticed the rather dense hedge of soldiers we have out beyond the bastions.'

'They seemed anxious,' Cecily said.

'As well they might,' replied Ferre. 'The current belief is that Essex will strike at Gloucester, for the siege there nears its fourth week, and pressure grows in Parliamentarian circles for it to be lifted. But Oxford remains a very ripe apple for His Grace to try and pluck. Wine?'

The women watched as Ferre reached for a crystal bottle perching at the edge of the table. He filled three delicate glasses with the dark liquid, sliding them over the polished surface.

'The enemy horde,' he went on after he had taken a sip, 'has been sighted around Wokingham, Colnbrook and Chesham these past days. They move north, avoiding our garrison, it seems. His Majesty's Council believes it is Gloucester for which they are bound, and thus he has returned to his siege.' Ferre set down his glass with a gentle clink. 'It does not go well, I am sorry to report. He wishes to take the city before Essex arrives. The clock ticks for our brave boys.'

Lisette looked across at Cecily. 'We must go there.'

'Gloucester?' Ferre asked before Cecily could answer. 'Perhaps not.'

Lisette gave him a baleful stare. 'Perhaps not? Miss Cade has suffered much to bring His Majesty this information.'

Ferre's face was suddenly stiff and implacable. 'I am aware of that, which is why I think it best that she does not die on the road before she may impart it.'

'You speak to me like I am a child, sir,' Lisette hissed.

Ferre grunted. 'I speak to you as though you are a woman.' He leaned back casually, studying the women through eyes that were black slits. 'I cannot, in all conscience, let you gallop off to Gloucester when the land between here and there is teeming with rebel regiments.' He looked straight at Cecily. 'Especially if what you say about your inheritance is true, Miss Cade.'

'Of course it is true, sir,' Cecily replied vehemently.

Lisette stood. 'Come, Cecily, we will take horses. We do not need his permission.'

'You have money, then?' Ferre said in a firm but inquisitive tone. 'To buy these mounts?' He grinned. 'Or are you intent on stealing them? It seems a trifle ironic that you should be strung up by your own side after surmounting such obstacles to get this far.'

The women glanced at one another and sat down in tandem.

Ferre's pleasantly benevolent expression returned. 'Here's what I will do for you, ladies. Lord Wilmot has—' he paused to snatch up a scrap of vellum from the table, scrutinizing a column of numbers running down one side, 'two thousand horse to the north of here, protecting us lest Essex change his mind and swoop down upon our virgin capital.' He tossed the vellum back on the untidy pile. 'A further detachment of harquebusiers leaves here the day after the morrow, destined to reinforce him. You may travel with them. I will see to it that Wilmot arranges safe passage from there to Gloucester. How does that serve?'

Lisette drained her glass. 'It serves very well, Mister Ferre.' And it did, for they were going to see the king.

Greyfriars, Gloucester, 29 August 1643

Night brought some semblance of comfort to Edward Massie. The bigger cannon ceased their murderous ministrations when it became too dark to see, and the musketeers in the vile Royalist rat-runs tended to filter back along their watery gullies to drink and whore, or whatever else the malignants did of an evening.

For the weary governor, there was no rest. He had returned, as ever, to his command post in the medieval friary, for it was ideally, if dangerously, positioned in the vulnerable sector of land between the South Gate and the East Gate. The building was strong, a muscular edifice of thick stone, but it had taken a pounding at the hands of the enemy batteries on Gaudy Green, and gaping holes had opened like black mouths in the roof and walls.

Massie cast a furtive glance at the ceiling directly above his head, checking for loose masonry. He allowed himself a rueful smile as he imagined what macabre fun the printers of *Mercurius Aulicus* would have with the news that Gloucester's chief rebel had been brained by a falling stone as he sat at his desk to plot against the king. It would be seen as divine retribution of the most poetic kind, and he wondered whether it was time to move his operation deeper into the city.

Comfortable that such a comical demise would not happen this night, he took his seat, tucking his long legs beneath the table and turning his attention to the never-ending pile of paper that greeted him each evening. There were inventories of powder and shot, of swords and tools captured during sorties and of food stocks. One report named the day's dead, while another described the progress being made on the twin countermines at the East Gate. The author complained of almost impossible working conditions, of mud so saturated that the task was proving futile. Massie thanked God aloud, his voice echoing about the high chamber, for if the city's countermines had run into difficulties, then so too would the Royalist works.

He leafed through the freshly inked ream. It appeared morale remained strong, while the secret gun port facing the wooden gallery over the eastern moat had nearly been completed. Soon they would be able to reveal the saker positioned within and blast the bullet-proof shield to splinters. The thought encouraged him, though it was tempered with concern as he returned with trepidation to the munitions inventory. Three barrels of powder was all they had left. He had used some of the precious commodity to mount a bombardment of the eastern trenches during the day, firing out from cannon placed at Friar's Barn, and, while he stood by that decision, it left their stocks woefully depleted. Would they even be able to fire the saker when the port was finally revealed?

A heavy knock at the door caused Massie to look round with a start. '*Come.*'

In walked three men. One was a sergeant who commanded this evening's guard at the entrance to Greyfriars. 'Sir,' he said, in the snappy manner of Stamford's blue-coated veterans. The volunteers of the Town Regiment were a little less staccato in their movements, not that Massie minded a jot.

'Well,' he said, setting down the papers and rising to his feet, 'what is it?'

The sergeant had an almost perfectly round face, with heavy, stubble-shadowed jowls and a wobbling set of chins. He reminded Massie of a fighting dog, all humourless brawn, yet now, in the guttering glow of the candles placed around the inner sanctum of Gloucester's war effort, his expression seemed almost to shiver with excitement. 'The messengers, sir,' he intoned, and Massie could have sworn he caught the hint of a smile. 'From Warwick.'

Warwick. The word had been so unexpected that Massie took a second to process it, and then he almost collapsed back in his chair. 'Praise be to God,' he whispered, a hand to his mouth. 'You made it through.'

The messengers grinned. One was young-looking, perhaps in his late teens, with lank sandy hair and a clean-shaven face. The other was probably in his mid forties, with thick, gunmetal-grey locks that fell in curls to his shoulders. The older of the two stepped forward a touch. 'All the way to Warwick and back again, sir.'

'And?' Massie reached to steady himself on the high back of the chair. He took a breath and clasped his hands tightly behind his back. 'What news?'

The older messenger cleared his throat ostentatiously, revelling in the moment. 'His Excellency marches to our aid, sir.'

Massie hardly dare utter the name. 'Essex?'

'The very same, sir.'

'You are certain?' Massie said, thinking of the trickery his opponents had used in the past. '*Certain*?'

The grey-haired man nodded solemnly. 'Aye, Governor, certain as God made the heavens.'

'Jesu,' Massie whispered. 'We are saved.' He noticed the unease on the second messenger's face. 'What is it, boy?'

The lad swallowed thickly. 'There is great consternation at His Excellency's strength, sir. His army bein' struck down with the plague so recently an' all. Some say he has ten thousand souls with him, sir. Others say two thousand.'

Massie nodded to show that he listened, but in truth his mind felt as though it danced in the thick beams above their heads. A relief force. Real hope for Gloucester's survival. If they could just hold out a little longer. 'Ten or two, it is something. Bless my soul, it is something.' He set his brown eyes on the men, darting between them, unwilling to let them break the gaze. 'Can you get through their lines again? I know it is asking much of you, but I will see that you are rewarded for the risk you take.'

'We could, sir,' the elder of the pair replied nervously.

'Just so,' Massie acknowledged. 'Get up on the hills. If you hear further news of his advance, light two great fires for me to see. Understood?'

'Understood, Governor,' the messenger said. 'But how will you know 'tis us?'

That was a good question and it made Massie pause. Only a few nights earlier a Royalist force had lit fires on Wainlode Hill, even going so far as to feign a loud skirmish in order to gull the city into thinking they clashed with a Parliamentarian army. Massie had dismissed the escapade as a devious ruse to make him throw open the gates, and time had proven him correct. How would this be any different? 'Light them at opposite ends of the hill, one twenty or so paces lower than the other.'

The messengers nodded and he dismissed them immediately, walking briskly back to the table. 'Just so,' he muttered quietly, forcing himself to remain businesslike in the duties that required his attention, despite the heartening news. The Parliament were finally on their way to save him, and yet, as he looked down at the paper with its numbers that told of dwindling powder, he could not help but worry. It would be a close-run thing, that much was certain.

Near Gaudy Green, Gloucester, 29 August 1643

Colonel Artemas Crow hated Gloucester. He hated it because it stood for everything that was wrong with the world. The new craze of social upheaval, of peasant disobedience, and of a Parliament that would not kneel to its rightful sovereign. Worst of all, it climbed from the sodden mud to scream defiance at the once all-conquering Royalist army, brandishing its ramshackle walls like some badge of honour, as though the mere existence of the cannon-frayed patchwork proved the fallibility of the king's cause. Crow had seen the Cavaliers forge a victorious path through the Roundhead ranks on so many bloody fields, taking territory, sacking towns and striking fear into the hearts of those arrogant enough to take up arms against Charles Stuart. He had jeered at the barefooted chain of prisoners who had been forced to march from Cirencester to Oxford in the snow to beg the king for forgiveness, and he had cheered at the news of the Cornish victory at Stratton. And yet it had all stopped. Juddered to a bloody, muddy, humiliating halt. At Gloucester.

'I would pay good money never to lay eyes on those crumbling walls again so long as I live,' he said as he pulled off his long boots. He propped his feet on the footstool in front, inspecting the stinking black hose that covered his feet with a wrinkle of his bulbous nose. 'Good money.'

The man standing before him was tall and thick-set, with a bushy beard of wiry black hair. An old scar made a horizontal cleft in his right cheek, dividing it into upper and lower halves. 'I still think we should storm the walls,' he said in a gruff tone that put Crow in mind of a growling mastiff. 'Lay ladders across the ditch to the north, where the rampart is lowest, and throw men at it. We have enough. The city would fall in an hour.'

Crow folded his arms. 'And then what, Major Triggs?'

Triggs scratched his beard thoughtfully. 'Then put the whole place to sword and fire, sir. Kill the men, rape the women, burn the houses.'

Crow laughed. 'And that is precisely what the King fears. We have gained a poor reputation with the common people, Major. A reputation for rape and pillage, as though we were an army of damned Norsemen. His Majesty would rather like to change that perception.'

'Then he will not take Gloucester,' Triggs said bluntly. He went to a battered little table where a stinking tallow candle flickered and spat against the closing darkness. He took it, pacing round the room to light three more for his colonel's comfort. 'I hear Essex marches even now.'

'Conjecture,' Crow said.

'Where there's smoke, Colonel, there is flame. We need to breach the walls quickly before the Roundheads reach us.'

Crow teased an errant hair from his bushy eyebrow, examining it between thumb and forefinger. 'Essex will not come. And if he dares, we will turn on him and crush his feeble army like ants beneath our boots.' He swept his hands over the spiked white tufts that grew in irregular clumps from his pate, and laced them behind his head. 'They could muster no more than two thousand foot and the same in horse. Pitiful.'

A wave of raucous laughter washed through from the next room, and Crow rolled his eyes in annoyance. This was one of the privations that made him sympathetic to Triggs' wish to wipe Gloucester clean off the map. There were simply not enough billets for the officers around the city, so, while the king made merry in his court down at Matson House, the rest of his men were left to find what shelter they could. The inns were crammed full; the storehouses, stables and barns were turned to quarters; every single house outside the walls was bursting with lice-ridden soldiery.

Crow might have been a full colonel, yet a little room in this pestilential hovel was all he had been able to find. It was scandalous, not least because the other three chambers in the rundown home had already been commandeered by grubby gangs of half-drunk pikemen. He had tried to turf out the surly mob upon his arrival, only to find that their officers had been forced to share with them. It was a disgrace to common decency, and another reason, if any more were needed, why Gloucester was simply the most wretched place in the whole of England.

'Tell me,' he said, 'how fares Dowdeswell?'

'The wound heals as well as can be expected, sir.'

'No fever?'

Triggs shook his head. 'None. But the blow was solid, took a good chunk out of his forearm. It'll be a long time before he can wield a sword properly.'

They waited while more shouts reverberated through the thin walls.

'But he'll live?'

'He'll live, sir.' Triggs could not hold his colonel's baby-blue gaze, and looked quickly at the floor. 'We failed you.'

'You did. But I am not surprised.' Crow moved his hands to his lap, straightening in his chair as the need to admonish the major grew. He had already bawled at Triggs, screamed in red-faced anger when the news reached him, but he could not help but labour the point yet again. 'I warned you, did I not? Told you to have a care with him. He's a real devil.'

'Give me another chance, sir,' Triggs muttered, crestfallen.

'I cannot risk it,' Crow replied as he brought his temper under control. 'I told you before that I could not risk a direct attack on Captain Stryker, for he is Rupert's creature.'

'But the—'

'The attempt the other night was under cover of darkness, and he was drunk. I heard his name mentioned at Council and sought his unit out.' It had been a terrible shock to discover that Stryker was still alive. God only knew what had become of James Buck, but Crow had a reasonable idea his agent would not be returning. He had gone to a deal of trouble to locate the billets to which Mowbray's regiment had been assigned, and yet more difficulty in ascertaining which taverns the officers frequented. But his men had spotted the one-eyed fiend eventually. 'That was your one chance, Major. You let him slip away.'

'Sir, I—'

Colonel Artemas Crow held up a broad palm for silence. 'Enough.' He closed his eyes and immediately saw Stryker's arrogant face. Christ, but it felt as though the hatred flowed in his veins instead of blood. 'Edberg, Buck and now you, Major. You have all failed me. The ugly peacock yet struts. Now leave me in peace, Major Triggs. I will deal with him myself.'

CHAPTER 22

The East Gate, Gloucester, 1 September 1643

The hole had been made in the old dungeon at the foot of the gate.

'Sally party, to me!'

Four blue-coated soldiers gripped their muskets in white-knuckled fists and pressed themselves up against the walls on either side of the newly made sallyport. They looked like night creatures, their faces darkened by dust and soot and their eyes glowing like hot coals in the gloomy dawn, and they stared hard at the near toothless sergeant as though in a trance.

'Have a care, you men,' the sergeant growled again, the lone incisor in his upper jaw jutting out between dry lips like a dirty fang. He kept his voice low, for, though they were on the inner face of the wall, it was no longer a secret that a company of human moles was busily tunnelling beneath their feet. 'No one gets killed lest I asks it of yer.' That elicited a few sheepish grins. 'Now where's that bugger got to?'

The bugger in question was a young man with straw-coloured moustache and close-cropped hair named John Barnwood. 'I'm here, Sergeant,' he hissed.

'You got what you're meant to've got?'

Barnwood's heart rattled like an antick in a cage, but he managed to affect a look of calm detachment. He had a small cloth sack in one hand and a length of smouldering cord in the other. He shook the sack. 'Three grenadoes and one match.'

The sergeant hawked up a wad of green and yellow phlegm, which he spat in a foamy ball at his feet. 'Then let's get this fuckin' thing over with.' He jerked a mucky finger at Barnwood's chest. 'You stay with me. I've orders to keep you alive, right?'

Barnwood was not about to argue. 'Right.'

The four bluecoats arranged themselves in single file and a ladder was passed up along their right-hand side. It was an awkward manoeuvre, for they had first to prop smouldering match-cords between their teeth and shift their muskets to their free left hands, but eventually they were ready. The lead man ducked through the hole and out on to the narrow lip of earth that ran between the outer face of the gate and the watery ditch, the rest following silently, with Barnwood and the sergeant in pursuit. Barnwood immediately grimaced, for the air stank. The ditch had been dug for defence but was quickly used for the city's refuse and, for the soldiers on the rampart, a convenient latrine. Moreover, it had filled with springwater and then rainwater, and the result was a stagnant moat that seemed to singe the hairs in Barnwood's nostrils.

He forced himself to keep the contents of his stomach down, biting back at the rising bile, for he did not wish his nausea to be misconstrued by Stamford's men as fear. This was, after all, his first raid, and he would damn well make a good fist of it.

'Go go go!' the gruff sergeant growled, shoving him between the shoulders.

Barnwood looked down to see the four bluecoats sliding sideways down the slippery glacis. They hurriedly laid the ladder across the stewing gully and scrambled across, the desperately weak-looking wooden poles, lashed together with twine, creaking as they bowed under the weight. Barnwood followed, noticing the wooden faggots and loose rubble dumped into the morass by Royalist engineers as he heard the raid's grunting commander breathing heavily at his back. He was frightened now, terrified, and with every inch of the putrid ditch he crossed, he expected to hear the scream of orders and din of musketry. But nothing came. He went on, dancing as nimbly as he could over to the far bank and into the Royalist works, the sack jangling at his hip with every rung traversed.

Edward Massie looked on from the fire-step on the east wall adjacent to the endangered gatehouse. He did not need his perspective glass for this work, for the action was immediately below his position, and, though the morning was overshadowed by a new host of grey clouds, he could see the operation unfold as though he were there himself.

'Is it worth the powder?' Thomas Pury asked at his side. The dour Puritan leader, along with Skaithlocke and several other officers, had scaled the wall to follow the garrison's first real attack in days.

Massie did not look round, leaning instead on the crumbling stone palisade in front. 'We cannot sit here and wait.'

'The enemy mines are not progressing as we'd feared,' Pury said as he adjusted his coat buttons. 'They have not yet filled the moat.'

'The surface petards, yes,' Massie agreed. 'They seem to be hampered by the springs, for the moat swallows their debris like quicksand. But underground?' He sucked at his teeth as he considered the report by some of the men in his countermines. They had claimed that they could hear the Cavalier digging crews through the walls of the muddy subterranean shafts. 'I believe they grope closer to our foundations every day, Thomas. They may already have cleared the moat. That is what this expedition has been tasked with discovering.'

'And if they find the mining work continues,' Vincent Skaithlocke said with grim relish, 'then we have a grenade expert from the Town Regiment to give the bastards pause for thought.'

Pury gnawed the flesh at the side of his narrow thumb. 'And nothing more of Essex?'

'No word,' said Massie sombrely. 'We only know that he comes hither. Therefore we must distract and delay the malignants for as long as we can, even at the cost of our precious powder.'

The group fell silent as their half-dozen raiders cleared the ladder, the blue-coated quartet tarrying briefly to fix matches to their muskets' serpents. Then they were moving on through the nearest saps. They had been long abandoned, having striven too close to the walls, their occupiers picked at by Massie's rebels, but the dark grooves might still hide hidden sentries and the watching group collectively held its breath.

John Barnwood peered down into the deep sap as he scurried past. It had been dug by brave men, he thought, for its proximity to the walls ensured it was within easy reach of the city's sharpshooters. A broken spade stuck out at an angle from the foot of the trench, while bits of wicker and wood were strewn along its length. He wondered whether one of Gloucester's cannon had put paid to the excavation here.

'Where now?' the gummy sergeant hissed to his flank as the musketeers dropped back to protect them.

Barnwood jerked his chin towards a spot just twenty feet away. 'There, by my reckoning.'

His reckoning was right, for they skirted another waterlogged and, thankfully, silent sap before reaching a flat stretch of sticky soil, at the centre of which was a large wooden board.

'That's it?' one of the bluecoats asked sceptically.

Barnwood did not know precisely what the soldier had been expecting, so he simply nodded. 'That's it.'

The musketeers fanned out around the square board, facing outwards to counter any threat from the Royalist lines, but the enemy, it seemed, were still blissfully abed. A few days previously, such a thing could never have happened, for the besiegers maintained a tight, watchful guard throughout the night, so frayed were their nerves by Massie's continual sorties. But the powder had ebbed away, Barnwood knew, and the raids had ceased, and the king's men had begun to sleep easy.

The sergeant crouched above the board and heaved it sideways, sliding it over the slippery ground to reveal a gaping hole.

*

'They're at the head of the mine,' Alderman Thomas Pury said in as excited a voice as Massie had heard him use.

'Pray God the fuses are properly cut,' Skaithlocke intoned.

Massie felt his fingers involuntarily grip the rampart. 'Barnwood knows what he is about, do not fear. If there is activity down there, he'll deal with it.'

'He'll damn well burn it,' said Skaithlocke.

Massie nodded. 'Just so, Colonel. Just so.'

Down at the entrance to the Royalist mine, John Barnwood was lighting a grenade. They had agreed to use just one, for there would be no time to loose the others, but Massie felt reassured by the city's explosives expert's insistence on taking three, in case the others failed. Yet the backups, he immediately saw, were not necessary, because Barnwood was standing astride the gaping maw, a clay sphere in his outstretched hand, and from its surface a bright light fizzed out to penetrate the gloomy dawn.

Massie sucked air into his lungs. 'Have a care on the walls! Fire on my signal!'

The explosion sounded strangely quiet in the depths of the tunnel, and for a fraction of a second John Barnwood feared his grenadoe had misfired, but then a tongue of flame lashed out from the hole to singe his eyebrows and he knew he had struck true.

He reeled back, staggering and slipping, and as his ears rang like the bells of Gloucester Cathedral, he was only saved from falling by the meaty embrace of the sergeant. Screams burst from the mine, the ground vibrated like an earthquake below their feet, and then more shouts ripped through the half-lit morn, raising the alarm across the labyrinthine network of saps. Immediately a swarm of soldiers rose like so many startled demons from their underground lairs, running between the trenches from their posts out of musket range to descend upon the mine that they now realized was under attack. They bellowed war cries and waved swords as they leaped the man-made valleys, splashing through the pools of brown water and skirting gabions and fences.

And now the mine itself spewed men up to ground level. Filthy, shirtless ghouls, coughing and spluttering amid a billowing pall of smoke, rolled out of its mouth to spill their guts and gasp for air. The four bluecoats fired, killing the miners where they lay, mouths still open for the breaths they never had time to take.

John Barnwood stared down at the reddening mud, horrified at the sudden deaths, but now more gun shots rang out, this time from the oncoming Royalists, and he knew there was no time to think. The sergeant collared him with a hairy fist, dragging him away from the fuming cavern and the twisted corpses with brute force and snarled urgency. The group raced back through the abandoned saps, thankful that no more Royalists lay between them and the ditch, bullets whining over their heads. Barnwood could hear the enraged cries of the enemy at their backs, the threats and curses clamouring in his ears.

And then the walls either side of the East Gate lit up, a huge volley of musketry rippling all the way along the summit, smoke drifting sideways to obscure the blue-coated men who had come to their aid. Barnwood did not look back, but he heard the screams well enough and knew that at least one of his pursuers had been hit. He slung the cloth sack over his shoulder and put every ounce of power he could muster into his pumping legs. They had done it.

Edward Massie let out a great sigh of relief as he watched the sally party scramble across their ladder and pull it through the tiny port. It had been an unmitigated triumph: the tunnel closed for at least a few hours, and some of the king's expert miners killed. But he was not altogether happy, could not join in the crowing celebrations that spread like wildfire across this sector of the tattered city, for the sortie had also confirmed his worst fear. The Royalist mine was still operational, despite the delays doubtless caused by the ever-seeping springs.

'We must double our efforts,' he said to Skaithlocke.

The hugely fat man had been turning to negotiate a safe passage to ground level, and he looked back in surprise. 'Governor? The mine is blown.'

'It will be resumed before long,' Massie replied, keeping his tone quiet so as not to dampen the spirits of the men around him. 'In truth, I had hoped Barnwood would not require his bomb. I'd wanted him to return to us with the message that the mine is filled with water, and that the malignants are no closer than when they started. Clearly that is not the case.'

'Then we persevere with our own mining,' said Skaithlocke.

'We must.' Massie stared down into the heart of the city. To his left, across the expanse of Friar's Orchard, the doughty citizens had already constructed a humble earthwork as a second line of defence. But it would not stop a concerted cavalry charge, and he was suddenly assailed by images of thrashing hooves and glinting steel. 'If we do not resist to our fullest endeavour,' he said with a small shudder, 'one of the mines will eventually succeed, and then all will be lost.' He pointed down at Friar's Orchard. 'Have them heighten the breastwork, make the earth wall much taller, and I will see to further measures.'

'Further measures?'

'See there, where the ground rises.' Massie pointed to a ribbon of raised land just behind the current defences across the orchard. 'We'll build a sconce just there. Place artillery on it.'

Skaithlocke nodded agreement and began his descent, while Massie simply stared down at the city he had come to love. If the Royalists found a way in, he would be ready for them.

The eastern trenches, Gloucester, 1 September 1643

Prince Rupert of the Rhine stalked through the saps like the angel of death, glowering at any who might dare meet his dark gaze. He reached the entrance to the mine, gave the steaming mound of mud and splinters a cursory glance, and stooped to stroke the muzzle of the gigantic poodle that had scampered up from Matson House in his horse's wake.

'What d'you make of it, Boye?' The dog licked its master's gloved hand and settled back on its filth-matted haunches, tongue lolling as it panted. Rupert straightened. 'I'd give a deal o' coin to hear his thoughts, you know, Killigrew.'

'Highness?' a small, pudgy-faced man with long, crooked teeth and tiny, shrewish eyes squeaked meekly some distance to the rear. He had been left behind, unable to keep pace with the long-legged warrior, and he bent double as he heaved air into his lungs.

'Boye has been at my side for as long as any brother officer, do not forget,' Rupert said. 'Even you, Ezra. He has seen it all, done it all, been in the midst of battle and survived it without a scratch.' He patted the poodle's head affectionately. 'You'd know what to do with this wretched place, wouldn't you, old friend?'

Boye whimpered and lifted a black-stained paw to scratch at a clump of mud that dangled from his shaggy coat. Rupert left him to it, taking an extra step towards the messy scene with his hands planted firmly on his hips. The attack had been so well executed he could hardly have done better himself. The mine was not destroyed, far from it, but the timbers bracing its entrance had been reduced to kindling, and some of the experts brought down from the king's Welsh mines had been killed, so the efficacy of the raid could hardly be denied.

'Sir, is that wise?'

Rupert spun round angrily. 'Is what wise, Killigrew?'

The aide's chinless head cracked open in a worried attempt at a smile. 'I fear we are in range, sir. Remember the stone.'

Rupert grunted, turning to stare defiantly up at the walls. He was well over six feet tall, elegantly dressed, with the broad shoulders and lean waist of a fighter. His hair was long and black, his hat adorned with a bright red feather, and the voluminous scarlet scarf at his waist bellowed his allegiance. All in all, Prince Rupert knew, he was a handsome target for the scurrilous criminals on Gloucester's almost laughably tumbledown walls, and he would not have it any other way. 'Let them try it,' he said, deliberately ignoring the memory of the pebble that had almost floored him a few nights previously. 'They couldn't shoot a dog in a box.'

As if his stentorian voice had carried all the way across the moat and scaled the wall, the rampart opened up, half a dozen shots cracking out from the bluecoats who clambered to get a look at the man the rebel press painted as a Germanic warlock who communed with Satan through his demon dog. Rupert spat derisively as each ball whistled past.

Ezra Killigrew shrieked, covering his black hair, plastered flat across his scalp with glistening lavender oil, with shaking hands. 'General, please!'

'Enough of your whining, damn your spavined hide!' Rupert snarled. He waved at the collapsed mouth of the mine. 'Look at this. Just blasted look, God melt your bones! They've ruined the tunnel. Confounded our efforts yet again.'

The aide shuffled backwards as another shot snapped at them, holing a gabion off to the right. 'It is bad news, sir.'

'You're goddamned right it is bad news, you obsequious little worm,' Rupert raged. 'Essex is en route, did you know that? He comes hither to lift this bloody ill-conceived siege and we slop about like so many pond-skaters. Christ, but we should have stormed when we had the chance.'

'Forth will not countenance it,' Killigrew proffered.

'Enough of Forth! The decrepit old booze hound was only too keen to sit outside and wait for the Puritanical bastards to surrender. Convinced my uncle it was the best course.' He waved a big hand, like the paddle at the end of an oar, at the defiantly resolute East Gate. 'Now look. They laugh at us like blue-feathered jackdaws.'

'We have the engines,' Killigrew ventured. 'Chillingworth's contraptions.'

'When will they be ready?'

'Almost ready now, sir, or so I hear.'

Rupert turned his back on the infernal city, calling Boye to heel and striding past the aide with splashing boots that splattered the cringing man's breeches. But he did not care. No indeed, he did not care for anyone at that moment. He had had enough of humiliation at the hands of the supposed genius Massie. Enough of the mockery at the hands of the Parliamentarian news-sheets, enough of bowing to the tottering fossil, the Earl of Forth. It was time to act.

Baynard's Green, near Bicester, 1 September 1643

Robert Devereux, third Earl of Essex and commander of the army of Parliament, squeezed his thighs together and his grey gelding moved off. Immediately he was greeted by a ripple of applause that swelled like a rising tide to roar across fields that had been transformed to a patchwork of bright colours by the mustering army. The force was huge, far larger than Essex had dared hope for when Pym sent him on his mission. Leaving the jubilant mob at Hounslow Heath, he had advanced northwards across a broad front, dividing his command into three columns to spread the burden of feeding and billeting the troops. The earl had led the main force, pushing up through Beaconsfield and Aylesbury, while the London Trained Bands forged a parallel route via Uxbridge and Chesham. To the west, a third column of six regiments, four infantry and two cavalry, marched up from Wokingham, through Thame, and eventually arriving at the rendezvous for the agreed muster.

Now here they all were. The young Lord Grey of Groby had come in the morning with the final detachment of cavalrymen down from Leicester, an arrival that, amid much rejoicing from the assembled throng, had brought Essex's unlikely army up to full strength. With the Trained Bands, who had somehow been released from London, he now inspected a force of 10,500 foot and 4,500 horse. Enough to challenge the festering Oxford Army and more.

Essex kept his back straight and his expression calmly poised, gathering the reins in one gloved hand and whipping off his broad, feathered hat with the other. 'Is it not a grand sight?' he said as he waved the hat to the bellowing crowd.

On horseback beside him were two men, both in their early forties. One was dressed in a charcoal-coloured riding cloak, with long arms and powerful shoulders. He tugged at the triangular tuft of grey hair sprouting below his bottom lip. 'Grand indeed, Your Grace. We shall give the Cavaliers a fright, and that's for certain.'

Essex beamed, for there were not many men in the country whose opinion he valued more. Major General of Foot, Philip Skippon was a hard, professional soldier who knew his business. A veteran of the European wars, he had vast experience, sound judgement and was well loved by the men. The earl replaced his hat, for the afternoon had turned cold, but he continued to wave at the deep units of his new army as they cheered his progress. 'You will command the first brigade,' he said.

Skippon nodded. 'How many will there be?'

'Five,' Essex confirmed, 'in the Swedish manner. Barclay and Holburn will each take a brigade, as will Lord Robartes. The Trained Bands will be taken by Mainwaring.'

'Very good, Your Grace.'

Essex glanced at the second man. 'Stapleton?'

Sir Philip Stapleton kicked forth to come alongside. 'Sir?' He had been a landowner in Yorkshire before the war, but, as protégé of Essex's confidante, John Hampden, had excelled in the army, seeing action at Edgehill and Chalgrove. When Hampden died, Essex had turned increasingly to Stapleton for advice, and, by turns, his star had risen.

'You'll take the horse,' Essex said.

Stapleton was a thin man, with pale skin and the hooded eyes of a man who rarely slept, but he nodded enthusiastically. 'An honour, Your Grace.'

They moved on, passing in front of the huge force, cheers ringing in their ears from bristling blocks of pike and musket. There were red coats and orange, blue and yellow, and grey and green. The bright tawny of the Earl of Essex was everywhere, in scarves tied around waists and chests, in hatbands and in ribbons adorning saddles and pike staves and sword-hilts. Huge standards waved in the chilly wind, swirled on thick staffs by seasoned ensigns and cornets. Skippon bowed to one phalanx of men when he caught sight of a particular red standard. It bore an arm and sword issuing forth from a cloud over a Bible. 'My brave lads!' he bellowed, receiving a renewed crescendo for his trouble.

They passed troop after troop of cavalry, gleaming in their pots and breastplates, formidable on the backs of the snorting beasts. The officers drew their long blades in salute, calling a huzzah to their general.

'If we do not smash them, gentlemen,' Essex said as the three commanders reached the artillery train, 'then I know not how it can be done.' He pointed at the rows of cannon, like an army of gigantic black toads squatting on the damp terrain. 'We have plentiful powder and ammunition.'

'How many cannon, Your Grace?' Skippon asked.

'Near fifty,' Essex said. 'We will unleash a veritable storm when the chance comes.'

'I pray it comes swiftly,' said Skippon. 'Does the King know?'

'That we intend to lift his siege? I am not certain.' He gazed back at the martial cavalcade that was now ready to strike out to the west. 'One hopes he fears for Oxford yet. It will make him dither.'

'Can we not try for Oxford, Your Grace?' Stapleton said, Yorkshire heritage lending a gentle accent to his words.

Essex shook his head. 'I'd dearly love to rattle that nest of hornets, I assure you. But the Parliament sees Gloucester as a talisman of the rebellion. A symbol of resistance. With the recent peace riots, the people need a hero, and Pym has decided that that man will be Governor Massie. If we can rescue him before his city falls, it will galvanize the public to our cause.'

'The Oxford Army may be frustrated at Gloucester,' Skippon warned as they turned their mounts for a second pass in front of the troops, 'but it is still a dangerous beast.'

'Agreed,' Essex said reflectively. 'It is a venture fraught with risk. But we must attempt it.'

'And if the attempt ends in defeat,' Skippon replied grimly, 'we may lose our entire field army.'

The supreme commander did not answer, for he could not afford to consider the alternative to glory. Skippon was right, the mission might be worth a great deal in Parliamentary propaganda, but it risked the destruction of the greatest rebel force raised since Edgehill.

So Robert Devereux, third Earl of Essex, closed his eyes and prayed, even as the raucous cheering gathered strength again. Because for all his good intentions, he could not win the war at Gloucester, but he could most certainly lose it.

Bletchingdon, Oxfordshire, 1 September 1643

Lieutenant General Henry Wilmot, first Earl of Rochester, swept into the stable block at his headquarters overlooking the River Cherwell and jumped from his saddle like an acrobat. He tore off his gloves, tossing them to a startled junior officer, and quickly unfastened his helmet. 'Where is the knave?'

The officer, a lieutenant who still fumbled with the lavishly fringed gloves, indicated a corner of the courtyard where a group of bustling harquebusiers were swirling and shouting excitedly, the hooves of their mounts rattling like a monstrous hail-storm on the cobbles. 'Yonder, my lord.'

Lord Wilmot, commander of His Majesty's Oxford cavalry, tugged the helm from his head, sweaty clumps of dark golden hair falling about his shoulders. 'Thank you, Wigram.'

Wilmot strode quickly across the open ground, pleased by the way the gallant cavalrymen, dashing, murderous peacocks all, deferred to him, swerving their whinnying mounts out of his path. They were Rupert's riders in truth, the Teutonic Knight's colourful rakehells who had terrified Parliament's forces up and down the land, but Wilmot had led them at Roundway, spearheaded the charges that destroyed Waller's entire Western Army, and now, gloriously, they believed in the young lord too.

Wilmot had been stationed out here to sit between Oxford and the advancing rebel multitude, watching for the roads they chose to take, and ready to harry them at every step. He had also been told to impede any move they might make upon Gloucester, which meant that, barring Christ snatching up Essex's pious men, he would see action one way or another. Wilmot felt alive, his limbs tingling with the smell of horseflesh and the promise of battle, and his generous lips widened in a broad smile as he reached the chattering group.

'Well? What does he have to say?'

The courtyard was hemmed by high brick walls, and in one of the corners, sat on his rump with shoulders thrust firmly against the brickwork, was a boy with curly hair the colour of russetted armour. Over him stood three of Wilmot's officers, all bare-headed but still dressed in the buff leather and grass-speckled plate they had worn for the day's patrol.

One of the officers, a man in his twenties, with short black hair and sharply trimmed beard and moustache, offered Wilmot a curt bow. 'Not a lot, my lord. Sweating like a sow in a shambles.'

Wilmot grimaced at the analogy. 'Delightful.'

'I niver did it, zir!' the lad bawled in an accent so thick that Wilmot found himself cocking his ear to the side as he spoke, as though that might help in disentangling the local drawl.

'Never did what, young man?'

The boy struggled to stand, but one of the looming cavalry-men thrust him back to earth with rough hands. 'Niver did whatever they says oi did, zir!'

Wilmot met the boy's brown gaze and wondered how old he was. No more than fourteen, he surmised. 'It is not what you did that troubles me, fellow, but what you said.'

'Then I zed nought, zir, 'pon my honour.'

'Honour?' Wilmot said with a smile. 'At least you're blessed with a sense of humour, I suppose.' He looked at the officer with the black beard. 'Good God, Percy, he's harder to under-stand than the folk at Breda.'

Percy grinned. 'Worse, my lord. Took him out near the bridge.'

'And?'

'Says he's a goat-herd, my lord.'

Wilmot peered down at the boy. 'Does he now?' He reached for the lace at his collar, tugging it gently down across his silver gorget so that it was straight. A robust hack out in the country-side inevitably resulted in dishevelled clothing. 'Good fellow,' he said when he was happy with the collar, 'where are your goats?'

The youngster scratched the curls at his temple. 'Zir?' He glanced between Percy and Wilmot, evidently gathering the latter's proper title, for he quickly added, 'M'lord.'

'Your goats,' Wilmot persisted. 'The ones you herd.'

The boy wrinkled his freckled nose. 'Oi can't rightly zay, m'lord.'

Wilmot breathed in deeply, letting the air out through his nostrils as he considered matters. 'Figments, young man,' he said after a moment. 'Of your dull-witted mind. You were spying for the rebels.'

'No, m'lord,' the boy protested weakly.

'Yes, boy, you were.' With that, the lieutenant general tossed his helmet to a waiting servant and drew his sword slowly, delib-erately letting the hiss of steel linger in the air between them as it cleared the scabbard's throat. He held the weapon up, exam-ining it for nicks, letting the afternoon light play along its length, before lowering it so that the tip rested against the prisoner's sternum. 'Now I am disinclined to befoul my blade,' he said coolly, 'but believe me when I say that I shall most certainly run you through if you give me cause.'

The youngster quailed, his bravado immediately folding like wet paper. 'I was, m'lord,' he mumbled. 'Watchin' you, that iz.'

Wilmot sighed. 'Well, I must say you are an even worse spy than you are a goat-herd.' The assembled troopers laughed at that, causing the boy to flinch. 'Still, you may help me now, should you wish to avoid being sliced in two.'

'Anythin', m'lord.'

'The Parliament men muster where?'

'Baynard's Green,' the terrified youngster blurted. ''Tween Bicester an' Brackley. Though they're on the move again.'

'Oh?' Wilmot asked, his interest piqued. He had been scouting all day in order to get a handle on the oncoming rebel army, and knew that they had been at Baynard's Green, but had no idea as to where next the wily Earl of Essex meant to march.

'T'ords Deddin'ton, mostly, an' some to Aynho.'

'Deddington,' Percy said when Wilmot looked to him for clarification. 'Due west of Baynard's Green. Aynho is north of there.'

Wilmot stared at the prisoner. 'West and north? You are certain?'

The lad nodded rapidly. 'Aye, m'lord.'

'Not south?' A shake of the head served as an answer, and Lord Wilmot withdrew his sword, sheathing it smartly. 'Well, you have been of great help, good fellow.' He looked up. 'Percy, take half the men. Oxford is not the target.'

'Gloucester?' asked Percy.

'Gloucester. But we'll stop them.' Wilmot cracked each one of his knuckles in turn and retrieved the helmet from his servant. 'By God, we will stop them.' He made to move, energized by the prospect of battle, eager to return to the saddle, but he caught a meaningful glance from Percy. He sighed, irritated by having to deal with the ginger-headed urchin. 'Oh, string him up.'

'What?' the boy cried, eyes popping from their freckled sockets. 'M'lord? No, m'lord, you can't!'

Wilmot ran his fingers through his sweaty hair and jammed the lobster-tailed helm back over his skull. 'I can do whatever I wish, good fellow. And you, sir, are a spy.'

'But you zed—' the boy babbled, trying in vain to shuffle backwards as if his feeble weight could push through the brick wall. 'You zed you wouldn't kill me if'n oi talked!'

Lord Wilmot, Earl of Rochester, stared down at the hapless prisoner through his triple-barred visor. 'I said I wouldn't run you through, and I shan't. But you're a rebel spy and you'll swing for it.' He turned away with a quick glance at Percy. 'Get on with it. Time is of the essence.'

The boy's screams faded as he was dragged away by a pair of surly soldiers, while all around the courtyard troopers fastened helmets and tugged on gloves. They hauled themselves up on to skittish mounts and called in boisterous tones to one another as though they were riding to hounds. Wilmot reached his own horse, the black stallion greeting him with a whicker and a shake of the head, and he stroked its soft mane, brushed to perfection by the servants while the lieutenant general had been conducting his unpleasant exchange with the local lad.

'Let us find some rebels!' he shouted to the massing men who clattered like so many mythical centaurs across the cobbles. 'Essex looks to Gloucester, but all he'll find is cold steel and warm lead!'

The men brayed a chorus of huzzahs, and Wilmot grinned broadly, feeling the stiff golden hairs of his whiskers tickle at his nose. And then he froze, because a new, quite unexpected voice had pierced his reverie.

'My lord Wilmot?' the woman said again.

Wilmot stared down at the speaker. She was small and lithe, dressed all in black and seated on a grey pony. Her hair was long and golden, though a lighter shade than his own, and her eyes were as blue as sapphires. Beside her, atop a slightly larger chestnut mare, was another woman. This one was a brunette, pale as a ghost, with large, brown and green eyes shaped like almonds.

'And who might you be?' Lord Wilmot asked, utterly thrown by this new vision.

The blonde woman, speaking with a French accent, offered a smile at his obvious discomfiture. 'I am Lisette Gaillard, and this is Cecily Cade. We are on king's business, my lord.'

CHAPTER 23

The eastern trenches, Gloucester, 2 September 1643

'It's a race against time,' Sergeant William Skellen droned. He lifted his musket, poked the barrel over the top of the stone-filled gabion, and took aim at a gunner whose head ventured just above the high parapet. He fired, cursing softly when he saw that the shot had missed.

Captain Stryker slopped down into the splashing grime at the bottom of the sap and nodded in agreement. The mining operation, set back by daring assault and inclement weather, was still not complete. The attempts to approach the walls with small parties of men under cover of darkness, thereby avoiding the bloody escalades so abhorrent to King Charles, had ended in abject failure. The artillery bombardments, though resumed with vigour now that a fresh supply of ammunition had finally arrived from the Royalist foundries, had done little more than smash rooftops and peck at walls that had been cleverly buttressed with cushioning turf. Even the saps, creeping closer to the city by the hour, had become waterlogged pits almost impossible to drain and painstaking to dig. 'A race against the Earl of Essex,' he replied, for the whole army now knew that a large, well-equipped relief force was marching to Massie's aid.

The laconic sergeant jabbed the butt end of his musket into the mud, leaving it there like a shortened flag pole, and delved into his snapsack. He drew out a scrap of salted meat. 'Race against ourselves, sir,' he said, popping the meat into his black-toothed mouth. 'Got to break in before the tawny boys reach us.'

Stryker eyed the meat greedily. 'Where did you get that?'

Skellen kept his face impassive. 'One o' the wenches at some boozin' ken, sir.'

'Did you a favour, did she?'

'Did her a favour, sir,' Skellen said.

Stryker decided it was best not to know more, and steered the conversation back to more pressing matters. 'Any luck finding Hatton?'

'None,' Skellen said. 'No one's seen him. You sure he's Skaithlocke's man?'

Stryker shook his head. That was just it, he was not sure. He suspected this man, Hatton, for no other men had deserted the rebel garrison at the time Skaithlocke had indicated, but perhaps the killer had come through undetected, and they were searching in entirely the wrong manner. Either way, they had found no trace of anything untoward. Perhaps, as Prince Rupert had said, it was indeed all simply another cog in Edward Massie's complex web of obfuscation.

'How d'you feel about it all now?' Skellen asked.

Stryker took a whetstone from his pocket and drew his blade. 'I wish I knew what the assassin intended.'

'Not that, sir,' replied Skellen. He pointed up at the walls. 'That.'

In truth, Stryker had tried to force their rebel odyssey to the back of his mind in recent days, but he could hardly deny Skellen the chance to discuss it. He looked down at the Toledo sword in his hand, gently running the stone along one of its cutting edges. 'They're good people.'

Skellen pulled off his cap and scratched at his ear. 'Aye, they are. I feel bad to think we'll soon have to kill them.'

Stryker knew that the statement was loaded. 'If you're asking whether the King will offer them quarter, Sergeant, I can't give you any reassurance. They've refused repeated calls to surrender. When we get over the walls, there's every chance there'll be a massacre.'

'Jesu.' Skellen slumped back against a large piece of timber that had been propped against the side of the sap to give it stability. The gabion sat immediately above them, shielding them from the men on the rampart. 'Are you glad we came back?'

Stryker was happy with the fine sharpness of his double-edged blade, and he put the whetstone away. He sheathed the weapon and sat next to the taller man. 'Yes.'

'Not just cos you're chasin' the assassin?'

'Not just that,' Stryker said truthfully. 'This is where I belong. We'll never speak of this again, understood?'

'No argument from me, sir.'

The pair stared away to the east. The area had been transformed by Roundhead fire and Royalist excavation to an obliterated no-man's-land. Lone gable walls climbed out of the mud, leaning precariously at strange angles. Blackened piles of rubble betrayed the places where family hearths had been. The Bible spoke of Armageddon, thought Stryker, and he found himself wondering if this was what the world would look like after that final battle.

Beside him, Skellen had produced a shard of biscuit. The sergeant tapped the granite-like scrap against his boot to rid it of the weevils lurking within. 'Want some?' he proffered.

But Stryker was no longer listening. Further to the south-east, along the old road that had once been the main conduit through the annihilated suburb, a man was striding alone, a huge metal tube in his hands. Stryker watched him closely, for something about the fellow had caught his attention. He stared a moment longer, and then it struck him like a thunderbolt.

He pushed himself off the rough timber perch. 'He has fair hair.'

'Come again, sir?'

Stryker pointed to the man. 'Skaithlocke said the assassin had golden hair.'

Skellen squinted along the road. 'Plenty o' folk do, sir.'

'What is he holding, Sergeant?'

'Looks like a duck gun to me, sir. Captain!'

Stryker was already running. He had leaped from the trench, sliding haphazardly as he hit the slick mud, but gained his balance in a frantic flail of limbs. And now he bolted through the desolate field towards the road, holding his scabbard out at the side so as not to trip, the enemy musketeers heralding his departure with a flurry of shots that all flew woefully wayward. He skirted the foundations of several buildings reduced to almost ground level, and burst out on to the road.

Still the musketeers took aim at his back, but he was out of range now, and he pressed on, closing the distance between him and the blond soldier with every racing heartbeat. Suddenly he was sure. It all made sense. The man had golden hair, as Skaithlocke had said, and he held a fowling piece; it was eight feet of iron and deadly at long range. He had seen one used at Lichfield during the winter, when a man had used one to shoot Baron Brooke through the eye from the very top of the cathedral spire. It was a sharpshooter's weapon. An assassin's weapon.

The man saw Stryker coming and his jaw dropped. Stryker drew his sword and bellowed at him to halt. To his surprise, the order was immediately obeyed.

'Mercy, friend, please, I beg of you!' the high-pitched plea tumbled from the blond man's mouth. His face had a look of unadulterated terror, and he released the huge gun, letting it squelch on the churned road.

Stryker held his sword level with the man's throat. 'Who are you?'

'Jeremiah Plant, sir,' the man whimpered through shivering lips. 'Local man, is all. Volunteered to fight for 'is Majesty, sir.'

Stryker looked down at the fearsome long-arm half sunk in the morass. 'Why do you bear this piece?' He noticed that a detachment of cavalry, probably fifteen strong, was coming up the road at Plant's back. If the man ran, he would be nicely trapped.

'I use it to shoot birds for the big manor over at Southam, sir. 'Tis my own gun.'

Stryker stared at Plant for a lingering moment, gauging the man's expression, but all he saw was fear. He lowered his sword, feeling the tension flow out of every muscle. He felt desperately foolish. 'My apologies, sir,' he said, sheathing the blade and stooping to retrieve the grubby fowling piece. 'A case of mistaken identity.'

Jeremiah Plant looked as though he might soil his breeches at any moment. 'M-may I go, sir? I've m' new billet to find.'

'Of course, Mister Plant. My apologies again, sincerely.'

'No matter,' Plant murmured, hurrying away towards the Astley's large encampment around Barton Hill.

'Christ,' Stryker snarled at himself when Plant was gone. 'You stupid bastard!'

'Weren't him, then, Captain?' William Skellen's sardonic voice sounded at his back.

Stryker turned, slapping a hand on to his face in embarrassment. 'This thing has me out of kilter, Sergeant.'

'I can see that, sir. Still, least you didn't fillet the poor bastard.'

Stryker laughed at that. 'I suppose that's something.'

'And he'll get over the fright,' Skellen added with the ghost of a smirk. His sepulchral eyes drifted over Stryker's shoulder as he spoke, taking in the approaching cavalry.

'I hope I get over the shame,' Stryker added.

'Oh, I reckon you will,' Skellen replied. He pointed at the horsemen who were now less than fifty paces away. 'You've got plenty else to think on, sir.'

Stryker frowned. He turned slowly, and as his gaze absorbed the cavalrymen stretched across the road, it felt as though the very breath had been squeezed from his lungs. Because, riding at the very centre of the bristling harquebusiers, was a person he had feared he might never again see.

'Hello *mon amour*,' the woman said. She was dressed all in black, perched nonchalantly upon a grey pony that scraped at the cloying muck with its front hoof.

Stryker looked from her long boots, past her breeches and voluminous cloak, to shoulders draped in thick tendrils of tousled gold. Her face was in the shadow cast by the wide brim of her hat, but he knew who it was, all the same. 'Hello, Lisette.'

Near Somerton, Oxfordshire, 2 September 1643

Lieutenant General Henry Wilmot, first Earl of Rochester, drew his sword. It was a beautiful blade, long, single-edged and gleaming. Its hilt swirled in the Venetian Schiavona style about his gloved fist like a ball of diamonds, calling his men to arms.

They came in their droves. He had almost two thousand mounted Cavaliers at his back, deployed around the pebbled ford, and the rasping sing of all those swords being drawn in unison was like an angelic choir to his ears. He peered at as many of the mad-eyed harquebusiers as he could through the slim bars of his visor, grinning wolfishly at any who caught his eye, and then stood high in his stirrups. '*To war!*'

'*To war!*' was the bellowed reply.

'For God and King Charles!'

Again the cavalrymen echoed his cry, and they were off, raking at their mounts' flanks, sending great fountains into the air as so many fetlocks thrashed through the ford. The horses whinnied and reared, their masters snarled into their pricked ears, whipping them to a frenzy of excitement, and the air chimed with jangling metal and pounding hooves.

Wilmot led the advance. Ahead, on the eastern side of the Cherwell, was another body of horsemen. These rode behind the twin cornets of Middleton and Ramsey, men who reported to the Earl of Essex, and Wilmot sensed they were here to keep him at bay. If that was the case, then he guessed Essex's main infantry brigades would be on the move. His scouts had informed him that the Parliamentary army had spent the night camped around Aynho, on the great river's east bank, which meant that they would now need to cross if they were to advance up the Severn Valley. Such a crossing made infantry terribly vulnerable, and Middleton had evidently been ordered to prevent the Royalist cavalry from cutting them to shreds as they crossed. Well, Wilmot thought as he spurred with gritted teeth along the bulrush-choked bank, they would see how difficult a proposition such an order would prove to be.

The Royalists galloped in a great line beside the bank. To their right was thick forest, dense and impassable, but up ahead the track opened out into a broad clearing, and it was there that Wilmot intended to be. He looked back with a whoop of joy, the thrill of the hunt pulsing through every vein and sinew. His men were at his back, flying across the muddy terrain like a flock of giant cockerels, such was the array of colours on display. Blues and greens and reds and purples flashed brightly as they careened through the mouth of the track and on to the open ground.

The Roundhead cavalry were cantering in formation across the small field. They spread out to meet the much larger force, drawing pistols, blades and carbines. The rebel officers screamed unintelligible orders as the space between the two parties evaporated.

Lord Wilmot leaned into his steed's powerful neck, smelling the musty scent of leather and sweat on the breeze-blown mane, and thanked God he was alive to see these days of glory. Roundway Down had made his name; today would make him immortal. He pointed his blade straight ahead as his thundering column spread out to envelope the Parliamentarians, noticed the enemy cornets fluttering proudly at their flanks, and steered his charge to pick them out. The standard bearers would die first.

'King Charles!' Wilmot screamed. 'Cold steel and warm lead!'

The musket volley took his immense force in both flanks. It shattered the grey afternoon, tearing through the Royalist cavalrymen on the outermost fringes of the column and sending panic through Wilmot's hitherto ebullient harquebusiers like flame through a dry thatch.

From Wilmot's position at the centre of the charge, he could not see what new threat lurked in the flanking woodland, only the huge clouds of yellowish smoke roiling out from a tree line suddenly transformed from rural serenity to powder-singed menace. He sheathed his sword as rapidly as he could, taking the reins in both hands and wrenching his horse's head roughly to the side, compelling the frightened beast to wheel back in a sliding, skidding circle that sent black clods of earth flinging up in every direction. He gave no order, for the unforeseen volley had done his work already. The king's cavalry had been caught by surprise and now faced the possibility of a sizeable force of infantry on the field. They were not about to hammer home the charge until they knew precisely what foe they faced.

Even as they rode back towards the track, a second rattle of musketry burst forth from the woods. Wilmot cast desperate looks at both the flanks, and though no one looked to be hit, every horseman seemed to shrink in his saddle, chin down and features clenched, as though he rode into the eye of a wintry storm. Except here and now the howling wind was the howl of man, and the stinging sleet was murderous lead.

He stood in his stirrups, craning over the bobbing heads of his men to squint into the trees. There, between two great boughs, he saw the glint of a bridle. And another, and another.

'Goddamned dragooners!' he snarled, as they reached the track that would take them out of musket range.

'Sir?' one of the nearer cavalrymen shouted above the din of hooves.

'Not infantry,' Wilmot called back. 'They have dragoons out in the trees.' And that would be a problem, he inwardly conceded, for the enemy effectively possessed mounted infantry: men who could ride quickly to each deployment, but bring full musket-fire to bear.

Wilmot twisted in his saddle as he guided his horse through the narrow opening that took them back to where they had started. He saw that the cavalrymen of Middleton and Ramsey were now advancing. 'Damn their brazen eyes!' he bellowed, thumping a fist against his breastplate. 'They attack me? The arrogant guttersnipes attack me?'

The Royalists watched as the rebel horsemen came on across the field. This would clearly be a hard day's work. Silently, Lord Wilmot cursed his luck and desperately racked his mind for a solution. There was none, other than to keep battering the Roundheads with his larger force and eventually drive them back. He prayed he could succeed in time to prevent Essex's advance across the Cherwell. Failure simply did not bear consideration.

Barton, Gloucester, ? September 1643

Stryker's billet was a tiny, windowless room on the upper floor of a stone building on Barton Street. It had been home to a young family, he guessed, for a rag doll had been left unceremoniously beside the downstairs hearth when first he arrived, and a battered pinwheel in a wooden chest that had since gone for kindling. There had been cooking pots too, and chairs and cups and jugs. But war had destroyed the once cosy place, chased the occupants away and left it as desolate as the saps a short way to the north. Now, as Stryker led Lisette Gaillard up the creaking staircase, he knew she would see little more than a stone box. There was just a rickety wooden bed frame, on which sat a straw palliasse that was grimy and uneven. Everything else had been stripped out by the Royalist army, looted or burned. Even so, Stryker had had to evict a pair of snot-nosed lieutenants to claim the dingy chamber for his own.

The sight of the place made him cringe as he drew Lisette inside, but she seemed not to notice. Instead she pushed the door shut behind her, the clunk of the lock sounding like a pistol shot in the silence, and they were plunged into gloom. They regarded one another wordlessly for what seemed an age, each letting their eyes grow accustomed to the dimness, each considering the weeks that had slipped by since last they met.

'How?' Stryker said when finally he found his voice.

'Lord Wilmot's men escorted us,' Lisette said. 'From Oxford.'

'Us?'

Lisette's stare hardened, just a touch, but he noticed it all the same. 'I have Miss Cade.'

411

Stryker felt his eye widen. 'You did it? You rescued her?'

'She is with the King now,' Lisette said, and her face was suddenly hostile. 'No thanks to—'

But the words would not come, for her mouth was suddenly blocked by Stryker's. He pressed against her, forcing her back against the door, and, though her hands were pushing at his chest, her tongue did not resist his. There they remained for a luxurious moment, fastened together in an embrace Stryker hoped would never end, but Lisette jerked violently back, breaking the trance.

She stared up at Stryker, still angry, and for a moment he thought she might slap him, but instead her hand reached out for his, squeezing his fingers and pulling them up to her face. He pressed his palm against her cheek; it was so warm in the chill afternoon. He lifted his free hand and threaded his fingers through the golden strands of her hair. She tilted her head, eyes closed, sighing at the touch. He leaned in to kiss her again, but this time she pushed him away so that he took a full pace back. She shrugged off her cloak, mud-spattered from the ride, and then the coat beneath, leaving them in a heap by the door as she stepped forth. She pushed him in the chest so that he staggered rearward, again and again, until the backs of his knees collided with the palliasse and he collapsed heavily on to its edge. And she was standing over him, tugging the string at the collar of her voluminous white shirt, glaring down at him. He took her thighs in his hands, let his palms snake up the brown wool and, with fingers that felt so out of practice, fumbled at the pewter discs holding her breeches in place.

Lisette was already pulling the shirt over her head. She tossed it casually away and stepped back so that he could see her. He swallowed thickly. She smiled down at him through the curtain of gold already tousled from his feverish attentions. Her skin was the colour of milk, her eyes like a cat's in the darkness, twinkling and predatory. Her hands moved to her breeches, finishing what his hurried fingers had started, and soon they were a mere pile at her ankles.

Stryker stood as though a fire had been lit beneath him, and he tore at his own clothes like a madman. Lisette watched in silence, the corners of her mouth twitching in a sardonic smirk as he struggled to unfasten his scabbard. He cursed, lifting the whole baldric clean over his head, throwing it to the foot of the palliasse, and ripping off the rest of his garments. She came closer, kicking off her boots. He reached out, grasping her wrists more roughly than he meant, and she mewed softly as he dragged her to the bed. They crumpled side by side on to the compacted straw, kissing hungrily, tongues twining, teeth clinking, exploring the flesh that they knew so well but feared they had forgotten.

Lisette pulled back. 'It is good to see you, *mon amour*,' she murmured.

Stryker tried to kiss her again, but she pressed a finger to his lips, urging patience. She rotated her hips a touch, lifting a knee, and slid across his stomach so that she straddled him. He stared up at her, watching her breasts sway behind the long, tangled hair, their dark tips brushing his chest in the half-light. She slipped a hand between their bodies, pushing her fingers down until she found him. He bucked at her touch, desperate that she guide him into her, and she eased back, gasping at the ceiling beams. His fingers dug into the soft flesh of her rump, while her nails carved red tracks from his chest to his shoulders. Nothing existed but the two of them. The siege, the rebels, the war. In that moment, nothing mattered.

'Why did you abandon me?' Lisette said later. She had told him of Cecily's rescue, of the time under Erasmus Collings' control, and of the huge army they had seen muster on Hounslow Heath. For his part, Stryker had listened with interest, though he knew that eventually she would bring matters back to this.

Stryker rolled on to his side to face her. He had no sheets in the Spartan billet, and they were naked together on the palliasse. Their skin was clammy where their bodies touched. 'I did not. I was ordered to Bristol, Lisette, and then here. The Prince sent me into the city.'

'You've turned spy now?'

Stryker ran a finger along her flank, over her hip and down the sweep of her buttock. Her skin was so smooth. It never failed to amaze him. 'Aye. Or, at least, I was spying until a few days ago.' He dragged his gaze back to her face, pushing the hair from her eyes with a delicate finger. 'You have to believe me, Lisette. The high command lost their hunger for the mission when Hopton was injured.'

'Injured?' she said in surprise. 'He lives still?'

Stryker nodded. 'He was burned badly, but recovers well by all accounts. They put him in charge of Bristol after it fell.'

'She will be happy to know that.'

'She?'

'Cecily.'

Stryker looked away. 'You did well to rescue her.'

Lisette tapped his shoulder. 'Christ, Stryker, do not look so bloody sheepish. I know what happened.'

'You know?' Stryker replied tentatively.

Lisette ran a hand gently over him, from the scab on his forehead, down past the fresh bruises of recent weeks and to his shoulders, arms and chest. She explored each scar as she had so many times before. There were new ones, and she paid them extra attention, as if committing every blemish to memory. 'You should have told me it was you she seduced.'

'She did not seduce me, Lisette,' Stryker argued.

'No? She is very beautiful.'

'She tried,' Stryker admitted, as something inside compelled him to speak the truth. It was as if all the lies he had told in Gloucester had been more than he could stomach any longer. 'I confess I was tempted. But I refused her.'

Lisette's probing fingers froze at a straight white scar along his abdomen. 'Tempted.'

'Tempted,' he repeated. He pushed his fingers through the hair above her ear. 'Nothing more.'

Lisette looked at him. 'What if I were to tell you that she regrets what happened?'

To Stryker's relief he felt Lisette's hand move again. 'I have thought about Gardner's Tor many times. What I would say to her if ever I saw her again.'

'And?'

'And I suppose she did what she had to do,' he said, thinking of his own duplicity in recent days. He flicked her earlobe tenderly. 'She did no more than you'd have done.'

She chuckled at that. 'True.' She pressed herself into him suddenly. 'She told me she had feelings for you, *mon amour.*'

'Oh?' Stryker said with a deliberately lascivious grin.

She reached down to grasp at his crotch, squeezing hard enough to make him bite his lip. 'You go near her and I'll chop off your bloody stones, understand?'

They both laughed, and as soon as Lisette loosened her grip, Stryker rolled her on to her back, moving between her legs and pinning her wrists beside her head. He slid down, pushing his face in the warm cleft between her breasts, and began to move his hips. Lisette moaned.

And someone knocked at the door.

Matson House, Gloucester, 2 September 1643

'Won't see me?'

The supercilious courtier, resplendent in a salmon suit that was decorated at every possible opportunity with brilliant white lace, shook his head with a condescending smile. 'I'm afraid not, miss.'

Cecily Cade was standing in the stone porch of the king's headquarters. She had parted company with Lisette as soon as they reached Gloucester, begging half the cavalry escort to see her safely to Matson. For her part, Lisette had wanted to find Mowbray's regiment, and Cecily had actively encouraged her to go. But now, as she stared into the smug face of the man who denied her entry, she wondered if the Gallic firebrand might have had better luck. 'Won't see me?' she spluttered with unconcealed incredulity. 'You do not understand, sir. What I have to tell the King is of the utmost importance.'

The courtier folded his arms. 'With all due respect, madam, you are not the first person to claim such import in order to gain audience with His Majesty.'

Cecily Cade stepped forwards, startling the courtier as she took the exquisite lace of his collar in her small fist. 'Now listen to me, you jumped-up little peacock,' she hissed, her face just an inch from his. 'I have risked my life time and again to bring this information to His Majesty, and I'll be damned if I'm to be denied an audience now.' She released him and he stumbled back over the threshold. 'Do we understand each other?'

The courtier stared at her from within the darkness of the house's interior, eyes wide and white as though he were a frightened creature peering at a predator from the safety of its cave. 'We do, madam,' he muttered hurriedly. 'That we do. But he cannot—he is not here.'

'Well where is he?'

'Inspecting the army, madam. He has ridden out to the north. We have brigades camped all around the city perimeter, and he would visit each one before the final push.' He stepped closer again now that her aggression seemed to have abated. 'Essex comes hither,' he said, casting a furtive glance over Cecily's shoulder as though the Roundhead earl would appear at Matson House at any moment. 'We must take this vile city before he gets here.'

'Which way did he go? I would ride after him.'

The courtier spread his palms to show that her guess was as good as his. 'It is a big leaguer, madam. There are thousands of soldiers here.' He moved aside, waving her in. 'I think it best you await His Majesty here, at Matson. Where it is safe.'

Cecily Cade did not wish to wait. She had been through too much to get where she was. But then, she thought, her journey was at an end. Collings and his blackcoats could not reach her now, and the king was but a few hours away at most. She had succeeded. In the shade of the stone porch, Cecily Cade breathed a deep, lingering sigh of relief. 'When will he return?'

'This evening, so I understand.'

Cecily nodded, stepping past the salmon-clad fellow and into the king's temporary court. 'I will wait.'

Near Hook Norton, Oxfordshire, 2 September 1643

Robert Devereux, Earl of Essex and commander of Parliament's forces, looked back along the huge train of man, beast, wagon and gun. Evening was drawing in, the murky light of dusk exacerbated by a new bank of heavy clouds, and he could not see the tail of his huge force.

'Is everyone across?' he asked, turning to an aide.

The man was panting, a sheen of sweat making his pink cheeks shimmer, and his mount stooped to drink thirstily from the small stream that ran beside them. 'Aye, Your Grace. All across.'

'Middleton?'

'I have just ridden from there, Your Grace,' the rider said. 'He held the malignants back with few losses. They skirmish yet, for Wilmot would doubtless harry our rear, but the Cherwell has been successfully forded.'

'Excellent,' Essex said happily. He looked around at the faces of aides and senior officers. 'Good work, gentlemen. We will make camp here.'

'Young Middleton has done a rare job, Your Grace,' Major General Philip Skippon said as he leaned across his horse to stroke its twitching ear. 'Outnumbered, but stood firm. If we make it to Gloucester in one piece, we'll have much to thank him for.'

Essex nodded agreement. 'He has done great work this day.' He looked at the breathless aide. 'See that he is recalled now that we are safely on this side of the river. Tell him we'll set pickets to protect us from Wilmot. His men may rest.'

'What awaits us on the morrow, Your Grace?' Skippon asked as the aide raced away.

'The morrow is Sunday, General, and we shall not swerve from our devotions, whether we are hounded by Wilmot or Satan himself.' He paused for the chorus of huzzahs to wane. 'I should like an open air service, if the weather permits.'

'That'll stir the blood,' Skippon said.

'Indeed it will. And then on to Chipping Norton. It is twenty miles short of the Cotswold escarpment, so I should like to rest there the night. We shall need all our strength if we are to press westward through the hills in good time.' He looked around the group, raising his voice. 'Never fear, gentlemen. We shall relieve Gloucester yet.'

Llanthony Priory, Gloucester, 2 September 1643

All Stryker could do was stare.

The business for which he had been so abruptly ripped from Lisette's arms was to be the king's final throw of the dice. For days – weeks – under the sultry sun and the torrential rain, a crew of local artisans had slaved amid the workshops of the priory, assigned to give life to the sketches of Doctor William Chillingworth. Stryker had remembered Mowbray speaking of the strange mechanisms, but nothing more had come of it, and, in truth, he had all but forgotten the idea as he had slogged in the sopping trenches out to the east.

But now, it seemed, the mad plan had come to fruition, for the men of Stryker's red-coated company had been ordered to one of the priory's forecourts. There they had encircled three wooden contraptions that looked for all the world like gigantic lizards. They were effectively wheeled pontoons of rough-hewn timber, set upon huge axles, with retractable bridges attached towards the front by dozens of thick ropes.

'The blind will protect you,' Prince Rupert of the Rhine announced as the incredulous musketeers looked on. The king's tall nephew had apparently taken it upon himself to end the siege quickly now that Parliament had a formidable army on the move, and his first act was to begin the mobilization of Chillingworth's timber monsters. He had hand-picked the troops that would storm the walls, borne on the beasts' long backs, and Mowbray's unit was the first on his list. The sharp-faced general, Boye panting noisily at his knee, went to one of the engines and patted the screen of stripped planks that rose to the height of two men above the front axle. 'The men stand behind it so that they are protected during the approach. The wood is thick enough to repel bullets and small shot. You'll see there are holes through which you may return fire when closing with the enemy.'

'What happens when we reach the moat, General?' a plate-eyed Lieutenant Hood asked, as he stared enthralled at the alien engines.

'You will pull these ropes,' Rupert said, reaching out to grasp the thick cord that connected the hinged drawbridge to the front of the vehicle like a great, lolling tongue. 'The drawbridge will rise. Then you will drive – pushed by the men behind – directly into the moat.' Rupert waited for the smattering of horrified gasps to die down. 'The ropes are released, the bridge falls on to their walls, and you charge up to glory.'

'Miss Gaillard's back, then,' Lancelot Forester said as he came to stand beside Stryker.

'She is.'

'Well, I presume?' Forrester asked in a matter-of-fact voice. Doubtless he had spoken with Skellen and been regaled with the details of how the captain had taken the Frenchwoman in his arms when first she had appeared like an apparition amid the devastation of Barton Street.

'Yes, Forry, thank you.'

Forrester lowered his voice so as not to irritate the irascible prince, who was busily explaining the more intricate workings of the drawbridge to Lieutenant Hood and a group of redcoats. 'I heard she came into camp with another young lass.'

419

Stryker looked pointedly at his friend, who now casually examined his fingernails. Clearly he was not as disinterested as he made out, for he had made enquiries of his own. 'Cecily Cade, aye.'

Forrester whistled softly. 'Managed to extricate her from the crop-heads on her own, eh? Very impressive.'

'Indeed,' Stryker said, trying not to take the bait.

'Bet she's none too happy with you, old man.'

Stryker rounded on him. 'Have a care, Captain Fo—'

'Captain Stryker!' Prince Rupert's voice cracked loud and crisp across the forecourt.

Stryker shot Forrester a caustic glare and turned to the general. 'Sir.'

'Brief the men,' Rupert ordered. 'Familiarize yourselves with the engines now, so that you all know how to deploy them when the time comes. You attack in the morning.'

CHAPTER 24

The Cathedral, Gloucester, 3 September 1643

I t was Sunday, yet there would be no day of rest. Not even a sermon.

Indeed, as the whispering congregation were ushered out of the shot-scarred church, they could only pause to pray for themselves, whisper lonely entreaties to the God that had kept them out of the clutches of the enemy for so long, and against such odds. There was no time for anything else, for soldiers had come, marching down the nave with powder-darkened faces and tattered blue coats to cut short the preacher before he could launch into his righteous tirade. They were carrying orders for every able-bodied parishioner to proceed directly to the East Gate.

Perhaps in days gone by, at the beginning of the siege when nothing was certain, they might have chosen to ignore the young governor with his narrow, ashen face and sorrowful gaze, putting such a summons down to youthful impertinence. But they had grown to respect him with each daring raid, each new earthwork and each countermine. He had believed in the city's will to survive, and they had begun to believe in him. Now, if Edward Massie needed help, they would happily leave the crimson-cheeked clergyman to bawl at the high beams.

The men and women hurried through the rubble-strewn streets, inured to the craters left by exploding mortar shells, blind to the decapitated chimney stacks and hardened to the sight of the gaping holes punched by round shot into rooftops and walls. They had lost people – friends and kin – but somehow the horrors of life within the beleaguered walls had become commonplace. What mattered was that they held out. After all, they had heard the news of Essex's advance. They did not know where he was, but they believed he was coming for them. A few more days. Just a few more days.

It appeared the Royalists scurrying about their miserable ant-hills in the section of trenches beyond the eastern wall had constructed a new, formidable battery from which they might launch a new bombardment of the gate. If that was the case, Massie had surmised, then perhaps their cursed mine beneath the moat had finally reached its target, the new artillery redoubt being part of a strategy of softening the defenders' spirits before the charges were ignited down in the sopping depths. A second line of defence, therefore, needed to be constructed, and it was to this task that the hardy citizens of Gloucester were quickly set.

'I want a strong breastwork here,' Governor Edward Massie called as whole families assembled for the morning's work. He pointed a skinny white finger at the ground where he stood, tracing an invisible line from one side of the road to the other. 'It must run all the way across Eastgate Street, lest the enemy break through the gate. We'll have a trench in front, deep as we can make it, and we'll place cannon at the flanks.'

Soldiers of various descriptions – Stamford's blues, the men of the Town Regiment, the smattering of dragoons that had been trapped behind the walls, and Backhouse's cavalrymen – began directing citizens to the day's toil, handing out spades and picks, and moving carts and sledges into position for the removal of debris. Further along the east wall, cannon fire boomed out from the new gun port. Overnight, Massie's secret plan to place a saker opposite the Royalist gallery had come to fruition, and, though its iron shot did not penetrate the thick wooden slats, the pounding to which the men filling the moat were subjected had served to slow their progress significantly. Down at the fresh works, the townsfolk cheered its every shot.

*

They had laboured with soil and stone for more than an hour, digging and hefting and scouring and sweating, when a great, despairing cry rose up from the south. As one, the citizens in the workforce stopped in their tracks to peer through the warren of battered houses at the great edifice of the South Gate. From the bastion and the walls on either side, men were frantically waving, calling a shrill alarm that made the folk at ground level stare in wild-eyed panic at one another. Massie was already running from the fresh breastwork, trailed by his entourage at a brisk jog that did nothing to salve the panic of his garrison.

Men and women were following suit, clambering up the earth glacis to the rampart running from the East Gate to the South Gate, and risking having their heads picked off by sharp-shooters in the saps below in order to get a look at the sight that had caused such consternation.

A great murmur rippled along the walls as hundreds of pairs of eyes settled upon a piece of desolate land to the south. It was the sound of dismay; a city gripped by sudden collective fear. Because out in the bleak wastes, as though conjured from the bowels of hell itself, three monsters crawled.

Near Llanthony Priory, Gloucester 3 September 1643

Stryker checked his musket for a third time. It was primed and ready, the charge kept safe beneath the pan cover, the match perfectly poised to ignite the fine grains when called upon. What a strange life it was, he thought silently as the engine lurched into juddering motion. He had gone back to his room at Barton, lain with Lisette for a few more precious hours. But then it had been time to return to the front, and he had left her, naked on his palliasse, only to be crammed on to the back of a timber machine and told to succeed where so many other Royalist schemes had failed.

Now he found himself towards the rear of one of Chilling-worth's great leviathans, braced between two ranks of men as they wobbled and jerked their way across the landscape. The engines were heavy and cumbersome, so the doctor had designed large handles that jutted from the back of the wheeled pontoons so that teams of men could push them as though they were vast barrows.

'I feel like a bloody Greek,' Captain Lancelot Forrester complained at Stryker's side. He was similarly armed, his bandolier loaded with extra powder flasks so that he rattled like a wind chime, his forearm wrapped in a length of spare match.

Stryker peered beyond his friend and over the vehicle's open flank. The terrain was slick and cloying, the engine's huge cart-wheels already beginning to slip. 'Except this horse isn't getting into Troy.'

'You do not think this will work?' Forrester asked cautiously.

'I think we rush into this attack because the King fears a relief force appearing on the hills. We are ill-prepared.'

'Uneasy lies the head that wears a crown,' Forrester muttered. 'That's *King Henry the Fourth*, part two. And never more worthy a quote, I am sorry to say.'

'Don't be like that, sir,' an excited Lieutenant Hood said. He had been enthused by the sight of the mechanical beasts, eager to board and be part of the first unit to cross Gloucester's wall. He grinned when Forrester rolled his eyes. 'We drive straight into the ditch, sir.'

'I'm quite aware of that, Tom,' Forrester said witheringly.

'Straight into it!' Hood went on, unaware of the weary disdain his ebullience engendered. 'And the engine's body – where we now stand – will become the bridge across the moat. Then we merely drop the drawbridge on to their rampart, and run up it.'

'And simply leap like a shoal of salmon into poor Gloucester town,' Forrester said, 'where the evil Massie and his horned minions will lay down their arms to us.'

'I pray so, sir, yes,' Hood replied, still apparently oblivious to the captain's sarcastic tone.

A flurry of shots came from the city. They were mostly wayward, flying high and wide, and too weak to do any damage at this range, but still the men ducked behind the timber screen. The musketeers at the front thrust their long-arms through holes cut into the log shield and played at the walls, if only to let the garrison know that the fight's leaden traffic would not all be one way.

On they rumbled, thrown shoulder to shoulder with each jolt as the wheels plummeted in and out of the deep ruts. At one point the engine slewed to the left, and the packed musketeers peered out to see that the wheels had become stuck on that side. Stryker ordered a handful to exit the rear of the vehicle and lend their muscle to the effort, and amid much snarling and cursing, the wheels jerked free.

But worse was to come, for it quickly became apparent that the wheels, though still in motion, were digging deeper and deeper tracks as they went. They were sinking. The ground, firm as iron at the start of the siege, was little more than slurry, and the unfathomably huge engines were simply too heavy to make it as far as the walls.

Stryker's engine seized on one side, and he could see that they were not simply stuck this time. They had been sucked into the mire. The wheels on the opposite flank were spinning madly in the air as the men pushing the contraption wrestled to get it squared and moving. But the garrison men were firing now, loosing a shower of lead from up on the rampart, and the bullets were clipping the wooden screen, zinging off the wheels and pecking the mud all around.

'Get movin'! Get movin', you lazy bastards!' someone shouted.

'Heave!' another called.

Stryker pushed his way back to look down at the toiling men who worked to combat the swamp-borne inertia, and immediately realized that they were not going to win the fight. He leaped off the back, planting his feet with a splash between the long handles. The grimacing soldiers who manned them looked like teams of galley slaves, sweat-stained and straining.

Stryker moved out from the safety of the engine to stare up at the walls. Massie's musketeers lined the bushel-plugged palisade, jeering and firing by turns. He swore as a musket-ball clipped his shoulder. It had glanced off a soggy spar, losing its murderous rage, but the blow served to make him duck low, and he found himself staring at one of the wheels. He watched in stunned despair as the long spindles slowed, the wheels digging a deep rut in the watery earth. Desperately he sought solace in the other two engines, but he could see that they were both floundering like ships in a storm, neither so much as budging in the gluey terrain. And he was turning, shouting at the men to abandon the engine and retreat, for the wheels were simply sinking with every shove the teams at the back gave. It was a lost cause.

The South Gate, Gloucester, 3 September 1643

The men on the walls cheered, raising muskets high and crowing to the pregnant black clouds. Their women and children cheered too, waving any garment they could find that carried a flash of orange or tawny in jubilant mockery of the pathetic engines.

Edward Massie watched the scene with something akin to disbelief. He had almost wanted the engines to reach the ditch, if only to see what the intriguing contraptions were capable of, and now that they languished like scuttled galleons out in the southern marsh, the engineer in him felt somehow deprived.

'A sign,' Vincent Skaithlocke rumbled at his right hand. The huge colonel had borrowed his perspective glass, and cradled it to his face with hands that made it seem like a child's play thing. 'A sign of God's will, if ever I saw one.'

'It was too wet,' Massie said, ever the pragmatist. 'We'd have been in trouble if they'd used them in the dry.'

'But they could not wait,' Skaithlocke said. 'They are frightened, Governor. They must know Essex closes with them by the hour. It was a desperate move.' He lowered the glass with a broad grin. 'God is with us.'

'I pray you are right, Colonel,' Massie replied, turning away.

'Wait.'

Massie looked back. 'Wait? What is it?'

The glass was back at Skaithlocke's eye. He had it trained upon the nearest of the impotent machines. 'Stryker.'

Massie frowned. 'Surely not.'

Skaithlocke handed the leather tube to the governor with an expression that was so ashen it was startling. 'Not many could be mistaken for him, sir.'

Massie scanned the glistening mud, tracing a path from saps to shattered buildings, to upended gabions, piles of trench tools and beyond one of the many burial pits that now dotted the surrounding land, until his view was filled by the dark shape of the siege engine. At its flank, frantically ushering red-coated soldiers back in the direction of the priory, was a tall man dressed in black, with a dark feathered hat. He was mostly obscured by the brim, but enough could be discerned to see that a patch of pale scar tissue blighted one half of his face. Indeed, he seemed to have only one eye.

Massie sighed, blowing cold air through his nostrils. 'Stryker.' He thrust the perspective glass into his belt. 'A great shame. He played us for fools.'

'A shame?' Skaithlocke replied, and it sounded as though a petard had erupted inside his throat. 'The villain. The fucking, double-dealing, pope-coddling villain.' He turned away from the governor, looking to descend to ground level.

Massie watched the corpulent soldier go, his great slab of flesh juddering like a bowl of whale blubber where it hung across his breeches. 'A shame,' he called after the strangely furious mercenary. 'Nothing more. After all, what has his betrayal cost us? We are undefeated. Unbowed before all the King's might.'

To his surprise, Skaithlocke marched away with a face that was twisted and crimson with rage.

Near Gaudy Green, Gloucester, 3 September 1643

'Majesty.'

'Wh-wh-what?' King Charles stammered. Perched on a fine roan gelding, he was furious since witnessing his lumbering siege engines meet their ignominious end. 'What is it?'

The horseman, who had thundered up to the royal party from the east with his breathless report, gently urged his mount to walk through the midst of the group. They moved aside for him, stunned by what they had just seen into unnatural deference. 'My lord Wilmot continues to skirmish with Essex, Your Majesty.'

'Good,' the king retorted waspishly, expecting nothing less. He turned back to the sad forms of his heavy machines, slumped and slanted in the mud, Goliaths with no Davids to be seen.

'But he reports that he has been unable to prevent His Excellency's march westwards.'

That grasped the monarch's attention, and his head snapped round, brown eyes like discs. 'Where is he?'

'Chipping Norton in the main, Your Majesty,' the messenger replied, brushing grass mulch from his sleeves.

The king tugged at his little beard. 'In the main? What is that s-s-supposed t-to mean?'

'His vanguard overreaches, somewhat. They have gone as far as Oddington.'

A huge warrior in full breast- and backplates, a broad, feathered hat and buff-coat laced with silver crashed his way through the group. The silk and satin entourage parted like the Red Sea for his black-nostrilled destrier, averting their gaze from the challenging rider and his bullish glower. 'They're spreading themselves too thin, Uncle,' Prince Rupert of the Rhine barked, showing that he had caught the last part of the exchange. 'Let me join Wilmot. We may destroy Essex's force in detail before he even reaches Stow. Let me crush them, Your Majesty.'

'V-very well, Rupert. Take the rest of the horse and put the hateful rogues to the swo-swor—'

'Sword, Uncle,' Rupert snapped, his flaring temper governing his tact. Immediately he realized his mistake, and turned his charger around, kicking the coke-black flanks before any more damage was done.

But the king seemed not to notice. He simply stared out at the abandoned engines again, crestfallen and deflated, a small figure on a large horse, overshadowed by Gloucester's towering defences. 'Falkland?' he said in a weak voice.

Lord Falkland, the grim secretary of state, was staring, slack-jawed at the floundered engines. He could not bring himself to look at his sovereign. 'Majesty?'

'Come with me, F-Falkland,' Charles said, shaking his reins deftly. 'I am eager to seek an exp—an explanation for this.'

Outside Matson House, Gloucester, 3 September 1643

Cecily Cade had waited.

She had sat in a large, rectangular reception room the previous afternoon and stared at the walls. She had peered out of the window, examined the high beams and even resorted to counting the scuff marks on the polished floorboards, rubbed raw by the riding boots worn by the king's visitors.

But he had not come till late. King Charles, as the courtier had told her, had spent the day inspecting his troops, blessing their endeavours and encouraging their officers. She had hoped the regal progress would not take long, but the city was big, the camps vast and the terrain difficult, and that made the whole affair an arduous and time-consuming duty. In the end the royal entourage had returned, but the hour had been late, and Cecily had been conveyed to a small antechamber at the rear of the building in which the bustling staff had arranged for her to stay. They had been kindly enough, she had to admit, despite their innate air of stuffy superiority, and she had rested her head on the most comfortable pillow she had felt in all her life. By the time King Charles was home, Cecily Cade was enjoying the deepest sleep she had had since that fateful day on a deserted Dartmoor road, when her father had been murdered and her life turned upside down.

In the morning, woken by birdsong and the sound of children shouting, Cecily had risen with renewed hope. The children, she was told, were the princes of the realm; Charles and James. If they were present, then surely he would be too. She had paused only to splash water on her face and straighten the creases on her filthy shirt, before going to seek an audience. Only to discover that King Charles had already departed. He had gone, it was said, to view the final assault on the city. The besiegers had some specially designed siege engines, throwbacks to the time of Richard the Lionheart or the Black Prince, and Charles had been eager to witness their long-awaited deployment.

That, she told the salmon-suited courtiers, was quite enough. After all the privations, the torture and the threats, running for her life one minute and hiding like some frightened rabbit the next. She was done with waiting.

Cecily Cade marched out of the leafy grounds and turned on to the deeply rutted road running past the great house. Cavalry-men and foot soldiers shared the thoroughfare with thundering messengers, carriages plain and ornate, and carts carrying pay chests, baggage, ammunition and powder, and she could instantly see by weight of traffic which direction would lead her to Gloucester.

One of the Matson staff came running from the house in her wake. 'Miss Cade! Miss Cade!'

She turned, and recognized the man who had first admitted her to the Royalist headquarters. 'What is it?'

'The King is aware you await him.'

'Then why does he ignore me?' she said angrily.

'Because the taking of Gloucester is his sole concern, Miss Cade. His every thought is bent on it.'

'Then I shall speak to him as he tends to his siege, sir.'

The courtier looked up and down the road with a look of sourness. 'It is dangerous, Miss Cade. There are armed men everywhere.'

'Then give me a horse,' she said simply.

He grimaced, as though the request caused him physical pain. 'I cannot, Miss Cade. You know I cannot. The royal mounts are not mine to give.'

He reached for her wrist, but she shrugged him off roughly. 'Then I will walk, and your worries be damned, sir. Where has he gone?'

After a second's hesitation, the man sighed. 'Gaudy Green, Miss Cade. North of here.' He offered a smile of resignation. 'I have a horse you may borrow.'

On Bristol Road, Gloucester, 3 September 1643

The road through Gloucester's southern suburbs had once been a furiously pumping artery for trade and commerce. Now the shops and houses were all gone, burned and smashed and shot to ruin. But the road remained. It conveyed soldiers to and from the trenches, linked the Earl of Forth's command centre at his fortified leaguer beside Llanthony Priory with the king's court at Matson House, and divided the batteries of Severn Street and Gaudy Green. For such a barren landscape, Bristol Road teemed with life, and it was here that a man who wished to go unnoticed had come to view the advance of the Royalist behemoths. Except they had failed. Miserably and laughably. Yet another lesson in abject humiliation that Gloucester had heaped upon King Charles.

Nikolas Robbens trudged with his back to the city. He stared at his boots as he walked, his mind in seething turmoil. The ridiculous abandonment of the siege engines had been an amusing distraction, but one that did nothing to alleviate his black mood. The king had barely ventured from Matson House since his return from Oxford. Robbens had waited and watched, walked the roads and moved between camps, always with his snapsack slung across his shoulder, its cloth-wrapped secret within. He had prayed to see the monarch, to get close to him, but the most powerful man in all England seemed to have hidden himself away. Then yesterday, a breakthrough. The chirurgeon who had been assigned to examine him at one of the casualty clearing stations up at Kingsholm had mentioned that His Majesty had ridden through the area reviewing the troops. Robbens had been furious to miss him, compelled as he was to have his phoney cough reviewed, but at least, he consoled himself, the king had finally ventured out of his lair.

The chirurgeon had given the man he knew as Hatton another two days' leave of duty for recuperative purposes, and Nikolas Robbens had gone back to the hunt. But still nothing. He had come out this morning, wandered down from Kingsholm, in the hope that the elusive king would make an appearance at Llanthony Priory to watch the engines advance, but Robbens had seen neither hide nor hair of him. Now, as the afternoon wore on, he would traipse back around the insolent city to his billet, hoping all the while that the heavy clouds did not compound his misery.

It was with outright astonishment, then, that he caught his first glimpse of a small man trotting atop an exquisitely groomed roan. He had a narrow, pale face, with an auburn beard and slim eyebrows. His hair was a shade darker than his whiskers, and fell to shoulders encased in burnished armour. He wore a sleeveless buff-coat beneath the breastplate, and it seemed to glimmer in defiance of the glum day, laced as it was with brightest gold. The rider's arms, free of the hide layer, shone even more brilliantly, for the coat the man wore was of emerald green, adorned with tight swirls of yet more gold. Across his torso, from left shoulder to right hip, ran a blue scarf that matched the feather in the man's large hat.

Nikolas Robbens stood in the middle of the road and gaped like a mortar muzzle. The man was diminutive, almost childlike, yet his bearing spoke of innate authority, and his garments oozed wealth. Beside and behind him rode more men. Some were nearly as ostentatious in their clothing, while others were heavily armed and brooding on fearsome destriers.

Robbens moved to the side of the road as the royal party clattered past. He bowed low, but straightened as soon as they had their backs to him. For he needed to see where they were going if he was to follow.

Llanthony Priory, Gloucester, 3 September 1643

Captain Stryker found Lisette Gaillard in the large forecourt where Chillingworth's sorry engines had been displayed the previous night. She waited beside one of the brick buildings that had been the mathematician's secret workshop for so many weeks, and which was now abandoned and empty, bits of rope and piles of sawdust the only signs of the frenetic activity that had once taken place within its walls.

'You lived,' she said wryly. She was wearing the masculine clothes that she favoured when conducting her covert work, but pulled down the hood of her cloak when she spoke.

Stryker and his men had fought their way back from the marshy wastes. Thankfully Massie had not sent a raiding party out to cut them off, but the timber monsters had striven close enough to be within musket-shot of the walls, and the ebullient defenders on the bulbous southern bastion had sprayed them with lead as their panicking cargo had attempted to evacuate. Stryker had arranged his men behind the stricken vehicles, which had become more akin to beached vessels in the slop. He and Forrester had ordered them to fire in teams of three and four; reloading as their comrades shot at the crowing rebels, and giving fire again. They had retreated that way, backing away from the engines but always fighting, until they were comfortably out of range.

Now, filthy, tired and hungry, the red-coated infantrymen trudged back into the priory complex like a ragged pack of wolves. They peeled off bandoliers and coats, propped muskets against the ancient monastic walls, and slid to their haunches.

Stryker went to Lisette, snaking his hands about her taut waist. 'I lived. The bloody things sank.' He shook his head, still shocked at the shame of the ill-fated enterprise. 'Just sank into the mud.'

'And Essex is on his way.'

Stryker blew out his cheeks, blinking a speck of stinging dirt from his eye. 'And Essex is on his way.' He stared down into her blue eyes, and a terrible knot pulled tight in his chest. 'Would Collings really have hanged you?'

Lisette's gaze did not falter. '*Oui*. He intended to let his men have me first.'

Stryker swore. 'Forgive me. I should have ignored him. Gone to London and damned the consequences.'

'Ignored the Prince?' Lisette said in apparent amusement. 'Then it would have been you with a stretched neck.' She went to the tips of her toes and kissed him lightly. 'I was angry. I thought you had abandoned me.'

'But no longer?'

'No longer. We all must do our duty in the best way we can. Yours was with the army.'

Stryker moved back a touch to survey the scene. His men stood, sat and lay all around the forecourt. Some chewed bits of iron-tough biscuit, others drank smoke from their pipes, and a few tended their weapons. Simeon Barkworth and Will Skellen were engaged in their good-natured but foul-mouthed sniping, Ensign Chase brushed a gloved hand over the precious company colour, and Tom Hood was earnestly debating the merits of Swedish and Dutch battle deployments with Captain Forrester. They were good men all, and he felt guilty at having ever considered leaving them. He shook the feeling off, lest his expression betrayed him, and quickly counted the group. He had not lost anyone, and he knew he should be thankful for that, but the glory and optimism they had all felt during the heady summer of victories had well and truly gone. He wondered if Gloucester, a place that held such affection in his heart, would prove to be the trigger for a difficult autumn. He prayed not.

'*Mon amour*,' Lisette said suddenly, her tone urgent.

Stryker looked round to see a bright cavalcade of expensive-looking horses and expensively dressed men clatter and stamp through the archway leading to the workshops. They were the peacocks of the court, each one replete with power, not a real soldier among them.

'Up!' he called, though the order was not necessary. No one could fail to notice the new arrivals, and none would risk being caught on his rump by this visitor. Every man scrambled quickly to his feet, doffing caps, hats and helmets, bowing low and keeping his peace.

'I would speak with Ch-Ch-Chillingworth!' King Charles announced as he dismounted. 'Where is he?'

Out on the road, a pair of guards wearing dark green coats and deeply hewn scowls stepped into the path of Nikolas Robbens.

He lifted his hands in supplication, offering a friendly smile. 'Well met, gentlemen.'

The larger of the greencoats stepped closer, levelling a glinting halberd at Robbens' chest. He had small, black eyes and tufts of red hair sprouting from below his Monmouth cap, framing a broad face from which the skin was peeling in large, weeping strips. 'Name?'

'Johan Hatton,' Robbens lied. 'I am a gunner.'

'Regiment?'

'None. I was with the rebels until recently. Swam the river to enlist with the cause of justice.'

The sore-faced soldier looked down at him along a fleshy crimson nose. 'Purpose 'ere?'

'I'm due to meet with the Earl of Forth within the hour. He builds a new redoubt, and looks to my advice.'

The second sentry, a remarkably tall man, so slim he seemed to be devoid of all fat and muscle, gave a small sniff. 'Dutchie?'

'Half Dutch. Loyal to King Charles, and praying, in my own small way, that I might help his cause.'

'Don't like the look of 'im,' the first soldier grunted.

The tall man leaned down to speak into his comrade's flaky, red ear. 'They said blond 'air, didn't they? This cully's bald as bleedin' round shot.'

Robbens struggled to keep his face impassive. Christ, but they knew he was here. Knew he was coming. But how could they? He battled with his racing heart, breathing deeply through his nose to settle himself. At least they were looking for a man with fair hair. He inwardly thanked Slager for suggesting he shave his prized locks, just in case. 'The earl has requested I attend him.'

'His Majesty visits Llanthony,' the man with peeling skin said.

'Then I hope to catch a glimpse,' Robbens replied.

'And no one may carry loaded weapons in his presence.'

Robbens frowned. 'The place is surely full of soldiers.'

'Soldiers,' the thinner of the two said, 'what belong to proper regiments. Besides, the main camp's out at the leaguer, not in the priory.'

Robbens forced another smile and held up his palms. 'Search me, gentlemen, by all means.'

The stocky greencoat moved in, patting Robbens down roughly, his tall companion standing with grim threat behind. Eventually he stood. 'On with you.'

Nikolas Robbens felt the sweat prickle at the nape of his neck as he strode confidently between the guards and up to the archway through which the king's entourage had cantered. His heart began to calm and his aching jaw began to relax. He was not to be denied.

King Charles was a full head shorter than Doctor William Chillingworth, but that did not cow him in the slightest. When the theologian, scholar and mathematician had appeared like an ashen-faced spectre from the doorway of one of his workshops, the diminutive sovereign had marched up to him and launched into a scarlet-cheeked tirade, finger thrust up into Chilling-worth's face, quivering with rage now unchained.

'Th-th-the engines f-failed!' Charles blustered. His stammer grew worse with the fury of the moment, but for once he did not seem to care. 'F-failed, Ch-Chillingworth!'

'The ground was hard, Your Majesty,' Chillingworth bleated. His face was white, the silver hair at his temples seeming to spread even as he spoke.

'W-when?'

'At the beginning, Your Majesty. Weeks ago, when first I arrived. It was all perfect.' Chillingworth looked as though he might weep. 'Perfect.'

The king gritted his teeth and stepped back. As though a veil had been lifted, he seemed to notice the red-coated soldiers who stared, transfixed, at the remarkable exchange. He balled his tiny fists at his sides. 'And now it is n-not.'

Chillingworth placed his flattened hands together as though about to pray. 'The rain, d'you see?' he whined in a high, weak voice, like a scalded child pleading with an angry parent. 'The rain and the springs that seem to leap out at every turn. They have ruined the soil, Your Majesty. Turned it to marsh, and my structures cannot move under such conditions. The engines became stuck,' he added, as though the fact was not agonizingly apparent for all who had witnessed the machines limp to a pathetic halt. He closed his eyes. 'Terribly stuck.'

Charles looked as though he might say more, but the realiza-tion that he had such a large and astonished audience seemed to push the words back into his throat. He turned to look up at one of his mounted aides. 'Then we must return to the mine. It is r-ready, yes?'

The horseman winced. 'It is not, Your Majesty.'

The forecourt was surrounded by buildings of different shapes and sizes, from large, brick workshops all the way down to meek sheds of rotting timber. Nikolas Robbens now crouched in the shadowy recesses of a shed.

He watched in silence as the king berated his shame-faced men, dozens of bedraggled soldiers in mud-spattered red coats looking on. As silently as he could, Robbens unslung the snap-sack from his shoulder and eased it to the dusty floor between his feet. The sentries had not thought to check the bag, and he thanked God for their negligence. Then again, what serious weapon could he conceal within such a small space?

Carefully, he took the steel bow from the bag. The balestrino was exactly what he had requested and, to his credit, Slager had delivered a fine piece. It was sturdy but light enough to wield quickly, small enough to conceal and, with a powerful draw-weight, could kill a man if the bolt found the right mark. Today, that mark would be the throat. He had imagined, in the moments he had played this day over and over in his head, that he would pick out one of the brown eyes that now creased at their corners as the king rebuked his obsequious lackeys. But now, in this drab afternoon, he knew that such a shot would be too great a chance to take. Targeting the eye would have been a profound statement, one that would seal Nikolas Robbens as one of the foremost assassins of the age, but the risk of missing was simply too high, even for an expert marksman.

He looked down at the weapon, caressing it in his hands for what, he knew, would be the last time. He flicked the powerful string of twisted cord, revelling in its tautness. He snaked his thin fingers over the rear of the weapon, gently brushing the beautiful surfaces of the octagonal stock, then tracing the length of the central quarrel channel with his nail. The gorgeous stags, etched into the bow by an expert in the craft, seemed to leap just for Robbens, as if they knew what he was about to do. He closed his eyes and prayed.

'Do we not have the men?' King Charles demanded in a high-pitched voice raised to a shrill whine by distress. 'Enough t-tools, candles?'

Lucius Cary, second Viscount Falkland, the king's morose secretary of state, wetted his lips nervously. 'We have it all,

Your Majesty. But the ground is like a sponge. It is painstaking work.'

'Y-you blame the weather as well, Falkland?' the king said, his words querulous. 'We are undone by water whichever way we t-turn.'

'Not undone,' Falkland protested. 'Merely set back.'

'Set back?' the king replied in disbelief. 'Set b-back until when, may I ask? Are you n-not aware of the treasonous army marching towards us by the hour?'

'Lord Wilmot and the Prince will have five thousand horse betwixt them, sire. We have further reinforcements en route from Oxford, and Rupert's brother is summoned from Exeter.'

'And will Prince Maurice arrive in time?' the king said through tight lips. 'I th-think not. We must t-take this confounded city now. Now!'

Hooves rattled through the archway, cutting short the king's rant. All eyes turned to the forecourt's narrow entrance.

'Your Majesty! Your Majesty, please!' The woman sat astride a snorting dun that shook its bridled head madly as she hauled it to a stop. She was swathed in a charcoal-grey riding cloak, her brown hair flowing down her back, her gaunt face like a pearl in the gathering dusk.

King Charles scowled up at her. 'Wh-what is the meaning of this?'

'My name is Cecily Cade,' the woman said breathlessly. She swung a leg across the saddle, plummeting to earth. 'My late father was Sir Alfred Cade.'

The king stared in wide-eyed confusion. 'I remember him.'

She nodded rapidly, doubling over in a deep bow that seemed to waver as she gasped for air. 'I would speak with you, Your Majesty. A matter of great import.'

Charles had regained his composure, and he clasped his hands at the small of his back as he inspected the newcomer down his long nose. 'Is not the matter at hand of g-g-great import, Miss Cade?'

'Your Majesty, I—'

'You requested an audience,' he said, his voice suddenly cold, 'and you will receive one.' He turned abruptly on his heels. 'But at a time of my choosing. N–not yours.'

Stryker was as startled by Cecily's pallor as he was by her unexpected entrance. She was a shadow of her former self. His inability to keep her safe had brought her to this. She was still a beauty, dark-eyed and fragile, but her cheeks were hollow, the fine wrinkles at the corners of her mouth were more defined, and her lips had lost their fullness.

She stumbled into Lisette's waiting arms.

'Miss Cade,' Stryker said.

He might have thrown ice water in her face, for she stared at him in bewilderment. 'Captain.'

Stryker felt suddenly embarrassed between the two women. 'Good to see you well.'

She was already looking at Lisette. 'He would not listen.'

Lisette offered a consoling smile. 'Give him time.'

If the Frenchwoman had been aiming for calm, she was well wide of the mark, for Cecily's face suddenly filled with a scarlet hue, as though a fire had been fanned within her. 'Time? Time?'

'You are here, Cecily,' Lisette persisted gently, the compassion in her voice startling Stryker, for he had not considered her capable of it. 'You are not going anywhere, and you are safe. The King will listen.' She shrugged. 'But at this very moment, his grand siege is failing. His plans for the war crumble about him. He can consider little else.'

'I cannot,' Cecily mumbled softly, then louder, 'I *will* not wait.'

Stryker was alarmed by the desperation in Cecily's voice. When last he had encountered her, she was cool and level-headed, effortlessly manipulating whomsoever she saw fit. 'Do not do anything foolish, Miss Cade.'

She rounded on him. 'Foolish, Captain?' Her tone was becoming bolder now, echoing in the forecourt, and more of the rag-tag assembly was turning to look at her. 'I have protected my secret for too long. Too many good people have suffered for it. You know that more than most.' She made to accost the king, who was deep in discussion with several members of his entourage, but Stryker took a fistful of her sleeve. She pulled against him, leaning her entire weight into the tussle until she dangled at arm's length like a landed fish. 'I will *make* him listen,' she hissed.

In the gloom of the sagging timber shack, Nikolas Robbens depressed the thumb trigger on the upper surface of the crossbow's steel stock, ensuring it would move freely. All seemed well. He reached into the snapsack again and brought out a steel shaft, barbed at the tip with a razor-sharp bodkin that had been dipped in his own faeces and allowed to dry so that the wound, if not immediately fatal, would be infected, ensuring a slow, agonizing death. He turned the bolt in his hand, letting the wan light dance along its shaft. One bolt was all he had. It was all he needed. It was all, he reflected with a pang of fear, he would have time to loose before the guards descended. He closed his eyes, swallowed hard to clear the acidic lump that had formed at the back of his mouth, and waited for the feeling to pass.

Outside, the king was speaking to the dourly upholstered Lord Falkland and a flamboyant-looking staff officer swathed in silver and purple, whom Robbens did not recognize. They were busy now, but Robbens sensed that he would soon take his leave. He knew he must act.

He placed the bolt on the ground and turned the screw at the base of the stock. The creaking cord eased back, inch by groaning inch. He gritted his teeth, prayed that no one would hear, and stared out through the open doorway at the men milling about the courtyard. The king had turned and was walking back to his horse as he spoke to one of the officers. A mad woman ranted in the background. It was now or never.

The bow was fully spanned, and he snatched up the bolt, setting it in the quarrel channel so that the nock at the bottom

441

end of the shaft nestled perfectly against the straining string. With a final, deep breath, he placed the empty snapsack over the bow, concealing it for the last time, and stood.

Stryker held Cecily firm. She writhed against him, jerking her wrist in his iron hold, but he would not let her enrage a king whose temper was already dangerously frayed. 'Stay here,' he ordered.

She tried to twist away. 'Damn you, Stryker, let me go. Let me go!'

But her words were suddenly quiet in his ears, as though she spoke from behind a wall, for his eye had settled on a point a little way along the courtyard. Or rather, it had settled on a man. He was rather nondescript, dressed in plain breeches and coat, his frame bone-thin and his face unassuming. His head was completely bald, and across his forearm was a snapsack, empty and limp. What caught Stryker's attention did not register at first. It was as though he knew this man yet could not fathom why, like some half-memory from childhood.

And then, with thudding, pulse-quickening, gut-churning understanding, he realized. The man had strands of coloured thread looped through the left lobe of his ear. As he turned his head they moved with him, sliding along his shoulder, and to Stryker's mind it was as though they were a beacon for him alone.

He surged forwards without thinking, releasing Cecily and bounding across the forecourt with a bellow of warning.

Nikolas Robbens held out his right hand, dragging the draped snapsack away with the other to expose the balestrino, revelling in the cold touch of the steel. A tiny weapon, easily concealed, beautifully crafted, accurate and powerful. An assassin's bow.

The world seemed to slow. He was less than ten paces from the king now, and he called out, even as another shout echoed between the low buildings. Charles's head jerked round at the hail, exposing a lace-fringed neck. Robbens shut one eye and took aim with the other. The next moment something hit him.

*

Stryker collided with the assassin's flank with all the force he could muster. The would-be killer was tougher than he looked, and Stryker had the dread feeling that the frail man might yet resist, but his legs gave way, crumpling before the force of the soldier, and he collapsed like a tree in a gale. People were shouting all around them now; bodies swirling like autumn leaves. Stryker heard a jolt as they fell, felt a powerful blow kick through their bodies, and wrenched the man round so that his arm pointed away from the crowd. The assassin landed on top of Stryker with his face turned to the sky. A woman screamed. Stryker saw that the bow had been fired.

Nikolas Robbens heard the scream and prayed as he fell. He prayed his shot had flown true, prayed God had guided the bolt even though the shot had been so cruelly disturbed. A woman was screaming, and he hoped it was because her sovereign's life-blood was pumping over the filth. The man beneath him was clawing at his face, so he tossed the spent bow away and swept back his elbow in a vicious blow. It missed, for he felt soft earth, but the second strike connected, jarring his bony elbow joint in a manner he knew would be agony if the all-consuming need for survival did not smother any but the most base of senses. He had imagined a glorious end. A murder, a quiet prayer, and a quick death at the hands of the king's armoured protectors. But the king was not as well guarded as he had expected, and Robbens' every instinct shrieked at him to fight. He lashed his arm down again, gratified by a muffled yelp that came from below, and then the grasping hands were free, the vicelike arms falling away.

Robbens felt a surge of elation as he scrambled to his feet. He had done it. There, in the centre of the courtyard was the thing he most yearned to see. The king was gone, as though vanished to nothing. Men clustered around the place where he had stood, shouting and bustling and tearing their own clothes to fashion bandages Robbens knew would be worthless.

He looked for a way out, hardly believing his luck. The yard was teeming with musketeers, but their weapons were not loaded. Stunned into slack-jawed inaction by the sudden attack on their king, they were now regaining their senses, moving in from their small groups on the forecourt's periphery. They would have him surrounded in moments. He had to think fast. And then he saw the horses.

Stryker's hands went to his nose, feeling the blood gush between his fingers and turn his vision to a blurry crimson. All around him men bellowed. It was chaos. He released one clamping palm and pushed it into the soft earth behind, heaving himself to a sitting position. His head swam, images tumbled, colours melded and parted. The king's entourage had descended from their prized mounts, converged on one place like wasps around a sugar plum. He knew with sickening certainty that he had failed. The king was dead.

He cast his gaze away. A horse was turning. A lone rider when all others had rushed to their stricken monarch's aid. The assassin.

Stryker shook his head, spat out a torrent of blood, and forced himself to stand. Sure enough, the man who had wielded the crossbow with such calm efficiency was winding the reins of a big grey about his knuckles, lashing them at the terrified beast in order that it should carry him towards the archway and out on to the road. It seemed to slew sideways, hooves skittering and head thrashing, unwilling to obey this unfamiliar master. Stryker knew it was only a matter of time before he gained control, and the redcoats around the yard could not hope to block the path of a galloping warhorse. For a second he thought of running anyway, reaching the sentries at the entrance to the priory complex and ordering them to raise the alarm. But who could respond? The entire body of cavalry had gone with Prince Rupert, ridden into the Cotswold Hills to delay the Earl of Essex.

Then he remembered the lone harquebusier who had accompanied the king. He was now on foot, but his saddle would be holstered with pistols. He ran to the bay gelding, swung himself uneasily into the saddle, and coaxed the horse into a ragged trot.

Even as the beast hesitated, he could see the assassin's grey beginning to break into a more measured stride, and knew the killer would be away in moments. He drew one of the pistols and pulled the trigger, but nothing happened. It was not loaded. Swearing viciously, he kicked hard at the horse, causing it only to rear, and had to cling on lest he be thrown clean away.

Up ahead, the grey had reached the arch. And it was there that it fell.

Nikolas Robbens had known he was not safe. There was the packed Royalist encampment to negotiate, the teeming road and the surrounding miles of hill and forest. Yet he had started to believe that he might just escape when the tall, reed-thin soldier had stepped into the archway. Even then he had not been unduly concerned, for one man on foot could do nothing to stop a galloping horse.

But the man had carried a long staff. And on that staff was a monstrous three-fanged beast of oiled steel, comprising a hook, a sharp point and an axe. The soldier had stepped into the road-way as casually as though he were taking the air, bent one leg so that he was in a balanced crouch, and swept the halberd across the ground in a huge, savage arc. The grey screamed. It shuddered beneath Robbens, a spray of red mist jetting up and out in all directions, and then it careened forwards, toppling over its head and neck, flipping the Dutchman from its back as though he weighed nothing.

Robbens flew, and for a serene moment he wondered if he was already dead, rising up to heaven to leave this vile country in his wake. When he hit the ground, his arms snapped and his spine felt as though it shattered like glass, he knew he was mistaken.

'Well done, Sergeant!'

William Skellen doffed his cap as Stryker rode past. 'Pistol, sir?'

Stryker tossed him the flintlock and an ammunition pouch he found hanging from the bay's expensive saddle, then kicked out past the twitching grey until he had reached the prostrate form of the man who had broken his nose and killed a king.

'Hatton?'

The man's face was crunched into a perfect picture of agony. He broke into a racking cough that made him wail in pain, tears streaming down his cheeks, and Stryker realized he had been trying to laugh. 'Hatton never existed. I am Nikolas Robbens.'

Behind them a pistol shot cracked out, echoing around the priory and up to Gloucester's southern walls. Stryker looked back to see Skellen standing over the horse that he had so brutally and crucially maimed. It was still and silent, wreathed in powder smoke. Further back, scores of men were coming through the archway. Forth's fortified camp was on the rising ground beyond the old monastic site, and his regiments were spilling out of their billets at the spreading news. Out in front were Stryker's own men, his beloved redcoats, and they flanked a lone woman with long, golden hair.

'Nikolas Robbens,' the assassin said again. 'Remember that. My name will go down in history.'

Stryker took a knee beside Robbens, drawing the thin dirk from his boot. 'No, sir, it will not.' He drove the blade down through the assassin's eye as hard as he could, putting his entire weight behind the bone hilt, forcing the keen tip through flesh and gristle until there was no steel left exposed. He left it there to quiver in the bloody socket as Robbens shuddered, a small sigh escaping between his lips.

When Stryker stood, Lisette Gaillard was standing between him and Skellen. Her face was a mask of sorrow, bleak and colourless. '*Mon amour.*'

'He's dead?' Stryker replied.

She shook her head. 'No, Stryker. He missed.' She took a step closer, raising a hand to silence his intended words of relief. 'It is Cecily. The bolt hit Cecily.'

CHAPTER 25

The East Gate, Gloucester, 4 September 1643

Lieutenant Colonel Edward Massie, governor of Gloucester and talisman of a rebel city, rubbed his bleary eyes and stared at his chief miner. 'They're below us?'

The miner, a volunteer from the city with a relatively good understanding of tunnelling from his time digging in the Forest of Dean, grimaced apologetically. 'That's it, sir. Our counter-mine has reached their position, of that I'm sure.' He looked back at the gate. ''Tis just that, beggin' your pardon, sir, we ain't gone deep enough.'

Massie sighed wearily. He might have been angry at the start of the siege, but now, after so long hanging on to their liberty, the people of Gloucester did not need a tongue-lashing, even if he felt like delivering one. 'How far above them are we?'

The miner thought for a moment. 'Three yard. Maybe four.'

'Dig holes from our tunnel to theirs. Bore down into the ceiling of their mine. We'll pour water in and drown the lot of them.'

'Very good, sir.'

Massie turned away. He was hardly surprised at this setback. For all their valour and determination in resisting the mighty Royalist army this past month, he still felt the enterprise had been a failure. After all, the enemy had virtually reached the East Gate, the baying horde outside had not budged an inch since they arrived, the garrison was now down to its last few barrels of powder, and there was no sign of the much vaunted

447

relief expedition from London. It was just a matter of time before the walls fell, and what then? What reward did a courageous, defiant city gain if it fell at the last? Pure, bloody slaughter. He shuddered even though he felt warm in his buff leather.

'How does it progress?' Vincent Skaithlocke's deep voice boomed like a saker as he lumbered up to inspect the mine.

'We've reached them, 'Massie answered, 'but we're not deep enough.'

'Flood 'em out,' the massively overweight mercenary suggested.

'I have already ordered it.'

Skaithlocke nodded, threading his hands across his wobbling stomach. 'Any news from the spies, sir?'

'None. Were you expecting something?'

Skaithlocke shrugged nonchalantly, though his jaw seemed set more rigidly than usual as he spoke. 'I heard a rumour that the King had been hurt.'

Massie was taken aback. 'I pray not, Colonel! We do not fight this war against the person of His Majesty, after all. Merely against the way he governs his realm.'

Skaithlocke looked away. 'Yes, Governor, of course.'

'And I'll thank you to curtail those rumours if you hear them again.'

'Naturally, sir,' Skaithlocke said, rubbing his face vigorously with his palm.

Massie noted the wildness in the huge man's eyes, though he could not discern whether it was from fear at the impending Royalist attack or some other strain. 'What is it, Vincent?'

'Stryker, sir.'

'Stryker?' Massie echoed. 'Men turn their coats often in such wars as these,' he said, thinking privately about how closely he had come to enlisting with the king at the outbreak of the conflict. 'It is not for us to grow embittered. God will judge him for his deeds, have no doubt.'

'God will judge him, sir, aye,' Skaithlocke said. 'But I will send him for that judgement.'

'Come now, Colonel,' said Massie mildly, 'his betrayal hurts you that deeply?'

Skaithlocke nodded slowly, jowls tremulous, eyes hard as oak. 'It does, Governor. Indeed it does. I fear he has destroyed a particular ambition of mine.'

'Oh?'

'It matters not,' Skaithlocke said with a shake of his massive head. 'But one day. *One day*, I will kill him with my bare hands.'

Near Compton Abdale, Gloucestershire, 4 September 1643

The dashing, daring, all-conquering Cavalier horsemen were failing.

Prince Rupert had taken what remained of the king's cavalry and galloped into the hills to the east, joining Lord Wilmot's force in order to confront the advancing Parliamentarian army. But they had been outfought by the swirling rebel cavalry who had first kept Wilmot at bay to cross the River Cherwell, and then they had been confronted by a horde of infantry regiments the like of which had not been seen since Kineton Fight. Rupert had been vexed by the sheer size of the Roundhead army, harried by Essex's mounted fighters, and outmanoeuvred by the earl himself.

The prince slid down from his tired mount and took a scroll from his saddle bag. He unfurled it on a large stone that marked the crossroads where the main body of his beleaguered horsemen now mustered, planting a gloved finger at a specific point. 'Naunton. That's where they are.'

Wilmot was with him, and the lieutenant general dismounted too, craning over the young general's shoulder to see the inky scrawl. 'Christ, but we haven't delayed them at all.'

Rupert blasphemed too. It was all so starkly, painfully clear. The simple fact was that, for all their aggression, their speedy attacks, launching up from sunken roads and through forested hillsides, they had not been able to stem the tide. Essex's massive relief force had pushed through the open country from Oddington to Naunton like a hammer, smashing their Royalist harassers at every pass, every bridge, every slope, thrusting them ever westwards like so many grains of dust in a storm. For all Rupert's efforts, he had been unable to curtail the inexorable march.

'Do they move from Naunton?' Rupert asked.

Wilmot shook his head. 'Scouts say they're ensconced for the night.'

'Then we'll make camp here,' the prince said. 'Attack again on the morrow.'

Lord Wilmot straightened and went back to his waiting mount. Prince Rupert of the Rhine rolled his map into a tight scroll, and returned it to his saddle bag. He cursed softly as he watched the men walk their animals to the surrounding fields. Because he knew he had been beaten. The Roundheads were going to reach Gloucester.

Llanthony Priory, Gloucester, 4 September 1643

'It is tainted.'

Stryker, Lisette and Forrester stood in a dark corner of the infirmary. It was a moribund building, part of an ancient cloister that now stank of mildew, with a roof half collapsed and a floor caked in bird droppings. The trio had been there all night, and now, as midday loomed, they were finally able to speak to the chirurgeon in charge of Cecily Cade's care.

'Tainted?' Lisette asked. 'How?'

The doctor was a man who had the broad shoulders of one who had once been muscular and the belly of a man long run to fat. His face was round and ruddy, his brown hair thin and receding, and his blue eyes glassy and bloodshot. He rubbed stained hands on a filthy rag. 'Rubbed with something. Some kind of poison. I know not what, but the effect will be the same. It will fester and she will die.'

When Stryker had run to intercept Nikolas Robbens, he had released his grip on Cecily Cade's wrist, and she had run to the king. She had, Lisette later told him, moved in front of the monarch, desperate to say her piece, and the crossbow bolt, knocked off course by Stryker, had hit her thigh. It had penetrated the woollen breeches, the wickedly sharpened bodkin digging deep into her flesh, and severed a major vessel that the chirurgeons had failed to fully plug. She had lost a great deal of blood, the tide blooming around her prone form as she gasped at the scudding rain clouds in the priory's forecourt, and, though she had been taken to the casualty station immediately, tended by the king's best physicians, the wound had continued to seep through the night.

The doctor rubbed his tired eyes, leaving them smeared pink with the blood from his fingers. 'She is wakeful now. Speak to her while you can.'

The three moved to Cecily's bedside. She was deathly pale, her eyelids flickering and her lips trembling. A sheet covered her up to the neck, so they could not see the wound, but they knew it was bad.

'Cecily,' Lisette whispered.

The large eyes peeled open. They were as richly green as ever, flecked with the intricate patterns of brown that had once made them so alluring. Now the spark was gone, the glimmer faded. 'I am hurt, Lisette.'

'You will live yet,' the Frenchwoman said, laying a hand on Cecily's angular shoulder.

Cecily offered a weak smile. 'No. Apt, is it not? I always said I would die for my father's secret, and now—'

'Rest, Cecily,' Lisette intervened.

'Now you may carry the burden.'

Lisette shook her head forcefully. 'I do not care for the treasure.'

'But you know its worth,' Cecily persisted, some of the old defiance injected into her tone. 'It must be recovered, or what was this for?'

Lisette looked up at Stryker. He nodded. After all the blood-shed, he would be damned if the Cade family secret went to the grave with its last member.

'Captain,' Cecily said, her voice growing hoarse with every grating syllable. 'I hear King Charles intends to reward you for your service.'

Stryker stared at the walls in shame. 'Please, Cecily, I—'

'It is good, Captain. Very good. You deserve it.' She coughed, spluttering helplessly as though she were drowning. When eventually she had wrested control of her chest, she spoke again. 'I would apologize to you.'

Stryker shook his head, but she closed her eyes in exasperation. 'I would apologize for my behaviour on the tor. I felt I needed to escape. I did not trust that you would keep me safe.'

He almost laughed at that, embarrassed. 'And you were right.'

She smiled weakly. 'You are a good man.' A frail arm slithered out from beneath the sheet and she took hold of Stryker's hand. 'I want you to know that I did not play you as false as you might suppose. Lisette is fortunate to have you.'

'He is fortunate to have me,' Lisette retorted.

'That he is,' Cecily agreed. She paused to breathe, the sound laboured and rasping. When she had caught her breath, she looked at each of the trio in turn. 'There is a house. The gold is beneath it. In the cellars.'

Stryker leaned in, keeping his voice low. 'Where?'

'Silly.'

Stryker frowned, looking up at Forrester. 'She is delirious.'

Lisette slapped him hard in the midriff. 'No, you fool. *Scilly.*' She looked down at her stricken friend. 'I'm right, am I not? You mentioned childhood visits to the Isles of Scilly, Cecily. I remember.'

Cecily nodded, the movement almost imperceptible. 'Tresco, one of the islands. Father has a retainer there. Watches the house still, I believe. Find him.' She closed her eyes again, but this time the motion was slower, like molten wax rolling down the side of a fat candle. She took a lingering gulp of air, letting the outbreath carry her words. 'Find him.' She did not breathe in again.

They stayed with her for the rest of the day; sat around the blood-soaked palliasse as physicians and their assistants bustled in and out, tended to the increasing number of sick, dressed wounds and plucked flattened lead bullets from various mangled limbs. The night drew in, the tallow candles guttered and spat, the sounds of soldiers going about camp life drifted in from the buildings and alleyways of the priory and the raised leaguer beyond.

'How did you know?' Forrester said in the gathering gloom.

Stryker looked up at him. 'Know?'

'About that assassin. How did you know that was him? The bow was concealed.'

'Skaithlocke told me he wore an ear-string. I'd forgotten until I saw it hanging there.'

'Still, a balestrino,' Forrester said. 'Clever bastard.'

'I have used one,' said Lisette.

'Of course you have,' Forrester replied with a roll of his eyes. 'I'd expect nothing less, Mademoiselle Gaillard, though please do not regale us with the details. I'm sure I do not wish to know.'

'I am going,' she said suddenly, causing both men to look at her. 'To Tresco. I don't care what you say, Stryker, I am bloody going and that's the end of it.'

'I was not going to say a word,' Stryker said truthfully. 'Except that I will join you.'

'As will I,' Forrester added.

Lisette nodded. 'Then it is settled. For Cecily.'

They finally left the infirmary just short of midnight. It was cold and pitch-dark, though the archway leading to Severn Street was lit by the orange flames of pitch-daubed torches set into the dilapidated stonework. The two officers escorted Lisette through the gateway's warm light, glancing to the left to look up at Gloucester's wall, and made their way on to the muddy road.

'Well there's a sight to break a man's beating heart asunder,' a familiar, cackling voice rang out from up ahead.

The threesome stopped dead in their tracks and stared up at the lone horseman. He was short and stocky, and wore a yellow coat. His helmet was fastened to a strap against his saddle, allowing his shock of spiked hair the freedom to shine as white as snow in the glow of the torches. His wide, red face glowered down at them, tiny eyes twinkling above the huge, bulbous nose.

Stryker placed a hand on the smooth pommel of his sword. 'Colonel Crow.'

Crow spat. 'I heard tell it was you took the bolt, Captain Stryker. Had prayed hard that it was your brave leap into the murderer's sights that saved the King. Had dreamed all night of the sweet image of your cold, dead face. Wanted to come and piss on your corpse.' He placed a hand on his chest in mock grief. 'The disappointment is palpable.'

'You sent James Buck to kill me,' Stryker said.

Crow dipped his big head. 'I did.'

Stryker smiled. 'I killed him first.'

Crow eased his pliable mount into a walk, bringing him alongside the three on foot. 'You are a devil, sir.'

'And those men at the inn?' Stryker asked, ignoring the insult.

Crow twitched his brow in a manner that left no doubt. 'You are a difficult foe to vanquish, Captain. Rather akin to a dose o' the pox.' He dropped a hand from his reins and slipped it down to his saddle holster. In a heartbeat, a pistol was in his hand. 'Still, there is nothing that won't die, given the right medicine.'

Stryker lunged at the dragoon, pushing away the hand that held the pistol and taking a handful of the colonel's coat. He dragged him from the saddle, slamming him down on his back.

'How dare you?' Crow shrieked. 'How dare you, sir?'

'You were going to shoot me,' Stryker hissed, as Forrester stooped to rip the firearm from Crow's flailing fist.

'Unhand me, sir!' Crow cried. 'You would kill a senior officer? A colonel?'

'No, Artemas,' Stryker said. 'No, I wouldn't.'

He hit Crow hard in the face. The white-haired officer's head snapped back, his eyes rolled and blood cascaded from his nose. Stryker released him and stood. 'Let us be on our way.'

They left the yellow-coated officer lying in the mud. He screamed obscenities at them, swore that Stryker would pay, but they did not look back.

'You should have killed him, *mon amour*,' Lisette said.

'Probably,' Stryker replied as she threaded her arm through his. 'But I'll be in enough trouble for that punch. I don't think I can stomach a trial for murder.' That was true, he thought, though the reality was that he had seen enough blood spilled at Gloucester to last him a lifetime. He would not shed any more this night.

She shook her head in bewilderment. Forrester laughed. Up on the hills, two huge fires sprang into sudden roaring life to illuminate the dark crest for all to see. On Gloucester's tumble-down walls, voices rang out in a great cheer.

'They're here,' Forrester said. 'Essex has come.'

Stryker nodded, but for once he did not care. He walked with his woman and his friend into the night.

EPILOGUE

Gloucester, 5 September 1643

The fires on Wainlodes Hill blazed all night.

Gloucester's weary populace could barely believe their eyes as the flames licked the sky. Indeed, most thought it another Cavalier trick, the briers set to coax open the city's gates. So they did not move from their positions on the rampart, and the gates remained firmly shut. And still the fires blazed.

The morning brought more surprise. The folk packing the walls looked on in disbelief as a vast flotilla of small craft sailed down the river. They had been moored against the bank of the Severn beside the Earl of Forth's headquarters at Llanthony Priory, used occasionally to transport supplies or wounded soldiers in and out of camp. But now, strangely, spectacularly, they were leaving as one, released like a flock of swans to race southwards in their scores.

Governor Edward Massie watched from the high rampart in as much amazement as everyone else. He rubbed his sore eyes as a train of wagons and oxen was corralled in the priory's tangled orchards, each stacked to the brim with men and baggage, ammunition, powder and barrels of food. They formed up in a line, cajoled by drivers with whips and soldiers with muskets, and soon began to trundle away from the city they had striven so hard to bring to heel.

Thomas Pury, the dour alderman and Gloucester's civilian power broker, stood beside Massie. 'What are they about?'

Massie was unsure. He studied the priory again. Soldiers, rows and rows of them, were marching out through the gates and down Severn Street. The artillery redoubt had already gone, he noticed now; the big cannon hauled away under cover of darkness. 'They're leaving.'

'I don't believe it,' Pury muttered.

Massie looked at him. 'I can scarce believe my own words, Master Pury, and yet here I am saying them. They're evacuating Llanthony.' He leaned back a touch to shout along the rampart. 'Ho there! What news of the saps?'

When word came back that the musketeers to the east had abandoned their trenches, his heart began to pound. When men called up that they could not longer hear the vibrations of the Royalist mine at the East Gate, his eyes began to prickle. Because the Royalist army was retreating. Marvellously, miraculously, they were marching away.

'Thank you Lord,' Edward Massie whispered. He had done it. He had won.

But one man did not clamour for space on the wall. His attention was instead fixed upon a small cloth sack into which he stuffed clothes and provisions. He moved quickly, with a fleet silence that belied his massive frame, muttering constantly through lips that were taut with fury, whispering vows of the most heinous kind.

Vincent Skaithlocke was preparing to leave. He had heard the news of the Royalist retreat, for the jubilant shouts rang loud and triumphal in every street and home, and that could only mean that a relief force had finally come. He straightened, pulled the string of his bag tight, and slung it across the dusty floor to nestle in the room's corner. Gloucester had been saved, but what did he care? How could he possibly give Massie and his obsequious rabble a moment's consideration when all he had worked for had disintegrated? The city was full of the news. An attempt had been made on the king's life. But that attempt, the rumour-mongers claimed, had failed, the assassin slain in the attempt. Skaithlocke imagined Robbens' quarrel flying forth, pictured the leering face of Charles Stuart as the bodkin sailed impotently by. But Robbens did not miss. He never missed. Someone had intervened.

'Stryker,' Skaithlocke said, instinctively guessing.

He moved to the window of his chamber and stooped to peer out at the unsettled sky. He would wait for Essex. The earl would soon arrive and Gloucester's gates would be flung open, and then, with no companion save the simple thought of retribution, Vincent Skaithlocke would ride away. Because he had a new purpose in life. Revenge.

The dark clouds finally made good their threat as evening drew in.

As column after grumbling column of pikemen, musketeers, dragoons, gunners and harquebusiers trudged sullenly away from their hard-dug saps, heading south for the rendezvous at the king's headquarters at Matson House, the heavens opened in a torrential downpour that seemed to heap scorn upon the army's misery. They slopped through huge puddles and sucking ruts, growled oaths when they were set to pushing floundering carts out of the rain-sodden mire, and privately cursed the officers who had led them to this disgrace.

And disgrace it was, for they all knew they had failed. The grand swarm of king's men who had so brazenly crowed at the feeble walls had been held at bay by less than fifteen hundred men and a smattering of common families with delusions of grandeur. Essex, it was announced, was less than a day's march to the east. He would be coming for them imminently, with a force far larger than anyone could possibly have imagined, and the siege would be lifted. What mattered now was that the vast Royalist army move out of their stinking trenches and regroup to face the approaching earl, and thus the earthworks would have to be sacrificed for the greater good. At least, it was said, they had not been smashed in pitched battle. But all secretly knew that they were an army if not defeated, then certainly defied.

Captain Innocent Stryker marched at the head of his men as the rain pelted them in thick, diagonal sheets. He had his head down, his hat angled to shield his face, and simply watched his boots as they ploughed furrows behind the thousands of others. He felt the disappointment in leaving Gloucester without breaching its walls, but, for his part, his distress was tempered by the knowledge that the men, women and children of the rebel stronghold had not been subjected to the inevitable sack that he had witnessed so often before. He looked back briefly above the heads of his soaking men, squinting through the forest of pike staves that bobbed at his back. Gloucester rose out of the boggy terrain like a battered but unbowed warrior. He touched a finger to the water-beaded brim of his hat in private salute.

'Where we gonna get a ship from, sir?' Sergeant William Skellen's sardonic voice droned at his left ear.

Stryker looked up at the man who had felled Cecily Cade's killer. 'Been speaking to Captain Forrester, have you?'

Skellen shook his head. 'Miss Lisette, sir.'

'How is she?'

'Just fine, sir. Ridin' in the wagons at the rear. Suggested we put some men back there to protect her.'

'And?'

'And she was quite rude to me, sir,' Skellen sniffed.

Stryker laughed. 'I am not in the least surprised, Mister Skellen.'

'The ship, sir?' Skellen prompted.

Stryker's thoughts turned to a wind-battered island in the Atlantic Ocean. It was where he knew he must go; for Cecily's memory, and for Lisette's love. 'We'll find one, Sergeant,' he said simply.

Tresco was his future, that much was certain. But what future now lay ahead for the Royalist cause, he wondered? They had been humbled here, humiliated, and though they were far from beaten, it was all too easy to imagine the name of Gloucester ringing like triumphant church bells in every rebel town and city across the land. A reputation for success could so quickly roll and build that Edward Massie's famed defiance might prove

459

more costly to the king's war effort than any defeat in open battle. A creeping dread spread through him at the thought.

'Sotweed, sir?' Skellen asked, producing a plug of tobacco from a pouch in his snapsack.

Stryker clapped his sergeant on the back and put the war out of his mind as the rain lashed down. 'Thank you, Mister Skellen. Don't mind if I do.'

ACKNOWLEDGEMENTS

Without the hard work and encouragement of a number of people, it would not have been possible to write this book. I would like to thank my editor, Kate Parkin, who has yet again steered me through the process, and my agent, Rupert Heath, whose belief in the series was the first step on the road to seeing my rough scribblings become real books.

Much gratitude to the team at John Murray and Hodder. Caro Westmore, Hilary Hammond, Lyndsey Ng and Ben Gutcher in particular.

Many thanks to Malcolm Watkins of Heritage Matters, whose invaluable comments have, as ever, been crucial in tightening the historical accuracy of the manuscript. Reimagining such a complex event as this, however, inevitably comes down to the author's own interpretation of the available evidence, and all remaining mistakes are my own.

Lastly, much love and thanks to my wife Rebecca, and kids, Joshua and Maisie, without whom none of it would be possible, or half as fun.

HISTORICAL NOTE

By the late summer of 1643 the Royalist cause had reached its high tide. Major victories in the north and (as described in *Hunter's Rage*) west had been followed by the storming of Bristol – England's second city at the time – and the pressure was beginning to tell. The Parliamentarians were in deep crisis – politically as well as militarily – and it appeared as though the Great Rebellion was about to be crushed.

But within weeks of Bristol's bloody fall, the king's chance at victory had been squandered. The reason widely cited for this dramatic turning of the tide is the Royalists' failure to take Gloucester. With the momentum firmly in his favour, King Charles, it is (and was at the time) argued, should have marched upon London. The impact of the decision to stay and 'mop up' the last Roundhead stronghold in the region cannot be overstated. The delays at Gloucester not only damaged his army's morale, but gave his enemies the time and encouragement to regroup. The heroics of the city's citizens, not to mention their inspirational leader, Edward Massie, became something of an example for beleaguered Parliamentarians everywhere. Moreover, the Royalist army's failure to take Gloucester, and its subsequent failure to defeat Essex in battle at Newbury, had the twin effect of galvanizing the rebellion – from the grass roots right the way up to the political elite – and splitting the king's ever fractious court into a fatal spiral of recrimination and acrimony. People often think of the first English Civil War as being a relatively inevitable victory for a Parliament that was more united, organized and determined than its Royalist counterparts. This was not even remotely true until after September 1643. The siege of Gloucester changed everything.

As for the day-to-day events of the siege, I have tried to stay as true to contemporary accounts as possible, and, therefore, I believe *Assassin's Reign* retells much of the story as it actually happened. The Royalist army was indeed vast, led officially by the ageing Earl of Forth from his camp at Llanthony Priory, though Prince Rupert seems to have been an ever-present voice at the king's makeshift court at Matson House. As I have tried to show, the besieging force was camped right around the city, and must have made for a truly intimidating sight for those on the inside, though they concentrated much of their efforts on attacking the south of the city where the ground was higher and drier.

As for the rebels, they had around fifteen hundred fighting men, perhaps a dozen small artillery pieces and a relatively meagre supply of gunpowder. They were outnumbered, outgunned and the city defences were relatively weak. But they had a new military leader, who would become the Parliamentarian hero of the siege. Edward Massie was indeed the rather ambiguous character I have described. The twenty-three-year-old son (though he may have been twenty-nine) of a Cheshire gentleman, the governor had, at the start of the war, allegedly attempted to obtain a commission with the king's army at York, but sensing there would not be sufficient opportunity for promotion, he headed instead for London and the rebels. Though his name went on to become a talisman of rebel resistance, he was clearly a man whose ambition ranked higher than his ideals. I describe in the book how Massie sent secret messages to his old commander in the Scottish wars, one Colonel Legge, suggesting that, should the king appear in person before the walls, Massie would gladly surrender. This was, according to the Earl of Clarendon, the final encouragement King Charles needed to march upon Gloucester. Was Massie serious, changing his mind when the Royalists eventually appeared? Or was it all a ruse to confuse his enemies? We will never know for certain.

Either way, it is clear that Massie's leadership was at the very heart of Gloucester's unlikely resistance. He was an experienced engineer, and that knowledge proved crucial in taking the decision to fire the suburbs, in rebuilding the crumbling city walls, constructing sconces, ditches and breastworks, and countermining the Royalist tunnels. All these measures were successful in delaying the Royalist advance and damaging their collective morale, but Massie's greatest contribution was arguably his sheer charisma. He was later described (as part of a 'Wanted' notice) as being of '*brown hair, middle stature, sanguine complexion*', which leads one to think that perhaps he was not a great physical presence. But he led the people of Gloucester from the front. He walked the walls, paced the streets, offered solace to those in need, and, crucially, adopted a strategy of taking the fight to the besieging army. They would not sit and wait for the inevitable assault, which would surely engulf their patchwork defences. Massie arranged a series of raids through small ports in the walls to harry and disrupt the network of saps that were being dug all around Gloucester's perimeter. The sallies met with varying degrees of success, but the net effect was a populace that felt empowered despite their predicament, and an enemy constantly thrown into disarray.

Indeed, the Royalist army, huge and confident at the beginning of the siege, became increasingly frustrated and mutinous as the days dragged by. The boggy terrain cannot have helped matters, for Gloucester's natural springs made difficult work for the king's sappers, and torrential rainfall compounded the problem, rendering attempts to undermine the East Gate extremely hazardous.

Conversely, morale inside the battered walls seems to have increased as the siege continued. Defence of the city was shouldered by the entire populace, with Massie as their inspiration. Women ventured out into the Little Mead, within range of Royalist snipers, to graze cattle and cut turfs for the walls, while children acted as messengers and, in many cases, took up arms themselves. In turn, their courageous story bolstered the pro-war faction in London and, so soon after the peace riots described in the book, served to quash any notion of surrender in the capital. Indeed, John Pym and his supporters in Parliament saw Gloucester's heroic last stand as something of a propaganda coup, and quickly raised a relief force. With the benefit of hindsight, we can see that Gloucester was a major turning point in Parliamentarian fortunes, and I wonder if Pym, ever the strategist, had foreseen just such a conclusion.

One of the more noteworthy events of the siege was the introduction of Doctor Chillingworth's engines, rather witheringly mentioned by one rebel as *'unperfect and troublesome engines . . . (that) ran upon wheels, with planks musket proof placed on the axle-tree, with holes for the musket show and a bridge before it, the end whereof (the wheels falling into the ditch) was to rest upon our breast works'*. As described in the book, these impressive machines were built at the fortified camp, or leaguer, amid the ruins of Llanthony Priory. But, rather like the Royalist ambitions as a whole, they proved something of a damp squib. They were eventually recovered by the victorious garrison in a marsh to the south side of the town, which suggests they were actually deployed, albeit unsuccessfully. Presumably, then, they reached the marsh (which Chillingworth would not necessarily have factored into his plans during the earlier rainless days of the siege) and floundered. The attempt, as featured in *Assassin's Reign*, ended without even reaching the ditch over which the machines were designed to cross.

While in recent years the idea has been entirely discredited, it ought to be noted that the failure of the siege engines is often used as an explanation for the origin of the Humpty Dumpty nursery rhyme, which, in its earliest form, reads thus:

> Humpety Dumpety fell in a beck,
> With all his sinews about his neck,
> All the King's surgeons and all the King's knights,
> Couldn't put Humpety Dumpety to rights.

The beck might be the marsh or one of the many ditches in the ravaged terrain, the sinews would be the ropes attached to the bridge, and the surgeon might be Chillingworth himself. Personally, I feel the link between siege and nursery rhyme is most certainly a modern invention, but it would be remiss of me to ignore it here.

As for the conclusion of the siege, it happened much as I have retold, with the exception of the king's brush with an assassin's crossbow bolt. The garrison was down to its last few barrels of powder, and Gloucester would surely have fallen within a matter of days had the Earl of Essex not arrived in the nick of time. What is perhaps as remarkable as the siege itself is the manner of Essex's arrival. I chose not to focus on the relief force, feeling the story was better told around events at Gloucester, but it is no exaggeration to say that another entire novel could be dedicated to the story of how Essex's army negotiated the march from London to Gloucester, all the while threatened by the formidable Royalist cavalry led first by Lord Wilmot and later Prince Rupert himself. Anyone wishing to learn more of how Essex successfully outmanoeuvred the hitherto invincible prince, or, indeed, about the battle fought soon after at Newbury, would do well to take a look at *Gloucester and Newbury 1643: The Turning Point of the Civil War* by Jon Day (2007).

Ultimately, though, the Royalists dithered. Too shaken by the carnage he had seen at Bristol, King Charles' aversion to an all-out assault (as espoused by Rupert) meant that the siege just took too long. They needed to break into Gloucester before the Roundhead army arrived, and they simply ran out of time.

The other significant location in *Assassin's Reign* is, of course, London. While Stryker is negotiating his way through the Parliamentarian stronghold in the west, Lisette Gaillard and Cecily Cade must extricate themselves from the very heart of the rebellion. I must confess that the story arc is entirely fictional in this case, but it is worth noting that the peace riots really did take place and were perceived as enough of a threat that troops were eventually ordered to open fire on the protesters.

As for the main characters in *Assassin's Reign*, I am pleased to say that many were 'real' people, and I hope I have portrayed them as faithfully as possible. Aside from the senior commanders on the Royalist side – Rupert, Forth, Astley, Vavasour, Falkland and so on – all of whom existed, I would also note that Thomas Pury, James Harcus and Richard Backhouse were major players in the defence of Gloucester, though it should be noted that Harcus was indeed killed while he was '*too venterously looking what execution a granado had done*'. Other true-life figures include the bookseller, Tobias Jordan, and Major Marmaduke Pudsey. They were chosen to show how the city gave the rebellious rebuff to the king's demand for surrender, and the audacious way in which they delivered the message is recorded thus by an anonymous Royalist: '*Their backs turned scarce thirty yards, on clap they their hats in the king's presence, with orange ribbons in them.*'

Sadly, though, many of the characters in *Assassin's Reign* are figments of my overactive imagination. Colonel Artemas Crow, Stryker's nemesis from *Devil's Charge*, is a work of fiction, as are Erasmus Collings, Cecily Cade, Henry Greetham, Christopher Quigg, Skaithlocke, Nobbs and Robbens. There was, however, a rebel deserter during the siege who swam the Severn to join the king's army. His name is recorded as one Hatton, a gunner, and I have taken the liberty of using that man as Robbens' alias.

For the men of Sir Edmund Mowbray's Regiment of Foot, the future is far from certain, for the tide has turned at Gloucester. Stryker, Skellen, Forrester and the rest will, I'm certain, be in the thick of the action, for as autumn gives way to winter, blood will be shed in the snow.

Captain Stryker will return.